"A HAUNTING AND COMPELLING
SUSPENSE TALE."
Andrew Greeley

*A father has forgotten his troubled heritage . . .
but a son remembers.*

*Drawn by the anger and loyalties learned at a grand-
father's knee, second generation Irish-American
Jamie McGuire has vanished into a world of
explosive secrets and brutal betrayals. Now Jamie's
father, Michael—an advertising executive with no
allegiance to any cause—must rescue his lost son
from a violent place where revolution is the faith and
freedom means death. But it may already be too late,
for Jamie has been chosen to play two indispensable
roles in a bloody, long-running international drama:
scapegoat . . . and martyr.*

――――――――――――――――

"A galloping good read."
San Francisco Examiner

"A good, serious, entertaining, and ironic novel."
Norman Mailer

"Enough plot twists to satisfy
the most jaded John Le Carre fans."
Fort Worth Star-Telegram

(More praise on the following pages)

BY PETER MAAS

FICTION
Father and Son
Made in America

NONFICTION
Manhunt
Marie: A True Story
King of the Gypsies
Serpico
The Valachi Papers
The Rescuer
Underboss
The Terrible Hours

PETER MAAS

FATHER AND SON

HarperTorch
An Imprint of HarperCollins*Publishers*

This is for Sam Cohn and Arlene Donovan

This is a work of fiction. Names, characters, places, and incidents are products of the author's imagination or are used fictitiously and are not to be construed as real. Any resemblance to actual events, locales, organizations, or persons, living or dead, is entirely coincidental.

HARPERTORCH
An Imprint of HarperCollins*Publishers*
10 East 53rd Street
New York, New York 10022-5299

Copyright © 1989 by JMM Productions, Inc.
Author photo © 1999 by Jonathan Becker
ISBN: 0-06-100020-5

First HarperTorch paperback printing: May 2002
First HarperCollins paperback printing: March 1990

HarperCollins®, HarperTorch™, and ◆™ are trademarks of HarperCollins Publishers Inc.

Printed in the United States of America

Visit HarperTorch on the World Wide Web at www.harpercollins.com

10 9 8 7 6

ACKNOWLEDGMENTS

This book is a work of the imagination. Still, for certain incidents that occur in it, I acknowledge the counsel and insights supplied to me by members, past and present, of the Federal Bureau of Investigation, the U.S. Customs Service, the Bureau of Alcohol, Tobacco and Firearms, the New York Police Department and the U.S. Attorney's Office for the Southern District of New York; and also by members, equally past and present, of the Provisional Irish Republican Army, the Ulster Defense Association, the Royal Ulster Constabulary, the Special Branch of the *Garda Siochana* in Dublin and the British secret security service, MI5.

Somehow, the thought that this would be a "fiction" removed many of the constraints that I otherwise might have encountered.

A number of investigative journalists as well were of great help, principally among them Kevin Cullen of the Boston *Globe* and Nick Davies, formerly of the *Guardian* in London.

I wish, finally, to acknowledge the expert guidance of my editor, Michael Korda.

Prologue

It was one o'clock in the morning, the Saturday after Labor Day. Clouds scudded across a half moon. At the far corner of the armory immediately below the roof, a floodlamp cast just enough light to reveal a row of National Guard jeeps and trucks in the rear parking area. There was a faint smell of the sea.

"The hell I'm doin' this for?" Bernie Quinn grunted, on his knees, severing another link in the fence with the big wire cutters.

"To save your fookin' soul," Dowd said. Seven years in Boston, and Dowd still hadn't lost his Belfast accent. That had its advantages. "Ah, this is Kevin Dowd, y'know," a fellow would say. "*He's* from over there. He can tell you what it's like there. He's been in the middle of it all there, y'know." Unmentioned was that Dowd was very good at cracking safes and vaults.

Squatting down behind Quinn, Dowd contemplated his bullet head, bull neck and massive shoulders and arms. Overall, Quinn had the graceful appearance of a heavy tank, as well as many of its functional uses. It was hard to conceive of anything or anyone standing in his way. He also was a testament to the wayward nature of life. The incident, still historically recalled in stupefied amazement in Boston's organized crime circles, had occurred three years before Dowd's arrival. At the time two Irish gangs, the Somerville and Charlestown mobs, were dominant in the city, with the Italians running a poor third, when on an August Sunday afternoon on the sands of Salisbury Beach, Bernie Quinn, then seventeen and a Somerville recruit, suddenly flung himself upon the ripe, baking body of Maureen Durkin, the girl friend of one of the Charlestown chieftains, pulled down her bikini top and proceeded to sink his teeth into her left breast.

In the ensuing bloodbath over the next two years, sixty-seven members of the two gangs met violent ends, including Quinn's two older brothers, both pillars in the Somerville mob. Yet Bernie himself escaped final retribution. Once, coming out of a Somerville redoubt, the Gaelic Tavern, he took two .38-caliber slugs in the belly, but after a week in intensive care returned to the street as good as new. On another occasion, set upon by three Charlestown assailants, Quinn singlehandedly broke the neck of one, fractured the skull of the second and in a kind of postscript to Salisbury Beach chewed off most of an ear of the third, suffering in the process a knife slash in the cheek, which his widowed mother, with whom to this day he continued to reside, sutured herself to avoid incriminating medical records.

All this carnage at last enabled the New England Mafia, headquartered in Providence, Rhode Island, to achieve the supremacy it had sought in Boston rackets, a situation only recently being rectified under the aegis of Thomas Ahearn, who had inherited the mantle of the Somerville mob after two of his predecessors in the job became the objects of High Requiem Masses, the first for making the mistake of starting his own car in the morning, the other riddled from behind at close quarters by a burst from a MAC-10 submachine gun held under a raincoat in a crowd exiting Boston Garden after a hockey game. "At least he went happy," it was said at his funeral. "The Bruins won."

Ahearn, a skinny man of fifty with Savonarola eyes as black as pitch, started the Irish on the way toward the semblance of parity in a daring sitdown with remnants of the Charlestown mob during which he managed to reach even the dimmest minds present with his clarity and vision. "Them fuckin' guineas are laughin' all the way to the bank," he cried. "We got to cut out this crap, we want to get somewhere. The smart thing, Jesus Christ, is forgive and forget. Think about it. Else you want some fuckin' dago always tellin' you when you can go to the toilet?"

Ahearn had long since absolved Quinn for his transgression. It was, he decided, a simple matter of unbridled youthful lust, and besides, Bernie had straightened out. "You want the truth," Ahearn said, "that Durkin broad asked for it, layin' there like that, tits hangin' out, practically showin' her snatch and everything." Noting Quinn's apparent indestructibility, Ahearn also had appointed him his personal bodyguard. And it was he who now dispatched Bernie to be with Kevin Dowd on Saturday night outside the armory's chain-link fence. "He's a good lad," Ahearn told Dowd. "You'll need his muscle." Not to mention, Ahearn reflected, his own interest in knowing exactly how everything had gone, if there had been any screw-ups he should know about.

The fence surrounding the armory grounds was eight feet high, topped with five strands of barbed wire. He had directed Quinn to cut a walk-in opening in the fence roughly five feet square from the bottom. The Riley kid, crouched next to Quinn, kept bending in the section of the fence Quinn was working on to reduce the tension, and the Ford van that Dowd had backed up by the fence in the motel's parking lot hid them from the view of anyone who might happen to glance outside in their direction.

Ever since he had checked into the motel on Thursday, Dowd parked the van in the same spot to get cruising police patrols or motel security people used to it, but there hadn't been a sign of any so far as he could tell. All summer long the motel had been filled with tourists who couldn't find better accommodations on the shore or were stopping by to visit the House of Seven Gables over in Salem and to ogle the old stocks for the witches. Now after Labor Day, though, it was nearly deserted.

Dowd had taken a room on the third floor, the top one, which gave him a clear look at the armory. It was a utilitarian structure, made of red brick, about two hundred fifty feet long and sixty feet high and maybe a hundred wide. A swath of neatly trimmed lawn separated it from the highway. The main entrance was on the far side. A driveway led up to a swinging gate. There was a diner on the highway just past the driveway that did a fair amount of business, but it closed up around one A.M. Promptly at midnight a cop in a squad car would come by, beam his spotlight at the gate to check the lock. Then the cop would go into the diner and emerge five minutes later carrying a sandwich bag and a container of coffee. That was it until armory personnel arrived at eight o'clock.

Dowd had picked this weekend because Donny Moran's nephew, who was a member of the unit attached to the armory, reported that no drills or maneuvers were scheduled. The nephew said the alarm for the vault ran on a leased telephone wire; there weren't any motion alarms inside and no alarm for the rear door through which Dowd intended to break in.

All told, Dowd figured he had three hours or so to get the job done. Directly opposite him, across the armory parking area, Ed Herlihy was making another, smaller cut in the perimeter fence. A thicket of trees and bushes about twenty yards wide ran right next to it. Beyond the thicket was a street and on the other side of the street a row of ranch houses with cars out front, so he could leave his own car there without attracting notice. From the cut, he'd be on the lookout for anything unexpected. And it was another way out in case something went wrong.

After his initial complaint, Bernie Quinn had not said another word, and Dowd wondered whether he

was actually mulling over the prospects of salvation.
On the other hand, Quinn wasn't much for small talk.
When Quinn cut through the last link, Dowd got
Herlihy on a low frequency walkie-talkie, the kind
children played games with, that wouldn't be picked
up on a police scanner.

"Ed, how you doin'?"

"I'm done."

"Oh, that's fine. Keep a sharp eye, mind you. We're
ready."

"Roger and out."

Who was Roger? Dowd always thought, and never
remembered to find out.

The armory's rear door was a fire door. Dowd
popped the lock with a jimmy in a matter of seconds.
Except for the front offices, the armory was window-
less. He flipped on a bank of lights. The steel vault
door was on his left. Twenty feet up, in the right
front corner of the armory, he saw the telephone
trunk line coming into the terminal box, and all the
other lines snaking out of it. He followed the line
from the vault. It looked like a simple open and
closed loop. When the vault was shut, the power
probably registered around six hundred ohms. When
the vault was opened, it dropped to zero and an
alarm went off at the security company.

Dowd climbed a ladder to the box. Inside he found
the alarm line neatly tagged "P" for private and "S"
for security. He clamped on a resistor, hooked its two
wires to the same screw lugs that held the ones from
the line and then he clipped the line. Theoretically
he was home free. But just in case the security com-

pany had a meter monitoring slight power variances, he decided to wait for a reaction.

"I jumped the line," he told Herlihy. "Let me know if somebody shows up."

"Understood," Herlihy said.

"Roger and out," said Dowd, feeling foolish.

After ten minutes, Herlihy said, "All clear."

Now came the hard part. The Riley kid angled the chisel against the steel sheeting on the face of the vault door while Quinn swung the sledgehammer. The idea was to dig into the steel and peel it off. The kid didn't look too comfortable holding the chisel, and Dowd didn't blame him. The noise was deafening. Dowd was counting on the armory's thick walls and cavernous interior to smother the sound, and when he checked with Herlihy on the walkie-talkie, Herlihy said he couldn't hear a thing.

Twenty minutes into the pounding, Quinn was starting to make some headway. But sweat was pouring down him, and Dowd called for a breather. Quinn appeared insulted. "What the fuck?" he said.

Dowd tried to mollify him. "You're too valuable, Bernie," he said. "You have to pace yourself, don't you know." Striding edgily around the armory, Dowd spotted some pickaxes and changed the routine. They'd each take turns, one, two, three, with the pickaxes. This seemed to drive Quinn to greater fury at his turn, as if he were now engaged in an athletic competition. Gradually the results could be seen as the asbestos insulation between the outer and inner steel sheaths of the door came into view.

Dowd used a crowbar to pry off strips of the splintered steel. He was five foot nine, and standing next to Quinn he was not particularly imposing. But he had muscular shoulders and powerful wrists and hands. Every morning, no matter where he was, Dowd executed fifty fingertip push-ups. He had gotten into the habit in the Kesh. That was Long Kesh, the internment camp the British established on the outskirts of Belfast. At first, the British government portrayed the Kesh as a sort of a fresh-air rehabilitation center where a fellow, with some encouragement, could restore mind and body. Dowd had to hand it to the Brits. When word began getting around that the Kesh might be a little more than that, they solved the problem by simply knocking it down, constructed a new concrete prison in its place with huge cellblocks shaped like an "H" and renamed it the Maze. Like magic, Long Kesh, the Brits announced, no longer existed. And somehow the thought of a proper prison to house recalcitrant members of the Provisional Irish Republican Army was far less offensive to the civilized world.

After an hour and a half, the innards of the vault's combination lock were exposed. Dowd ripped away more of the asbestos to get a clear look at it. He studied the mechanics of the lock for a moment, played with the gears and got the tumblers lined up. Then he pulled the vault door open.

"Ah, yes," he said. "Lovely."

The glistening M16 rifles were stacked in wheel racks. More than he could easily count. At least a hundred, he thought. Next to them were a dozen attachable 40-mm grenade launchers. There were ten M60 heavy machine guns. And eight .45-caliber automatics. Fifteen electronic night vision binoculars hung from hooks. In the back of the vault was a pile of shrapnel flak jackets.

Bernie Quinn started to trundle out the first rack of M16s toward the rear door of the armory when Dowd stopped him. "Let's sweep away the asbestos first," he said. "It clogs those wheels and it's the devil to pay." Over the walkie-talkie he asked Herlihy, "Ed, all clear?"

"It is."

"Well, come over then and give us a hand."

Dowd was afraid it would be too noisy to push the racks across the parking area. So the rifles and the rest of the booty were carried by the armful to the hole in the fence and put on the mattresses lining the van's interior.

It was still dark out. The whole operation had taken three and a half hours. Dowd sent Herlihy on his way. He had the Riley kid wire back the severed section of fence. He instructed Quinn to drive the van straight to the country place Thomas Ahearn had in New Hampshire.

"Tommy already told me," Quinn said.

"What a memory," Dowd said.

Then Dowd walked around the motel to a pay phone. He dialed a number and heard Ahearn say, "Yeah?"

"Piece of cake," Dowd said and hung up.

He went to the motel entrance. An elderly black porter was mopping the lobby. The porter opened the door, peered at Dowd and said, "Must've been some night."

"Love at first sight," Dowd said.

"Those were the days," the porter replied.

In his room, exhilarated, he could not sleep until he did his push-ups. He awoke at noon when Herlihy came around for him. He looked out his window. Everything was quiet. The chain-link fence appeared untouched. He checked out, having prepaid in cash under the name of Jason Kaminsky, and Herlihy drove him to his two-room apartment in South Boston in a dilapidated building on West Broadway. Dowd liked it there. The neighborhood reminded him a little of the Falls Road in Belfast, even to the Chinese takeouts, especially when it rained.

He lived alone, without a woman. It had been that way ever since his escape from Northern Ireland. He had been taken over the border into County Donegal, into free Ulster, to the village of Maas set in the hills overlooking Gweebarra Bay on the west coast. On his first night a girl had been brought to him, auburn-haired with milky white skin, and she strove mightily to please him, knowing him to be a hero of the struggle. But he could no longer achieve an erection. Not that night, nor the next two. And after that he stopped trying. He would be, he told himself, forever a celibate warrior in a holy cause, like a Jebbie. The concept intrigued him. In the Kesh, he had read *The Sun Also Rises* and could never figure out whether Jake Barnes's impotence stemmed from a physical or psychological wound suffered during the war. None of the other lads in his cage knew either, despite much conjecture, and Dowd had never met anyone else learned enough to ask.

He slept for another two hours. Then, bathed and refreshed, dressed in blue jeans and a polo shirt, he crossed West Broadway to the Four M's saloon. The

M's stood for the brothers Moriarty, although there was but one currently available on the premises, the oldest having been fatally knifed in an altercation over money owed following a New England Patriots game and the other two serving extended sentences for running a major loan-sharking ring.

Dowd felt at ease there. Strangers entering without an introduction were immediately assumed to be federal agents. A back exit went through the kitchen, and another was by way of the cellar. The police, though, were quite accommodating. Three shooting deaths had occurred at the bar in recent years because of drunken disputes, but in each instance the sidewalk outside, where the bodies were deposited, was accepted as the actual site of otherwise inexplicable crimes that had no witnesses.

Crossed flags, the Irish Republic's tricolor and Old Glory, were painted above the entrance. On the wall panels inside were murals depicting the neighborhood, including a faithful rendition of South Boston's main employer, the Gillette plant, complete with the roof sign that said, "Right Guard." Many of the young toughs who caroused in the Four M's were shock troops in the street melees against integration of the Boston public school system. That their brethren in Belfast and Derry were treated like local blacks was a reality far beyond their comprehension, so Dowd never bothered to get into it.

He had a corned beef sandwich on rye and a stein of Michelob draft. The one thing ironically missing at the Four M's was a pint of Guinness, much less one decently pulled. Indeed, the best he could find was in a pub over in Cambridge, frequented by, of all people, students from Harvard.

Dowd went to the rear of the saloon, where there was a line of video games. He was very good at them, and he bent forward now in intense orgiastic pleasure, annihilating one enemy alien after another zooming across the screen. For Dowd, every alien was a Brit.

The next day, Monday, when news of the armory break-in was discovered, authorities described it to reporters as a thoroughly professional job. A National Guard spokesman, however, was quoted as saying that the stolen weapons were "virtually useless," since the bolts, as required by regulations, had been removed and stored elsewhere.

Oh, how they cover their asses, Dowd thought, just like the politicians. It was the first thing he had looked for when he was in the vault, and the bolts were all there, not that a good machinist couldn't have replaced them anyway.

Then, that afternoon, young Jamie McGuire told Dowd that the trawler was ready to go.

PART
I

Chapter

1

The memory of a June morning now ten years past hammered mercilessly at Michael McGuire, each detail of it, every nuance.

Jamie had just turned nine, and Michael McGuire was then an account supervisor in the New York advertising agency that he had started working for in the mailroom. Not too shabby, he would think, for an Irish kid out of the Inwood section of Manhattan—which might have been Oshkosh as far as Madison Avenue was concerned—the son of a subway motorman, who had gone to Cardinal Hayes High School in the Bronx, joined the ROTC to help get him through Fordham University while living at home, and paid back the army with three years of service in the Counterintelligence Corps in West Germany.

That morning the sun was a shimmering metallic yellow, about the span of Michael McGuire's hand above the horizon, when he came out of the house toward the boat. Jamie had been right behind him clutching his new rod. "Dad," Jamie had said, "why does the sun look like that in the morning? Why isn't it, you know, red like when it's going down?"

"I think it's because all the pollution in the air hasn't started yet," he said. The truth, of course, was that Michael McGuire didn't really know and hadn't even thought about it before. The question pleased him, though, and he wondered again if he had been that inquisitive and outspoken when he was Jamie's age. But he couldn't remember.

The boat was wooden, a secondhand Lyman lap-strake inboard, nineteen feet long. Considering that she had to be sanded down and painted and varnished every year and the bottom given a new copper coat, one of those glossy new outboard fiberglass jobs would have been a lot more practical to maintain and run around in, especially in the shallow stretches of Moriches Bay on the south shore of Long Island. But the Lyman drew just two feet at the propeller guard, so you only had to be truly careful when the bay was at dead low tide. And with the weight of the inboard engine, you could go out of the inlet into the ocean, if it wasn't too rough, without that skitterish, bouncing sensation McGuire often felt when he was in somebody's outboard. Besides, Mary Alice had fallen in love with the Lyman's traditional workmanship the instant she saw her and said, "That's what I want for my birthday, for all of us," and the next day he went back to the boatyard and got her, and the first thing he did after that was to have *Mary Alice* put on her transom.

Michael McGuire had been anticipating this morning all winter long in the city, the time when the schools of bluefish migrating up from the south would finally hit the Long Island shore and he would take Jamie out with him. Late last summer, after he bought the Lyman, he had gotten a bamboo pole for Jamie to fish for snappers, the voracious baby blues that swarmed around the wetland fringes of the bay after the spawning season was over, slashing into clouds of frantic little silvery shiners and killies before heading into the Atlantic.

It was such a perfect introduction to fishing for a boy. He remembered how when he was a kid on vacation in the Catskills with the rest of the family, *his* father had played cards and drunk beer all day with other union members while he went off by himself to the lake with a pole and a bent pin and a slice of bread and waited for hours for a bite that never came. It was a wonder he ever tried fishing again. But wasn't that what being a father was all about? To be better.

He had shown Jamie how to insert a snapper hook into the tail of a shiner and push the shank through to the shiner's head, and where to clip the red and white bobber to the line and toss it near the leaping baitfish that came out of the water and then fell back in like a splatter of raindrops and to watch for the bobber to dip under the surface when a snapper hit. Almost instantly the bobber had gone under and he would never forget how his son had cried out, amazed and delighted, as he swung in the wriggling six-inch snapper. Within an hour, a couple dozen more snappers were taken, and Mary Alice deep-fried a batch of them so you didn't have to worry about the bones and served them up with scrambled eggs, and Michael McGuire had said, "Next year, we'll go after the real thing," and Jamie looked at him solemnly and said, "Is that a promise?"

The weekend before that June morning, after they had all come out from the city, he had driven with Jamie down the Montauk Highway to the tackle shop in Hampton Bays to pick up the trolling rods and reels he had left over the winter for reconditioning, the ones he would use later in the summer in the ocean along a sandbar that ran for miles off the beach, and to retrieve the eight-foot beautifully whip-like graphite casting rod that he had commissioned for himself, and to get one of the fiberglass rods in stock for Jamie to start out with.

"Which one should I pick?" Jamie had said, and Michael McGuire said, "You've got to decide for yourself, son. Try them out and take the one that feels best for you. That's the only way you can tell." Then after Jamie had chosen a bright red rod that had some nice action to it, he bought him a Shake-speare spinning reel, and while the eight-pound test line was being spooled on it, one of the men standing around the shop said to Jamie, "Well, boy, you going to get yourself a big fish?"

"Yes, sir, I am," Jamie said.

"Better be ready then. I hear those blues are run-ning up the Jersey coast. They'll be around here any day now."

Michael McGuire felt a rush of pride at the way Jamie was conducting himself in the shop, confident but not cocky, not acting up as a kid his age might. He was wearing cutoffs and his Spider Man T-shirt.

He was nearly four foot nine, lean as a whippet, with a mop of jet black ringlets, blue eyes, almost violet, like Mary Alice's, and a freckled nose. It was amazing, McGuire always thought, how closely Jamie echoed her fine-boned face without a hint of his own blunt features to be found.

In the car, driving back from the tackle shop, Jamie said, "Dad, does eight-pound test mean if the fish is more than eight pounds the line will break?"

"Not exactly. It's all a delicate balance. It's partially how much the fish weighs and how much give the line has, and how much drag is on the reel and how you play the fish with the rod and how you have to be careful not to jerk the line when the fish comes out of the water trying to throw the hook or when you're reeling it in close to the boat and it suddenly takes off again. The thing is to make it all as fair as possible for you and the fish. For instance, there's some pretty big blues in the ocean off the point at Montauk, and those party boats go out after them with wire lines, but it doesn't make any difference how big the fish are if you're using wire, it's just a matter of horsing them in, and for me that's not what fishing is all about."

Now, as Michael McGuire started the engine and listened to the lazy, throaty sound of the exhaust spewing water before he eased away from the dock, Jamie said, "Hey, there's Mom," and he looked up and saw Mary Alice in her white cotton nightgown waving at them from the deck of the house and they both waved back. The house was at the tip of a miniature peninsula that jutted into the bay from the barrier beach. A developer had jammed twenty summer cottages on it before anyone had thought about zoning, and when you drove in, the sense of it was, well, a little tacky. But once you were at McGuire's, right at the end, you had no sense of any of this.

The view due north was three miles of uninterrupted bay, and east and west it was even more expansive, made all the more imposing by the million-dollar vacation homes you could see along the ocean beach itself, as if his cottage was an integral part of the picture. He had rented it for two thousand dollars one season and bought it for twenty-five the next on a fifteen-year mortgage. He'd added on an extra room for Jamie, and with waterfront property prices suddenly zooming, it already was worth close to three times what he had paid for it. It was another reason why Michael McGuire considered himself one of the luckiest fellows around.

He wheeled the boat in a wide turn and, gradually throttling up, sped west, knifing through the glassy stillness, reveling in the glistening sheets of spray shooting out from both sides of the bow and in the serenity of this hour of the day. A mile or so north a big cabin cruiser moved through channel markers of the coastal waterway. Soon the waterway would be filled with other boats, but right then there wasn't another sign of human activity in the bay. Off to the left three cormorants, necks outstretched, flew in frantic haste a few feet above the surface. The cloudless western sky was still just dark enough to display the palest gold sliver of moon. Michael McGuire, behind the wheel, glanced at Jamie next to him, at the profile of his face peering so intently forward, and couldn't resist tapping him on the shoulder. He

smiled at him when he looked up, and saw Jamie
smile back and give him a thumbs-up. It was a magic
moment. Michael McGuire had never felt closer to
his son.

The first place they would try was a hole about
ninety yards across where sand had been pumped
from the floor of the bay a couple of years before in
a vain effort to fight beach erosion. They'd drift over
it casting to see if anything was there. Michael Mc-
Guire slowed the boat, then cut the engine at the
edge of the hole. At first, there seemed to be an absolute silence. But then McGuire heard a slap on the
water and another, and spotted little eddies after
each slap. They were coming from mossbunkers that
the blues loved to feed on. He could just imagine all
those blues down there driving the bunkers up.
There hadn't been any wind at all, but now, right on
cue, a breeze sprang up, ruffling the water just
enough to help obscure a line and leader.

As Michael McGuire attached lures to the leaders,
Jamie said, "Do fish have breakfast like people do? Is
that why it's best to fish in the morning?"

"That's part of it, but the main thing is that the
tide's turning and that gets everything in motion, and
the best tide is outgoing, like this one, bringing all
that good stuff around to feed on."

He told Jamie to stand on the engine housing for
more height and said, "Okay, let's give it a shot," but
when Jamie whipped the rod around, the lure
slammed against the boat.

"Oh, Dad!"

Michael McGuire suppressed his irritation. For
Christ's sake, don't be a little-league father, he

thought. "It's okay, son. You forgot to release the bail."

In his next try, Jamie let the line go free too soon, and the lure went almost straight up before landing in the water, too close to the boat. Still, there was a telltale swirl right behind the lure.

"Relax, Jamie. They're out there. Wait till the rod's past your shoulder, and remember to snap your wrist."

This time Jamie made a lovely cast, sending the lure out in a graceful arc maybe a hundred feet before it hit the surface with a soft plop. Almost at once, as he began taking the line in, there was another swirl and the rod bent quivering, and Jamie was shouting, "I've got something!" and a blue came straight up at least a foot out of the water trying to throw the hook, and then Jamie was saying, "I'm reeling in, but the line's going out, should I put on more drag?" and Michael McGuire said, "No, he's running now, let the rod do the work," and suddenly the line went slack and he said, "He's coming back, reel, keep tension on the line." The blue abruptly changed direction again, breaching the surface in a frenzied leap forward. Michael McGuire watched the line cutting through the water, circling the stern of the boat. "Follow him around, Jamie, keep your rod up," he said. Then the blue headed back in once more, barely breaking the water. "Keep reeling, he's tiring," he said. Close by the boat, spooked by her, the blue desperately renewed the fight, silvery flashes exploding first one way, then another. He leaned out for the line, sliding his hand down it until he could grab the leader, and then reached for the fish with a small gaff and lifted him into the boat. "Good work, son," he said, "he's a beauty, close to three pounds," and looked up at Jamie, standing on the engine housing with a big proud grin on his face.

By now they had drifted past the far side of the hole, and Michael McGuire started the engine and turned back in a wide sweep to begin over again, and on their second pass Jamie hooked another blue and brought him in on his own, and then Jamie said, "Dad, aren't you going to fish, too?" So the next time around they were both casting and each of them got one, and working in silent tandem they kept bringing in more blues on every pass.

If it had been a commercial, Michael McGuire thought, it could not have gone better. It was clear that Jamie was enjoying himself hugely and that there was an intense camaraderie between them, as tangible as it was unspoken. He felt the tenseness in him recede. He hadn't realized how uptight he had been, or just how important this morning really was to him. Every time he picked up a newspaper or a magazine, there was always something about the failure of parental relationships. Some rich guy's kid had overdosed on heroin, or some otherwise apparently respectable kid had gone on a murderous rampage, or some other kid had committed suicide; and always there was an expert comment in these stories about loneliness and the lack of communication, that the kid hadn't had anyone to turn to.

Michael McGuire wondered if other fathers worried the way he did, but he didn't know, because he had kept all of this to himself. And even though he knew that kids in the beginning were supposed to be tied to their mothers, he secretly envied Mary Alice's easy closeness with Jamie, how he would walk in on them unexpectedly and find them chatting away, giggling about something, or at the piano singing together or to one another. He'd feel so helplessly left out. He couldn't carry a tune to save his life.

Once, he had let his frustration show. "What was that all about?" he asked Mary Alice after a prolonged conversation she and Jamie had in the kitchen, and she said, "He wanted to know what 'boisterous' meant," and he said, "How come he doesn't ask me?" and Mary Alice had looked at him with amusement and said, "Actually, it's a little more complicated. First you had to hear all the details about Timmy Abernathy's birthday party, about the vast array of toys Timmy received, including a remote-controlled car, an item, I was reminded, that is missing in this household, and how the Gelb girl, I think her name is Samantha, suffered, apparently to everyone's great glee, an embarrassing moment of incontinency—those are my words—and then, finally, getting to the nub of it, the news that Mrs. Abernathy had barred David Hoogenboom from the party because he was too boisterous, and what was that? I think Jamie figured you wouldn't be too interested in all of this, and I also think he was probably right."

The previous summer Michael McGuire had taken Jamie to see the Yankees play. Every kid loved baseball. He remembered how his Uncle Jack had taken him to the old Polo Grounds to watch the Giants, and how Uncle Jack pointed out the way Mel Ott raised his right foot forward and out just before swinging the bat, which, according to Uncle Jack, accounted for all the home runs Ott socked down the right field line, and how he had absorbed and treasured this information and solemnly relayed it to the other fifth-graders in acolyte training at the Church of the Good Shepherd. But with Jamie it had been a disaster. After two Cokes and two hot dogs, he was squirming so in his seat that McGuire had to take him home before the third inning was over. In retrospect, he realized that Jamie had never exhibited the slightest interest in baseball, that it all had been a fantasy of his.

So when the snapper fishing went so well, and Jamie wanted to fish more with him, Michael McGuire had felt such a surge of emotion. It was as though he had at last connected with his son in a new bonding that they could build on together. Lost in this reverie, he hadn't been paying attention to the blue he had on the line. After coming out of the water the blue had run straight at the boat and before he could react, it was under the hull, and then the line snarled around the propeller and snapped.

"See, nobody's perfect," Michael McGuire said. Ordinarily, he would have been furious at himself. But now he was secretly glad he had been the first to lose a fish.

"Relax, Dad," Jamie said, laughing, working his own blue. "Got to keep your eye on the ball, you know."

The sun was up a good deal higher and Michael McGuire could feel it beating against the back of his neck. The day was in full bloom and it was going to be a hot one. They made two more passes without a strike and he knew the fishing was over.

"Let's pack it in, son. They've stopped biting."

"How many did we get?"

"Let's see," Michael McGuire said, trying a rough count. "I think eleven."

"Who got the biggest?"

"You did. That first one. Right there." He put his hand on Jamie's shoulder. "That was all right, wasn't it?"

"Hey, are you kidding? It was the best!"

Michael McGuire put the rods in their holders. He went to start the engine when Jamie said, "Dad, can I take her back?"

"Sure."

Michael McGuire stood, letting the wind wash over him, while Jamie crouched behind the wheel. The early morning tranquillity of the bay was gone now. Sunlight bounced blindingly off the surface. Weekend sailors were beginning to crowd the waterway. Right in front of them a Sunfish sailboat maneuvered erratically.

"Watch out for that guy," Michael McGuire said. "He doesn't know what he's doing."

"Don't worry, Dad. I see him."

Jamie slowed to reduce the wake and curved around the Sunfish and then suddenly gunned the engine so that the *Mary Alice* leapt forward, planing over a slight chop that had kicked up. McGuire started to tell him not to go so fast, but just then Jamie turned toward him, grinning conspiratorially, and so he didn't say anything at all.

Michael McGuire had always done the docking, and when they were fifty yards away, Jamie automatically stood up to give his father the wheel, but now he said, "No, you take her in," and was pleased at the way Jamie handled the boat, nosing her in, taking into account the direction of the wind, smoothly throwing the engine into neutral at just the right moment without McGuire saying a word, then reversing for a second before bringing her gently against the dock bumpers. He had a real instinct for boats, Michael McGuire thought.

Then, after the bow and stern lines were set, Jamie cut the engine and jumped out of the boat and raced toward the house, shouting, "Mom, look at what we got!" and Mary Alice came out, wearing white shorts and a gingham shirt that showed off her slender tanned legs and a hint of firm breasts that let you know they were there but didn't beat you over the head with their presence. She was such a fine-looking woman, Michael McGuire thought, with her close-cropped lustrous black curls and a face with marvelously sexy freckles multiplying in the summer sun; and now, standing on the bulkhead as Jamie helped him lift the trash can filled with blues onto the dock, she stared down at them and said, "My two fishermen."

Without being told, Jamie removed the rods and hosed them off and hosed down the boat as Michael McGuire on the dock began to scale and fillet the blues, except for the two biggest, which he gutted, leaving their heads on. Mary Alice would marinate them in pimento to get out the oil, and he'd broil them whole over charcoal for the friends they were having for dinner that night.

"Can we go out again tomorrow, Dad?" Jamie asked.

"Sure."

"And can we go trolling for the big blues in the ocean when the time's right?"

"You bet."

"What's the biggest blue you ever caught in the ocean?"

"Well, that was three years ago, and it was a record blue around here that summer."

"How big?"

"Nineteen pounds, four ounces."

"What'd it look like?"

"It looked like Moby Dick to me. You know who Moby Dick was?"

"No."

"You'll find out. There's a wonderful book about him that I'll get you."

"Wow," Jamie said, "as big as Moby Dick."

"Hold on," Michael McGuire said, laughing. "To tell you the truth, I was exaggerating a little. But you'll understand what I mean."

In his sleep, when he dreamed of this, the nightmarish part always began when he started coming awake, rising through successive levels of consciousness, struggling desperately against it, actually hearing himself in the dream protesting its inevitability, dreading it, and then awakening with terrifying swiftness, bolt upright, coated with sweat.

Jamie, oh, my Jamie. You were all I had left, he would say to himself. And would silently weep.

Chapter

2

"**W**ho is this guy?"
O'Dwyer said.

"Scotland Yard," Frank Twomey said. "An inspector."

"Yeah? What's his name?"

"MacGregor. Thomas J. MacGregor."

"Hey, how about that? A real Scotch guy in Scotland Yard."

"You're hilarious," Twomey said. "It's a real bonus having to listen to you all day, every day."

Twomey and Jimmy O'Dwyer were agents attached to the Brooklyn/Queens office of the Federal Bureau of Investigation. Normally they worked organized crime; but the night before, the supervisor had called Twomey over and told him that he and O'Dwyer were to pick up this Scotland Yard inspector in the morning and take him where he had to go. For some interview on Long Island.

"It's a courtesy," Twomey told O'Dwyer. "Hands

across the sea. They do it for us when our guys go over there. And besides, we have to be there to make it official. We have to write it up, how it went."

"So what else is new?" O'Dwyer said. He gazed around at the traffic that they were stuck in on the 59th Street bridge going into Manhattan. "Why us?"

"Because we're available. It's no big deal. We finished the Paulie case, and unless you have Alzheimer's, I'm taking off tomorrow, Friday, to see Nellie in Washington." Twomey had been out of the FBI Academy almost five years, and O'Dwyer had only been a year and a half behind him, but sometimes, Twomey would think, he was like Jimmy O'Dwyer's father confessor. "I'm sorry it's over, the Paulie case," he said.

"Yeah, I never ate so good. Those sausages and peppers were something else. You know, they make those sausages right on the premises. And that fettucine with the cream and butter and cheese. Right on! I'll tell you one thing, wiseguys know how to eat."

The Paulie case had been a big score, three capos bagged, with defense lawyers screaming all over the place, and they both were going to get commendations. Paulie's was a restaurant in Queens alongside the East River with a spectacular view of the Manhattan skyline. The joke was that Paulie Delvecchio and his brother Dante, a lieutenant in the Gambino crime family, neatly divided housekeeping chores. Paulie did the cooking and Dante did the killing.

Frank Twomey had developed the lead from one of his street informants, a smalltime transvestite wiseguy named Winnie the Pooh, who, after having spent three years in the federal penitentiary in Lewisburg, Pennsylvania, on a hijacking rap, did not wish a return visit. "Just keep what you're doing within reason," Twomey had advised him, "and we'll keep, you know, a balance sheet." Winnie had tipped the balance heavily in his favor when he reported that Paulie's restaurant was the laundering machine for a mob-controlled interstate bookmaking ring. Monday was payoff day for losers, and while to a large extent these transactions were in cash, others were checks; and on Tuesday morning these checks passed through Paulie's for forwarding to the various banks involved. Apparently it had been going on for years.

Twomey and O'Dwyer kept the restaurant under surveillance for more than a month, noting and photographing the comings and goings, especially on Tuesdays. They also of necessity became regular customers. Paulie's clientele included major dons and their underlings in the city, and Brooklyn and Queens political figures with their snouts in the trough, as well as dedicated gourmands drawn by the three-star rating *The New York Times* had accorded the kitchen.

One night O'Dwyer nudged Twomey and said, "Look who's here, two tables to your left." It was the Brooklyn D.A. A Paulie waiter handled his presence with aplomb. The waiter, in taking his order, said, "You don't need an American Express card for me to know who you are."

Nearby Paulie's, bordering the river, was an indoor tennis club. On weekends particularly, they had observed the parking area filled with Mercedeses, BMWs and Cadillacs, many of them chauffeur-driven. "I'm going to check it out," O'Dwyer had said suddenly, and when he came back, he said, "Jesus, you won't believe it. Two thousand a year just to join and sixty bucks an hour for a court."

"What do you care? You don't play tennis."

"Well, I was thinking maybe I'd start. You're always telling me to get in shape."

"Stick to racquetball," Twomey had said.

Now, on the 59th Street bridge, the traffic stalled, horns hooting, O'Dwyer said, "We should have taken the Triborough."

"You know, if they had a quiz show on TV called 'Twenty/Twenty Hindsight,' you'd be a real winner."

"I was watching 'Wheel of Fortune' the other night. Grand prize, a Trans-Am. Category, people. Three words. First word, three letters, first letter 'N.' Second word, four letters, third letter 'R.' Third word, six letters, fifth letter 'T.' I got it right away. 'NEW YORK GIANTS.' I could've had the Trans-Am."

Twomey finally got off the bridge and made his way down Lexington Avenue to the Halloran House to pick up Thomas J. MacGregor. The Halloran House was where the Justice Department parked everybody who came to New York, assistant U.S. attorneys, agents, you name it. There was some kind of a deal on the rooms.

He went to the desk clerk, who pointed to a stocky figure in a dark blue suit and white shirt pacing back and forth across the lobby. Old J. Edgar Hoover would have approved, Twomey thought, but Hoover was no longer among them. Twomey himself was wearing a light blue shirt and tan sports jacket.

"Inspector MacGregor? Frank Twomey, FBI. Sorry I'm late. The traffic coming in was awesome this morning."

"Don't mind. London's the same these days. Don't know where it's going to end."

He may be a Scot, Twomey thought, but he sounded pretty English to him, and immediately saw that he had a diplomatic crisis on his hands. Even though it was only a little past nine o'clock, MacGregor was puffing on a big stogie. O'Dwyer's occasional cigarettes were bad enough, but a cigar was beyond the pale. Twomey was on a health kick. He jogged six miles at daybreak three times a week, and worked out regularly with weights in the gym. He debated if he should say something, but decided the hell with it. He'd at least get him in the rear seat and lower the window. When they were by the car, though, and Twomey was saying, "Inspector, this is my partner, Jimmy O'Dwyer," O'Dwyer had the front passenger door open and was practically pushing MacGregor inside. He was sure O'Dwyer had done it on purpose. He could see the malicious grin on his face.

"You enjoying yourself, Inspector?" Twomey asked.

"Quite, although it's rather a quick trip. One of your lads had me to dinner last night. Larry Theomopolous. Took me to a Grecian restaurant. Belly dancers and all that. Different, you know."

Twomey had heard of Theomopolous. He was in Squad 431, Division Four. In the international arena, as they say. Foreign counterintelligence. The Middle East, North Africa, Western Europe. Tight-lipped guys. Not too many laughers there. He wondered why somebody from the 431 wasn't with MacGregor now. Probably this sort of babysitting was beneath them.

"Where to, Inspector?" Twomey asked. "We really haven't been filled in, except to be at your disposal."

"Glen Cove, I believe on your Long Island. This is the address."

Twomey decided to take the Midtown Tunnel. There was still a lot of traffic coming in, but heading the other way was fairly smooth.

On the Long Island Expressway, O'Dwyer said, "You after some big international fugitive, you don't mind me asking?"

"In a manner of speaking."

"What's the deal?"

"Terrorists."

"Terrorists?"

"Yes, the IRA."

"Hey, come on," Twomey heard O'Dwyer say from the back seat. "The IRA's not terrorists."

Twomey glanced sideways at MacGregor. The Scotland Yard inspector looked as if he were going to asphyxiate on his cigar, his face flushed, jowls quivering over his starched collar. Of all the times for O'Dwyer to come up with that line, Twomey thought. Thank God he hadn't told O'Dwyer the real reason why he was taking the next day off. All Twomey needed now was for this MacGregor to say something to Theomopolous and those other guys in 431. There'd be a real stink. Full internal investigation. Jesus! Twomey shot O'Dwyer a withering look in the rearview mirror.

"Inspector," he said, "what Jimmy here means is that it's hard sometimes to figure out what's going on.

You know the old saying. One man's terrorist is another man's freedom fighter. He was like talking generally."

"Oh, yeah, right," O'Dwyer said.

MacGregor appeared to have recovered somewhat. "Bloody terrorists," he said. "Blew up the bloody horses outside Buckingham Palace. Blew up Lord Mountbatten. Tried to blow up the prime minister."

"Yeah, right, I forgot," O'Dwyer said. "We going after a bloody terrorist right now? Maybe we should have backup."

That was a nice gung-ho touch, Twomey thought. O'Dwyer at least was making a stab at rehabilitating himself.

No, it wasn't necessary, MacGregor said. They were going, he said, to the residence of a Mr. Moses Weinstein.

O'Dwyer continued to try to work his way back into the inspector's good graces. "Hey, you mean the investment banker, the guy they call the Wolf of Wall Street?"

"So I'm told." The Weinsteins, MacGregor said, had hired an Irish au pair girl named Rita Carroll for their two children. Rita, he said, was the girl friend of Mick Connally, an IRA bomber known to have masterminded the attempt on the prime minister's life in Brighton. They had just missed Connally in his London digs. They had tracked him to Holland, but then the trail evaporated. Scotland Yard's only current lead was Rita. One way or another, Rita had to be in contact with Connally.

"Awesome," Twomey said when they drove up to the Weinstein home, a huge pillared white clapboard house with a great expanse of lawn sloping down to Long Island Sound. Mick Connally, he thought, could hide out there for a year before they found him.

Twomey rang the front bell. As soon as he had identified himself and asked for Rita Carroll, the black maid who had opened the door hastily closed it. A minute or so later, the door opened again. This time a thin woman in a blue silk dress, nervously fingering three strands of pearls around her neck, was standing there. "I'm Mrs. Weinstein," she said. "Is there something wrong? Is something the matter with Rita's papers?"

"Not at all," Twomey said. "It's a missing person case. We thought Miss Carroll could be of some help."

"Oh, I'm so relieved. She's so good with the children, but you never can tell, can you? Please come in."

They spoke to her in her sitting room, off a small bedroom. She was pretty in a plain way, Twomey thought. She wore no makeup. She had reddish, slightly kinky hair. On the wall was a calendar with the heading "Flames of Freedom." Almost every date was captioned, noting another milestone in the Irish troubles, and for this day, September 26, the caption read "19 newspapers suppressed, large number of arrests in Ireland, 1919."

She looked scared at the sight of the FBI shields, but Twomey saw her eyes turn blankly defiant when MacGregor was introduced to her. MacGregor got nowhere. Yes, she knew who Mick Connally was, she said. No, she had no idea where he was. For all she knew, he could be in China.

"We know you were with him in London just before the Brighton bombing," MacGregor said.

"Do you now," she said. "I don't."

Behind the inspector's back, O'Dwyer gave her a wink and a smile.

Afterward, on the way back to the city, MacGregor said, "She's lying. I'm going to request that a careful watch be kept on her. Sooner or later she'll bring us to Connally."

"I agree," Twomey said. "We'll write up a memo for the record."

He walked MacGregor into the hotel and said, "Well, good luck to you, sir. Real pleasure meeting you. And I want to thank you for being so instructive to my partner. We all need to hear the truth."

"What can I say?" O'Dwyer said in the car. "I fucked up. Do you think he'll do anything?"

"No, I think we cooled it. He may mention it, is all. He'll push, though, on that Rita Carroll you were giving the big wink to. You get a chance, you better tell her to mind her p's and q's."

In the morning Twomey drove back into Manhattan, to the 13th Precinct on East 21st Street. His father was a retired New York City detective. His uncle, a sergeant still on the job, was a kilted piper in the police department's Emerald Society band. There was a third brother on the dole in Derry to whom they sent a check every month. "I'll not be run out of my homeland," the brother had written once. "I'll die in my bed, unless they slay me first. God bless." Twomey's father had framed the letter.

With his family credentials, after graduating from St. John's University in Brooklyn, Frank Twomey had no difficulty being accepted into the FBI. He always remembered an evening when he was in parochial school and several of his father's police friends were at the house cursing the name of an officer who had exposed widespread corruption in the department. "He's a rat," one of them cried, "we shouldn't be washing our dirty linen in public," and Twomey, sitting on the stairs, listened as his father said, "I don't know the man from Adam. All I know is when he took an oath to enforce the law, it didn't say against everyone except other cops." He said, "Every man must decide right from wrong."

The department's bomb squad was headquartered in the precinct. Twomey took the elevator up and found Sergeant Monahan at his desk scrutinizing the sports pages of the *Daily News*. "Hello, Frankie," Monahan said, "you're looking well. What do you think? The Jets against the Patriots. Should I give the points?"

"I'll lay the bet for you at Paulie's."

"Oh, that's rich. Saw your picture in the paper and everything." Monahan looked around uneasily. "Let's go down to the cafeteria for coffee," he said, taking a manila envelope with him. There he slid the envelope across a Formica tabletop to Twomey. "Here's the requisition you want. For a carton. That's thirty cakes, a pound and a half each."

"I'm sure I won't use it. It's just a precaution."

"I trust not. I'll say it's a forgery." Monahan looked at his watch. "I've got to get back. There's talk the spicks are scheming to plant a device in the Statue of

Liberty. Doesn't that beat the devil? Well, best to your dad."

However unintentional, the irony was not lost on Twomey. But America hadn't grabbed off part of Puerto Rico, he thought. The whole island had voted. If only all of Ireland were allowed to vote.

He cut across lower Manhattan to the Holland Tunnel and then the New Jersey Turnpike. Just inside the Philadelphia city limits, he got off I-95 at the Academy Road cloverleaf and turned into the grounds of the police academy where the bomb squad there also conducted all of its explosives training. The sergeant he had been told to ask for was named Duffy, and when Twomey saw him, he thought that there must be a giant cookie cutter somewhere that turned out police sergeants. Duffy was as beefy and red-faced as Monahan. Except there was a difference. When Duffy handed him the requisition and Twomey said in all likelihood he wouldn't have to use it, Duffy said, "The fuck I care. Let them investigate all they want."

By the time Twomey got to Washington, he got caught in the rush hour, and Nellie was already in the room waiting for him at the Georgetown Inn on Wisconsin Avenue. They hadn't seen each other in nearly a month, since she had gone back to college, and they fell into bed immediately. She was in her senior year at Catholic University, majoring in sociology, and they were engaged to be married, waiting in deference to her father, a battalion chief in the New York Fire Department, until her graduation.

"It'll make him happy that way," she had said. "And what difference does it really make? I'm yours no matter what." They had both grown up in Elmhurst, in Queens, in St. Mary Help of Christians parish, although he was five years older than she and had never noticed her until they met seriously after he had become an agent and their parents were chatting following Sunday Mass.

They had cheeseburgers and beer in a saloon on M Street, and he told her all the details about the bust at Paulie's and how one of the handcuffed capos was yelling, "What is this, Russia?" and about O'Dwyer's loose lips with the Scotland Yard inspector and about how tough the girl Rita Carroll had been.

"We have to find someone for Jimmy," Nellie said, and he said, "There's one thing for sure, whoever she is, she'll never get a word in edgewise," and they laughed and returned hand in hand to the room. In the morning she said, "Can't you stay tonight?"

"No, I have to get back."

"What's this all about?"

"It's just as well you don't know."

"So that's it, is it," she said. "What's her name?" And then she kissed him. "Frank, I know you have to do what you have to do. Please don't get into trouble."

He went across the Theodore Roosevelt bridge to Route 66 and then hooked into I-95 again. Somehow it didn't have the same resonance that old 66 did. The signs along the way, though, rang with the past. Falls Church, Warrenton, Manassas. Up ahead, Fredericksburg and Richmond. History had been one of Twomey's favorite subjects in school, and blue and gray ghosts flitted across the fields in his mind's eye.

He drove past the ramp for Quantico Triangle and

the main sentried entrance to the marine base. A little farther down I-95, he turned off at Exit 49, and almost at once he was inside the base. It had never ceased to amaze Twomey that you could drive right into the most famous U.S. Marine Corps complex in the country just like that, and nobody stopped you. Suddenly, off to his right, armed marines in camouflaged fatigues were charging up an incline. A line of tanks was silhouetted against the horizon. There was a volley of fire from a rifle range, and another.

After a couple of miles he went by an electrified fence that bordered the road. Within were grass-covered mounds where they kept the stuff. Sticking out of each mound was an air vent, like an unblinking eye. Even if you didn't know what was stored in the bunkers under those mounds, the explosives and ammunition, the whole vista had a sinister sense to it.

When he got to the grounds of the FBI Academy, he parked, flashed his shield at the reception desk in the Administration Building and went upstairs. Richie Donahue of the Hostage Rescue Team had said that there was an exercise that morning and to come by after lunch when it would be quiet. Twomey walked by the recreation room with its rows of pool and Ping-Pong tables to the huge cafeteria. All you could eat for two bucks. Standing in line with his tray he had to laugh. They were still featuring chow mein as one of the entrees. He selected Swedish meatballs, hoping for the best, macaroni with cheese, severely overcooked string beans and chocolate cake.

It was as though nothing had changed. The FBI recruits were in blue shirts, the cops plucked from various police departments coast to coast in red. The cops had been carefully chosen for specialized training. They were ones that Washington considered the most promising candidates to advance in their local departments. The bonds were maintained. It was like creating an auxiliary FBI, for the exchange of information and future cooperation, no questions asked. Each graduating group, together with family and friends, was treated to a spectacular of the FBI in action, complete with helicopters, the Hostage Rescue Team and an explosives display.

That was how the stuff was obtained.

After eating, Twomey drove down past a shooting range, an obstacle course and a bedraggled airliner. The inside of the plane was lined with automobile tires to absorb the live ammunition and stun grenades used in practice rushes. Nearby was a large rectangular roofless structure whose outside walls consisted completely of tires stacked on one another. The walls inside were constantly rearranged for other Hostage Rescue Team rehearsals.

Twomey saw Donahue waiting in fatigues, on his haunches, chewing a blade of grass. He'd been in Twomey's academy class. From Hoboken, New Jersey, he looked right out of a John Wayne movie. "Hey," Twomey said, "lean and mean."

"They keep us running, for sure. How are you? I hear you're the bane of the Mafia."

"Only in restaurants."

He directed Twomey to a field about two hundred yards away with a number of derelict cars, also used for rescue and bombing practice. "Over there, by that Pontiac," Donahue said.

He dragged out two cartons from underneath the

Pontiac that were marked "Property of the U.S. Marine Corps." The cartons contained the military explosive Composition 4, which had a punch second only to a nuclear device. It looked and felt like ordinary putty. It was practically impervious to climate conditions. Besides its power, the beauty of it was that you could shape it any way you wanted to and expertly focus its force. And without a blasting cap it was perfectly harmless. You could throw it against the wall. Light a match to it. A little went a long way. The Philadelphia police had utilized a bit of it for a bomb that was dropped on the heavily fortified house of a militant black group resisting eviction, and the resulting inferno destroyed nearly two hundred neighborhood homes.

"You take the cakes out of the cartons," Donahue said, "and remove that green paper they're wrapped in, and they're untraceable."

"It's appreciated, Richie."

"No problem. Glad to help the good fight. Those fellows don't take American hostages."

The requisitions Twomey had brought with him were a hedge against the remote possibility of being stopped and searched by an MP patrol. You just didn't take any unnecessary chances. That was why he was driving straight back to New York. All he needed was to have his car stolen overnight. He could visualize the headlines now. FBI agent's car found. Ninety pounds of explosives in the trunk. Says he doesn't know how they got there.

It was past ten o'clock that night before he turned into the street in Woodside, off Queens Boulevard by New Calvary Cemetery, and located the shingled two-story frame house with an attached garage. He rang the bell. A tall, slender, elderly man wearing a tie and cardigan opened the door. John L. Mooney had a freckled face and sparse, fading blond hair combed straight back. He had the precise air of an assistant bank manager, which he was. He peered at Twomey through gold-rimmed spectacles.

"Mr. Mooney? Frank Twomey."

"Oh, yes, I've been expecting you. Please come in."

"Thanks, but I'd just as soon not leave the car on the street."

"Of course. How thoughtless of me. I'll open the garage door. I don't have a car myself, you know."

In the garage Twomey unloaded the two cartons and carried them to the basement. "We have to get rid of these boxes and wrappings right away," he said, and Mooney immediately produced several other cartons. He saw Twomey staring at them. The new cartons were for floral displays. "I get them from Flower and Fauna around the corner," Mooney explained. "Especially handy for elongated objects."

He insisted that Twomey have a cup of tea in his book-lined study dominated by what appeared to be one of the original proclamation copies of the 1916 Easter uprising in Dublin. Addressed to Irishmen and Irishwomen, it began: "In the name of God and of the dead generations from which she receives her old tradition of nationhood, Ireland, through us, summons her children to her flag and strikes for her freedom."

After Twomey left, Mooney waited a few minutes and then walked to a pay phone on Queens Boulevard and put in a person-to-person call to a Patrick O'Malley at the Excelsior Yacht Club in Boston.

"Speaking," Kevin Dowd told the operator on the first ring.

"Jake here. The merchandise from Virginia has arrived."

"Fine, very fine. A young lady name of Rita will be around to get it tomorrow. About noon, I'd say."

3

She stared at Michael McGuire from inside the silver frame on the table, her hair longer then, her eyes so merry, just the hint of a mischievous grin crinkling the right corner of her mouth.

He remembered that on their first date Mary Alice Turner said how wonderful it must have been to be raised in all the warmth of an Irish family.

"I wouldn't go overboard on that," he had said. "Besides, I'm not Irish. I'm American."

"You know what I mean."

"Ah, faeries, dancing under the moon, a Druid land, a Druid tune."

"That's Yeats, isn't it?"

"It is, yes," he said in a mock brogue.

"Don't tell me you're trying to escape your past?"

"I'm giving it my best shot," he said. Right from the start, he told her, he'd had two career choices. To be a subway motorman like his father, or anything else.

"You made the right decision," she said. "I never take the subway."

She wanted to know where Inwood was exactly. Wasn't it somewhere in Queens? Everybody thinks that, he said. But it was at the northern tip of Manhattan. When he grew up there, it was mostly Irish, because that's where the borough's bus barns and subway yards were.

"There's a wonderful big park there," Michael McGuire said. "When I was a kid, I used to go down to this marsh where there were wild ducks, all kinds of ducks, and swans and herons—can you imagine, right here in the city?—and huge tulip trees fifteen feet around, and fields of jack-in-the-pulpit and mayapple and jewelweed. Have you ever seen jewelweed? It grows wild, kind of yellow and orange with reddish spots."

She looked at him almost as if she were seeing him for the first time and said, "I'd never guess you knew things like that."

He could feel his face redden. "Well, I went on a couple of nature walks," he said, "and, you know, you remember things like that. There were a lot of Indian caves, too. I explored one once, and I found a real arrowhead. I still have it, I think."

At her insistence, when they decided to marry, he introduced her to his mother and father. She wanted to make it a grand occasion, so she booked a table at the Four Seasons restaurant. After the old man had made it past the reservations desk and the maitre d' and the captain had ushered him to their table in the

Pool Room, he had the look of a death row prisoner on his way to the gas chamber.

"I'll take a rye, straight up, you don't mind," he said, grabbing the arm of the busboy serving a basket of rolls.

"Pop, that's not the waiter. He's a busboy."

"Busboy, is he? I never seen a busboy dressed up like that." Four ryes later, he was as stiff as a billy goat. "Very fine," he kept saying, "very fine."

In contrast, Michael McGuire's mother, Nora, sat primly alert, surveying the elegantly subdued setting of chic Manhattan at dinner around a bubbling pool, determined not to give an inch. She was wearing a dated little veiled hat tilted over her forehead. He was certain it was on prominent display every Sunday at Good Shepherd, along with the white gloves she was now fastidiously removing.

"Michael is our pride and joy," she told Mary Alice. "Of course, we can't forget his sister, Doreen, up in Utica. She's married to a young man in the transportation business, as I'm sure Michael has told you."

That was some promotion, he thought. It was as if his mother was daring him to contradict her. Doreen's husband was a truck driver, and he had not seen his sister in years. Nor had he ever mentioned to Mary Alice that he even had a sister.

"Yes, Michael's told me how close you all are," Mary Alice said.

"I understand you're not Catholic. Would you be married in the church?"

"Mom, come on, you know I haven't been to Mass since college."

"Nothing would please me more," Mary Alice said.

His mother's eyes gleamed triumphantly. "I think I'll have the lamb chops," she said.

In his cups, the old man said, "Turner? That's Brit, ain't it?"

"Yes, more or less. I'm half English. Why do you ask?"

"They've taken our land, don't you know?"

Mary Alice appeared startled. It was the first year of John F. Kennedy's presidency, and the biggest mention Ireland was getting then in the papers was that he was going over to visit his ancestral village.

"There's nothing my father enjoys more than fighting a battle that's over and done with," Michael McGuire said.

"It ain't over yet."

"Well, dinner is," he said, and after he put them in the car he had hired to take them back to Inwood, he said, "See, what did I tell you?"

"But they're your parents. They're family. You owe them."

"Up the violins," he said, letting it go at that. She'd already told him that when she was a college senior her father had absconded from his brokerage firm, together with his secretary, with three million dollars.

"What's amazing is that he's never been caught. I used to have these fantasies of him lolling in a hammock on some tropical island. He's probably living on a very respectable street in Flint, Michigan. Taking the money was the most imaginative thing he ever did."

"What about your mother?"

"Oh, she married a widowed dentist and moved to Arizona. We see each other once a year. All she talks about is my father, and how could he have done what he did."

Instead of a church wedding after they went downtown to get their license, he suddenly said, "The hell with it. Let's get married right here. Now."

And without telling anyone, they checked into the Plaza for a weekend honeymoon. When he took her in his arms in the room, he said, "I'm glad you're an experienced woman. Show me what to do."

"That's terrible," she said, laughing. "That's the all-time worst."

"I love you so much," he said. "Don't ever dare leave me."

"We'll make our own family," she said.

When Mary Alice became pregnant with Jamie, there was a major complication. She began leaking amniotic fluid and had to spend nearly ten weeks in the hospital in bed. A series of new mothers had occupied the other bed in the room, but it was temporarily vacant one evening when he made his nightly visit.

"You won't believe this," she said. "Remember Rachel who had a baby girl, her third in a row? It turns out she's a Hassidic Jew, and this morning before she left to go home, her rabbi came by to commiserate with her. You hear me? *Commiserate!* He said that maybe the next time out she'd have a son. Can you imagine? I was so mad I almost got up and punched him in the nose."

"How did Rachel take it?"

"She just lay there blubbering."

Then Mary Alice began to cry.

"Hey, what's this?"

"The doctor was here. He told me I'm going to make it, he didn't think I would. But he said I couldn't have any more. My insides are all screwed up. Oh, Michael, I had two abortions. I'm sure that's why."

He kissed away her tears. They knew it would be a boy, and he said, "Come on, we already have him. That's what counts."

Finally she managed a smile. "I'm sorry. You're right. We will have him, won't we?"

It was her idea to have Jamie baptized a Catholic, but Michael McGuire did not argue. The old terror, he thought. The Baltimore Catechism drumming at him on his deathbed. "Who made you?" "God made me."

"It's for continuity," she said. "He can make up his mind when he grows up, but at least he won't have to knock on the door."

"When are you coming out of the closet?"

"I just might do it," she said. "I think John the Twenty-third is swell."

She was determined that Jamie be admitted to one of the city's elite private schools. After he took the Educational Records Bureau tests, though, they got back mimeographed rejection notices without even the hope of his being placed on a waiting list. "Listen," Mary Alice raged, "he may not be as smart as we think, but he's not retarded either." She found a child psychologist recognized by all the schools, and the reason for Jamie's failure was quickly established. The tests had been designed to establish how far a child barely out of infancy could progress. But Jamie was the kind of kid who if he figured he couldn't finish something didn't bother trying. Once the game rules were explained to him, he did stupendously well, and warm personal acceptances subsequently flooded in.

•

Jamie was in the seventh grade when his life, and Michael McGuire's, would be forever changed.

The boy was on spring break, spending a week in Florida at the home of a schoolmate's grandparents. Michael McGuire was looking forward to a respite when he and Mary Alice could be completely alone. That night, a Friday, they were going to the theater.

In the afternoon at the office the hysterical call came from the housekeeper, Dahlia. There'd been an accident. Mary Alice had been taken by ambulance to the hospital, the same one where she had given birth to Jamie. She had been standing on top of a folding ladder putting up new living-room curtains when she lost her balance and toppled off headfirst and was knocked unconscious.

By the time he reached the hospital, she'd been X-rayed. A slight concussion was the diagnosis and she was being held overnight for observation. Their family physician, an internist, had been alerted; but when Michael McGuire asked him on the phone when he was coming to see her, he said that he didn't think it was necessary. He said he had talked to the resident on the case and it seemed pretty routine. Mary Alice had had a nasty fall. She'd have a headache and be a little woozy for a while, but there was no reason she couldn't go home in the morning. The physician ex-

cused himself. He was just leaving for a weekend in
the country and gave McGuire his number.

When he tiptoed into her darkened room, she was
awake and he said, "Hi." There was a bruise on her
forehead and he saw three or four stitches just below
and across her lower lip.

"It was so stupid," she said. She pointed at the
stitches. "Plastic surgery. First thing."

The next day he brought her back to the apartment and put her right to bed. He made her a tuna
fish sandwich for lunch, but her mouth hurt too
much to eat it. Later, after she had slept, he brought
in a bottle of champagne.

"That's the ticket," she said.

On Sunday she seemed much better. But in the
afternoon while they were talking he noticed how her
speech suddenly got slurred, as if she were drunk.
After about twenty minutes, though, the slurring disappeared. Then that night it happened again. The
eerie thing was that she didn't appear to be aware of
it.

He insisted that their internist bring in a neurolo-
gist to give her a thorough examination. Then she
was back in the hospital. She had passed out while
being examined. But when he got to the hospital, she
was sitting up in bed looking fine. "I'll be okay," she
said. "Don't say anything to Jamie when you talk to
him. It'll only upset him." They were the last words
he ever heard her say.

Around eight o'clock in the morning the internist
phoned. Mary Alice was in a coma. Michael McGuire
found him waiting outside the room she had been in.
It was empty. She was in intensive care. A nurse had

discovered her comatose when she had gone in for a wake-up temperature reading.

"What happened?"

"I, we, don't know."

"You're telling me she's lying here in this fucking hospital in a coma and nobody notices it?"

The internist's hands fluttered aimlessly.

"Are you saying my wife may die?"

"I, uh, the prognosis is not good."

This cannot be taking place, Michael McGuire thought. He wanted to scream his rage, send his fist into the internist's ashen face, trash everything on the station desk behind which nurses and various attendants were studiously averting their gaze. Instead he barely managed to whisper, "Show me where she is."

When he saw Mary Alice, the tubes and wires connected to her, the flickering monitors measuring her vital signs, his stomach turned over. He sat beside her, holding her limp hand. He closed his eyes and kept pinching her as hard as he could. When he opened his eyes, he told himself, she'd be awake from the pain. He tried to pray, begging forgiveness for his lack of faith, promising to change. But this came off so hollowly, even to him. Then he tried to will her back.

Jamie was due to return that day from Florida. During the ride in from the airport, Michael McGuire said nothing about Mary Alice. The idea of saying anything within earshot of a stranger, the driver of the car he had hired, was more than he could bear. Or was he only grabbing hold of an excuse to put off the inevitable? He felt himself beginning to unravel, and he could not allow that to happen, not now.

He tried to concentrate on Jamie's description of his visit to Disney World. "You would have gotten a kick out of one thing, Dad," Jamie was saying. "They have all these hedges all over of elephants and camels and giraffes and things. 'Cept they're not real. I asked someone how they kept them clipped and he said they didn't have to. They were made of concrete and painted green to look like hedges."

Oh, Jesus, Michael McGuire thought.

Two of Mary Alice's best women friends were waiting at the apartment, along with Dahlia. "Where's Mom?" Jamie said.

He took Jamie into the bedroom he shared with Mary Alice. And now he prayed fervently, however unfocused, that he'd be given the strength and the tongue to say the right words. "Mom's very sick," he said. "She's in the hospital."

"What's wrong?"

"Well, it was an accident. She fell, she fell off a ladder, and she hurt herself very badly. She hurt her head."

"Why didn't you call me?"

"Because I didn't want to worry you. Because nobody knew how bad it was going to be."

"Can I see her?"

That was a decision Michael McGuire already had made. He remembered how it had been when he was in the intensive care unit by her side, his stomach doubling up on him, bringing him to the edge of throwing up. Rightly or wrongly, he was not going to subject Jamie to that horror. He would not allow it to be the last image Jamie had of Mary Alice.

"The thing is she can't talk," he said. "She's in a

special place where they're trying to do everything they can for her."

"Is she going to be all right?"

They were sitting next to one another on the bed. He took Jamie in his arms. He felt the rigidity in his son's body. He stared vacantly past Jamie's shoulder, not knowing how to answer. He saw a framed portrait of the three of them on Mary Alice's bureau. His eyes welled with tears. He thought about letting himself go, of sharing all of his terrified grief. But this simply was not his nature, and he fought again, as he had in the car coming in from the airport, to control himself. "I hope so," he said. "I just don't know, son. We're just going to have to hang in there together."

One of the women present, whose name was Elizabeth Carter, had gone to college with Mary Alice. Divorced and a free-lance writer, she had a son whom Jamie knew and often played with, and she had him come over now; and after Dahlia had fixed them dinner, the two boys went into Jamie's room. "He seems okay," Elizabeth said when she looked in on them. "They're both bent over a chessboard. Hardly noticed me."

"That's good," Michael McGuire said. He'd been steadily sipping Jack Daniel's on the rocks, automatically refilling his glass. "But if the worst happens, what am I going to do with him without her?"

"You're a good father," Elizabeth said. "He's lucky to have you. You'll do fine. That's the least of it."

"I'd like to believe you. I think we've gotten a lot closer. But let's face it. For the really important things, the secret things, the connection is still with her. And when you get down to it, that goes for me, too."

Everyone left around ten. He told Jamie to try to get some sleep. "If you want to," he said, "why don't you go into the big bed. I'd like that. I'm feeling kind of lonely." And Jamie said yes, that would be fine. So Michael McGuire kissed him goodnight and said, "I'll be along in a while," and then fixed himself another Jack Daniel's and sat there thinking about Mary Alice, and about how he had come to depend upon her so much, for her love and intelligence and wit and her unwavering support, and about the awfulness of this time, the unfairness of it.

He peeked into the bedroom. Jamie seemed to be sleeping peacefully on his back, not stirring at all. He must have gone off the moment his head hit the pillow. The only jarring note was the old beat-up Snoopy doll he was holding that he always went to bed with when he was a little kid. Mary Alice had resewn it again and again. Michael McGuire tried to fathom what he'd been thinking inside, what dreams he was having. But he couldn't tell. Right then Jamie's face appeared so serene and innocent and vulnerable.

At eight in the morning the phone rang. Instantly awake, Michael McGuire got it on the first ring. It was the hospital resident. He glanced at Jamie, who had not moved. He put the call on hold and took it in the kitchen. A new X-ray procedure called a CAT scan had discovered a blood clot buried in Mary Alice's brain. It was located in a critical spot, beyond surgical help, and it was getting bigger.

"There's no hope?"

"It's very bad. I'm sorry."

He hung up and poured himself a straight vodka and downed it in a gulp. It was at that precise moment, he would later reflect, that he began a personal withdrawal, purposely numbing himself, as though he were physically amputating wounded limbs of his body, cauterizing his nerve endings instead of embarking on an emotional catharsis that might enable him better to glue himself back together. And he would wonder, without ever really knowing, how this had truly affected Jamie.

Word was spreading about Mary Alice. He had his secretary come up from the office to handle the calls. He went back to the hospital to sit by her side, but he was only going through the motions now. She looked exactly the same. Finally he whispered, "I'm going to miss you so much."

People started dropping by the apartment that afternoon, and he had Dahlia order in food and liquor. He continued to drink, vodka in a Bloody Mary mix, not gulping it down like the first vodka that morning, but still sipping steadily, pacing himself, creating a barrier against the pain knifing through him, a pain that would not go away.

He asked Dahlia to stay over, and after the last people had left and she had gone to bed and he and Jamie were alone, Jamie looked at him very hard and said, "Is Mom going to die?"

"Yes," he said.

Jamie flung himself into his arms and began to sob uncontrollably. He held him close, feeling Jamie's body convulse. The sobs grew louder. He felt the hot wetness of Jamie's tears. Michael McGuire wept silently for his son. Oh, Jamie, please, let it all out, he thought, and get rid of all those Furies. He wished that he could do it for himself.

At last, after many minutes, the sobs got softer and the spasms started to ease and then ceased, and Jamie said, "I'm sorry, Dad," and he said, "Hey, there's nothing for you to be sorry for."

He stared into his son's red-rimmed eyes, gripping his shoulders. "What I'm sorry about," he said, "is that you had to find out so soon how rotten life can be."

He went to see Mary Alice one more time, and then could not face it anymore. She lingered on for another day and a half. People were in the apartment all the time now to be with him and Jamie.

"Why are they having such a good time?" Jamie asked, and Michael McGuire said, "They're not. They're just trying to cheer us up," and a while later he overheard Jamie explaining to one of his friends, "They're here to cheer us up," and somehow afterward, in his memory of all of this, that was one of the first things that would always come to mind.

Then it was over. He took Jamie aside and told him, "Mom's gone," and this time there were no tears left to be shed.

After the funeral Michael McGuire arranged for Dahlia to live with them full-time instead of only coming in during the day. "Jamie's going to need you," he said. "We both are." He kept Jamie out of school for a week. When he returned, his grades did not suffer noticeably. Everyone agreed that this was a good sign. Swimming was a big school sport, and Jamie had displayed considerable ability on the junior varsity. He left the apartment promptly at six each morning to get in his laps. In the evenings he sometimes played the piano, but mostly the guitar that Mary Alice had gotten him the year before. Michael McGuire would hear him playing and singing quietly for hours on end in his room.

About three weeks after Mary Alice's death, Anthony Seth-Jones called. He was in Washington, over from London, and he'd be in New York the next night. He offered his condolences. "It's a damnable shame," he said. Michael McGuire wondered how he knew, but, of course, it was Seth-Jones's business to know things.

He had met Seth-Jones in Germany when he was assigned to a liaison post with British army intelligence. Seth-Jones was a captain, several years older, but the young American shavetail and he had hit it right off. At that time the Cold War was in full swing, and the order of the day was to organize espionage networks against the Soviets.

After he left the army, Seth-Jones had joined MI5, the British secret security service. Every so often he would pop up in America and give Michael McGuire a ring. When Mary Alice met him, she asked, "What do you do exactly?" and he said, "My dear, I watch the sun setting over the British Empire. It's quite interesting work." And afterward, in bed, she said, "He's so English with that red face and bushy mustache and his tweed jacket. How can he possibly be a spy?" McGuire had groaned theatrically and said, "Honey, he isn't a spy; he catches spies," and she giggled and said, "Well, can't they see him coming?"

He told Jamie, "He's a little stiff, but he's really

very nice. We were together when I was in the army in Germany."

In the apartment, Seth-Jones said to Jamie, "I understand a bit of what you are going through. My own mother passed on when I was about your age. My father was in the service and I was sent off to what you in this country call boarding school. At least you have your father with you, and I know you will give him the support that he needs."

"Yes, sir, I will," Jamie said, and after a while he said that he had some homework to do; and then Michael McGuire could hear the strains of the guitar coming from his room.

"He's a good lad," Seth-Jones said. "Like his father. I saw that the moment you entered my office in Hamburg. Seems like yesterday."

"I worry about those days sometimes, some of the things we did."

"Don't. Ours was not to reason why. You must think of it in context. What had to be, was."

Over dinner that Dahlia had prepared, Seth-Jones said, "Iris and I have separated. Pitfalls of the office, I imagine. Too much apart, even when we weren't. Luckily, no children."

"How is the office?" Michael McGuire asked.

"As you may gather from the press, we in the United Kingdom appear to have an inexhaustible supply of pansies doing Ivan's dirty work. I believe we have spotted one flowering in the Washington embassy, which has brought me briefly to these shores."

They had coffee and brandy, and then Anthony Seth-Jones departed. "Chin up, old chap," he said.

•

Chapter

4

The banker, Mooney, was the last to arrive in the corner booth, set apart from the other tables. Over the sound system the Clancy Brothers could be heard singing "Four Green Fields."

John Scanlon, in whose popular eating and drinking establishment, Scanlon's, on Second Avenue in midtown Manhattan, they had gathered, sat nursing a beer, his gray hair brushed with care, his conservatively tailored blue suit featuring a red square peeking from the breast pocket. He was a former vice squad detective who had diligently husbanded sources of income beyond his salary while on the job. Scanlon's was his flagship enterprise. In addition, in partnership with his brother Pat, who was a graduate in hotel and restaurant management from Cornell University, he owned a chain of nineteen saloons catering to a less fashionable clientele in Manhattan, Queens and Brooklyn, each called The Leprechaun.

They also had three pubs, two in Dublin and another strategically located outside Limerick near Shannon airport.

Mooney asked for his habitual cup of tea from the buxom waitress assigned to the booth. Her name was Tess. She was the wife of an IRA volunteer on the run. Her husband worked as a bartender at a Leprechaun in the Bay Ridge section of Brooklyn. Scanlon at this time had a dozen such in his employ, paying them off the books. Over the years there had been many of them, some overstaying a visitor's visa, others with false passports, still others with no entry record at all, the latter aided and abetted by the third man in the booth, Daniel P. Daugherty.

"And I'll take another Dewar's, dear, a touch of water, mind you," Daugherty now said with a conspiratorial wink at his companions. "It's a terrible sin, nearly mortal, but I've tried them all, Jameson's and Paddy's and all the rest, and I can't take them straight. I comfort myself with the thought," he said, "that Cardinal O Fiaich, Primate of All Ireland, the one hundred twelfth successor to St. Patrick, a man from Crossmaglen in South Armagh, where the Brits, you know, have achieved such local cheers they must take out their garbage by helicopter, that the good cardinal when he journeyed to Number Ten Downing Street to see old Iron Drawers herself, that wonderful Maggie, in a vain effort to mediate the H-Block hunger strike—'What are they trying to prove,' I'm told she inquired, 'their virility?'—he was offered a glass and when he asked for Irish whiskey and was informed there was none in the house, he settled for a Scotch, and he was a man of God.

"Now where was I?" Daugherty said. "Right, so anyway, there was poor Jimmy Walker of years gone by, mayor of New York, *Beau James,* a dapper and debonair joy for the citizenry in the midst of the Great Depression to behold, the very spirit of the great metropolis, forced to relinquish his post on corruption charges stirred up by a bunch of Republican legislators as crooked as they come and to sail off to Europe with his lady friend. Now this, of course, was of great discomfort to the revered sachem of Tammany Hall, Charlie Murphy, who'd put Jimmy in office in the first place, and when they were casting about for a new candidate and old McCooey, who ran Brooklyn, suggested this fellow John P. O'Brien, Charlie was in no position to argue much. All Charlie said was 'Is he one of us?' and McCooey said, 'That he is,' and Charlie said, 'Well, hell, in that case shove him down my throat,' and that's how O'Brien was elected the city's eighty-seventh mayor."

"Oh, that's rich, Dan," said Scanlon. "Where'd you hear that one?"

"My father, God rest his soul," Daugherty said. "You know how active he was in political affairs, coming off the docks and all. I'll tell you one thing, everything else aside, those crafty old-timers, bosses they called them and bosses they were, Daley in Chicago, Billy Green in Philly, Charlie Buckley in the Bronx, Prendergast in Kansas City, James Michael Curley of Boston, they were true patriots. At least when they got together to pick a president, they knew who they were picking, 'stead of what we got now, thirty-second TV spots put together by Madison Avenue and high-priced hired guns like they were selling cornflakes, which is what we end up getting."

"You should run for office yourself, the words roll out of you like sweat off a ballplayer's puss," Scanlon said.

"That's what the big guy says, just so's I don't run against him, he says," Daugherty said—the big guy being Cornelius (Corny) Gallagher, twenty-two years a congressman from Brooklyn, chairman of the powerful House Appropriations Committee, whose portrait occupied a hallowed place in Scanlon's along with such as John F. Kennedy and Thomas (Tip) O'Neill and under whose subtle auspices Daniel P. Daugherty had risen to assistant commissioner for law enforcement of the northeastern region of the U.S. Customs Service, stretching from Baltimore to, Daugherty was fond of saying, "all them watery WASPs in Bar Harbor, Maine."

The rub, though, was money, said Daugherty, his florid plump face flushing darker. "Nowadays you got to have the lucre," he said. "Did I ever tell you how old Joe Kennedy was needin' a bit of untraceable cash for his dear Jack's candidacy, and one fine Monday morning he calls the cardinal up there and he says, 'Your Eminence, how'd the collections go yesterday?' and the cardinal says, 'Well, now, let me see, yes, nine hundred fifty thousand, eight forty-two, somewhat disappointing,' and Joe says, 'I was thinking of a little exchange of funds, a diocesan contribution, say a million; as a matter of fact I'm making the check out right now,' and the cardinal said, 'Oh, that'd be most appreciated. Will you be sending the regular fellow over?'

"*Money,*" Daugherty said, "that's where it's at. Once the big guy calls me and hands me an envelope with ten K in it that I am to take to this fellow, and I'm on my way out the door when he says, 'Count it,' and I said, 'But Mr. Gallagher, I don't doubt you,' and he says, 'Yes, suppose the other fellow says there was only nine big ones in there. Let me tell you something, young man, and never forget it. The money never grows in the passin'.' "

" 'Cept for Jake here," Scanlon said. "Jake Mooney's someplace and someone slips him a ten spot, a fifty even, for the boys, and you can bet your beads that it goes right into the accounts, all right and proper."

"Of course," Daugherty said quickly. "That's what I mean. Jake's the exception that proves the rule."

They made for an odd trinity, indivisible only in their hatred of Britain, although for Scanlon and Daugherty the sense of an idyllic past was the overriding factor, imagined nostalgia for the sweet smell of turf, peat fires burning, and thatched roofs, for the salmon-filled streams, the blessed greenness of the land, the fabled pastoral innocence and joy, all brought into focus by the swirl of bagpipes up Fifth Avenue on St. Patrick's Day, all ripped asunder by the imperial invader. Scanlon's eyes would water instantly at a rendition of "Danny Boy." For Daugherty, the tales of how his grandparents were forced to flee the famine in steerage sufficed. Their sybaritic visits to the Ould Sod were marked by hoisting rounds in Dublin, attending the races and golfing on the great courses along the west coast lashed by the Atlantic.

"They've redesigned Ballybunnion, you know,"

Daugherty had reported. "You slice off the first tee now, you wind up in a cemetery."

"A cemetery?" Scanlon said.

"Yes, to be avoided at all costs."

John L. Mooney, however, born in County Mayo, the son of an impoverished stonecutter, had never returned after arriving in America as a boy to, as he said, "succeed at something." He had joined the army at the tail end of World War II and graduated from Queens College on the GI Bill. A bachelor and ascetic in creature comforts, the sole support of his aged widowed mother, his only indulgence season tickets to the New York Giants, he was obsessed not by the Irish past but its future. In his banking job he saw himself with quiet satisfaction gnawing underground at the roots of exploitation. His hero was the revolutionary socialist James Connolly, one of the executed leaders of the Easter uprising. Connolly's books and pamphlets filled his study, and in them he underlined favorite passages that called not only for the removal of the British army but also the establishment of a socialist republic. Otherwise, "England would still rule you . . . through her capitalists, through her landlords, through her financiers." Later Connolly had written, "The gun must be our court of last resort in the case of Ireland versus England." For Mooney, that was the final argument. There was no other way.

Daugherty ordered another Dewar's.

"I'm told the lamb stew is excellent tonight," Scanlon said.

Since he was the host, his guests dutifully obliged.

"Ah, it's good, it is, nothing like a good stew," said

Daugherty, who would have much preferred the prime shell steak listed on the blackboard. "Now to business. It went down well, I take it?"

"Yes," Scanlon said. "Not a hitch, thanks in large measure to our noble Jake." The proceeds of the six bank heists in Dublin, Waterford and Cork, he said, had totaled $1,300,000 and change in Irish pounds. The boys packed the pounds in two suitcases and put them in the trunk of the Ford Escort they got for the priest, and the priest had taken the ferry from Rosslare harbor in County Wexford to Cherbourg in France, and after that they drove to Switzerland and deposited the money in Crédit Suisse in Geneva, and next it was wired in various amounts to Jake's bank, to the phony accounts that he'd set up; and once it was there, Jake had transferred a million back to Ireland, to Scanlon's account in the Bank of Ireland as profits from his chain of saloons in New York. The million, by now well laundered, passed into the IRA's operational fund, which left three hundred thousand in Jake Mooney's hands for arms purchases.

"No problems at all, huh?" Daugherty said.

"None. I understand the priest brought along a blind fellow and a cripple. Said he was taking them to Lourdes. I think he actually did. Course, the boys were covering him all the time just to be safe, and they took the load on into Switzerland."

"No problems at the border there, either?"

"No, you know, the Swiss don't care what you bring in, long as it's money."

"What order was the priest?"

"Legion of Christ."

"That's a new one on me."

"Me, too," Scanlon said. "Must be militant, though. Least the good father is. He's got a relative with the boys, I understand."

Daugherty started on an Irish coffee. "God, John, this is first rate," he said. "You serve the best Irish coffee in New York, maybe the whole world."

"It's the real cream that does it. None of that stuff out of a can."

There was a reflective pause. Then Daugherty's face mottled in sudden anger. "We got to scratch and claw around," he said, "pretzel-bending left and right, for a lousy million, what have you. Country spends that much a day for the fuckin' Afghans, them other fuckin' niggers in Africa, just because of the fuckin' Rooskies. Give them goddamn advanced Stinger missiles, I read in the papers, knock anything out the sky, and we got to settle, we get 'em, for Redeyes, already fuckin' obsolete. Talk about fair."

"How much do these Redeyes cost?" Mooney inquired.

"Twenty-five thou per."

"We can't do better?"

"I tried with Julio."

"Julio?" Mooney said.

"Yes, Julio. Julio Gonzalez."

"Jesus, a Puerto Rican?" Scanlon said.

"No, I believe he's of the Dominican persuasion. The army's full of Dominicans, Jamaicans, so forth, you know. They join the army, they're eligible for citizenship in two, three years. Anyway, I say to Julio, I said, 'Listen, we're all comin' from the same place. I mean we got the same holy mother of God, the Virgin Mary, and don't that count for something?' I said, and he said he knew that, that he had taken that into consideration, which was why the price wasn't thirty-five thou. Course, there're the accessories as well. I don't have to tell you, the Redeye's no good without rockets. The rockets are six apiece."

"The main thing is," Scanlon said, "can we get them?"

"No problem, Julio says. Julio's a corporal in a reserve unit. They go on maneuvers, sometimes they drive to a big depot for the stuff, what they need, in Pennsylvania it is, Fort Letterkenny, he says. Julio's Uncle Augie's a master sergeant there, right in the arsenal. They draw their Redeyes, they requisition a few extra and, you know, drop them off. It goes on all the time. Julio says do I need some meat? He's got a friend up at the officers' club, West Point. Just tell him. The price is right, he says.

" 'Julio, suppose something goes wrong,' I said, 'just suppose, say, five Redeyes turn up missing on those shelves and it all hits the fan,' and Julio said no problem. There's a bird colonel down there in charge at the arsenal, and he finds out five Redeyes are missing in the inventory, he's going to tell Julio's Uncle Augie get right on this, make a trade with another arsenal that's short something else. That bird colonel's bucking for a star. It's his ass on the line, and he ain't going to let himself hang out to dry for five lousy Redeyes, screw up his career."

"So what's the next step?" Scanlon said.

"The next step is that I fix up a meet for Julio and Kevin Dowd, and they work out how it's to be done, the transfer, and Jake comes up with the cash."

Mooney nodded, sipping tea, and said, "Whatever

happened with that business about you and the Brits
and the customs commissioner?"

"Ah, yes," Daugherty said. "Over and done with.
That's some stiff, that Alan Nyquist, we got for commissioner, U.S. Customs Service. Dumb fuck from
Minnesota. How he got the White House to appoint
him, I'll never know, 'cept I do. I hear his mother's
loaded, big steel, big wheat and a big contributor. I
hear he wants an ambassadorship and I'm prayin'
and hopin' what I hear is right. The Brits bitch, Commissioner Nyquist jumps. The other side gets lucky
once in a while, you know, grabs an unaccompanied
bag off Aer Lingus, nabs some sailor bringing in
goods off a ship, opens up a crate by accident and
bingo, but it drives them nuts thinking about all what
else's going through.

"What cut it," he said, "was those two containers
went out of Port Newark marked 'Machine Tools,'
the ones with the pistols, semi-automatics and a machine gun. They knew about them ahead of time.
Had a tap in Dublin on one of the safe houses. That's
why they left the containers on the Dublin docks, an
army of Special Branch cops waiting to see who
picked them up, but nobody did because the lads
were tipped about the tap, and that's when the Brits
went bananas."

Daugherty said, "So that Brit intel guy they had in
Washington for undercover liaison, hell's his name?
Oh, yeah, Forbes, Brian Forbes, he corners Nyquist
and says, See, all these shipments are going out because the U.S. Customs Service, meaning me, is lettin'
them slip by, that I'm executive vice president of the
customs service Emerald Society, that I got special

squads which are called 'Danny's Boys' which are facilitating arms smuggling to the IRA, and I get my ass hauled down to D.C. and the commissioner says, 'There have been some very serious allegations lodged,' and I say, 'Really, from where?' and he says, 'I'm not at liberty to say.'

"Now I know that tap they had was illegal, can't be used here, whatever was on it, plus it would give the whole show away, and I say, 'Well, Commissioner Nyquist, there's any evidence against me, I'd like to be confronted by it, get myself an attorney,' and he says, glaring at me, 'That won't be necessary.' Then he circles around the stuff about the Emerald Society and Danny's Boys and what was that? and I say, 'Commissioner, I'm proud to be a member of the Emerald Society. My people over there were subsistin' on potatoes and then there wasn't any potatoes and tens of thousands of them were starving to death, and all the while the English landowners were shippin' out grain and beef and lamb like it was going out of style. My people, what was left of them, finally rose up to regain their freedom and independence, but a quarter of their country is still occupied and I don't pretend I love that. That's my right as a citizen, an American citizen, and it don't mean I don't do my sworn duty to uphold the law, and as far as Danny's Boys are concerned, I'm proud of that, too. I like to think all the boys in customs are my boys, you don't mind,' and he says, 'Well, just watch your step, Daugherty. I have my eye on you.' "

"That was the end of it?" Mooney said.

"No. Naturally, I tell Corny Gallagher what's up, and he gets on the horn to Nyquist and says, 'Commissioner, this is Congressman Gallagher'—Corny doesn't have to identify himself more'n that—'My attention has been directed to some upsetting rumors that a foreign nation, run out of London, is assuming an administrative role in our esteemed customs service.' Nyquist right away says that it isn't the case at all, but at the same time it has to be recognized, he says, that we do have a 'special relationship with the United Kingdom,' and Corny says, 'Yes, I'm aware of that. It got particularly special around 1776 when we threw the Redcoats out,' and that, you want to know," said Daugherty, "was the end of it."

"Let's get on with the rest of the agenda, Dan, could we?" Scanlon said. "Be here all night the way you get going."

"All right, yes," Daugherty said, "that brings us to the cannabis weed and Mr. Thomas Ahearn of the Somerville gang, Boston, Mass., and nearby parts. Now I'm the first to say I don't like doing business, any kind, with Tommy Ahearn, though I got to admit he put the guineas back in the bottle up there, so to speak. Now, too, my own son Stevie, he says, 'Pop, you ought to stop drinking, try a little pot. Relaxes you. Gives you a nice easy high. Doesn't do anything bad to your liver. Pop, your liver's got to be as big as Texas,' he says. 'Look around. Everybody's doing it. Real middle class. It's just a matter of time, they legalize it.' And I say to myself, you know, the kid's right. And it's not like it's real junk, like coke or horse. No one runnin' around muggin' someone for a fix, like they'll die if they don't have it, and that's the truth.

"Besides, what's headed for the lads this time," he

said, "can't go in no containers or via Aer Lingus. We got to have a boat, and Tommy Ahearn has the boat. So I told him he gets two freebies first and then the boat goes over for us. One hand washes the other. I told him he gets his bales dockside, my boys will pass them. Anything on the high seas, with the coast guard, that's his problem, nothing I can do about it, and that's the deal."

"Fine," Mooney said.

"One more thing, Jake," Daugherty said. "You tell Kevin Dowd when he has the meet with Julio on the Redeyes, be sure to say his name right—*Hoo*lio. Got that? He's very sensitive about it."

Chapter

5

In the early summer of 1979 after the death of Mary Alice, and after Jamie's school year was over, Michael McGuire took an extended weekend off and they went to the beach house on Moriches Bay on the south shore of Long Island.

They worked together for hours at the marina yard where the boat had been stored over the winter, sanding down the wood and revarnishing it, repainting the hull and scouring and coppering the bottom. Jamie had thrown himself into all of this with astonishing intensity. Getting the engine in shape and checking it over was a chore that was normally left to the yard, but he appeared to be especially fascinated by everything about the engine, and it was Michael McGuire who would knock off, leaving Jamie behind crouched next to one of the mechanics, asking about this valve, that wire.

Jamie's school reports had continued to note his

prowess as a swimmer and his musical ability, but also
that he tended to remain something of a loner, and
McGuire was pleased at the way he seemed to be
interacting so well with the work crew at the marina.
His original idea was to take Jamie back to the city
during the week, coming out on weekends until vacation time in August.

Jamie, though, settled the matter when he said that
the marina's manager had offered him a job for a
dollar an hour, half a day Saturday and Sunday off,
and that he wanted very much to have it. Michael
McGuire called the manager, who said that he had
been serious. "Jamie's a good kid," he said. "He's got
a real feel for boats and machinery. I'll start him out
mostly cleaning up and working the pumps, but he's
a quick learner, and everyone around here likes
him."

So Michael McGuire decided to let him stay, in the
care of Dahlia. When he checked in with her that first
week, she reported that Jamie was doing fine. He got
to the marina in the *Mary Alice* in the morning, and
if the weather was bad he would hitch a ride to work.
When he got home, she said, he would go swimming,
and right after supper he'd be in bed asleep without
even bothering to watch television.

He made sure to call Jamie around suppertime
every evening. These conversations were usually
brief and they left Michael McGuire vaguely dis-
quieted. They were all about surface things, like what
the weather was like, how it was going at the marina,
about how he wished he were out there instead of
being in the city. It was as if they were both corking
emotions, and he knew that it was his fault, that he

was setting the tone. But he did not know how to break out of the pattern, especially on the telephone, to reveal the anguish that constantly racked him. He wouldn't be breaking out, he told himself. He would end up simply breaking down, and he couldn't divine the consequences of that and therefore feared it. Maybe he should speak to a psychiatrist after all, and he decided to have dinner with one whom he had met through Mary Alice. They had seen him and his wife socially on and off, and it was this familiarity that caused Michael McGuire to approach him; but almost at once the psychiatrist announced over a martini that his wife of twenty-one years had left him and that only yesterday he had been forced to institutionalize one of his children for heroin addiction. So when he finally got around to asking, "How are you and Jamie doing?" McGuire said they were doing as well as could be expected and let it go at that. The hell with it, he thought, he'd just have to tough it out. Half the people at the agency appeared to be in heavy therapy, and he hadn't noticed much improvement on anybody's neurosis meter.

One evening on the phone Jamie spoke to him about the *Mary Alice* on the boat's transom. The stock bronze-colored letters had been individually attached. Jamie wanted to replace them with ones painted on directly in gold.

"It won't cost much, Dad," he said. "I can get a break on the price of the gold leaf and I'll do it myself. I already did it for another boat. All you need are the stencils. Is it okay with you?"

"Sure. That's a great idea."

"The way it is now," Jamie continued solemnly,

"one of those letters could fall off and we'd lose it, and we don't want that to happen."

"You're right," Michael McGuire said, and after he hung up he cried for the first time since he had held Jamie in his arms to tell him that his mother was going to die.

When he got out to the beach on Friday evening, Jamie gave him a kiss and a hug, and then said, "Come look," and McGuire followed him out to the dock. The *Mary Alice* had never looked more spanking and polished. The new lettering was in elegant script.

"That's terrific. You did a terrific job."

"I was hoping you'd like it."

"Well, I do. How could I not?"

After he had changed clothes, he started a charcoal fire for the steak Dahlia had taken out of the freezer, and went back to the dock to rake up a dozen of the clams he had planted alongside it. He had put them in rows, cherrystones and little necks, like lettuce in a garden. Every so often he would go clamming in the bay to replenish the supply. He made himself a vodka and tonic, and when the coals were beginning to glow under their gray coat, he roasted the clams until they had opened and squeezed some lemon juice on them and carefully added a drop of Tabasco sauce on each one. He made himself another drink and Jamie got a Coke and they sat there on the deck eating the clams, watching a marvelous sunset turn the underbellies of scattered clouds in the western sky purple and pink while the good scent of the smoke from the sizzling steak on the grill filled the air.

"This was Mom's favorite time," Jamie said.

"Yes, I know." Michael McGuire looked at him, at his sunburned face, at Mary Alice's violet eyes, at his biceps noticeably bigger from working around the marina, at his now trembling chin. It was a moment to say something very important, he thought, but he could not find the right words. "I think about her always," he said finally. "We just have to go on."

Then he promptly sliced into his left thumb carving the steak, and Jamie ran inside to get the hydrogen peroxide and a box of Band-Aids; and after he had wrapped a Band-Aid over the cut, the blood still came through, but after Jamie helped him put on a second Band-Aid, that seemed to do the trick.

"You okay, Dad? Should we go to the medical center?"

"No, it'll be all right. I get the dummy award, that's all. Come on, let's eat the steak before it's ruined."

Over dinner, Jamie said that he'd gotten a postcard from Paris, France, from one of his classmates who was traveling in Europe with his parents. "Were you ever in Paris, Dad?"

"Yes, a couple of times when I was in the army in Germany. It's really something to see. Maybe next summer, we'll go, you and me. You know, the first time I ever ate mussels was in Paris, and I'll never forget it. Did I ever tell you what happened?"

"No, what?"

"Well, I was taken to this restaurant and somebody said I should try *moules marinière*, which is mussels in French, so I said sure, and they brought the mussels and a finger bowl. I'd never seen a finger bowl in my whole life. I didn't know you were supposed to dip your fingers in it to clean them off after you finished with the mussels. I figured it was for the mussels, so there I was taking the mussels out of their shells in this rich wine sauce and carefully dipping them in a finger bowl full of lemon water before I ate them. You can imagine, I never tasted anything so bad, but I kept going. I didn't want anyone to think I didn't appreciate fine French cooking. The worst part was nobody said a word. I guess they were too embarrassed."

"Oh, Dad, far out," Jamie said, laughing. "That sounds like something I'd do."

"God, I hope not. Hey, by the way, I meant to tell you if you want any friends here, go right ahead."

"Thanks, but I'd be working all day, and they'd just get bored. Maybe later. And speaking of work, I better get to bed. See you tomorrow."

"Sleep well, son," Michael McGuire said. He poured himself a brandy and, sitting on the deck, he listened as Jamie played the guitar in his room for fifteen minutes or so and then saw the light shining on the grass from his room go out. Overhead the stars glittered, and the aroma of the sea enveloped him. There was a steady muffled roar of ocean surf.

He hadn't thought about Paris in years. His host that humiliating night with the mussels was a French army intelligence captain. The captain was trying to wheedle some information about a former German SS officer that the Counterintelligence Corps had squirreled away, but he could truthfully say he couldn't be of much help on that particular case.

The rest of that first week in Paris had been a sexual extravaganza for Michael McGuire, and on the deck of the house on the bay he recalled this; and because his thumb was starting to throb, he had another brandy and took three aspirins and went to bed. In his dreams a Montmartre whore named Danielle sidled toward him in a black garter belt and stockings. The Czech refugee Ina, her breasts swinging wildly over him in the bathtub, giggled as he came up spewing soapy water, and shouted, "Darling, you shouldn't disappear like that." Then Mary Alice suddenly intruded, saying, "I just might marry you." That was too much for him to bear, and he awoke and put on a robe and walked out on the deck. It was no longer dark. There was a line of crimson in the east. He was all alone. He said out loud, "How could you do this to me?"

The next day he had his first fight with Jamie since it happened. Jamie had left for the marina by the time he had awakened again. His thumb was still bothering him, so he went into the medical center in the village and one of the doctors put two stitches in it and then he went shopping with the list Dahlia had given him.

When he returned to the house early in the afternoon, Jamie was not around, and when he asked Dahlia where he was, she waved toward the bay and said, "Out there, swimmin'."

He stood on the deck scanning the bay and could not see Jamie anywhere nearby. Then he thought he saw something way out in the water, close to a mile off. He ran back into the house and got his binoculars. He trained them at what he thought he had seen, and then, horrified, he saw that it was Jamie, headed toward the far side at a point where the bay narrowed to about two miles; but still, to reach it,

Jamie had to cross the coastal channel where there was plenty of traffic. Michael McGuire could not believe it.

He ran to the *Mary Alice*, gunned the engine and took off after Jamie. He caught up to him just before the channel. Jamie was wearing goggles and flippers. If he noticed the *Mary Alice* alongside him, he did not show it. He swam with powerful, methodical strokes, like a goddamn machine, Michael McGuire thought.

Then Jamie was in the channel, crossing it, and all Michael McGuire could do was to stay with him, escorting him. His worst fears were realized when there were two warning blasts from a big cabin cruiser bearing down on him. The cruiser was still at least a hundred yards away, but it just as easily could have been closer. He ignored the cruiser, and then finally Jamie was past the channel, and the bay gradually started getting shallower. When the depth was about three feet, Jamie stopped swimming and stood up in the water, staring at him through his goggles, saying nothing.

"What the hell do you think you're doing?" Michael McGuire yelled. "Are you trying to kill yourself?"

Jamie did not reply.

"Get over here," Michael McGuire said, setting up the ladder.

Jamie remained motionless.

"You hear me, mister? Move it. Now!"

At last, with elaborate casualness, Jamie approached the boat and climbed in and took off his flippers and goggles. Michael McGuire could see the defiance in his eyes.

"I asked you a question. What the hell do you think you were doing?"

"Swimming."

"Oh, that's cute. That really is. You know you could get ground up like chopped meat in that channel?"

"I can take care of myself."

"Oh, can you now?"

"Yes. I've been doing it all week, and nothing's happened."

They were both shouting, a foot apart. Jamie's hands were clenched. Michael McGuire had a sudden vision of them in a fist fight one day. The thought sickened him. "And *nothing* is going to happen," he said. "This is the end of these little jaunts. You want to swim so much, do laps in a pool."

"It isn't the same."

"Then swim along the shore, not across the bay. Is that understood?"

"Why don't you just leave me alone?" Jamie said, eyes brimming with tears.

"Listen, when you're eighteen, I'll leave you alone all you want. Until you're eighteen, you're my responsibility. You don't like it, that's tough. If you're not getting the message, you can forget about the marina. You'll be back in the city. Is that clear?"

The confrontation left him spent. He had been right, he thought, but he had handled it wrong. It demonstrated to him how close to the brink he was, how he had to learn to control himself better against the unexpected. But Jamie out there in the bay asking for trouble had him falling apart. If a bad thing ever happened to Jamie, he did not believe he could go on living.

Somehow, though, there had been a catharsis of sorts. Jamie had sat hunched over by himself in the stern on the way back, but as Michael McGuire brought the boat up to the dock, he came forward to help with the lines and then he asked about the new bandage on McGuire's thumb.

"It's just a couple of stitches. They said it would heal faster."

"Does it hurt?"

"It did, until my attention was diverted."

"I'm sorry, Dad. I won't do it anymore."

That night they went into the village and had pizza and saw a movie. And in the morning, after a late breakfast, Michael McGuire said why didn't they go out trolling in the ocean for blues?

"What about your thumb?"

"I don't think it'll be a problem. I'll tape a sponge over the stitches and wear a glove."

Jamie ran the boat, and as they came out of the inlet into the ocean, Michael McGuire observed how expertly he maneuvered her. The inlet, which had been created by a hurricane in 1938, entered the ocean at an angle, and as a result a number of sand-bars had built up outside, one after another; so when the weather was rough the waves crested in serially, like surf on the beach. Over the years a number of boats had been swamped and people drowned. Today the sea was moderate, but still you had to be careful, and Jamie took the first three bars straight on and wheeled quickly to starboard between the third and fourth bars, which were farther apart, and then slipped neatly around the fourth one.

"Good going," Michael McGuire said. "That was well done."

When they got to the bar that paralleled the beach a couple of hundred yards offshore, Jamie throttled down and helped him set the lines. They put out three of them; the two outboard lures were rubber tubing to emulate eels, and the one in the middle was a large red-eyed white bucktail. Jamie began slowly to crisscross the bar. The day was dazzlingly clear and you could see the sandy top of the bar about six feet beneath the surface before it dropped off sharply on either side. Michael McGuire snapped open a can of beer, enjoying the crisp air and the dancing, sporadically white-capped sea. He looked at the campers on the beach and he saw some of them surf casting, and one of them had a fish, and he told Jamie to stay just inside the bar for a while.

A minute later the ratchet on the reel with the bucktail began to whine and the rod bent and quivered violently. Michael McGuire grabbed the rod. He could feel the fish at the other end and then he saw a big blue come thrashing out of the water two hundred feet away. Jamie threw the engine into neutral, so that the blue could be played fairly and the line, which was only twelve-pound test, would not part on its own, and he reeled in the two outboard lines to keep from fouling the line with the blue on it.

It was a good fish and it fought like hell. It first made a run away from the boat, and then as Michael McGuire carefully worked it back, it moved doggedly from side to side, breaching the surface several times in an effort to shake the hook. He held the rod high, trying to ignore the hurt in his thumb. I get this one in, he thought, and that's it. At last he brought the blue in to where it was about twenty feet from the side of the boat, and he could see it turning and twisting, flashing silver in the sunlight. Close by the boat, it plunged down one final time, and then, exhausted, offered no more resistance as he reeled it in and Jamie got the net under it.

"It's a beauty, isn't it?" he said. "I'll bet it goes twelve, thirteen pounds."

"Big as Moby Dick," Jamie said, grinning.

"Ah, yes. Well, it turns out the thumb isn't so great after all. I'll do the driving. You fish."

They trolled along the bar for another hour, and Jamie pulled in four more blues. Michael McGuire swung off the bar on the ocean side, and they drifted; and as the *Mary Alice* rocked in the swells, they silently ate the sandwiches Dahlia had prepared.

"Jamie," he finally said. "There are a lot of things I want to say to you, but sometimes I don't know how to do it."

"It's okay, I understand."

"The main thing is I love you an awful lot."

He started the engine and headed back to the inlet. He rode gracefully over the bars, which gave him a sense of control, however illusory, and then, opening the boat full throttle, sped to the dock. He had Jamie bring a fish to each of three neighbors, and sunburned and tired, despite his aching thumb, he took a dreamless nap. After dinner, as he was getting ready to return to the city, he was surprised to hear Jamie ask, "Maybe Grandpa and Grandma would like to come out for the week," and he said, "Sure, why not. I'll call them and see."

He had not spoken to his parents since the funeral, and even then the exchanges, the conveyance of condolences, had been awkward. They simply did not speak the same language any longer. There was no meaningful comfort they could offer, and they seemed to grasp that and, happily, didn't really try. They had remained on the fringes throughout, blood strangers.

His father had retired by now, having logged in overtime with a vengeance his final year to build up his pension. This was the major legacy of one of the city's mayors, who had entertained thoughts about running for president and decided to make himself look good by trading off immediate union monetary demands for contracts that called for pensions to be based on a worker's last annual income. Let the next guy worry was his motto, he'd be in the White House. Now these payments were helping to break the municipal treasury.

Michael McGuire had no idea what his father did with his days. Probably whiled them away at the Liffey Bar on 207th Street decrying the encroachment of the "spicks and spooks" into Inwood. He called without identifying himself and the old man interrupted testily, "Who's this?"

"Your son, Michael."

"Oh, my son, Michael, yes. What can I do for you?" He sounded cautious, suspicious. But when he found out what the call was about, his voice softened measurably. "That'd be fine, fine. Your mother would look forward to that, too."

"When can you go?"
"Anytime. My dance card ain't so full."
"I'll rent a car for you for this afternoon then."

In the city, Michael McGuire buried himself in supervising agency accounts. He received any number of dinner invitations, some of which he accepted, but more often than not he would stop by a saloon like P. J. Clarke's for a hamburger and beer or would scramble up some eggs at home.

Wednesday night, though, was poker night, and he increasingly had come to depend upon it to get his mind off things. One of the regulars he especially prized was named Harry Hollander, who whenever he was dealing invariably selected seven card stud. Hollander, Michael McGuire had discovered to his profit, would always go for a last card to fill in his hand, betting as though he already had it. He did not seem to care that this approach would cause him to lose nine times out of ten. It was that tenth win, pulling it all out with a dramatic flourish, that mattered.

He had an insouciant air and an impish grin that Michael McGuire found beguiling; and more to the point, in McGuire's present state, he appeared to be the ultimate survivor. Hollander had grown up a rich Manhattan kid. He had been married three times, to a spoiled Jewish princess, as Hollander characterized her, to a go-go dancer and to an airline attendant. For the princess alone, he had forked over $25,000 three years running to a famous fashion writer to include her on a list of the country's ten best-dressed women.

He also had been in prison in a federal minimum security facility for conspiring to run up the value of fringe stocks. "I didn't need the money," he told Michael McGuire. "I guess I did it for fun." The warden, as it turned out, was an avid follower of the stock market and soon recruited Harry to handle his portfolio. This meant Harry had to have access to a phone, and he naturally used it to manage his own accounts as well. There were also other advantages. Whenever his second wife, the go-go dancer, visited, they were allowed to picnic and frolic carnally after hours in a secluded parklike section of the prison grounds. "The only problem sometimes was the fucking mosquitoes," he said.

But according to Harry, the high point of his term was the great Ping-Pong match. When he arrived, the reigning champion was a Mafia power named Gaetano "The Gay Blade" Balamenti, a man of darkly handsome looks whose sobriquet derived both from his youthful expertise with a knife and the splendor of his custom-made suits and shirts. Balamenti had taken up Ping-Pong while putting in nearly five years in the harsh confines of the federal penitentiary at Fort Leavenworth, Kansas, on a labor racketeering conviction. He then was transferred to the camp, which was supposed to serve for him, along with a number of other mafiosi, as a sort of halfway house preparatory to a return to redemptive civilian life.

Harry Hollander had been there about five months when he happened to mention in the middle of some collegiate reminiscing with a Wall Street embezzler in the next cubicle that at his alma mater, Syracuse University, he had been the campus Ping-Pong king. Before he knew it, the whole place was electric with news of a challenge to Balamenti's supremacy.

"You're nuts," Hollander said he told the embezzler. "I haven't had a paddle in my hands since I was at Madam Ecstasy's house of fun and games on East Sixty-sixth Street."

"Harry, you've got to do it. The action is getting really outstanding."

"Where do you get the money to bet in prison?" Michael McGuire asked.

"You don't bet money. You bet push-ups."

"Push-ups? How do you get anybody to pay off?"

"Michael, if you were ever inside, you wouldn't ask a question like that. You pay up. I'm telling you, everyone was working out. Of course, I was a big underdog. My people kept Syracuse to themselves."

He trained rigorously for two weeks, Harry said. His slices and cuts came back. They were, he thought, his only chance against a top-spin slammer like Balamenti. The match was held over a two-day period, five games out of nine. At the end of the first day, he was down one game to three, but he rallied to take four out of the next five. The last game went to match point twelve times. "Let's face it," Hollander said, "a lot of social status was at stake here."

Afterward, he said, he and The Gay Blade became fast friends and still saw one another. "The Blade's in electrical contracting these days. I'm thinking of investing. The Blade bids on a job, I want to tell you, he has an uncanny way of getting it. He also has a great restaurant on Mulberry Street. Hidden ownership, of course, with the liquor license and what have you. I'll take you down there. You'll love him."

Somehow these exotic tales made Michael Mc-Guire's life more supportable. Hollander reminded him of the kid's toy with the round bottom that you pushed over and it kept popping back up. And it was while walking along the street that Wednesday night after the poker game, the week that Michael Mc-Guire's parents had gone out to be with Jamie, that Hollander suddenly said, "They coming after you yet?"

"Who?"

"If they haven't, they will. Maybe it's a little too soon."

"What are you talking about?"

"Women. Broads."

"Are you crazy? That's the last thing in the world I think about now."

"I'm not talking about you. I'm talking about them. Take it from me, *they're* thinking about it. You're reasonably young. You're successful. And you're single and vulnerable and straight. They're going to be all over you."

"Harry, you are the worst."

"Mark my words, Michael."

Driving to the beach on Friday evening, Michael McGuire resolved to be absolutely correct with his mother and father. After all, Jamie had wanted them, and there had to be a reason. Probably his mother. Jamie had to be yearning for some kind of maternal presence, some sort of a connection, a connection he couldn't provide himself.

"Dad, guess what?" Jamie said. "I just took Grandpa fishing and we got a big striped bass by the rocks in the inlet."

That's more than the old man ever did for me, Michael McGuire thought, and then reminded himself of his vow on the way out.

"We'll be leaving first thing in the morning," his father said defensively.

"You're welcome to stay."

"No, I get a little edgy, I'm out of the city too long."

He had to admit that the striper was a fat-bellied beauty, and after he had scaled and gutted it and closed the grill cover to bake it, he asked his mother if she'd like a drink and she said, "I'll take a little sherry, thank you." He poured some rye on the rocks for his father and made himself a vodka and tonic, and they sat on the deck as the sun went down.

"Come on now, Jamie," Michael McGuire's father said, "sing us a song, won't you?" and Jamie went to his room and came back with his guitar and began to sing in a sweet, haunting voice, still a soprano.

> In Mountjoy one Monday morning,
> High upon the gallows tree,
> Kevin Barry gave his young life
> For the cause of liberty.
> But a lad of eighteen summers,
> Yet as no one can deny
> As he walked to death that morning
> He proudly held his head on high.

His father, and then his mother, joined in the chorus.

Another martyr for old Ireland,
Another murder for the Crown,
Whose brutal laws may kill the Irish,
But can't keep their spirits down.

There was a silence after Jamie had finished the last verse that even Michael McGuire had to observe. Then after dinner, when Jamie had gone to bed, he said to his father, "He learned that one from you, didn't he? All that romantic Kevin Barry claptrap."

"Yes, he did. He deserves to know his roots."

"The only roots he has, whatever's left of them, are right here," Michael McGuire said, tapping his chest.

6

It would be the first general convention of the Provisional Irish Republican Army in nearly sixteen years, and in Dundalk, just below the border, Gerry McMahon said, "Jack, how ye doin'?"

Except that the "how" came out "high." While it still remained something of a mystery to him, McMahon recognized it as a fact of life that the Belfast accent was different, and that he had to be careful right now where and to whom he spoke. Once, when O'Houlihan recruited him as a driver for one of the cars that an American television news team had hired during the time Bobby Sands lay dying in his prison hunger strike, he heard the correspondent say to a cameraman, "As long as I've been coming to Belfast, the only thing I've truly learned is not to do a man-in-the-street interview—unless you intend to use subtitles."

McMahon had taken the train. He could have gone

by car on the motorway due south or the one west, off which there were multiple entry points into County Monaghan in the free state. The problem with a train was that you were trapped, while there was always a chance of making a getaway in a road-block. But unless an alert was on, the chances of random roadblocks were greater, and besides, McMahon liked the idea of riding a train. It gave him an opportunity to be alone, to free-associate, just staring out the window, lulled by the click of wheel on rail, and there was plenty on his mind.

Looming over the west side of the city of Belfast that Gerry McMahon was leaving, where he was born, raised and where he most surely would die, was Black Mountain. It was not a conventional mountain, some towering peak reaching skyward. It was rather like a massive shoulder hunched over the city, visible from every quarter and reflective of Belfast's own inelegant presence.

The city's population was about 350,000, a third of them Irish nationalists and Roman Catholic by baptism if not always commitment, the rest unionists loyal to the British crown and mainly of various Protestant denominations ranging from Church of England to militant homegrown fundamentalists. Belfast was a collection of tightly knit neighborhoods, enclaves really. For the Royal Ulster Constabulary, the British army and MI5, which directed and coordinated all security activities, it was a city of two colors, marked on their maps in solid blocks of green and orange. Green was for the nationalist enclaves. Sometimes there would be isolated bits of green in the big blocks of orange.

Most of the green blocks on the maps were in West Belfast in the shadow of Black Mountain, places called Andersontown, Turf Lodge, Ballymurphy, the Falls, the Lower Falls and, farther north, completely isolated, two others named the Ardoyne and New Lodge. This was the heart of the nationalist movement in Belfast where the Provisional IRA, the Provos, operated from, and from here the city dropped into undulating flatlands—split by the wide M1 motorway and the railroad and then the River Lagan that flowed northeast into the harbor—climbing again into the hills of East Belfast, which was entirely colored orange on the maps.

Within the city limits in this part of Belfast, on quiet tree-shaded streets, were large private residences with neatly clipped lawns and hedges and elaborate flower gardens reminiscent of those in wealthy suburbs across the United States. Here, in enclaves like Malone, lived Belfast's bankers, business executives and major bookmakers, its prominent lawyers, physicians and accountants, some of them, a distinct minority, even Catholic.

There also were, though, sprawling working-class areas with aged and grimy redbrick row houses as well as newer developments, called estates, with semi-detached housing fronted by tiny patches of grass, which were barely distinguishable from their counterparts in West Belfast. The only difference was a more prosperous air along the main shopping roads. And there were the sidewalk curbs, some for a few blocks, others stretching for miles, painted in the red, white and blue of the Union Jack, and the signs on buildings that proclaimed, "God Save Our Queen" and "One Crown, One Faith."

Central Belfast, sandwiched between the motorway and the river, with its department stores, smart boutiques, corporate headquarters, banks and airline offices, was completely cordoned off. No car could pass the barricades during the day without a special pass. At night cars were banned outright.

But aside from this minor inconvenience, you could spend weeks in East Belfast or downtown without any sense of real trouble. For that you had to be in West Belfast, dotted with heavily fortified stations of the Royal Ulster Constabulary or the British army barracks with their high walls and watchtowers out of which day and night rumbled the big enclosed Saracen armored personnel carriers with hatches on top for gunners, and smaller ugly armored vehicles called "pigs."

They would proceed down the Falls Road flanked by lines of soldiers in full battle gear. These troops crouched, whirled and aimed their weapons as if they were moving through some enemy-infested jungle. All around them, meanwhile, people went about their daily routine, many of them women wheeling babies in prams. It was like watching two different movies being filmed on the same set. The most hated of these soldiers were the paratroopers, identifiable by their red berets, who appeared to enjoy knocking down anyone in their way. The idea was to cow the local populace.

It had not worked very well. During Gerry McMahon's coming to manhood there had been some 2,600 bloody deaths. In Northern Ireland's population of a million and a half, one out of every twenty households had suffered a death or injury from bombings and shootings. McMahon had heard the American television correspondent remark that a comparable figure for the United States today would rival the mortality rate of its own Civil War. He had not known about that statistic before, and was impressed. It gave breadth, even grandeur, to the struggle.

Notification that the convention was to be held this Friday came suddenly in the morning and he left Belfast for Dundalk in the afternoon. Although it was August, the weather was more like November. Whatever else Belfast was, it was not famous as a magnet for summer tourists. There was a chilly light rain falling. When he stepped out of his house in Ballymurphy, the clouds obscured the top of Black Mountain and an adjoining one called Divis. Still, a British army helicopter circled over West Belfast, so inviolate with its heavy machine guns and high-resolution cameras that could freeze-frame a man's face as if he were only a foot away. Oh, how he'd love to knock one down, just one, to give them something to think about.

Cathleen Cassidy, his driver whenever the need for her arose, went along the Lower Falls Road past the Divis flats, a complex of crumbling six-story concrete apartment buildings around a tower of nineteen floors, the second-highest structure in the city. The sight of them never failed to enrage McMahon. They had been announced with great benevolent fanfare by government authorities to replace an ancient slum in St. Peter's parish put up for workers in the old linen mills, row houses fronting narrow walks that had a room and kitchen on the ground floor, with an outhouse in back, and two tiny bedrooms upstairs. But the project turned out to have been a quick trip from purgatory to hell. The new buildings had started falling apart as soon as they were occupied. A blackish slime fed by moisture spread over the interior walls. Sewage backed up in the plumbing lines. Asbestos floated freely in the air. There were no shops to buy food. Mounds of rubble were all the children had to play in. It got to be such a public embarrassment that plans were announced to raze them. But McMahon wondered if the tower would ever come down. Up there, on the nineteenth floor, behind the windows tinted black, the roof bristling with antennas, British intelligence maintained an unrivaled electronic and optical watch over West Belfast around the clock that would be hard to replace.

McMahon dragged deeply on a cigarette and smothered a cough. "You should try to stop that," Cathleen said.

"I know," he said. But death from tobacco was the least of his concerns. He felt a great guilt about Cathleen. She had started out as a member of the *Cumann na mBan*, the women's auxiliary of the IRA. He suspected that Mary suspected something, although nothing had been said. He loved Mary, the mother of their two wee ones. And he loved Cathleen, his comrade in arms, who handled an Armalite rifle as well as any man could. It was that simple and that complicated. He did not try to explain it further, even to himself.

McMahon had cheerful blue eyes with crinkles in

the corners and light brown hair that fell over his forehead. He was a lean five feet nine, and he was wearing a Donegal tweed jacket, a shirt open at the neck and corduroy trousers. At the train station, before getting out of the car, he put the Pioneers Total Abstinence Society pin on his jacket lapel. It was white with a small red Sacred Heart. When you received the sacrament of confirmation around the age of ten or eleven, you were automatically inducted into the society. At eighteen, if you renewed your pledge against the drink, you were given a green probationary pin, and after six months of good behavior you got the white one. Some innocents, upon seeing a wayward Pioneer reeling in the street, would rush to his aid in the mistaken belief that he was suffering a mortal seizure.

After the pin was in place, Cathleen said, "God bless."

"Ah, very appropriate, that," he said. "I'm off to be a better man. I trust I look the part." It was ironic, he thought. They called this a sectarian war, and yet Holy Mother the Church meant nothing to him. In the north the Brits financed the Catholic schools, and that had bought off the bishops—talk about your thirty pieces of silver. And in the south, in the free state, the bishops had made sure that the Republic of Ireland was the only nation in the Western world to ban divorce. If he were a devout Protestant loyalist, McMahon figured he'd have a few second thoughts himself.

Cathleen did not know the purpose of his departure and had not inquired. Nor had he volunteered anything. Out of habit, they did not publicly touch one another. The only time they had any physical contact was in bed.

Inside the station, the normal Friday afternoon crush was on. McMahon was carrying a small shoulder bag with a change of shirt and underwear and a toilet kit. At the luggage inspection counter, nobody stopped him. As he had expected, all he got was a curl of the lip from an RUC cop who eyed his Pioneer pin. It was the last thing that anyone would suspect the O.C. of the IRA's Belfast brigade, its commander, to have been sporting. And if he was singled out for some reason and questioned, he had all the particulars of the weekend retreat he was supposedly attending.

Out of the train window, McMahon saw the Union Jacks flying in the countryside. When the British had finally acceded to the partition of Ireland in 1922, six years after the Easter Monday uprising in Dublin, they carefully carved out six of the nine counties of the ancient province of Ulster to create what was called the Province of Northern Ireland, thus assuring that a solid sixty percent of it, the descendants of colonizers in a conquered land, was both Protestant and loyal to the crown. Having done this, they then declared that they would abide by a democratic vote regarding any future unification with the rest of Ireland. McMahon couldn't help admiring this marvelous sleight of hand. In an instant, a minority had become the majority.

The eastern counties of Northern Ireland, County Antrim, where Belfast was, and County Down, through which he was now traveling south, were overwhelmingly loyalist. As you moved into the counties westward, the percentages began to even out and then changed the other way as you got to overwhelmingly Catholic and republican Derry, Northern Ireland's second city, which the Brits insisted on calling Londonderry. But the ball game, everyone agreed, was in Gerry McMahon's Belfast.

The laughable part, he always thought, was that the Brits held all the Irish, loyalist or republican, in equal contempt. One of his favorite stories was from some of the lads who had been incarcerated in the Wormwood Scrubs prison in England. There also was a fellow held there from the Protestant paramilitaries, the Ulster Volunteer Force, and one day the lads were gathered at the end of a prison corridor when this Ulsterman was walking down it, and behind him a screw yelled, "Hey, you, Paddy, come here," but the Ulsterman kept walking, as nonchalant as you please, and the screw yelled again, and the Ulsterman at last turned around in amazement and said, "You mean *me?*" and the screw yelled, "Yes, you, you're a bloody Paddy, aren't you?" and later the Ulsterman had come up to the lads and said, "Christ, all this time I've been on the wrong side."

The last stop before the border was Newry. It was here that the first dependable homemade mortar bombs had been unveiled and left the Brits and their RUC toadies in such shock. The bombs, which looked like miniature missiles, had been shaped and welded out of steel pipe and tested on the Donegal coast, using industrial tubing to launch them, and then trucked around south of the border and up along a cattle path into South Armagh to Newry. A mortar battery had been placed in a lorry about five hundred yards from the main police barracks and set off by a radio signal, the kind used to control model airplanes. So much for the dumb Paddys, McMahon had thought. It had been a night spectacular, the bombs streaking skyward like a fireworks display, decimating the barracks and killing nine cops.

The ride from Belfast to Dundalk took little more than an hour. McMahon knew he was across the border when he saw the big white letters on a stone wall, "Up the IRA!" Along the ridges of the hills that rose from the free state, he could see British army observation posts. On these same hillsides, in 1970 at the age of seventeen, he had trained to become an IRA volunteer. And that was the most significant fact of all, far more significant than bombs raining down on a police barracks, or the ambushing of eighteen paratroopers on a country road, or all the other glorious triumphs *and* all the terrible defeats and fiascos, infinitely more significant than the horror of Bloody Sunday when the paratroopers cut down thirteen unarmed civil rights marchers, or even the greater horror of the hunger strike in the H-Block cells of the Maze prison.

The struggle had spanned centuries, of course, but it had sputtered throughout, like grease in a frying pan when the heat was turned on and off, a few years here, a few there. But now for the first time there had been a generational jump of continuous sustained combat. That was the difference. The kids like McMahon, who had known no other life, were now the commanders.

At the Dundalk station he looked across the tracks at the gleaming vats of a subsidiary owned by the

Guinness brewery set behind big plate-glass windows. It was, he joked, his great moral failure. Guinness was part of the establishment, the enemy. Yet he could not forswear his pints of Guinness stout. He fantasized the final day of victory when Guinness would be nationalized and he could down it in peace of mind as well as body. "Now that's worth a bit of fightin' for, isn't it?" he had teased Cathleen.

He walked over the rail bridge and went three blocks to the pub where Jack O'Connell was waiting in the dark rear and said, "Jack, how ye doin'?" although he had not seen O'Connell in almost ten years. They had trained together in the hills northwest of Dundalk, and after they had returned to Belfast Jack had been named by an informer in the shooting of a Brit lieutenant. It had been a wonderful shot that Jack had squeezed off, right between the eyes at two hundred yards. McMahon knew this because he was part of the ambush party.

O'Connell, though, had escaped in a garbage truck from the Crumlin Road jail and had fled to the free state. The time was highly charged. The hunger strikes were going on and O'Connell would be on trial without a jury, in which a policeman's unsupported word was considered proof, before a British judge who had just acquitted two RUC cops for gunning down an unarmed suspected IRA volunteer. In his ruling the judge had commended the two cops. "You brought the deceased to justice," he said, "and in this case, I am pleased to say, to a final court of justice." That remark got around pretty well, and for once, although the IRA was outlawed in the south as well as the north, the Irish Republic refused extradition on the grounds of murky and contradictory evidence.

Jack went to work in the Dublin offices of the IRA's political arm, *Sinn Fein*, which in Gaelic meant "Ourselves Alone." He was the wisest fellow McMahon had met in the movement. When they had both been interned in Long Kesh, the literacy of some of the lads was, well, limited, but Jack had conducted one of the most successful classes ever. He had started them out on smuggled copies of *Playboy* magazine and then said, "You think the pictures are good, wait till you learn the words."

McMahon was as sure as he could be that O'Connell sat on the secret seven-man Army Council which conducted overall operational planning. And he'd bet anything that Jack had a major hand in the convention site. It was to be at a Cistercian monastery south of Dundalk on the bank of the River Boyne, in itself a poetic touch. You could argue back and forth that the subjection of Ireland began in the twelfth century with the English King Henry II. But there was no disputing that the die was cast three hundred years ago at the Battle of the Boyne on July 12, 1690, when the troops of William of Orange crushed what appeared to have been the last great Irish rebellion. That was what the loyalists thought anyway, for each July 12 the Orange Order, with their bowler hats and sashes and puffed chests, marched to the thump of tribal drums all through the streets of Northern Ireland commemorating victory forever over the Fenian papists.

Using the monastery had been a genius stroke. The Cistercians, the "White Monks," like their Trappist offshoot, took vows of silence, communicating with one another in a private sign language. Independent of the bishops, only the old abbot and his assistant abbot dealt with the outside world. The abbot was a holy man who believed in forgiving but not forgetting. Ten years before, the youngest son of his sister, himself the father of four, had been fatally shot north of the border after being caught in the fire of British soldiers chasing a Provo fugitive. Worse yet, instead of admitting their error, the British had announced that the dead man was also a terrorist.

The problem was that the area around Dundalk was a hotbed of republicanism, and the Special Branch of the *Gardai Siochana*, the Irish police, was all over the place. The abbot, however, handled this quite nicely. There were frequent retreats at the monastery, and when the *Garda* inspector, a religious man who enjoyed chatting with the abbot—"We're not so different," the inspector once reflected, "we both hear confessions"—came by on a routine visit, the abbot took care to observe that the following weekend the monastery would be host to a gathering of the Pioneers.

"Ah, bad news for the local pubs, that," the inspector said, immediately making a notation that there would be no need to investigate a sudden influx of vehicles on the monastery grounds.

"God works in wondrous ways," the abbot said.

And now in the pub in Dundalk, McMahon drained his Guinness, and O'Connell said, "It's time."

On the way, McMahon said, "John Bingham's been located."

"When's it to happen, then?"

"Soon. Sunday night, I'm thinkin'. Before he takes off again. I wonder, should I mention it?"

"I don't see why. He's fair game, the murderous bastard."

"I intend to do it myself."

"All the more reason."

"The weapons are different. Something's got to be done. I won't keep silent about that."

"Don't. You may be surprised, pleasantly."

"How long will it go on?" McMahon asked.

"The convention? Twelve hours at the most. We can't dare more than that."

"No. I mean the war."

"A long time," O'Connell said. "Perhaps past our time. It's a disservice to say otherwise. There's been too much talk of next year, or in three years, or five."

"It's hard to tell people there's no end in sight."

"But there will be an end if we keep the pressure on, that's the thing. The truth is we haven't won, but the Brits haven't either, and all the while they thought they had."

"Why don't they just go?"

"Ah, Gerry, it's because we're about all they've got left. Us and the Falkland Islands."

Along with its agricultural sheds, the monastery consisted of three main structures—the original thirteenth-century castle, a large manor house built in the 1700s and a modern, twenty-year-old dormitory facility. Extending from the house were stables converted into guest quarters to keep visitors separated from the monks. And in the house itself was a great oak-paneled hall where the delegates assembled. Behind one of the panels, the abbot had advised, was an underground passageway for any of the lads on the run in case something untoward occurred.

One hundred fifty-three delegates attended, representing all IRA departments and units, north and south. Much of the old military organization, especially the battalions and companies in the north, existed only in the loosest way to retain a sense of history and tradition. Vulnerable to informers and penetration by British intelligence, they were used to police crime in local neighborhoods in the absence of any help or interest from the RUC, to pass on tidbits of information and sometimes to fetch or dump arms.

The fighting core of the Belfast brigade, tailored for urban guerrilla warfare, was limited at any given moment to sixty active service volunteers divided into three- or four-man cells that were constantly collapsed and re-formed. Because they were always on call, very few had jobs. Most, to keep them off government registries, were paid salaries equivalent to what they would get on the dole. They used pseudonyms with one another. It was a lonely, elitist life. They stayed away from other IRA members and sympathizers and republican drinking hangouts like the Gaelic Athletic Association clubs. Only McMahon, as the O.C., and his adjutant and the brigade security officer knew who all of them were.

The majority of the convention delegates were from the Irish Republic, but this meant little. Whatever the numbers, the convention was simply a confirmation of the power swing northward, to the men

on the line in actual combat. It had begun in 1970 at
the last convention after the civil rights marches,
when the loyalist mobs ravaged Catholic enclaves
while the old Official IRA, headquartered in Dublin,
was caught unawares and the legendary initials were
jeered throughout Belfast and Derry as standing for
"I Ran Away." That was when the Provisional IRA
was formed, permanent now although the Provo tag
had stuck. Both a Northern and Southern Command
were created, theoretically on an equal footing. But
it was the north that now called the tune while the
south, except for hit-and-run incursions across the
border, was gradually relegated to providing safe
havens, raising money and collecting and storing
arms and explosives.

The Northern Command had called for the convention, and in an effort to keep his actual status
secret, Gerry McMahon was there simply as an ordinary delegate from the brigade's first battalion. He'd
been O.C. for only three months, and supposedly
Terrance McBride was still brigade commander, but
poor McBride was facing a death sentence from cancer of the colon, although that was still a secret, too.
Not even the Belfast active service volunteers were
aware that McMahon was now in charge. Sooner or
later, the presumption was, word would leak out, and
not necessarily from an informer. It was the Irish
curse, as if silence were a mortal sin. Some fellow
would hear something and pass it on to some other
fellow over a glass or two. "Guess who's wearing the
big stripes?" he'd say, and the Brits would hear about
it, and then McMahon would be hauled off to the
Castlereagh interrogation center in East Belfast and

given a going over, and if he didn't break during the seven days they were allowed to have him, he could be slapped in the Crumlin Road jail as a known terrorist. But since there had been such an international outcry over the kangaroo courts that the Brits had established, he might just be targeted for assassination by one of the police death squads, or the trained undercover killers of the British army's counterinsurgency detail—the Special Air Service, as it was euphemistically called. Or, more likely, he'd be placed under intense scrutiny, watched where he went, whom he came in contact with, a rising star in the MI5 computer system. Or, just maybe, none of this would happen.

Whatever you said about the Provisional IRA, McMahon thought, it was democratic to a fault. The main purpose of the convention was to vote on allowing candidates of *Sinn Fein* to take seats in the Irish Republic's parliament, the Dail. This struck a raw nerve among southern old-timers. Since partition in the 1920s, which the IRA had never accepted, abstentionism had been the order of the day, to preserve the purity of the struggle. The Northern Command had argued that it was a moribund policy. Widespread political support in the south was critical. How could you expect young people to back those representatives who then sat on their asses out in the cold? It had worked well in the north in local elections. You had to offer your constituents the ballot as well as the bullet.

The debate raged. McMahon was surprised and moved by the passionate voices of IRA men of other times, men in their fifties and sixties, who had held the rifle and had been wounded and hunted and imprisoned and had dear friends and relatives killed before their eyes and who spoke darkly of the betrayal of a fundamental principle if abstentionism were abandoned, how the forces of corruption and co-option would worm their way insidiously into the cause. Finally, though, balding Joe Callahan, seventy-one, once chief of staff, once an hour away from the gallows for shepherding an illegal arms shipment into the free state before his sentence was commuted, rose to address the delegates. "You all know who I am," he said. "You know I never wear a tie because I don't fancy nothin' around me neck." And then in choked tones he had declared that the life blood of the cause depended on constant renewal, that the torch had been passed to a new generation and that, right or wrong, its wishes must be respected. "They're the ones who will have to fight on until British rule is ended," he said. "If you don't believe this, we might as well all go home." After that the motion carried overwhelmingly.

To McMahon's astonishment, the next item on the agenda, the removal of sexist language from the original IRA constitution and an amendment to it that enunciated the equality of men and women within the ranks, produced almost as much furor. And now the voices from the past lost him. A woman's place was to bear children, not arms, they said, and to comfort and sustain her man, a woman was too soft to stand up to torture, a woman gossiped too much. "Who would look after the children if their mother was arrested?" one of them cried. McMahon felt like asking whether they believed a woman was entitled to an orgasm, but he didn't want to call attention to himself, and then he didn't have to. The motion passed.

The delegates reaffirmed a pledge not to attack government institutions and forces in the twenty-six counties of the Irish Republic. They also endorsed a strategy already put in place by the Northern Command that warned vendors and contractors to cease doing business with the British army of occupation in Northern Ireland under the pain of lethal punishment. The idea was to force London to use troops instead, making them more vulnerable to attack. Too many IRA targets had been RUC cops and loyalist paramilitaries. The Northern Command wanted more boxes containing the corpses of British soldiers shipped home so that families in Liverpool and Manchester and Birmingham would begin asking why their sons were in Northern Ireland, what were they dying for?

Afterward, the convention by secret vote elected a new IRA Executive which would set future policy. The Executive then withdrew to select the seven-man Army Council and to pick a chief of staff, who in turn appointed his headquarters personnel and chiefs for both the Northern and Southern commands.

On Saturday morning when McMahon was summoned to meet the new chief of staff, he found himself looking at Jack O'Connell. Which made sense. A northerner in the south with the freedom to coordinate activities. But the new northern commander was Denis Dillon, and it took McMahon some moments to appreciate the bold design of this. Dillon had been elected on a *Sinn Fein* slate to the British parliament at Westminster, although of course he never actually took his seat. It had been a bitter blow to British claims that IRA "thugs and hoodlums" were an anathema even to Irish nationalists. Everybody knew that Dillon was in the IRA, but the trouble was that neither the Brits nor the RUC were ever able to prove it. During the years of internment, while hundreds of Provo suspects were swept without trial into Long Kesh, Dillon had gone across the border into County Monaghan, sticking like a sore thumb into the soft underbelly of Northern Ireland, and led a legendary series of commando raids. Then he resurfaced in Derry, and after his dramatic election he became the focus of press and television attention around the world. A round-faced, pipe-smoking man, educated and articulate, who attended Mass and wrote learned articles on the works of Oscar Wilde, James Joyce, Samuel Beckett and William Butler Yeats, he had said in one of his most famous interviews, "The Brits are now attempting to criminalize eight hundred years of Irish patriotism. They are masters at self-deception." His celebrity shielded him from normal retribution, an informer's word or a cop's sworn testimony. He would have to be nailed in the act, an unlikely event. As for the rest, his armored car and constant escort would have to do.

Still, the elevation of *Sinn Feiners*, however notable, to command roles concerned Gerry McMahon; and as if reading his mind, Dillon said, "The armed struggle continues, comrade. Nonetheless, if we've made mistakes, and we have, it is in the area of military elitism. If we want a unified thirty-two-county nation, we have to have thirty-two-county support. That means we have to engage people politically as well as militarily, in community groups, trade unions, in co-operatives and tenant organizations, with city workers and working farmers and small business entrepreneurs. Everyone wants peace. *We* want peace. But we're tagged as godless men of violence. Thieving gangsters, the bishops and the establishment lackeys call us. Their morality is the morality of the ruling class. They say we're the enemies of the people, and I'll grant them some of that. We are enemies of people who enslave, who torture, who discriminate, who exploit, who misrepresent and manipulate. It's in this context that the armed conflict must be pursued. Because the hard, inescapable fact is that the Brits have never given up anything willingly, beginning with the United States of America."

"In that case, speaking of America," Gerry McMahon said, "I'll be needing the firepower of M16 rifles to supplement the Armalite. American plastic explosive. Night scopes. Laser beam detonators, as the Brit convoys are using scramblers against our remote radios. And for the helicopters, the Redeye missile. The politics I'll leave to those better qualified."

"We're aware of the wanted equipment," Dillon said, "and it's being looked after. You'll be informed in due course. Soon."

McMahon glanced at O'Connell and then said, "I should tell you the lads have located John Bingham."

"Yes, so we've been told. It's sanctioned."

Later that afternoon, McMahon asked O'Connell, "Why didn't you tell me of your august appointment?"

"How could I? I'm no seer. I didn't know myself."

They drove up into the sun-dappled heathered hills near Dundalk, where they both had trained for a month. There had been eighteen of them, with three Lee-Enfield rifles, four revolvers and an allotment of twenty bullets each, under the direction of a County Tyrone man who had been a paratrooper when the Brits were still trying to hang on to Cyprus.

"That shipment Dillon was talking about," McMahon said, "it's big?"

"The biggest. Kevin Dowd is handling it. In Boston, in America. You remember Kevin from the Kesh?"

"I do, yes." Then McMahon suddenly said, "Do you remember the way to the Faerie Hill?"

"My, this is a sentimental journey."

McMahon had never forgotten it. The steeply inclined country road a couple of miles from their camp flattened out for about twenty yards before rising again. The fellow driving the car had come to a dead halt in the flat part and put the gearshift in neutral, when all at once, without anyone touching the shift or the accelerator, the car on its own started moving forward, slowly gathering speed up the rise for at least another fifty yards until the road dipped down once more.

Now, with O'Connell, the same thing happened. McMahon got out and walked the length of the rise, clearly five or six feet higher than where the car had been stopped. "It has to be an illusion," he finally announced. "The whole hillside is tilted in some fashion and this rise isn't really rising."

"No, you're just trying to rationalize," O'Connell

said with a smile. "It's the faeries. IRA faeries doing the impossible."

McMahon stayed in a safe house in Dundalk that night, and rode the early morning train back to Belfast. He had only been home a few moments before Mary returned from Mass with the wee ones, Deirdre, eight, and Sean, four. Mary looked drained, he thought, the dark circles under her eyes. It had all taken so much out of them. But she was forever committed. He saw that always when they went to the Milltown cemetery to place flowers on her da's grave, killed in the 1969 savagery. He recalled how she had brought him oranges when he was in the Kesh, laced with vodka she'd inserted with a hypodermic needle, and their frenzied lovemaking when he was released that had produced Deirdre and Sean.

In the afternoon he took Sean to Corrigan Park to kick a ball with him and afterward bought him an ice cream and told him about a magic place he had been where the faeries made a car go uphill without any power; and then, with Sean on his shoulders, they silently watched the Saracens and a British patrol from the Black Watch regiment go past them along Whiterock Road.

They had pork chops and carrots and mashed potatoes for supper, and when the dishes were done he told Mary that he was sorry, that he had to be off again, probably for the whole night.

She did not ask where he was going.

Gerry McMahon and John Bingham had grown up across the street from one another in the Shankill district, a block from the Falls. There weren't any Catholics anymore in the Shankill. Now the wall separated it from the Falls. Built by the British in a land where there was no peace, the wall was called "The Peace Line." The wall was twenty feet high. It had been originally constructed of corrugated steel and cinder block. Parts of it were being gentrified in brick. It snaked across municipal thoroughfares, through backyards, past churches and factories. It was topped with razor wire, television monitors and mesh-covered lights. Except for Berlin, there was nothing else like it in the world.

But before this, while the Shankill had always been predominantly Protestant and loyalist, there was a sprinkling of Catholic families like the McMahons. McMahon and John Bingham had, of course, gone to different schools, but Gerry could remember how the two of them had played ball together most every afternoon. And in a kind of stupefaction that gripped him to this day, Gerry could also remember how, when he was a wee one, he asked his da why they couldn't paint the curb in front of their house red, white and blue as the others on the street did, or why on the twelfth of July he couldn't step to the drums celebrating the Battle of the Boyne.

Then in August of 1969, after the civil rights marches began and people were singing a song he'd never heard of, a song called "We Shall Overcome," mobs from the Shankill had poured into the Kashmir section of the Falls shooting and burning and looting, and his da, never supposing that his own neighbors would turn on him, had rushed off to help defend it. Gerry was at home with his ma and sister when the

crowd suddenly gathered outside, and first the rocks
and the exploding petrol bottles had come crashing
through the windows, and they were forced into the
street in front of the jeering crowd while the cops
stood by taking in the spectacle. Gerry had seen John
in the crowd and heard him yell through cupped
hands, "Gerry McMahon, you Fenian bastard, one
day I'll cut your fookin' balls off."

They made their way to the house of his ma's parents in the Falls, and later that night when his da
caught up with them, his da said he'd been to the
police station and was told they could return to
gather up what remained of their belongings. Mc-
Mahon had never seen his father so dispirited. And
in the morning, while they were salvaging what they
could in a borrowed lorry, a crowd assembled again,
watching silently this time, and just as they were to
go, McMahon saw Bingham toss another petrol bomb
into the lorry, and now they possessed nothing beyond the clothes on their backs.

Afterward McMahon enlisted in *Na Fianna Eireann,* the IRA's junior wing, "The Soldiers of Ireland," where he learned Irish history and twice
brought guns to a jump-off house for IRA operations; and then when he was seventeen he was accepted into the actual IRA, swearing allegiance to its
constitution and to bear arms against Great Britain
until British withdrawal and the reunification of the
whole of Ireland.

He heard that Bingham had joined an Ulster Vol-
unteer Force gang led by Lenny Murphy, the
"Shankill Butcher." The name came from the way
Murphy horribly dismembered his victims, nineteen

of them, all ordinary citizens, all murdered simply because they were Catholic. The IRA finally caught up with Murphy as he was departing a rendezvous with his mistress, but Bingham, having gained managerial experience running a string of massage parlors, regrouped the gang. Within the past six months, there had been eight more sectarian killings masterminded by him. He made no secret of it. Journalists recounted the high drama of being blindfolded and taken to interviews with him in the dead of night. They wrote that he was surprisingly gracious and witty and refreshingly candid. "There's terrorists and terrorists," he was quoted as saying. "My kind of terrorist just wants to hold on to what he's got." Asked about a Catholic father of five, gunned down while going to work, he said, "Look at it as a form of copulation control. He was like every other fookin' Fenian, breeding like fookin' rabbits, they are. And this one wasn't too smart, was he? You don't go around sayin' you want so badly out of the British Empire and next march brazenly into a shipyard takin' jobs away from them that's loyal to the crown."

But then Bingham went too far. A young Protestant woman who had married a Catholic was shot dead in her bed with her husband. Although the cops tried to hush it up, her belly had been slit open from her vagina to her breasts and her husband's severed penis stuffed inside her. A crude note alongside her body said, "You should know better, dearie."

All over West Belfast, McMahon picked up the angry street talk. The theme was constant. What good was the great IRA? An IRA intelligence unit pinpointed a new residence Bingham had moved to with his wife and seven-year-old daughter in a loyalist enclave called Ballysillan north of the Shankill. Surveillance tied down three attack possibilities. An Ulster club that Bingham frequented in the afternoon and early evening. During his trip home from the club. Or the home itself.

McMahon decided on the home. An attack on the club required too many men so deep in hostile territory, and Bingham always had an escort when he traveled from place to place. At home he'd be less on the alert. "We'll be sending a message," McMahon told his adjutant, "that we can go anywhere we want. It'll brighten up their dreams."

In any event, it wasn't going to be easy. Bingham lived off Park Road in a small estate named Ballysillan Crescent, really a narrow street that curved back up a hill to another dead-end street cutting across it at the top, like the serif on the letter "J." Bingham's house was on this second street, the third from the end closest to the road. Driving directly in was out of the question. There was only one entry and exit, with no room to maneuver, and a car in the middle of the night would spark immediate attention.

There was, though, a stretch of open ground, perhaps fifty yards wide, between the main road and the street Bingham was on. That's how they'd go in, dashing straight up the open ground, bypassing the rest of the estate. McMahon figured they would have no more than three minutes to do the job once they were there. His personal feelings about Bingham, his memory of him, did not enter into his calculations at all. And ordinarily he would have waited for a more opportune time. Bingham wasn't the answer. The

Brits were. Bingham was something you found when you turned over a rotting log. Anywhere else, he'd be a police matter. His demise would not alter the course of the war. The irony was, McMahon thought, that he was probably doing the Brits a favor getting rid of Bingham, and given the ravings of the Protestant fundamentalist minister Ian Paisley, who cried for republican blood from the pulpit, there was sure to be someone else ready to take his place. But Bingham had magnified himself into a ghastly symbol of the moment. The IRA's reputation as the community's guardian was on the line.

That Sunday night around eight o'clock, as McMahon was helping to clean up after supper, the owners of a dark blue Ford Cortina and a maroon Volvo in Andersontown received knocks on their doors and were told that the IRA was requisitioning their vehicles for a brief period while they and their families were to remain at home in the presence of an IRA volunteer.

Both cars, equipped now with police radio scanners, were parked near the jump-off house by the time McMahon arrived. Besides himself and Cathleen, there were four more active-service men. Only he knew who everyone was. And as far as they knew, except for Cathleen, he was just another volunteer acting as operations officer for this particular mission.

Then McMahon revealed what it was. He spread out a map and explained the procedure. Bingham's wife and little girl would be in the house, he said. No harm was to come to them. Within the hour four teenage scouts from *Na Fianna Eireann* showed up at intervals through an alley carrying backpacks containing three walkie-talkies, two Armalite rifles with folding stocks so they could fit, as the saying went, in a box of cereal, a Uzi submachine gun, also with a folding stock, a nine-millimeter Browning automatic and a Colt .38 pistol.

At eleven, the phone rang and a voice said, "The bird's nested in. Everything's on the green. Luck."

McMahon got into the Cortina next to Cathleen, two of the volunteers with them, one carrying a sledgehammer. The other two would trail them in the Volvo, to create a diversion if something went wrong. This stage of an operation always had McMahon on edge. It was the most unpredictable, therefore the most dangerous. You never knew when you'd hit a roadblock, even though an intelligence network kept a constant lookout for them. He relaxed a little once they were passing through loyalist enclaves on Woodvale Road and then the Crumlin Road. The chances of being stopped were much less here, one of the perks of fealty to the crown.

Shortly after midnight, Cathleen parked below Ballysillan Crescent. The Volvo was about a hundred yards behind them. There was nothing special on the police scanner. With only one streetlamp on the corner, it was quite dark. They donned black ski masks. "All right, lads, let's be off," McMahon said.

Crouching low, they moved up the open space to where Bingham's street dead-ended. The only light visible was in a ground-floor window of his house. A Union Jack hung from a flagstaff over the entrance. They crept up the front steps and McMahon peered through the window. A woman, presumably Bingham's wife, was knitting.

"Give it a go," he whispered to the volunteer with the sledgehammer.

The door instantly gave way. McMahon charged in, his Browning in hand. A staircase was directly ahead of him. Right at the top of the stairs he saw a door already starting to close. He bounded up, but the door snapped shut just as he hit it with his shoulder and bounced off. It was made of steel.

He pumped two rounds into the lock, smashing it, and with the added weight of the volunteer who had come up behind him, forced the door. Bingham was on his knees, frantically trying to get under a bed.

"Not another move," McMahon said, leveling the Browning at him. He pulled up his mask. Bingham turned, sitting on the floor. Their eyes met. It was the first time McMahon had seen him since he had thrown the petrol bomb into the lorry.

Bingham's eyes widened in sudden frightened recognition. He raised a supplicating hand. "For the love of God, Gerry, don't!" he pleaded.

McMahon heard a child's voice calling from another room. Jesus, he thought, don't come in, not now, and then he said, "John Bingham, I execute you in the name of the Irish people." He squeezed the trigger and watched the left side of Bingham's head dissolve in a geyser of blood.

Downstairs the volunteer covering Bingham's wife with a Uzi in one hand and holding a walkie-talkie in the other called out, "Condition red. Time to go."

Outside, lights were being turned on. As they hurried toward the Cortina, Bingham's wife began screaming behind them. "What is it?" McMahon asked Cathleen.

"There's a report of shots being fired. There's cops nearby, but they're confused. They're still asking for the location."

"On our way then."

A police car, and a second, raced past them from the opposite direction. "It'll be ten minutes before they can seal off anything," McMahon said, "and we'll be far gone. Nice work, lads."

He spent the rest of the night with Cathleen in the tiny house she shared with her sister and brother-in-law. Lying in bed next to him, she said, "Are you all right?"

"Never better."

"I was worried tonight."

"Why?"

"All at once I had this terrible feeling about an informer. Why are there so many informers?"

He lit a cigarette and saw her anxious eyes in the glow from the match. "Ah, well, it's our religion, you see. You feel so good when you come out of confession."

"You shouldn't be making fun of me. I'm serious."

"So am I," Gerry McMahon said.

PART
II

Chapter

7

Far removed from these events, and indeed before any of them had occurred, Michael McGuire, struggling to piece together his shattered life, discovered that Harry Hollander was right about the women. The first was Mary Alice's close friend Elizabeth Carter. She and her son, Tommy, came out to the beach for a week late in the summer. It had all been very correct and, he thought, very pleasant; and then in the fall in the city they would see each other occasionally on weekend outings with the boys and sometimes during the week, just the two of them. To tell the truth, he dreaded the prospect of shepherding Jamie alone through adolescence, magnifying in his mind all the mysteries which that passage entailed and which, everything else aside, appeared to him to be infinitely more sophisticated and complex than his own childhood. At odd moments he found himself contemplating the idea of creating a new family unit with Elizabeth, one that would provide stability, and for Jamie a sibling in fact if not blood. That fantasy evaporated when he asked Jamie what he thought of Tommy Carter, and Jamie, as though reading Michael McGuire's mind, replied without enthusiasm, "He's okay, I suppose." One night sitting with Elizabeth on the sofa in her living room, she suddenly reached over and unzipped his fly and groped inside until he pulled her hand away, and she looked at him and said, "I'm sorry. I guess the chemistry just isn't there," and he departed feeling as regretful for her as for himself.

Sex, which had always been such an elementary part of his life, ceased to be. He dreamed continually of Mary Alice. She'd be alive, and then dead. Sometimes this would happen in the most terrifying circumstances. He would be holding her and making love to her and suddenly she'd disintegrate in his arms, and he would cry out like a confused child.

Other women tried a different approach, through Jamie. At dinner one evening, he was seated between a divorced former model who had two small children and an extremely wealthy divorcée named Monica DuChamps, who at least didn't have any. He ended up in a cab with both of them. Since Monica lived the farthest away, he was directing the driver there when she leaned over and whispered, "You're taking the wrong one home first."

In her canopied bed, the sheets were silk. He'd never been in a bed with silk sheets. The feel of them was incredibly luxurious. He wondered how much they cost. The fringe benefits of a life being kept in silk sheets briefly occupied him. When she slipped in beside him, however, he felt nothing. Oh, what the hell, he thought, he'd go down on her and maybe that way he would get into it. But she stopped him. "It's not that important," she said. She was from Youngstown, Ohio, born Monica Grabowski, the daughter of a steelworker. Her last, late husband was a French industrialist whose name she had retained. "He was sixty-seven when we got married," she explained, "so it wasn't exactly a roll in the hay every night, but he was rich, I'll say that." It was the most inhibiting remark Michael McGuire had ever heard.

After she met Jamie, she said, "What a captivating child. The owner of the New York Yankees is a friend of mine. I'll take him to a baseball game. I'll arrange for a ball to be signed by the team. He'll adore that."

"I don't think so. He doesn't like baseball."

For the first time, Monica seemed nonplussed. "I thought all boys loved baseball."

"Well, this one doesn't."

It took her no time at all to recover, however. "Jamie," she said, "how would you like to have tea with me at the Plaza?"

"*Tea,*" he said, making a face.

"You don't understand. Tea's just an expression. You can have anything you want. Hot chocolate, an ice cream soda. All sorts of scrumptious cakes. And perhaps afterward, we'll have time for a little shopping."

"How was it?" Michael McGuire asked.

"Great," Jamie said. "Guess who was there? Barbra

Streisand. I saw her. And Mr. Spock, I mean the guy who plays Mr. Spock in 'Star Trek.' "

"Mr. Spock was having tea at the Plaza?"

"Sure. Everybody has tea there. It was really neat."

Jamie was lugging a large bag with the logo of F A O Schwarz, the toy store opposite the Plaza Hotel on Fifth Avenue, and Michael McGuire said, "What's in there?"

"You won't believe it," Jamie said, blushing. "It's the Bally Computer System for video games. Look at this! It's got Galactic Invasion, Zzzap and Dodgem, Seawolf and Missile and a whole bunch more. And a joystick for flying and a real wheel for car racing."

Michael McGuire knew how expensive it was, having cased various models on the market the previous Christmas. "Didn't I get you something like this?"

"But Dad, it's the best. It's so cool."

"You'll have to return it."

"How come?"

"Because I said so."

"But Monica didn't get it for you. She gave it to me."

There was an undeniable logic in that, and the best Michael McGuire could manage was "You don't think I had anything to do with it?"

Jamie stared at him curiously, and then Michael McGuire was stunned to hear him say, "Dad, are you going to marry Monica?"

He was almost grateful for the way the question suddenly forced him to crystallize his thoughts, the idle vision of being kept in silk sheets. "No, I'm not. What makes you ask?"

"I don't know. She's kind of nice, and you're going to marry somebody, aren't you?"

"You think I should?"

"Maybe."

"Well, it's not going to be Monica."

"Why?"

"Because, for one thing, I don't love her."

"Dad."

"Yes?"

"Can I keep the Bally anyway? I mean, she did give it to me."

Michael McGuire felt so miserably alone. "Okay," he said, "you win."

Friends told him that a divorce caused more psychological havoc in a child than a parental death. A divorce ripped a child apart, with all the divided loyalties it conjured up, burdening a child with enormous feelings of guilt for perhaps being responsible for the divorce in the first place. The finality of a death, as awful as it was, did none of this, and would only strengthen the bonds between Michael McGuire and Jamie.

However supportive these pronouncements were designed to be, they privately enraged him. How could anyone know what was churning inside of him? Or inside Jamie? Not even he knew that. It was like telling him he was lucky not being black and living in South Africa.

Small matters became monumental, like the advent of Mother's Day. He had always despised Mother's Day, knowing it to be an advertising gimmick, right

behind the birth of Christ in the chase for a buck.
Now it was rearing up before him like a coiled rattle-
snake. He considered taking Jamie out of school and
going off somewhere until it was over, but he concluded that this would be a pitiful evasion of reality.
In the end, Jamie confronted it better than he did.
He came home from school with a Mother's Day card
he had made. The borders had artfully crafted cur-
licues and cupids with arrows and in the center was a
photograph of Mary Alice and underneath in script
it said, "For Mom, We Love You and Miss You." It
was signed "Jamie," and Jamie said, "You have to
sign it," and he wrote "Michael," and then there was
the bad moment when Jamie's eyes teared finally and
he said, "We don't have anyone to give it to," and
Michael McGuire said, "Yes, we do, we are giving it
to her memory," and put it on the mantel in the living
room.

He met Allison Ashley at Harry Hollander's. She was
blond, her hair expertly colored and coiffed so that
the ends flipped up demurely around her neck. Unlike the other women at Hollander's, flitting about in
chiffon and taffeta and black slip dresses that displayed pushed-up bosoms, she stood coolly in a corner in a tailored gray skirt and jacket with velvet
lapels and a white silk blouse that had ruffled cuffs.
For all of this, she exuded a profound sexuality. Michael McGuire could see from the swell of her jacket
that she was remarkably full breasted. He wondered
what other secrets and excitements lay hidden beneath her composed exterior.

"You need a refill," he said. "What can I get you?"

Her pale gray eyes shifted lazily, surveying him. "Thank you," she said. "Perrier, please. No lime."

The ultimate Episcopalian lady, he thought when she told him her name. Yet he did remember thinking that he had never encountered an Episcopalian lady with the kind of currents he felt running through her. Later, much later, after it was too late, he discovered that her name was originally Carol Steinberg. The fact that she was Jewish would have been, in any event, of no consequence to him, except that it might have helped make her elusive sensual nature more explicable. The important thing was that it meant a great deal to Allison Ashley.

"We were playing one of those games the other night," he said. "The first question was who's the most memorable person you've ever met."

"My father," she said without hesitation.

"Really. Why?"

"Because he's so gracious. Whenever I call him for advice about the stock market, he's always ready to provide it even if he's suffering one of his frightful migraines. They're so bad that he never sees people anymore. He has to spend most of his time in a darkened room, in his bathrobe. He had to give up riding, which he loved."

In fact, her father had been a rabbinical student who, having abandoned the Talmud, was imprisoned for check forgery as well as the theft of securities and had been deceased for five years. He also had changed the family name—to Stone. "So you see," she would eventually explain, as if she were dispensing a primer in logic, "it was no big deal switching from Stone to Ashley."

She was, she said, an investment banker, which was an acceptable exaggeration, since at that time she was a trainee in the mergers and acquisitions department of a Wall Street firm.

The dinner was a buffet, and Michael McGuire stayed with her. A fellow in a group sitting nearby was saying loudly, "I don't see how you can sleep away every morning. For Christ's sake, it's the early bird that gets the worm," and she suddenly leaned over and said, "What about the worm?" and one of the women in the group said, "Yeah, Larry, *what* about the worm, you're so smart?"

The quip amused Michael McGuire. It was the sort of thing, he thought, that Mary Alice might have said.

Again later—too late, he ruefully had to acknowledge—he said to Hollander, "Why didn't you warn me?"

"How was I to know you were going to marry her? You sure didn't let me in on it."

"Even so."

"Hey, Michael, you know, every man to his own spinach."

The truth was that he didn't tell anyone. His worst moment, though, after it was over, was when he happened to be passing Jamie's room, and overheard Jamie saying to an unseen friend, "He didn't ask me about her. If he had, I would have told him," and Michael McGuire had hurried away, too embarrassed to hear the rest.

She said that she was thirty-three and had never married because she cherished her independence.

And right off he was pleased to note that she didn't cater to Jamie. He had begun to believe that he was incapable of raising Jamie. One minute he'd be yelling at Jamie for spending hours in front of the television and in the next giving in to him about a new video game. What Jamie needed was the even hand of a strong woman. Dahlia had been a blessing, but a housekeeper couldn't be expected to oversee Jamie's homework on the nights, often many in succession, when he was involved in crash projects for the agency. One evening she came by as Jamie was about to have supper. "You can't eat with hands and fingernails like that," she said, "go wash them," and although Jamie shot her a dirty look, he did scrub up. Another time when he was after Jamie to get his room in order, she calmly said within Jamie's hearing that her father once had the same problem with her and when she refused to heed him, she returned from school to find her bed tipped over and all of her possessions, even the clothes in her closet, piled on top of it. "I spent two days putting everything back together," she said, "and from then on, I kept everything very neat." Jamie said nothing as he listened to this, but Michael McGuire observed that conditions in his room markedly improved.

And witchlike, she magically revived a sex drive that he had begun to fear was in permanent eclipse. He'd invited her to fly to Los Angeles with him for a client meeting. He always stayed at the Beverly Hills Hotel and had reserved a suite with an outdoor patio. There was a bouquet of flowers with a welcoming note from the manager and a complimentary bottle of champagne. She read the note and in the first real emotion he had witnessed in her, she exclaimed, "I like it!" and pirouetted around the sitting room.

After the bellhop had put away their luggage, she went into the bedroom and sat on the bed against the headboard, her knees drawn up. She had no underwear on at all. He watched her slide a finger between her legs, a crooked grin on her face. And suddenly it was happening. A miracle, he thought, like going to fucking Lourdes and throwing away your crutches. He was enormous. For the first time, in all of this bad time, he felt confident, in control.

"Yes, oh, yes," she moaned, and before he knew it, she was shrieking, "Give it to me!" and he thought, Christ, the whole goddamn hotel must be hearing this, and he got a hand over her mouth to muffle her cries. It was just the beginning. Somewhere he had read an article questioning multiple orgasms for a woman and he thought, Well, here's exhibit A for the defense.

When they returned to New York, he proposed that she move in with him, to try it out for a while, and she said, "No, not being married would be bad for Jamie."

They were married in Virginia, which required no waiting time. "Don't involve Jamie in this," she said. "It'll only make him feel guilty about his mother. Once it's done, he'll accept it because he didn't have anything to do with it." She showed him a watch she had bought, a quartz chronometer that had everything you could think of for a watch to do short of walking a dog. "Give it to him afterward as our wedding present," she said. "He'll like that."

He did not confide in anyone else either, out of the

fear, of course, about what they might say. The day of the marriage, after they got back, he took Jamie on a walk through Central Park, broke the news and gave him the watch.

Jamie just gazed at him.

"Is there anything you want to know?" Michael McGuire said. "Any questions you have?"

"No."

"Look, if you do, I'm here."

"What difference would it make?" Jamie said.

The marriage lasted nearly a year, the last quarter of which was punctuated by vicious quarrels grounded in his knowledge that he had made a disastrous error in judgment. These shouting matches inevitably culminated in marathón rounds of sex. One night she presented him with silk curtain cords to tie her wrists and ankles to the bed posts. He felt silly, but she suddenly made the scene very real. "What are you doing?" she cried. "Don't, please don't," and he found himself attacking her with a rapist's savagery, and afterward she said, "God, that was wonderful." It was the last time they had sex.

After his lawyer gave him the bad news about the divorce settlement, he tried to fathom how he got into this mess. For sure, it wasn't love. At first, he told himself that it was for Jamie's sake. Then he decided that this was a cop-out. He'd done it totally and self-ishly for himself. But friends in heavy analysis contended that it was actually very simple. He had felt a deep anger at Mary Alice for having left him alone with Jamie, and out of guilt for thinking this, he punished himself by marrying Allison. Finally, though, he concluded that whatever else it was, it had been an act of sheer hubris, like a guy building a house on an ocean dune and thumbing his nose at nature.

On the surface Jamie seemed okay. They had one conversation about her. "I just wish you had told me first," Jamie said.

Waves of humiliation enveloped Michael McGuire. He couldn't abide fools, and night after night he had lain in bed thinking how foolish he'd been. "It was a mistake," he said. "I didn't want to get you involved in it. Hey, look at the bright side. You weren't."

The thing was to move on as best he could. After Allison, at least, there had not been any more sexual hang-ups. He had a succession of liaisons of varying lengths, all of which ended upon the realization that marriage was not in the cards. Although the subject was never raised, Jamie appeared to sense that there was no permanence in these female comings and goings, and the tension between them, as far as Michael McGuire was concerned, perceptibly eased, and so did his remorse. It would be the two of them, he thought, and he'd settle for that now, and for as much of the good past as he could re-create.

Jamie would leave the apartment at five-thirty every morning for swimming practice, and by the end of his sophomore year in the upper school, as they called it, he was the top varsity swimmer. His coach, Jamie said, wanted him to attend a swimming camp in Canada during the summer. It would be the first time they'd been apart for any period of time, the first time Jamie hadn't spent the summer working at the marina where he had become so expert in the handling and maintenance of boats and a sought-after mate, despite his age, on charter fishing trips.

Michael McGuire flew to Toronto and drove two hundred fifty miles north through Ontario to visit the camp. Jamie's regimen was so severely structured that he could do little more than wander around watching him in training and competitive workouts. But he liked the way Jamie measured up against the other boys, some of whom had come from England and Brazil and even Japan to attend the camp. He was disappointed that he couldn't have supper with Jamie. It was a strict camp rule that every boy had to eat at his assigned table. And then after supper, there was an intramural softball game Jamie had to play in as part of the overall competition between cabins. He had never seen Jamie with a glove on before. Jamie was assigned to right field, of course, where the fewest balls would be hit, and when he came to bat he struck out and came away head down, but then the next time Jamie was up he hit a towering drive for a triple; and after he had slid into third base, he turned toward Michael McGuire, sitting on a rise overlooking the field, and gave him a thumbs-up and a big smile.

That night he was led by lantern to a guest cottage about three hundred yards from the main camp that nestled in a lakeside pine grove. He poured himself a brandy from the flask he had brought with him and sat in the screened porch as a brilliant three-quarter moon shone on the water. A vast silence surrounded him. The pine scent was overpowering. He shivered slightly in the cool air, so crisp that you felt it could suddenly shatter, like glass. Every breath a guinea in the bank of health, he thought. Where had he heard that? Some movie, he remembered, but he couldn't recall which one. He had another brandy, and another.

Almost against his will, he thought about Mary Alice. How proud she would have been of Jamie, how if she were only here she would have made such a joy out of this trip, how they would now be talking animatedly about Jamie while they snuggled under the quilt he had seen on the bed. He poured himself a brandy, emptying the flask, and, slumped in a chair, he held up his glass and called out, "Here's to one of the luckiest guys in the world," which he had formerly believed himself to be, and then muttered, "Jesus, McGuire, how maudlin can you get?"

He tried to be at Jamie's school swimming meets and attended auditorium recitals of a soft rock group that had Jamie as the lead singer. Once, Jamie performed solo, in which he sang a number of popular Irish folk songs, but then he ended with a haunting nineteenth-century ballad that was obviously unfamiliar to his audience. It was called "Skibbereen," and Michael McGuire vaguely remembered it from his childhood. It was about how absentee English landlords drove poor tenant farmers off the land so they could replace them with more profitable flocks of sheep. It began with a boy asking his father why he had abandoned "Erin's Isle" despite "her lofty scene and valleys green, her mountains rude and wild." Somehow Jamie's young voice conveyed all the melancholy and sinister overtones of that time, and the other students remained hushed for a moment after he had finished before they broke out in applause and cheers.

Jamie's grades were uneven. He excelled at calculus and computer programming, which was a good thing, since Michael McGuire was helpless in those areas. He did rather well in English, was abysmal in Latin, and very rocky in history, especially European history during his senior year.

"Dad, it's so boring," Jamie said. "All Mr. Pitts wants are facts, names, dates, places. We never get into anything. There never are any discussions."

"Well, kid, it's his course and you're stuck with it if you want to get into a decent college." So before every quiz or test, Michael McGuire would drill Jamie by rote on the subjects to be covered and they'd inevitably wind up yelling at one another.

"When was the Treaty of Olmütz?"

"Eighteen forty-eight."

"No, goddammit, it was eighteen *fifty*. How many times are you going to get it wrong?"

One evening Jamie said, "Dad, do you know who Wolfe Tone was?"

Michael McGuire tried to think. "Yes, no, okay, I give up."

"He was like the George Washington of Ireland. He even came to America and was befriended by Tom Paine."

"Is he part of the course?"

"No, that's the point. He isn't even mentioned."

"So what happened to him?"

"In seventeen ninety-eight he was captured by the British. He was tried for treason and condemned to death by hanging."

"All of a sudden you're very sharp on dates. He doesn't sound much like George Washington to me."

"He was, in spirit anyway. He was very influenced by the Revolutionary War."

"How come you're such a big expert on him all of a sudden?"

"I found this book at Grandpa's."

"I thought so. You ever think he's not in your course because he isn't important?"

"But there's practically nothing in it about how England conquered Ireland. Just a couple of paragraphs that they did."

"Come on, Jamie, it's all over and done with. What happened, happened. What's going on there now is a bunch of retarded religious nuts, Protestant and Catholic, right out of the Middle Ages, killing each other like crazy Arabs."

"But, Dad, Wolfe Tone was a Protestant, and mostly with other Protestants he founded the United Irishmen, which was what the Irish Republican Army is today."

"Oh, boy, the IRA. Now we're for terrorists."

"Dad, were the soldiers at Valley Forge terrorists?"

"Jamie, you and I both know that isn't the same. I really don't want to waste any more time on this."

Michael McGuire thought that was the end of it until Jamie received a failing grade on a major paper in an ethics and morality class that the school required for graduation.

"What's this all about?"

"Well, I wrote about the ethics of a supposedly democratic country holding part of another country in thrall."

"In thrall?"

"Yes."

"You sure have a knack for asking for it. Who's the teacher?"

"He's English, so what do you expect? He's the school chaplain. They exchanged chaplains for a year. Reverend Crow went over there, and this guy, Reverend Billingsgate, came over here."

The school was affiliated with the Episcopal church. Michael McGuire felt a flicker of dormant Catholicism, and this time he went to bat for Jamie.

"My course involves personal morality," the Reverend Billingsgate told him in clipped tones. "Your son strayed quite far afield, I'm afraid."

"It is ethical behavior you're teaching, isn't it?"

"Thank you for your interest, Mr. McGuire."

He took it up to the headmaster, although he kept this from Jamie, and the upshot finally was an unsaid accommodation. Jamie still was failed on his paper, but got a minimal passing grade on the course, which lowered his overall average to a level where Michael McGuire despaired of acceptance by the kind of college he had hoped for.

As it turned out, he didn't have to worry.

"I can get into Harvard," Jamie said.

"Harvard? How?"

"Swimming. Coach says they really need swimmers. Yale's been killing them. Coach says Harvard has special categories for quote a well-rounded student body unquote, like if you're black and play the flute and from Idaho, you're in. *If* you're not a retard."

Michael McGuire ignored the gibe. "Harvard," he said. "Jamie, that's terrific."

He could barely contain his excitement when Jamie was assigned to Weld Hall, the residence that John F. Kennedy had lived in during his freshman year.

"What's the big deal?" Jamie asked, and Michael McGuire said, "It's hard to explain. I remember staying up all night to see if he won. I don't know, it's just very special to me that you're going to be where he was. I guess I'm showing my age, or something."

At Thanksgiving, he was dismayed that Jamie wasn't all that enamored with Harvard. "It's okay, Dad," Jamie said, "but there are a lot of rich kids sitting around talking about money. It's not that they're not smart. It's just that they can't wait to be lawyers or on Wall Street, like that's all there is."

"Hey, Jamie, give it a chance. I can't believe everybody up there is that way."

By the Christmas break, Jamie's attitude had improved discernibly. He had fallen in with some other students and joined them in a musical group that played for functions both on and off campus. "It's pretty good, Dad," Jamie said. "Fifty bucks each." His wish list of presents included a new guitar and also ski equipment. He was going to Vermont with friends for the last half of his vacation. Michael McGuire got him everything he asked for. The call came the day he was to return to Harvard. He'd torn up his knee.

"I'll come up," Michael McGuire said.

"No, Dad, it's all right. I'm being taken care of. I'll just be in a cast for a while."

During the winter, whenever Michael McGuire would phone him in his room, Jamie was always out, although he would dutifully return the call in a day or so and would report his knee was coming along fine.

Then, later on, there was the call from a fellow at another agency, who said, "I was up in Cambridge last week and caught your son singing at that pub. He's really great."

Michael McGuire was too embarrassed to do more than mumble his thanks. When he finally got through to him, Jamie said, "Oh, yeah, right."

"How come I'm the last on my block to know?"

"I was going to tell you. I wanted to make sure it worked out first."

"Where's all this taking place?"

"It's called The Crooked Plough."

"Ah, yes. Yeats on the heavenly constellations. 'The Pilot Star and the Crooked Plough,' often called the Starry Plough, what the Irish call the Big Dipper."

Michael McGuire picked up the surprise in Jamie's voice. "I didn't know you knew that."

"Give me a break."

Jamie laughed and said, "Well, then, when are you coming up to hear me?" and Michael McGuire thought how eerie it was, how there would be this wall of tension between them, and it would suddenly dissolve and there'd be an easy camaraderie, like that day he had first taken Jamie fishing.

Then the wall was back up. "Listen, how come you're never there when I call?"

"I've kind of moved in with someone. Uh, you'll like her a lot."

"Her? Who is her?"

"You'll meet her when you're here."

Michael McGuire was so astounded that he decided not to push it over the telephone. He'd never discussed girls with Jamie, mostly because he never knew quite how to broach the subject. He had listened to other parents complaining about how their offspring spent hours on the phone with the opposite sex, but not Jamie. He'd even imagined a scene with Jamie in which Jamie said that he was gay and he had to be sophisticated and understanding enough to accept it. But three-quarters of the way through his senior year, around the time of the ethics and morality crisis, Jamie had shown up with a cute brunette who attended a fashionable New York school for girls. One morning Michael McGuire arose early for a glass of juice and saw a pair of satin high-heeled party pumps neatly parked by the front door. His only reaction, he remembered, was relief, and soon after that the calls came in constantly and he found himself pining for the days when there were no calls.

The next Friday evening they had dinner at the Ritz-Carlton in Boston, where Michael McGuire was staying. He ordered a martini and a Coke, and Jamie said, "Dad, if you don't mind, I'll have a beer."

"Of course, sorry about that." How dumb he was, he thought. He studied Jamie again. He was a big strong kid, grown up almost. It was that choirboy face, Mary Alice's face, that fooled you.

They were nearly through eating when Michael McGuire said, "So tell me about her."

Her name was Ingrid Gerhard, Jamie said. She was born in Germany and came to the States when she was seventeen. She was a nurse at Massachusetts General. She was a terrific skier, and he had met her at the lodge near Stowe when he hurt his knee. She had gotten him right in to the best orthopedist at the hospital, a guy you usually had to wait weeks to see, and she'd taken care of him while he was recovering, made sure he did all his rehabilitation exercises. And she had made him study like hell, which was why his grades were so good. She was on duty now, but she'd be at The Crooked Plough later.

"The college doesn't care that you're not living at Weld Hall?"

"No, why should it?"

"I keep forgetting. The times, they have really changed."

"Well, I've got a couple things I have to do. See you. I go on about eleven." As he got up, Jamie grinned and pointed at his knee. "Look, Dad, no limp."

The name of the courier out of Belfast was Sean Walsh, although this, of course, was not mentioned. As usual, the call on the overseas line had been made to the banker, Jake Mooney.

"My sister's payin' a visit," the caller said, and gave the Aer Lingus flight number. "Arrives this Friday. You can't miss her. She'll have a white rose pinned to her coat. Ah, she loves those roses." Mooney passed the information to Daniel P. Daugherty at the U.S. Customs regional office in Boston.

There would be no record of Walsh ever having left Ireland or entering the United States. He first traveled to Dublin by car. He was dropped off at Dublin airport, where he went to a particular ticket agent on duty and paid in cash for passage to Shannon. The ticket agent gave him his Shannon boarding pass and also punched out a second boarding pass reserving the same space for New York via Shannon. Since Shannon was a domestic flight, Walsh did not need a passport. When the plane safely landed in New York, the computer passenger list was automatically wiped clean.

At Shannon, Walsh spent the hour-and-a-half layover in the international lounge area, again bypassing customs and passport control. Then he reboarded, this time using his pass for New York. At Kennedy airport, he made sure that he was the last passenger off the plane. On his lapel jacket he had the white rose he'd been carrying in his travel bag. As he stepped onto the air bridge, the enclosed movable ramp that extended from the terminal gate, a customs agent, dispatched by Daniel P. Daugherty, was waiting. "You Mr. Mooney's friend?" the agent said; and when Walsh nodded, the agent unlocked a door directly behind him on the ramp and led Walsh down the stairs to a customs car parked on the tarmac.

"Trip okay?" the agent said, waving at a security guard manning a gate reserved for government vehicles.

"Yes, thank you."

"This is for you," the agent said, and handed Walsh an envelope. Inside were ten ten-dollar bills. He dropped off Walsh at LaGuardia for the shuttle flight to Logan airport in Boston. "Well, good luck and have a nice stay."

Walsh had brought the final requisition list of

weapons and explosives, and Dowd was now going to have to relay through him the arrangements he'd made with Tommy Ahearn of the Somerville mob for a boat to transport them. Ahearn, of course, had been delighted with the idea of being able to land two protected loads of marijuana in return for one-time use of the boat for the hallowed cause. "Do they give you a medal or somethin'?" Ahearn asked, and Dowd assured him that he'd be long remembered.

Dowd met the plane and took Walsh to his apartment in South Boston. "What's your pleasure, me boy?" he asked.

"I'll have a wash-up and then I wouldn't say no to a pint."

"I know just the place," Dowd said.

The Crooked Plough was six blocks down from Harvard Square on a corner. When you entered, there was a long bar on one side and a line of small tables on the other. Beyond the bar it opened up into a larger room with more tables, and in the rear there was a small bandstand with a microphone. By the time Michael McGuire arrived, it was already jammed with students and young professionals. He squeezed in at the end of the bar near the back room. The noise was deafening and he wondered how anyone would be able to hear Jamie in this din. But when Jamie was introduced, it grew abruptly quiet.

He softly said, "Hello," and began singing songs of the Irish struggle, and then he said, "I'd like to sing a new song for you. It's called 'Back Home in Derry' and it was written by Bobby Sands, the poet and patriot who, as you know, was the first of the ten hunger strikers to die in the Long Kesh H-Blocks, not for better food or better conditions, but to preserve their status as political prisoners. He wrote this song to commemorate Irish freedom fighters of long ago who were sent to the penal colonies of Australia. He sang it to his comrades in the dead of night through the keyhole of his cell door until he was too weak and drained to do it anymore."

> *In 1803 we sailed out to sea*
> *Out from the sweet town of Derry*
> *For Australia bound if we didn't all drown*
> *And the marks of our fetters we carried....*

In the silence that followed after he had completed all the stanzas, someone yelled, "Give us Kevin Barry," and someone else clapped and shouted, "Yes, Kevin Barry," and then Jamie sang that.

There was a man standing next to Michael Mc-Guire drinking a glass of Guinness. Michael McGuire noticed that he had tears in his eyes. He was with a younger fellow, about Jamie's age, Michael McGuire thought, who was quietly mouthing the lyrics.

"Ah, that lad," said Kevin Dowd, "like a nightingale he is," and Michael McGuire wanted to say, He's my son, you know, but he did not.

He watched Jamie go to a table where a girl was sitting. As he approached, he saw her slip an arm protectively through Jamie's. For Jamie or for herself? he wondered.

"Dad, this is Ingrid," and she shook his hand and

gravely said, "I am very happy to meet you, Mr. McGuire."

She had a pretty, roundish face with flaxen hair cut short, not beautiful but somebody who'd catch your eye, and a full, healthy body. You sensed from her erect posture that she was in great shape. He could see that she was older than Jamie. She had a German accent, but not a harsh one. Echoes of his past came to him. Bavarian, he thought, and when he asked her, she said yes, she was from Munich originally.

When Jamie excused himself for a moment, he asked her how old she was, and as if daring him to make something of it, she said, "Twenty-eight," but all he said was, "Really? You don't look it."

Jamie was saying, "I was hoping Ingrid could spend some time at the beach after the term is over," and Michael McGuire, enveloped in sudden vertigo, managed to reply, "Uh, sure, that'd be nice, glad to have her."

He looked away, and almost in relief he saw the man who was Kevin Dowd staring intently at them. "Jamie, do you know who that guy at the bar is, the one in the dark green sweater?" and Jamie said, "I haven't a clue. I think I've seen him here once or twice before." Then Jamie smiled and said, "He's probably a fan."

8

On the Monday morning after the IRA execution of John Bingham, Brian Forbes was in his MI5 office in London leafing through the weekend security traffic out of Belfast.

Officially, MI5, the nerve center of British counterintelligence, did not exist. Officially, therefore, whatever it did never happened. In MI5, depending on the vagary of your private religious beliefs, either your First or Eleventh Commandment was "Thou shalt not get caught."

Its unmarked six-story headquarters, incongruously set in elegant Mayfair, occupied an entire block on the north side of Curzon Street just past the bend curving down from Berkeley Square, not much more than a stone's throw from the private night spot Annabel's and the gambling clubs like the Clermont, where the British upper crust, either monied or aristocratic, or both, carelessly drank, dined, danced and gamed away the evenings.

The ground floor, housing computer banks, was fronted in solid concrete, windows blocked over, the rest of the facade faded red brick, the upper windows cloaked in drawn heavy lace white curtains.

A cobblestone alley on the west side led around to a courtyard barrier and a secured basement garage. A narrow steel canopy hung over the unmarked main entrance on Curzon Street. Inside a glass booth in the modest lobby, a uniformed bobby checked off names on a registry before issuing passes to rare visitors, who then waited in a small room for their escorts to appear. Facing elevators, once manually operated, now automated in a bow to modern times, rose slowly to landings with vaulted ceilings and teak-inlaid walls of another era. Wide hallways at each end of the landings ran parallel through the building. The color scheme in the offices off these corridors was monochromatic—beige walls, beige filing cabinets, beige desks. The only personal touches in sight were an occasional photograph framed in leather or silver of a wife, children, a favored hunting dog.

For a brief period, until he had to ask her to desist, a single rose decorated the desk of Brian Forbes every morning, placed there by his adoring secretary, with whom he was now having an affair. Affairs, though, whether heterosexual or homosexual, while frowned upon, were tolerated, given the fallibility of human nature, so long as they were known by "B" branch, the personnel directorate, and preferably confined to "the office," as MI5 was called within its ranks. MI5's sister operation, MI6, the Secret Intelligence Service, which conducted espionage overseas, was referred to as "the friends," a characterization that did little to reflect the rivalry and suspicion between them. Forbes alway found it ironic that the Americans were called "the cousins," so infinitely more familial.

From his office window, parting the curtains, Forbes could look down across the way at a fashionable French restaurant frequented by celebrities. The restaurant had been a godsend. Forbes, obedient to his oath of secrecy, did not discuss security matters with his wife, Priscilla, and that left little else for them to talk about. The tension between them was increasingly palpable. He began finding empty gin bottles in the clothes hamper and behind a shelf of books.

So he'd say, "I saw Elizabeth Taylor."

And Priscilla would seize upon this intelligence as if it were the Soviet order of battle for World War III. "Really? Was she fat?"

"Rather chubby, I'd say."

"*Really*? What was she wearing?"

Or, "You'll never guess who I spied today."

"Oh, who?"

"Robert Redford. At least I think it was Robert Redford."

"What was he like?"

"A bit on the short side. Surprisingly so, as a matter of fact."

"Yes," Priscilla would reply solemnly. "I've read that somewhere."

It had not been that way when Forbes had been posted as MI5 liaison in Washington. They'd leased a garden apartment across the Potomac in the old part of Alexandria, Virginia, where so many U.S. government workers lived. Priscilla was immediately invited to join the local garden club. When someone asked her what Forbes did, she'd simply say he was a commercial attaché at the embassy, and that would be the end of it. But here, back in London, it was more difficult. If inquiries were made about her husband, he worked for the Ministry of Defense. If pressed further, the work was secret. "You know how they feel," she was to explain. "Russians under every bed, that sort of thing. Silly, isn't it?"

"At a party, when we go to one, I can't even ask someone else what he does," Priscilla complained, "for fear he'll ask me about you." The upshot was that they hardly ever ventured forth socially. "B" branch had a staff of counselors and pyschologists to deal with stress situations; and when Forbes had discovered his wife's excessive drinking, he briefly considered and discarded the idea of seeking help, since this same branch also played a decisive role in career advancement. It was perhaps, he thought, pure paranoia, but wasn't paranoia the whole reason for MI5's existence—paranoia at what enemies of the state were doing, planning to do, capable of doing? Perhaps he should have married within the office. He thought that having a child might make a difference, but Priscilla proved barren, which only triggered more tension, and subsequently the affair with his rose-bearing secretary.

And there was a more cogent paranoia. Forbes had graduated from Bristol University, academically one of the most esteemed of the so-called redbrick and plate-glass universities. Still, even though MI5 and to some extent MI6 had stepped up recruiting in these institutions, the upper echelon continued to be ruled by Oxford and, especially in MI5, Cambridge elitism. All you had to do was muse on Sir Anthony Blunt, Cambridge, MI5 officer, arrogant surveyor of the queen's art collection, for decades a KGB mole reporting to his Moscow masters, unrepentant to the end, protected to the end by the Cambridge crowd.

Supposedly this was no longer true. Forbes wondered. He had risen rapidly in MI5. Still, he did not lunch at the right clubs, like White's or Athenaeum, settling instead for a bite at an MI5 haunt around the corner, the Pig and Eye. He wondered if his background presented an insurmountable obstacle to his ambition. He had an athlete's build, like a light heavyweight, and wore dark gray and blue suits with discreet chalk lines, although they were off the rack from Marks and Spencer, the department store, not bespoke on Savile Row. He wondered about his nose, somewhat flattened from youthful amateur boxing.

His school marks had earned him a grant to attend Bristol. He had thought to enter the business world, climb the corporate ladder. A member of the career advisory board at the university, on retainer by MI5, had steered him toward the service. There was an aura of glamour to it, the thrill of being on the inside and the sense of superiority engendered by serving one's country in such a special way. His security check, "vetting," it was called, was "most positive," showing him to be the son of a career warrant officer in the Royal Fusiliers, his politics comfortably Tory.

The glamour aspect, of course, turned out to be an illusion with the possible exception of "K" branch, which played cat and mouse with the Soviets and had been made so famous in the fiction of John le Carré. Forbes always thought that if he'd been running KGB operations in the United Kingdom, the time to strike would have been when the BBC serialized "Smiley's People." There wasn't a member of MI5, Forbes included, who had not been tied to his television set. "B" branch's recruitment section reported an immediate upsurge in applications and recommended more such programs, all the better to skim off "the cream of the crop."

After training, he was detailed to "F" branch, which was charged with ferreting out domestic "subversion," and assigned to a section that dealt specifically with Provisional IRA activity on the home front.

A year later he was transferred to Northern Ireland, where he began to learn of the bitter competition between Her Majesty's intelligence and security services. MI5's original charter had covered the British Empire, but there wasn't much empire left. It had been reduced to a scattering of liaison officers in Australia, Hong Kong, the British army headquarters in West Germany, the Bahamas, Canada and, of course, Washington. So besides the British mainland, Northern Ireland was about all the action that was left. But MI6 claimed that, since the bulk of IRA support came from the Republic of Ireland, it should be in command.

The infighting had gotten so vicious that a Belfast-based intelligence coordinator for Northern Ireland was appointed to oversee the activities of both secret services, as well as the undercover killer teams of the Special Air Service and the Special Branch of the

Royal Ulster Constabulary, the main components arrayed against the IRA. The new man, however, was Sir Maurice Oldfield, an owlish bespectacled retired former MI6 chief. MI5 immediately saw this as an unacceptably slick maneuver by the hated "friends" to exercise control. For years, MI5 had known Oldfield was a closet homosexual, but had stayed quiet about it because of the embarrassment of Anthony Blunt. Once Blunt's past became public, though, all wraps were off.

It was Oldfield's habit in the late afternoon two or three times a week to visit a pub in a village by an inlet off the Irish Sea. Leaving his driver outside, he would sit at a table by himself steadily drinking. He was beyond caring. He had just received a diagnosis that indicated stomach cancer. MI5 operatives planted an angelic young man at the pub. After their third encounter, the young man rose to go to the lavatory. Oldfield followed. Photographs were taken. There were leaks from unattributed sources to the press.

Oldfield confessed to sexual transgressions dating back to his school days. "I've been very silly," he was said to have said. Mrs. Thatcher, the prime minister, accepted his resignation. It was only after his death from cancer that the details of his disgrace finally surfaced. The coordinator's post remained in force, but from then on it was run by MI5. "A" branch technicians even installed a system in the Irish Republic to intercept all microwave phone calls coming in and out of Dublin and dared anyone to complain.

Forbes was assigned to the main army headquarters in Lisburn, just south of Belfast, where the bulk

of the MI5 contingent, some sixty of them, were stationed, roughly divided between analysts and handlers. Forbes was a handler, running informers
against the Provos. It was exciting, dangerous work
that often brought him into the street, and he loved
it. He had an instinctive knack of knowing when to
cajole, threaten or comfort a "grass," slang for an
informer. Although everyone used it, the word was
an English import, from a Cockney song that had a
line in it about "whispering grass."

He built by far the best network MI5 had, and his
tour was extended from the normal eighteen months
to three years. At first, for Forbes, it had been an
abstract game of wits, and then it got very personal.

One night he received a frantic call from an informant named Tony Dolan. "They're on to me, the
bastards, I think," Dolan had said.

"Come in, come in," Forbes told him.

"I can't, you see. There's the wife and kids. I've
packed them off to her family's place near Cooks-
town in Tyrone. I must join them. The wife, you
know, she don't know."

"Where are you?"

"In a public phone. I'm going home, get my things,
let things blow over."

"I'll be there straightaway."

Dolan lived in a housing estate in Andersontown
in West Belfast. When Forbes arrived, Dolan was
throwing clothes in a satchel. Not ten minutes later
there was serious thumping at the front door.

"Jesus, Mary and Joseph, they find you, it's the end
of us both. Get in there," he said, pointing to a large
armoire.

Crouched inside the blackness of the armoire,
Forbes felt the sweat running down him. He drew his
pistol. From the voices, it sounded like three, maybe
four men. There was a slight scuffle and he heard
Dolan say, "Oh, no!"

There was a strange whirring sound. Then muffled cries from Dolan. Should he burst out of the
armoire, Forbes thought, try to take them by surprise? Forbes would always wonder. Was it simply
that the odds against him were too great? Or was it
that he was simply afraid? He would never know. He
would simply have to live with it, always.

Suddenly he heard the front door slam. There was
silence, except for a dreadful moaning. Forbes
waited another minute and then came out of the armoire, holding his revolver in front of him. The
room was empty, save for Dolan. He was on the floor,
on his belly, his hands tied behind his back, a rag
stuffed in his mouth. His face was turned sideways,
toward Forbes. Tears were running down his cheeks.
His trousers were rolled up. Blood was trickling from
holes behind each knee. Usually for kneecapping, the
Provos used guns. Perhaps they'd been worried about
the noise. This time they'd used an electric drill.

Forbes unbound Dolan's wrists. He took the balled-
up rag out of his mouth. Dolan did not move. "Help
me," he whispered.

Forbes hesitated for a moment. Were they still out
there? That was when the shame truly came. Dolan
had not given him away. There would have been no
kneecapping for him. Instead, it would have been a
bullet in the head. "Hang on," he told Dolan.

He edged out the back door, vaulted a fence and

ran to his car parked a hundred yards away on a main thoroughfare, Glen Road. He used his radio and waited until the ambulance from the Royal Victoria Hospital raced past him.

He spoke to a doctor at the hospital about Dolan's chances of recovery. The doctor looked at him as if he had just been asked if the sun would rise in the morning. "Well, I'd say his running days were over," the doctor said.

Two days later, Forbes bypassed the chain of command and went directly to Stormont Castle, to the office of MI5's chief in Northern Ireland, Roger Gravesend, whose official title was director and coordinator of intelligence. The castle, replete with battlements and turrets, in a grove of trees on the side of a hill dominating East Belfast, was where the real power lay, where London ruled by fiat.

He had only met Gravesend once before, when he first arrived in Belfast. Forbes had instinctively liked him. Like Forbes, he was from a redbrick university, Manchester. Forbes remembered him as an energetic no-nonsense man in his early fifties, without airs, who chain-smoked American Marlboro cigarettes. "Welcome to the mess," Gravesend had said.

On the crest of the hill, above the castle, was Northern Ireland's House of Parliament, twin Union Jacks flying. It was a great wedding cake edifice, like something Mussolini might have commissioned. How ludicrously out of proportion for a province about the size of his native Yorkshire, Forbes thought as he drove up the mile-long gated drive that led to it, an empty statement of past glory. It was in fact now almost literally empty, the Ulster parliament having been dissolved as a result of the new round of troubles that began in 1969.

No, Forbes told the receptionist and then a senior staff member, he did not have an appointment. It was a private, urgent matter. He would wait all day, all week, all month, if necessary.

After three hours, he was ushered into Gravesend, who clearly was not in an amiable mood. "Ah, yes, Forbes," he said. "This had better be quite captivating."

"Yes, sir. I realize that, sir. Sir, you've heard about Dolan, Anthony Dolan?"

"I have. Unfortunate. One of those things. You're not here because of that?"

"I am, sir. We have to do something for him."

"Why? He's been blown, obviously. He's of no further use."

"Not to us, but he is to the Provos. Hobbling along the Falls Road, crippled for life, a sad walking example, if you'll pardon the expression, of what happens to anyone who cooperates with us. I have a dozen other Dolans on the line. What do you think they'll think?"

Gravesend lit another Marlboro, drawing hard on it. "What do you have in mind?"

"I'd like to get him out of sight, out of Belfast. Spread the word that British medical science has made him almost as good as new. I'd like to have him sending back letters and cards, postmarked through London, saying that he's never been happier."

"And where is this utopia we'll be dispatching him to?"

"I'd suggest New Zealand, sir. He was originally a

country man. He spoke to me of his love of salmon fishing. I understand the salmon fishing is quite good in New Zealand."

Gravesend tugged at his chin. "Yes," he said at last. "You're right, of course. Consider it done."

"Sir."

"Really, Forbes, what is it now?"

"I've had this thought. My people have pinpointed some IRA dumps. Rather than seizing them, it occurred to me that we might replace a number of their detonators with defective ones, so that when they arm a device, it'll blow up in their faces. They'll believe it's their fault, for a while at least."

Gravesend looked at Forbes as if he were seeing him for the first time. "Rather nasty, that," he said.

"Yes, sir."

"Draw up a memo for me. Mark it for my eyes only. And Forbes," he went on.

"Sir?"

"Try not to be so melodramatic in the future."

After Forbes had left, Gravesend jotted some notes for inclusion in Brian Forbes's personnel file. They said, "Resourceful, inventive, dedicated. Without scruples."

When Forbes was next posted to Washington, D.C., as an MI5 liaison officer in the embassy, it was in large measure a continuation of his tour in Northern Ireland. At first, IRA arms purchases generally had been made in Europe. But the Provos discovered that their suppliers, mostly German and Belgian, with no ideological feel for the cause, often tipped off these shipments in order to be allowed to engage in bigger, more lucrative operations elsewhere. So more and more they became dependent on dedicated sources in America.

Overall, though, Forbes was amazed at how adept the British Information Service, the foreign office's media arm, had been in making terrorism in Northern Ireland exclusively synonymous with the IRA, equating it with such universally detested terrorist groups as Direct Action in France, Italy's Red Brigades and West Germany's Red Army Faction—and as far as murderous unionist paramilitary operations were concerned, presenting the picture of a stalwart British Tommy, gun naturally in hand, keeping a bunch of mad Irish religious zealots from slaughtering one another. A prominent American columnist, with impeccable liberal credentials, actually wrote that Northern Ireland's sole salvation lay in a British policy of "enlightened colonialism."

The Provos, of course, had contributed mightily to this by an early strategy of bombings that caused a great number of innocent civilian casualties. They had tried to rectify matters by phoning in warnings to British security headquarters, but these warnings had been purposely ignored to stir up public outrage. And there was always the Paddy factor—the bomb aimed at troops or the police that went off prematurely.

Not even the leak of a comprehensive secret intelligence analysis of the Provisional IRA, signed by the commanding general of British forces in Northern Ireland, J. M. Glover, seemed to make any difference. It concluded that the Provos were "committed to the traditional aim of Irish nationalism, that is the removal of the British presence from Ireland" and that evidence concerning the IRA rank and file "does not support the view that they are merely mindless hooligans drawn from the unemployed and unemployable."

Still, the harangues right out of the Reformation by the Reverend Ian Paisley weren't helping. The pope was "the anti-Christ" he thundered from the pulpit. "Victory for our enemies would put us under the jackboot of priestly tyranny. To submit to Dublin and Rome would be worse than death!" Forbes always had a laugh over that one. If a third of the Provos ever made it to Sunday Mass, it would stand as a bloody miracle, he thought, but this sort of stuff did not sit too well with the conservative Catholic community in America.

On a more immediate level, Forbes began monitoring sympathy for the republican cause among U.S. law enforcement agencies that were layered with personnel of Irish extraction. The Bureau of Alcohol, Tobacco and Firearms did a workmanlike job tracing guns upon London's request, but hardly ever initiated investigations. While the counterterrorist units of the FBI appeared first rate and the agency as a whole was highly disciplined, Forbes reported increasing pockets of anti-British sentiment. Indeed, the head of the New York unit, who was especially energetic on the IRA, had been transferred, although Forbes was told that it was because of a fuck-up on an investigation having nothing to do with Ireland. The real hot spots were police departments along the East Coast and the U.S. Customs Service.

Pipers in the Emerald Society band of the New York Police Department had even gone to the Irish Republic and marched in County Donegal in memory of the dead H-Block hunger strikers.

Worst of all, though, was the customs service. The last straw was the trial of a group of IRA sympathizers in New York charged with conspiring to ship weapons to the Provos. The case appeared airtight until a customs agent, subpoenaed by the defense, testified that the arms dealer used to entrap the alleged conspirators had been previously involved in some CIA operations in Latin America.

Forbes immediately contacted an FBI counterterrorist supervisor. "How did they get on to that?" he asked.

"One of Danny's Boys," the supervisor said.

"So it's Daugherty again?"

"Yeah. Daniel P. himself."

"What will happen now?"

"You can wave goodbye to this one, is what. The defense'll claim they thought it was all authorized by the CIA. The CIA screws up so much, juries believe anything. Listen, Brian, you lucked out with me. I don't make laws. I just try and enforce them, even the ones I don't like. But you got to understand, a lot of people, especially concerning Ireland, don't go along with that."

This was too much to swallow. Forbes personally lodged a bitter complaint to the head of the customs service, who seemed genuinely concerned, but then, in the furor that followed, all behind the scenes, Forbes was suddenly withdrawn from Washington.

• • • •

During Forbes's American tour, the security coordinator for Northern Ireland, Roger Gravesend, had become MI5's deputy director general, and in London when Forbes reported to him for a debriefing, Gravesend said, "You've been returned to us, you know, gratis Congressman Cornelius Gallagher—of Brooklyn, I believe. How does a single congressman manage to exert such extraordinary influence?"

"Well, sir, it's rather unknown, even in the States, but the fact is that while any proper congressional committee can *authorize* expenditures, for, ah, for example, the customs service, if Gallagher's committee, the Appropriations Committee, doesn't allocate the funds, it's quite meaningless."

"How quaint," Gravesend said. "In any event, you correctly did what you had to do. Time for you to move on. Time to let the cousins know we mean business. We have some due bills for allowing our airfields to be used for those bombing runs on Libya, and I can assure you the prime minister is most determined to collect on the Irish issue. By the way, you didn't bring any Marlboros back with you, did you?"

"Yes, sir. I did take the liberty."

Shortly thereafter, Forbes was made Gravesend's special assistant for Northern Ireland.

The job was newly created, another jerrybuilt attempt to get a handle on what had become a bureaucratic nightmare that defied MI5's otherwise tidy organizational charts of branches and sections.

It annoyed Forbes that he wasn't a branch director. But as Gravesend said, the whole thing had gotten

too bloody unwieldy, a group of fiefdoms implacable
in their determination not to give up an inch of territorial imperative. There was, just to begin with, at
the center of the storm, the security coordinator's
office in Belfast. But its effectiveness essentially
stopped at the border of the Irish Republic, where it
still had to contend with MI6 as well as the Special
Branch of the Irish *Gardai*. In theory, the *Gardai* and
British intelligence were supposed to work hand in
glove, but collegiality wasn't advanced one whit after
the discovery that MI5 had subverted a key file clerk
to keep it abreast of what was going on at *Garda* headquarters inside Dublin Castle.

Forbes did not delude himself that he could truly
resolve anything. More than a century ago, there had
been a horrendous string of bombings and political
assassinations by what was then called the "Irish Republican Brotherhood." Afterward, Sir William Harcourt, the home secretary at the time, a cabinet post
to which MI5's director general still reported, had
warned, "This is not a temporary emergency requir-
ing momentary remedy. Fenianism is a permanent
conspiracy against English rule which will last far beyond the term of my life and must be met by a permanent organization to detect and control it."

Harcourt had written these words in 1883, and he
was long gone. It was insane, Forbes thought, that
the will of Great Britain could be thwarted by a bunch
of dumb Paddys less than an hour's flight from where
he was sitting, but there it was, with no end in sight.
Over lunch at the Pig and Eye, a research type in "S"
branch had remarked that in fact the Irish struggle

for independence, dating back to the twelfth century, was now the longest one in history currently active.

Who was the previous record holder? he inquired, and was told, "The Vietnamese, against the Chinese, the Japanese, the French and the Americans. Fourteen hundred years." Forbes didn't know whether it was true or not. He did not want to think about it.

For Brian Forbes, the ideal scenario was for Gravesend to rise to the director generalship and for him, in turn, to be given the elite "K" branch, where there was a mutual adversarial respect between MI5 and the KGB, true gamesmanship in the main arena. In the meantime, to help make this happen, he would do his best to keep the lid on Northern Ireland, keep all the intelligence channels open, the data flowing, make sure Belfast got what it needed. Control was the operative word. It hadn't escaped Forbes that old Sir William Harcourt in 1883 did not hint at the possibility of victory over Irish nationalism, only control.

And that delicate control was in jeopardy.

On Monday morning in his office after sorting through the Belfast weekend traffic, Forbes could not have cared less about the demise of John Bingham. Bingham had been a bloody nuisance. Indeed, more than once he had toyed with the idea of having an undercover squad from the Special Air Service dispatch Bingham. Whatever acclaim the Provos would get among local Catholics was far outweighed by the damage Bingham's murderous spree could cause in world opinion, especially in America.

What did attract his attention, though, was an intelligence report that the IRA was planning a general army convention in the near future, within the month. Surveillance by MI5, the SAS and the RUC Special Branch was being stepped up on the known leadership. Undoubtedly it would be convened in the free state, and what a haul this could be! He'd notify Dublin at once.

But on Tuesday all of Forbes's good humor vanished. A confirmed report came in that the convention, in fact, had been held the previous Friday. And *that* wasn't amusing. The Provos must have planted the first rumor to throw them all off. They must be enjoying a jolly laugh. He wondered who the new boys were, and what they had in mind.

Pacing, Forbes stopped at the window and parted the curtain. Below, across the street, a chauffeured Bentley had stopped in front of the French restaurant. He watched as two men got out and then a woman. Very blond. Photographers appeared out of nowhere. The woman stopped and struck a pose for them. Forbes noticed how professionally she pivoted her right calf sideways, knee slightly bent, hand on hip. She was a famous film star, he knew. He tried to remember her name to get through another evening with his wife.

But he couldn't concentrate. How had the IRA pulled this off? Why hadn't he been forewarned? Why a convention now after all these years? What had happened to the informer network?

Forbes returned to his desk. He began to rethink the Bingham assassination. It had been extraordinarily daring, and so expertly planned. Darting right into the heart of rabidly loyalist territory controlled

by Ulster Volunteer Force gunmen, where even the
RUC was unwelcome. According to intelligence
charts, Terrance McBride was the Provo brigade
commander in Belfast. McBride had gone on the
chart when Forbes had been stationed there. Suddenly Forbes knew that McBride wasn't capable of
masterminding the Bingham affair. He'd been
around too long. Too old, too cautious. Happy to
settle for a sniper shot at a stray soldier, hope that a
planted bomb went off without a mishap. What was
going on?

Great unease seized Forbes. He couldn't explain it.
He just had this feeling that something was afoot that
could change the status quo, *control!*

It was the same kind of instinct he'd once had about
Billy Dugan, code name "Clara," who at first glance,
or even second or third, was the last person you'd
imagine would turn out to be what he was.

At long last, he decided, the time had come to ac-
tivate Clara. This meant that he would have to return
to Belfast, because Clara, of course, would talk only
to Forbes.

First thing, he would clear it with Gravesend. He
wondered if Gravesend, immersed in his exalted
new position, even remembered Clara. But Forbes
did. He remembered the exact words he had said to
Gravesend in Stormont Castle. "Why don't we do
what the Russians did to us? Why don't we insert a
mole and just let him be until we need him?"

Billy Dugan!

There hadn't been a need for him, and now there was.

Sitting behind his roseless beige desk, surrounded by beige filing cabinets, in his dark gray double-breasted suit from Marks and Spencer, Forbes instantly summoned forth the memory of his first sight of Dugan in the army holding center at the old Springfield Barracks off the Falls Road.

The dingy brick main building was for the police, its front door heavily sandbagged. To get in, you went through a gate to a side entrance by the parking area reserved for official vehicles. The holding center, separate from the main building, was in the rear, a big shed made of corrugated steel.

Late one evening, Forbes had gone there to meet with a couple of army intelligence chaps. He happened to glance through a one-way glass window just as Dugan was standing at the receiving desk holding a piece of slate with his name, the date and time chalked on it, getting his picture taken. It was obvious that this wasn't the first time for him. You could tell that by the way he automatically clutched the slate in the palms of his hands so he wouldn't leave any fingerprints, not that it mattered anymore. Technically, under the law, the army still couldn't take prints. But when the internment sweeps had begun in 1971, army intelligence, anxious to build up its files, had lifted the prints off these slates until the word got around. It was wonderful, Forbes thought, how in an environment where normal civil liberties were a joke such little legal niceties lingered on.

Dressed in jeans and a windbreaker, Dugan was a burly man with wiry red hair, but that wasn't what caught Forbes's attention. It was his eyes. Not defiant, not furtive, not even fearful. They were, well, blank, he thought. But with a special sort of deadness in them. On the other side of the one-way glass, Dugan was about twelve feet away. Forbes kept peering at his eyes. They were eyes that didn't care, he decided. About what, though? About himself? About where he was? About being arrested? Or, Forbes reflected, about something else. But *what*? Then Forbes thought, Could it be the movement itself, the cause, that he no longer cared about?

He'd read psychological evaluations of burnt-out cases, of people who weren't even aware of what had happened to them. One was a young MI5 officer who had been a handler—*yes!*—in Northern Ireland, who then had been transferred back to London, to "K" branch penetration of a Soviet network, and who had been turned by the Russians. It was established that neither greed nor ideology motivated him. "I just wanted to set things right," he said. The sentencing chief justice had denounced him as "puerile." You snapped under the stress, the case studies said, and became childlike, a blank slate for someone or something to fill in for you, so you could have some kind of meaning to your life again.

"I remember a friend of mine telling me he was going out to buy a pint of milk," the officer had said at one point, "and I followed him to see if he really was."

"And was he?"

"Yes."

"Why didn't you believe your friend?"

"I don't know. There are so many lies."

Behind the glass, Forbes had watched Dugan being led behind the cloth drape of one of the cubicles lining the end of the receiving area. He'd be there until he was taken to an interrogation room. The procedure had always remained the same. The army could keep a prisoner for four hours. Then he was either released or turned over to the Royal Ulster Constabulary for three days of questioning. An application could be made to the courts to keep him an additional four days before charges were formally lodged and he was arraigned. No one could ever remember an application being turned down.

Forbes spoke to the Royal Anglian lieutenant who headed the squad that had brought Dugan in. There'd been a tip, the lieutenant said, that an operation was being set up in a house in Ballymurphy. Four men in the house had been taken. Three handguns and two rifles had been found. In the dark a shot had been fired at one of the squaddies guarding the rear of the house. Just as they were closing in, a car was spotted approaching the house and then wheeling quickly away. Dugan and two other men had been apprehended in the car.

As soon as the receiving area was clear, Forbes walked over to Dugan's cubicle and parted the drape. Dugan was sitting on the rubber tile floor, knees drawn up, hunched against the far corner of the cubicle. When he looked up at Forbes, his eyes were still strangely lifeless. Close up, Forbes could see that his face was pitted with acne scars.

Forbes didn't smoke, but his informants were forever asking did he have a fag, and so he always made sure to have a couple of packs with him. He offered

Dugan a cigarette. Dugan just stared at him. "Come on now, it won't bite you," Forbes said.

Finally Dugan reached for it. Forbes lit the cigarette for him and left him two more along with matches. "Cheerio," he said. He thought he saw Dugan's hand trembling a little.

Curious, he had Dugan punched up on the computer. On the record, Dugan was a tough customer. He had been initially picked up in 1971 and sent to Long Kesh. He was then twenty, recently married and had listed his occupation as an apprentice carpenter. These internment roundups, which were conducted in wholesale lots without specific charges or trials, were designed to break the latest chapter in the troubles brought on by the civil rights marches. They had exactly the opposite effect, galvanizing support in nationalist enclaves throughout Northern Ireland, even among those hostile to the IRA or ambivalent about it.

And the Long Kesh cages—each a compound surrounded by barbed wire with three Nissen huts holding a hundred men that was run along prisoner-of-war lines—became a breeding ground for radicalization, for basic military indoctrination and training. Dugan was detained for a year, during which his first child, a boy, was born.

Four months later, according to his record, he was picked up again for possession of a handgun. He was interrogated for only three days, which indicated he was considered low level, not worth the bother. As an IRA volunteer, he refused to answer questions, citing the Geneva convention regarding the rights of military prisoners. His defense was that the alleged weapon he was carrying was just a starter's pistol for sporting events and that he'd had it in his belt as a show of force to maintain crowd control during the celebration of St. Patrick's Day. He was returned to Long Kesh for another fifteen months. During his incarceration, a second child, a daughter, was born. It was noted that while in the Kesh, Dugan was believed to have been selected for IRA officer training.

After his release, an informant reported that he was the quartermaster for B Company, Second Battalion, Belfast Brigade. Two attempts were made to pick him up for questioning. But he was on the run, no longer living at home. Then a random roadblock snared him in a car loaded with rifles and explosives. This time, Forbes saw, he was apparently given the full seven-day treatment at the main police interrogation center at Castlereagh in East Belfast. When he appeared for arraignment, he had a broken arm and three broken ribs. A police spokesman explained that he had been received at the center in that condition after having tried to escape the roadblock.

The days of internment without trial were over. Instead, there were the Diplock courts, invented by an English jurist, Lord William J. K. Diplock. They were not exactly out of the Magna Carta. A single judge presided over a trial. There was no jury. The burden of proof about whether a confession was "voluntary" or not rested with the defendant. In the absence of direct evidence, the testimony of a soldier or police officer would be considered sufficient. So, generally, would be the testimony of an informant. In accordance with IRA regulations at the time, Dugan refused to recognize the court. In any event, he had been caught red-handed, and in January 1976 he was sentenced to twelve years.

At that, Forbes thought, he was lucky. To replace the Long Kesh cages, construction of the Maze with its concrete H-Block configurations, based on a German design, was nearing completion. And beginning March 1, 1976, anyone convicted of using violence to achieve political ends would be denied prisoner-of-war status and be treated as a common criminal. Which meant, among other things, the wearing of prison uniforms. The symbolism was enormous, the ultimate step in criminalizing the Irish rebellion, and it first led to the blanket protest in which IRA inmates, some of them for as long as three years, remained in their cells huddled naked, unwashed and unshaven, in urine-soaked blankets, their shit smeared on the walls. When this failed, the hunger strike began, and it was only after Bobby Sands and nine other volunteers slowly died, one after another, that the uniform requirement was finally lifted.

The hunger strike, Forbes knew, was a watershed blunder for Britain. Community support for the IRA, which had been tailing off, dramatically revived. The Paddy factor, it seemed, worked both ways. Throughout all of this, simply because of the date of his conviction, Billy Dugan had remained in one of the old cages within the two-mile-long walls of the Maze. While conditions in the cages had grown increasingly unpleasant, they were nothing compared to the H-Blocks. If he didn't act up, a prisoner usually served two-thirds of his sentence, and Dugan was released after eight years.

Now he was headed back in—and this time to the H-Blocks.

Two days after he had first seen him, Brian Forbes went by the Castlereagh interrogation center. The routine beatings had been dropped after the European Commission on Human Rights declared Britain guilty of torture and inhumane and degrading treatment of Provo prisoners. They had been replaced by sensory deprivation techniques. A prisoner being interrogated was left under glaring lights in a small, totally white room, the walls perforated with hundreds of small holes, like pegboard. The heat was turned up. It was amazing, Forbes thought, how quickly the hallucinations and the disorientation came. They said that the holes as you stared at them grew large and then receded, wavered and danced every which way, until a man didn't know where he was. Almost as good as the old-fashioned methods. Better even. Left no visible marks.

A criminal investigation detective told Forbes that Dugan had been given the bag treatment as a lark. A prisoner was ordered to get up on his toes and bend forward against a wall, bracing himself with his fingertips. His body would begin to quiver. Then a cop behind him would cock a revolver and press the barrel under an ear. The cop would say he'd had enough. He would count to five and pull the trigger. At five, another cop would burst a paper bag filled with air. More often than not, the prisoner fainted, the first step in breaking him.

"What happened?"

"Just shuddered a bit. Didn't seem to care really.

He's been through it all. Waste of time speaking with him."

"I'd like a chat anyway." Forbes had to be careful. The IRA wasn't the only organization with informers, and he did not want to attract undue attention to Dugan. "London seems to think he may know something about a bombing in Manchester. I know it's no use, but it's not up to me."

When he saw him, Forbes noticed that Dugan had some difficulty getting the proffered cigarette into his mouth. "You're in a fine mess," he said.

Dugan didn't answer.

"Or perhaps life in the Maze, or at the very least twenty years of it, doesn't amount to a mess."

"What's that to mean?"

"A British soldier saw you taking off in that car."

"I was just drivin' up that way. You see all them soldier boys, what's to do?"

"A British soldier was also shot at. That's attempted murder."

"I know nothin' about that. I heard no shot."

"Oh, didn't they tell you? They have a grass, a supergrass you could say, who says that the shot came from the car you were in."

"That's not fookin' so."

"Who says you and your friends were going to the house to plan an operation, the ambush of a British patrol. I suppose that's not so either, eh, Billy?"

Dugan did not reply.

Ah, the truth, Forbes thought, that part stings a little, doesn't it?

"Of course, it's not for me to say," Forbes said. "It's up to the Diplock judge to decide. And with your record, your denials will receive full consideration, I'm sure. Here, have another smoke."

Then Forbes got down to it. "Tell me," he said, "how's that wee lad of yours? And the girl? I'll wager you haven't been with them for a total of a year's time since internment. Since they were *born*. Pity."

He saw Dugan's blank eyes tearing.

"And your wife, Billy, how's she?"

The eyes came alive at last, flashing rage. "That first time them troops took me, they kicked in the door, knock they could've, and they come right into me bedroom and rousted me out, and me wife, half naked she was, clutching the sheets and askin' could she please have a moment to put on a robe, and one of them soldier boys gives her one, he does, with his rifle stock and says, 'Get up, you Irish bitch,' and she's tryin' to cover her private parts and that soldier boy says 'Look at them titties, real standups, aren't they?' "

"It's rather a nasty business, all this," Forbes said. He thought about hiding in the armoire and hearing the whir of the electric drill and Tony Dolan's muffled cries. "The trouble with you chaps," Forbes said, "is you swallow your own nonsense. You keep telling each other we'll be leaving, and there'll be a general amnesty. But we're not leaving. Someday, perhaps. But not in your life, or mine, as things are. In the meanwhile, you're in the Maze for good. What's the gain?"

"You'd love me to tout, wouldn't you? A nice new grass, so you's can put some other lads away. It's no go. Go fook off."

"I'm not suggesting that. I'm your friend. You'll

never have to testify. I just want information now and again. Stop things before they get started. Actually save lives. The quicker things settle down, the quicker we leave. Nobody will ever know."

For the first time, Dugan held out his hand for a cigarette.

"Think about it," Forbes said. "Think about your wee ones growing up through all those years seeing you for an hour once a month until they get tired of it, the uselessness of it, until one fine day they get you back to bury you."

Afterward, Forbes went to see Roger Gravesend at Stormont Castle.

"Another bright thought, is it, Forbes?" he said.

"Thank you, sir. I'm afraid so." Then he told him about Billy Dugan. They'd been using informants only for tactical purposes, he said. It was a short-sighted policy. With Dugan, they had a chance to insert a mole inside the Provos, the way the KGB had employed Anthony Blunt. Let Dugan percolate, for years if necessary. Wait for an important moment, when it really counted. He already was in the quartermaster side of things, critical for strategic intelligence.

"How do you propose to break him? An event, I take it, that has yet to materialize."

"Sir, the fact is he's already broken. Only he doesn't fully realize it yet."

"And the rest of the legend?"

"Have the grass against Dugan recant. It has additional value. It will demonstrate that the Diplock courts in fact epitomize fairness under the most trying of circumstances."

"We'll have to free those other two in the car with him."

"What's the difference?"

Gravesend reached hastily for a Marlboro. He's just like Dugan, Forbes thought. Must have his pacifier.

Gravesend expelled a lungful of smoke. "Ah . . . yes, I quite agree. Bloody good. Just make certain our Billy doesn't backslide."

Forbes had no concern on that score. In the normal course of events, Dugan would be transported to the Crumlin Road jail to await trial. The IRA's Crumlin battalion commander—part of the Belfast Brigade's ghostly Fourth Battalion, as it was called, encompassing all Provo prisoners in the area, including the Maze—would hold an inquiry. If Dugan confessed that he had talked, he would be absolved as long as he revealed what questions were asked, what he'd said. The Provos made it a practice to keep their word and it had proven to be an extremely effective tactic, although the unfortunate fellow would always remain a marked man.

If Dugan stayed mum, though, and the truth was learned, he was a dead man, and he knew it. Dugan was whipped. Forbes was certain that he didn't have the stomach to play double agent. His choices were to go along with Forbes or face the prospect of life in the Maze.

* * *

Time was running out. Dugan had to be recruited before he entered the Provo support system at the jail.

"Billy," Forbes said, "I've done all I can for you. I won't be seeing you again unless you cooperate. It's for your own good."

"It isn't fair."

"Come off it. Is it fair for you to waste away in the H-Blocks for them? The more bullets and bombs, the longer we'll stay. You being put away won't change anything. Be a man. Your own man. Think of your family."

Dugan worked one cigarette till there was practically nothing left of it, and used it to light another. "How will you's keep anyone from knowin'?"

He's hooked, Forbes thought. "You let me handle that, Billy. Trust me. Remember, I'm your friend."

"None of the lads will suffer harm because of me?"

"Not unless it's of their own doing."

"I'll never have to testify?"

"Never. You have my word."

"And I'll only speak to you?"

"Agreed."

"All right. What's to be done then?"

"You'll give me a rundown on the organization as much as you can. Names. Where they fit in. Aspirations. Contingency plans. What's the thinking? What's the morale? What's the worries? I'll put it all down and you will sign a statement attesting to its veracity."

"I'm not so high up, you know."

"I have every confidence you will be. You're smart. They're lucky to have you. You're doing them a favor they can't appreciate. Tell me, what was your grand-mother's name?"

"Clara, it was."

"That'll be your code name, Billy," Dugan said. "Clara! Marvelous. That's just what we want. To make things clear, clarify them. Remind you always of your grandmother. Your family. Your wee ones. What comes first in this vale of tears."

Forbes locked his eyes on Dugan's. "One more thing for now, Billy," he said. "I know you're not doing it for this, but I'm seeing to two hundred quid a month for you. Help out a bit. Put a little extra on the table. Remind you always of me."

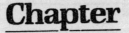

9

At the end of the semester, Jamie phoned and said that he and Ingrid would be driving down from Boston in her Honda directly to the beach. They'd take the ferry across Long Island Sound from New London to Orient Point on the north shore.

Michael McGuire was disappointed. "You don't want to come into the city first?" he said. He'd been looking forward to taking Jamie to a couple of plays, getting caught up over dinner, just the two of them, in some good steak houses. He'd nearly forgotten that Jamie wasn't coming alone. Oh, well, he thought, there would be time later for all of that.

"I just want to take it easy. Lie in the sun. Take out the boat. Is the boat in the water?"

"No, I was waiting for you."

"Well, I'll do it. We're leaving Wednesday morning. When you get out for the weekend, everything'll be ready."

Michael McGuire had been seeing a young copy-writer on and off. She was cute and smart, and he thought briefly about bringing her with him. But he quickly discarded the idea. She was thirty-five, prac-tically this Ingrid Gerhard's age. Okay, that was stretching things, but still it made him feel uncom-fortable. It wasn't exactly the father and son reunion he'd had in mind, he and Jamie weekending it with two young women. He was, he concluded, a lot more middle class than he had believed possible.

He arrived Friday evening at sunset. There was just enough chill in the air for the fire that was crack-ling. "Hey!" Jamie said, embracing him, and he felt the strength in Jamie's body.

"Hey yourself," he said. "Some muscles."

He'd been working out twice a week in the weight room, Jamie said. They wanted him back on the swimming team. Ingrid stepped out of the kitchen. She and Jamie were both wearing gray sweatshirts and jeans. "Good evening, Mr. McGuire," she said.

"Michael, please," he said. "You make me feel like you're talking to my father."

"How is Grandda?"

Michael McGuire caught it right away. *Da*. It was as though Jamie was working on two levels. But he let it go. "As irascible as ever," he said.

"I've got to get into the city to see him."

"Yes, so you two can continue plotting the over-throw of British imperialism."

"Oh, Dad, come on."

Michael McGuire put his bag in his room. He had

the unsettling sensation of being a guest in his own house. He changed into slacks and a sweater, put on topsiders and came out and mixed himself a martini. "Make anything for you guys?"

"No, thanks," Jamie said. "We'll stick to beer."

"The *Mary Alice* okay?"

"Take a look."

They walked out on the deck. Michael McGuire paused to admire the last golden red streaks of the sunset. "Boy, it never fails, does it?" he said. Then they walked down to the dock. The brightwork on the *Mary Alice* gleamed in the dying light. He listened to the water lapping against the hull, the creak of the lines. He noticed how neatly the excess on the lines was coiled on the dock, how precisely the spring line was set. "You haven't lost your touch," he said.

"Thanks, Dad, but it's no big deal. I love this boat and everything she means."

"Yes," he said, and all the might-have-beens flashed through his mind again.

Ingrid was coming out of the kitchen when they returned. "God, that smells great, whatever it is," Michael McGuire said.

"It's sauerbraten," Jamie said. "Ingrid's been working on it for two days. We're going to have sauerbraten and red cabbage and potato pancakes."

"Sauerbraten!" Michael McGuire said and then— instantly regretting it—"When in the world did you start up with sauerbraten?" The words had just popped out. His excuse to himself was that Jamie had never been what you could call an adventurous eater. He felt his face flush. He did not look at Ingrid.

"Around the time Hitler invaded Poland," Jamie said, laughing.

Grateful for the chance to banter his way off the hook, Michael McGuire said, "The mind boggles at your increasingly impressive grasp of history."

"What can I say? You sent me to Harvard to be educated. By the way, I'm doing a paper for a fall course in public policy. It's called 'The Liberal Dilemma over Northern Ireland.' The idea is that liberals gather together and wring their hands about the Middle East, Central America, South Africa, and then somebody, like me, says, 'How about Northern Ireland?' and their eyes roll back in their heads. They don't want to hear it. They've got these cultural hang-ups about the Brits, the Magna Carta, Princess Di. Makes you wonder why Washington, Jefferson and Adams went to all that trouble. Worst of all, they can't get a handle on it. Everybody's white and worships the same God—no Yahweh, no Allah, no heathens even. How does that grab you? My professor says it's intriguing. If it doesn't work out, he said, I can turn it into a standup comedy routine."

"Jamie, there's a word for you. Incorrigible. But speaking of Hitler, I notice Germany and England manage to get along pretty well now, and you can't say they didn't have their problems."

"Yes, perhaps it is because England does not occupy the Ruhr," Ingrid said.

In the exchange with Jamie, Michael McGuire had nearly forgotten her. She was staring at him with great intensity. "Touché," he said. "Okay, I surrender. And I'm starving. As we Irish say, up the sauerbraten!"

He went to bed early, right after coffee and a brandy. What a role reversal, he thought. All those times past when he had been in this room with someone, and Jamie had been in his room alone, playing his guitar. Still, he was doubly glad he hadn't brought out the copywriter. Things were complicated enough as they were. He drifted off to the sound of the rock group, The Police, on the stereo in the living room, singing "Can't Stand Losing You."

They were still asleep when he awoke in the morning. He saw at once how neat and tidy everything was. Somehow he had figured to find everything in a mess. After he returned from tennis, he saw them lying head to head on the bulkhead, on their stomachs, sunbathing. He experienced a stab of unfocused envy, and then the thought occurred to him, for which he immediately castigated himself, that Jamie had found a mother he could sleep with. When they heard him, they got up. She was entrancing in her bikini. Round, full breasts, rounded hips, not a glimmer of fat, sturdy legs, maybe a little on the short side. Later, in the afternoon, acting as lookout when they went water skiing, he helped her climb back into the boat and felt the resilient, almost rubbery tone of her skin.

When they returned to the house, she stayed on the deck with him while Jamie went inside to shower. It was the first time he had been alone with her. They sat silently watching the constant boat parade across the bay before she said, "You have a wonderful son."

He readied a modest disclaimer to the usual follow-up compliment, that it was undoubtedly because he had been such a terrific father. But it didn't happen. Finally he said, "Thank you."

She must have been born, he thought, about the time he returned from his German tour and was discharged from the army. He said, "What made you leave home?"

"Well, you know I was married before."

"No, I didn't."

"Yes, to an American officer, a captain. When he was transferred back to the States, he decided to continue in the military. It was a very unhappy time for me. It reminded me of too many bad things. I was a late child. My father was in the German army. He lost a leg at the very end of the war. He did not participate in what you call Germany's rebirth. He was very bitter about the war, about Germany's defeat."

"And you weren't?"

"No, how could I be? I hated everything the Nazis stood for and I despised my country for it. And when I became divorced, I didn't want to go back. With my training as a nurse—you know, they said, 'My god, she was trained in Germany'—it was easy to get in any hospital I wanted."

"Jamie knows all this, of course."

"Of course."

She hesitated. "I was searching always for something. I'm not sure of what. But I found it in Jamie. He is such a caring person. I realize what you are thinking," she said. "I'm nearly ten years older than he is. But I will stay with him as long as he wishes."

Her frankness left Michael McGuire nonplussed. He didn't know what to say. Then he said, "Whatever makes Jamie happy, makes me happy." He hoped it didn't sound too evasive.

On Sunday she packed a lunch and they went fishing, and out on the water searching for the blues, the years fell away. He even had to smile when he heard Jamie say, "Listen, *Liebchen*, just relax. Wait till the rod's past your shoulder and snap your wrist." Echoes of himself.

They caught three fish, and while Jamie hosed down the boat Michael McGuire scaled and gutted them. He would be driving back to the city after dinner, and he couldn't put it off any longer. "I was by the marina," he said, "and they told me you wouldn't be there this summer. They were awfully disappointed. They're building up their charter business and they said a lot of people were especially asking for you."

"I'm sorry, Dad. I was going to tell you. The thing is that Ingrid can't get off this summer, and I want to be with her, and this guy offered me a job as mate on a commercial trawler out of New Bedford, sometimes Gloucester. It'll be good, tough work, get me in real shape, and the pay's good, the price for swordfish is sky high and, well, that's what I'm going to do."

Michael McGuire wanted to say, Jamie, Ingrid's very nice and all that and he really liked her, but, for Christ's sake, Jamie, she's ten goddamn years older than you, and you've got your whole life ahead of you, and how much time are you going to have with her anyway on a trawler out of New Bedford, sometimes Gloucester? He wanted to say, Think about it for a minute, Jamie, use your head! He had regretted so much not saying things to Jamie which he hadn't said before because of his own blocks, but this time, when he wanted to, in a way that counted, he was completely flummoxed. What the hell could he say that would make a difference? Jamie hadn't even asked him what he thought of her. And that was the devastating clincher.

"I like how that young fellow sings," Kevin Dowd had said to Sean Walsh. "Makes me homesick, he does. The usual fare around here is 'McNamara's Band' or 'Sweet Rosie O'Grady.' "

It was the Friday following Michael McGuire's visit to The Crooked Plough, and this time when Jamie had finished, only Ingrid was at the table with him.

Dowd said, "I'd like to shake your hand, lad. You sing like an angel, or the closest I'll ever get to hearin' one. Can I buy you and your lady a drink?"

"Thanks, no, we've got to be going," Jamie said. "By the way, what's that accent?"

"Belfast, it is."

"Belfast!"

"Well, mind you, with a wee bit of Boston mixed in. I've been here awhile. But Sean here's just come over. You want pure Belfast, give him a listen."

"Hey, sit down, will you? This is Ingrid. The drinks are on the house. What'll you have?"

"Guinness would be fine."

"Right, Guinness. I'll have one, too. Four Guinnesses—uh, make that three and a white wine," he told the waiter when he saw Ingrid make a face.

"Where'd you learn them songs?" Dowd asked.

"Some I got myself. Mostly from my grandda, though."

"He's there, is he?"

"No, he lives in New York. But *his* grandda's from County Cork and was in the Fenian uprising, the one in eighteen sixty-seven."

"Not a vintage year, 'sixty-seven," Dowd said. "Arrests, betrayals, executions. That was a year the Brits had nothin' else to do."

"It isn't over, though, is it?" Jamie said.

"For sure, it's not," Dowd said, his face suddenly hard. Later, Ingrid would remember that, the way Dowd's face was.

"Are you a student here?" she asked Walsh.

"Oh, no, I would like to be. But I have other work to do."

"How old are you?"

"Twenty-five. Why do you inquire?"

"It's just that you look younger. That's why I thought you might be a student."

Kevin Dowd said, "Sean here was in the Kesh, y'know," and Jamie stared at him and said, "You were in Long Kesh?" and Sean Walsh said, "Yes," his voice so soft that Jamie and Ingrid had to lean forward to hear him.

"What happened?" Jamie said.

"I was nicked carryin' a carbine to someone."

"He was three years in the Kesh, in the H-Blocks," Dowd said, "during the dirty protest, the blanket protest, he was part of it."

Jamie was transfixed, Ingrid would remember, as if Sean Walsh had descended from outer space. "What was it like?" Jamie asked.

"Well, each H-Block has four wings with twenty-five men to a wing, one to a cell with heavy steel doors. The crosspiece of the 'H' is the administration section where the warders—them's the guards—are, and each block has its own walls, so it's isolated from the other blocks, so as to break up all the prisoners."

"No, I mean, what was it like to be in there?"

"Well, we wouldn't wear the prison garb, so we didn't have nothin' except the blankets," Sean Walsh said. "We had three blankets and a mattress and a water container and a pot to piss in and a towel, even though we wasn't washin' up. And we put our shit on the walls with sponges we made from the mattresses. The warders, some of them, used to kick over the pisspots on the blankets."

There was a toneless quality to Walsh's voice, none of the pent-up rage you'd expect.

"You seem so calm about it," Ingrid said.

"Do I now?"

No one spoke for a moment, and then Jamie said, "Did they, uh, physically abuse you, or was it, you know, all psychological?"

"Oh, I can say for a fact it wasn't only psychological," Walsh said. "There was once when a warder come in to search me cell and kicked me so hard with his boot that me"—he hesitated, glancing at Ingrid, blushing—"that me, ah, testicles disappeared, and in all the pain that was jumpin' through me, I reached down, holdin' meself, and I didn't feel nothin' except a great fright, wonderin' where they could be, so it was psychological, too, I suppose you might say."

Jamie ordered another round of Guinness and

said, "I don't know how you hung in there like that. *Three years.* Unbelievable!"

"You don't let yourself think in terms of time," Walsh said, "of one week, a month, a year. You just went from day to day, else you'd go insane. Actually, four or five individuals on the blanket did go insane."

He was also lucky, he said. He could speak Gaelic, so he gave classes in it. There was a gap under his cell door for him to shout out the words. He kept part of the wall free of shit and used his Saint Christopher medal to scratch out the lessons on the concrete surface.

"Could you read books or have a radio?"

"No, not at all, nor any exercise outside. We could only go out for Sunday Mass. But we could sing. They couldn't stop that."

"Sing him the H-Block song," Dowd said. "He'd surely want to hear it."

And Walsh quietly began to sing, and then Jamie, picking up the chorus, joined him:

> *So I'll wear no convict's uniform*
> *Nor meekly serve my time*
> *That Britain might brand Ireland's fight*
> *Eight hundred years of crime.*

"Hey, I've got to write that down," Jamie said.

Dowd said, "You should tell him about that warder, what he said, and what you said."

"Well, the stench was terrible foul, you know. You never got used to it even after the washdowns," Walsh said, "and one fine day a warder come in, not a bad sort he was, and sniffed around and looked at me in me filthy blanket sittin' on me filthy mattress and he said 'You couldn't get me to do this for two million pounds,' and I said, 'Oh, you couldn't get me to do it for that either.'"

Jamie was near tears, Ingrid could see, and so was she. After hearing that, she remembered, how could anyone not be?

"That's fantastic," Jamie said.

"No, it was the truth," Walsh said.

Without warning, Kevin Dowd's eyes narrowed. "What the hell's the use of all this?" he said. "You're just a rich college kid and all this singin' the patriot's game is just a lark, a spectator's sport for you."

Jamie flushed. "Hey, wait a minute. What do you want me to do? Apologize because I wasn't in the Kesh?"

"Don't mind Kevin," Walsh said. "He don't mean that. You must understand, compared to Kevin, I've done little enough. Kevin's taken the Brits on face-to-face in armed combat."

As subdued as he had been angry a second before, Dowd said, "Ah, Sean's right. I meant no offense. I lost my head in memories."

"I just want you to know," Jamie said, "that maybe I'm not a poor kid, but I'm not rich either. Like I've worked plenty around boats, earning my own money. You see me on a boat, you'd understand. I'd do anything to help the cause if somebody'd tell me what it was."

Dowd stared at Jamie. "Boats, eh?" he said.

"You've got it," and then Jamie said, "Listen, here's my—our—address and number. Maybe you guys could come by sometime and we could talk some more."

Afterward, in Ingrid's apartment, Jamie said, "Jesus, with guys like that Sean, the Brits don't stand a chance. Look at what he's done, and look at me. That other guy was right. I wonder what his story is."

"Jamie, it's not your country," Ingrid said.

"It's my other country."

"Go see that lad," Dowd told Walsh on Sunday morning. "Make amends. I don't know what got into me. But he didn't take it lyin' down now, did he? I like that. Inquire more about him and the boat business. I'll be returnin' in two days."

Then Dowd left in the Ford van that Tommy Ahearn had lent him to attend a major event on the gun circuit, a big sales show held annually in a National Guard armory at Newburgh, New York.

His mind drifted in the monotony of driving. He worried about how he had snapped the other night. Was he losing his grip? No, he decided, it had been as he said. It had to be the memories. Sean had resurrected them.

And the first memory was always the spinning sky above him as he lay face up in the grass in Andersontown, his life oozing out of him. He'd been so stupid, him who should have known better, toting a .38 when the undercover sergeant had suddenly grabbed him from behind at the bus stop. In the struggle he'd gotten the sergeant in the leg, but, of course, they always came in pairs, and the sergeant's sidekick across the way pumped the bullet into his stomach.

He'd managed to toss the .38 off in the grass, and in all the confusion of the wounded sergeant and the people running around and screaming, and the cops and more soldiers, the wee one—only eight, he was, they said—picked it up and gave it to his da, who gave it to the IRA block man. And then he was in the ambulance, and the medical attendant was scrubbing his right hand and wrist with alcohol, it smelled like, and he mumbled, "What the hell are ye doin'?" and the attendant whispered, "Least they won't find no gunpowder, corpse or no."

At the hospital it was thought he would not last the night. But he did. Then he was informed that the bullet had so mangled his bowels that a colostomy had to be performed or he would die. "I'd rather die," he cried.

He believed, still believed, that this was just a way to punish him more, so when they finally let the solicitor in to see him, he said he would only submit to an operation that would suture his torn insides. He counted on the surgeon, once he was on the table, to do his best, and he was right. Three times during his recovery, armed guards stationed outside his room pulled out the tube running down his throat to drain the poisonous buildup of fluids. They claimed that he must have done it to himself in his sleep.

After two months he was transferred to the Crumlin Road jail. His solicitor said, "Well, they have no weapon, no forensic evidence against you."

"Sure, and that'll save the day," he said.

That was when the great escape took place. The wonderful, stupendous, incredible great escape! The thought of it still left him breathless. There were always escape plots, going over the walls, burrowing beneath them, and he had said, "Why don't we go out the way we come in, through the front door?"

The purity of it, the sheer audacity, seized them all, and the brigade headquarters gave its blessing. Two .25-caliber automatics were smuggled in, one through an Ordinary Decent Criminal, as the Brits called them, whose visitation rights were far less stringently monitored than the Provo prisoners, the other in the dirty diapers of a baby brought by his mother so his father could touch and cradle him.

At gunpoint, eight of them took over the visiting area in the jail's "B" wing, herding everyone else into the holding pens. He and another volunteer dressed in guard uniforms. Two others took the pass cards of solicitors on hand to confer with clients and put on their suits, coats and hats. The remaining four stayed in their own clothes. As bold as brass, they marched through three interior gates and then the front gate, as if they were headed for the Belfast High Court directly opposite the jail on the Crumlin Road where the Diplock trials were held. The normal access to the courthouse from the jail was through an underground passageway, but at each gate Dowd briskly said, "Didn't ye hear? There's been a disturbance down below," and they were waved through. And why not? After all, the courthouse across the road bristled with machine gun posts and pillboxes manned by soldiers and cops.

As soon as they were outside, they began running up the road toward two waiting cars the brigade had set up. It took a second for the startled sentries to react. Still, by the time they reached the cars, bullets were whining by them. They had to take cover in front of each car. Some of the pursuing cops and soldiers had caught up to them, crouched now behind on the trunk of the closest car, firing. Dowd's automatic jammed. It seemed hopeless anyway. And it was at that moment that he became a heroic figure in the movement. In the guard's peaked hat and tunic, he suddenly stood up, raised a hand and shouted, "Police, police! Don't shoot!" and in the frozen instant, they piled into the cars and roared off.

The next night he was over the border in the free state, County Donegal, his picture on the front page of every paper in Ireland and Britain. Three months later, bespectacled, with a new mustache and hair dyed black, equipped with an Irish passport in another name, he flew from Shannon to Amsterdam and then Toronto, was supplied with a New York State driver's license and a card that attested to his honorary membership in the Patrolmen's Benevolent Association of the New York Police Department, and crossed into the United States without incident. For a time in New York City he worked off the books as a bartender in one of John Scanlon's pubs. In Belfast, he'd been an electrician's apprentice, and he diligently applied himself to advanced vocational school locksmith and circuitry courses and then journeyed to Boston, where he found employment cracking safes and vaults for Tommy Ahearn. He also had coordinated four arms shipments, but nothing comparable to what was now being planned.

And that had brought on more strain. In his meetings with Daniel P. Daugherty, Daugherty had been less than enthusiastic about bringing in Ahearn, until

Dowd said he'd welcome alternatives, keeping in mind their cash position.

The Army Council was going to have to swallow it, too, or else come up with a better solution. It wouldn't be the marijuana deal with Ahearn in return for the boat that would concern the council. The issue would be Ahearn himself. The council hated to go to outsiders, and gangsters like Ahearn were always trading off with the law.

But Dowd figured he had an ace in the hole. For all of his cunning, Ahearn was afraid of the IRA, the passion it stirred, the retribution he believed it could exact, its ability to undercut him even in the Somerville mob if it ever felt betrayed.

Dowd would send Sean Walsh back to Belfast with all of this, and the decision would be made one way or the other. Dowd also wanted Walsh to return with some definitive good news about what would be in the shipment. Which was why he was on the road this Sunday morning.

There must have been two or three thousand people milling about on the immense drill floor of the Newburgh armory by the time Dowd arrived.

Inside the entrance the National Rifle Association had a recruiting booth soliciting signatures to uphold the inalienable right under the Constitution of all Americans to bear arms. The sound system was blaring out patriotic airs. Dowd signed and got a red, white and blue button that said "NRA." "Got to keep up the pressure," the fellow in the booth said. "Fucking Commies are everywhere, trying to subvert us."

"I couldn't agree more," Dowd said.

The show was a mecca for gun collectors seeking vintage weapons. Even Dowd paused to admire a pair of dueling pistols with inlaid ivory handles. But the bulk of the items for sale were very up to date. All the major manufacturers and dealers had elaborate displays. There also were dozens of independent sellers who simply set up a couple of card tables to show off what they had. You were supposed to have a driver's license for identification. Dowd had three. More often than not, though, in the hectic activity, this formality was dispensed with.

Moving back and forth from the armory floor to his van, Dowd bought four new Winchester semiautomatic Mark III twelve-gauge shotguns, twenty Sturm Ruger Mini 14s easily convertible to fully automatic, sixteen .308 Heckler & Koch model 91 semiautomatics and ten Remington Woodmaster carbines with Weaver K-4 telescopic sights. The transactions were in cash. There would be other purchases he would make later, like MAC-10 submachine guns in Florida. Ohio was for handguns, with accommodating outlets in Cleveland, Columbus and especially in Steubenville at a store owned by a County Mayo man. In and out. No waiting for a gun license first, sales records kept on site.

Late that evening, Dowd drove the van to New York City, to Queens, and parked in Jake Mooney's garage.

"Tea?" Mooney said.

"Yes, thanks."

"Have you eaten? I can scramble up some eggs."

"No need. I stopped at a McDonald's. How's your mother?"

"As well as can be expected at her age. She's asleep. I have to have someone in now, a lovely girl from Limerick, to look after her while I'm at the bank."

Dowd gazed at Mooney. This frail, freckled old man was tougher than all of them, he thought, tougher than him, or Sean Walsh, or Gerry McMahon, or the rest. All these years, here in America, he could have walked away at any time. But he had not, never giving up, forever pursuing the quest when it appeared to be finished, when five rifles was like a miracle.

He'd once asked Mooney what it was that sustained him, and Mooney said that when he was a wee lad in Killarney and news of the partition agreement had come, that all of Ireland wasn't going to be free and united, someone had said, "This wasn't what the fight was for, was it? We'll just have to keep on."

"It goes well?" Mooney asked.

"So far, so good. Tomorrow's the big day for the Redeyes. But the truth is I'm worried about the boat. Is it the right boat? I'll go along, of course, but what do I know? We have an Irish Republican Army. Unfortunately, no Irish Republican Navy."

"You'll find a way."

"Will I?"

Mooney walked him to the subway stop on Queens Boulevard. "Take the R train into the city," he said. "Get off at the Fifty-seventh Street station. It's only a short walk to the hotel. The room's reserved in your name, paid in advance."

The next morning, in the Sheraton City Squire,

while Dowd waited in his room, he recalled Daugherty's injunction and kept repeating to himself, "*Hoo*lio, *Hoo*lio."

Julio Gonzalez was thin and swarthy, hair slicked back with brilliantine. He was wearing a flower-print sports shirt in hues of orange and yellow flopping over suntans. He looked more like a lookout for a sidewalk three-card monte game than the purveyor of Redeye missiles.

After some preliminaries about how warm the New York spring was, and how hot the summer would be, Dowd said he would want five launchers.

"No problem," Gonzalez said.

"And fifty warheads with battery coolant units."

"No problem."

"And all the training manuals."

"*Hey,* no problem."

They talked about delivery dates. The middle of August would be best, Gonzalez said. There were all kinds of exercises and maneuvers going on. The arsenal at Fort Letterkenny in Pennsylvania went crazy in August, Gonzalez said, rolling his eyes. He would deliver the goods to a warehouse in Brooklyn where Dowd and his people could inspect the package. Once they were satisfied, Dowd would have the cash brought in. The exchange would be made then and there and everybody would go his own way.

Dowd said he couldn't go along with that. He'd pay after he was able to get the Redeyes safely out.

"Now we got a problem," Gonzalez said.

Dowd argued that the way it stood, he could lose the money and the missiles.

"How?"

"Somebody could jump us."

"Who?"

"The feds, maybe."

"Hey, we are businessmen. We ain't rip-off artists," Gonzalez said. He rose and started for the door.

Dowd saw the Redeyes slipping out of his grasp. "Listen to me," he said. "It's for both our benefit, don't you see? *I* could be a fed."

Gonzalez whirled. "You a fed?"

"No. But that's what I mean. We can't be too careful."

Gonzalez edged back into the room. "What you got in mind?" he said.

"Hostages," Dowd said. "I'll give you two of my people. You just have to give me one of yours. We have to have time to stash the Redeyes. When we pay, the hostages are released. Now, what could be fairer?"

"How much time?"

"Twelve hours."

"Too long."

"Six then."

"Hokay, you got a deal. Ten down."

"Try him with five first," Daugherty had counseled. "He sees all them Ben Franklins staring him in the face, he'll start swooning like his joint's being copped."

"How's five for starters?" Dowd said, spreading out the hundred-dollar bills fresh from Jake Mooney. "What I mean, five or ten, it's good-faith money, is all."

Gonzalez hesitated, then scooped up the bills.

They traded phone numbers. Dowd gave him the

one for the Excelsior Yacht Club in Boston. "That's area code six one seven," he said. "You ask for Patrick O'Malley. If I'm not there, I'll get the message."

"What's that name again?"

"O'Malley," Dowd said. "Never mind. Here, I'll write it down for you."

As he was leaving, Gonzalez said, "You want any meat? U.S. prime. I got a connection at West Point."

Dowd suddenly had the feeling that if he had enough funding, he could equip an entire division, top to bottom. "Not right now," he said.

"I've been with Jamie McGuire," Walsh told Dowd when he returned to Boston. "I saw him Sunday night and again last night. He's to be trusted. I have no doubt he's committed to us. If he'd been in the Kesh, he would have been on the blanket with me. He's no spoiled rich kid. He's had his troubles. His ma passed on when he was a wee one. He don't make a big thing of it, but it's there. He knows what sorrow is. I told him a little about you. The escape and all."

"And?"

"He didn't get excited or nothin'. Just listened very intently. He said he understood why you were short with him."

"How does he know about boats?"

"He's been around them since he can remember. His da took him fishin' all the time. He worked in a boatyard. He hired out on charters. He's been around the commercial trawlers like the one you say we're to use. He's smart. I think he senses somethin's on."

"Well, I'll give him a looksee. Perhaps you spoke too loosely."

"You told me to make inquiries. And I did. To my satisfaction." Walsh chopped off the words. There was a lot of defiance in his voice.

Dowd was taken aback. Walsh sounded like the McGuire kid did at The Crooked Plough. At the age of thirty-eight, he suddenly felt old.

The boat Ahearn had leased was a fishing trawler based in New Bedford. The trawler was named *Sea King*. The captain and the crew were Portuguese. "There's nothin' but them fuckin' Portugays down there in fuckin' New Bedford," Ahearn had said. "Even the fuckin' D.A. is Portugay. The captain, I looked him up, he was busted a couple, three years ago for smuggling in a hundred K wortha Canadian swordfish. Got a suspended sentence. The fuck they got to smuggle in swordfish for, that's such a big deal? Anyway, he's got this big gold front tooth. 'Captain,' I says, 'I got somethin' for you to bring in fill your whole goddamn mouth with gold,' and he just grins, says when does he get started? Course, I don't say nothin' about the other trip, the one over there. But them Portugays don't care, believe me, hardly speak American, long as they get theirs."

Maybe so, Dowd had thought. But it was one thing to pick up a marijuana load a couple of hundred miles out, and quite something else to sail across the North Atlantic with an arms cargo. Somebody had to be on that trawler that he trusted, someone knowledgeable, who could tell him what shape the trawler was in, whether she could make it, how much she could carry, how capable the captain was, somebody *committed.*

For sure, Ahearn was not your knowledgeable seafarer despite the thirty-five-foot Chris-Craft cabin cruiser that he kept at the nearly all Irish Excelsior Yacht Club in Boston, a satisfying testament to his status in the community. On weekends, he loved to don a blue blazer, white trousers and braided cap and have his bodyguard Bernie Quinn drive him to the club. The trouble was that Ahearn was subject to violent seasickness at the slightest suggestion of waves. So mostly the Chris-Craft remained in her berth, venturing forth into Dorchester Bay only on the calmest of days, while Ahearn entertained assorted politicians and business associates on board with drinks and buffet spreads catered in the club's kitchen.

Dowd had Jamie take the cruiser out and immediately saw the way he handled her with practiced ease. And he saw something more, how the minute Jamie took the wheel, he took command, calmly issuing orders to his neophyte crew, Dowd and Walsh.

Still, Dowd hesitated. "We could bring a Kerryman over who knows the sea," he told Walsh.

"But what would he know of American machinery and equipment? And on the New Bedford docks he'd stick out like a Brit squaddie in the Falls. You'll do no better than Jamie McGuire, mark me."

"Perhaps we need no one."

"You said yourself we do."

Dowd pondered it for a week. When he finally sounded out Jamie, he did it cautiously. "It'd be a seagoing trawler," he said, without saying from where or when.

"What condition's she in?"

"That's somethin' I would want you to say."

"You'd best tell him about the blowy," Walsh said.

Blowy? For a moment Dowd did not remember. Blowy was a Belfast street name for marijuana. In Belfast it also meant explosives. Odd, Dowd thought, dwelling on the irony. Or maybe a portent.

"How do you feel about the weed, grass?" he said.

"Not much. Just about everybody I know smokes a joint, including yours truly."

"We're beggars, not choosers," Dowd said. "The trawler will first be used to bring in two loads of the weed. I can't go into the details, but arrangements have been made to assure safe passage. Still, I can't deny there's a danger. Somethin' could always go wrong."

"No coke, or anything else?"

"No. And you understand, this must remain among us."

"I'd have to tell Ingrid. If I can't tell her, it'll stop right here. I'll forget I ever met you. She'd know something was up, anyway."

Finally Dowd said, "Only her."

"All right then. You do what you have to do, don't you? Count me in."

"Are you going to tell your father?" Ingrid said.

"He'd never understand."

"I'm not sure I do."

"All my life I've been a kid," Jamie said. "I don't want to be a kid anymore."

PART

III

PART

49

10

The morning courier plane from London circled low over Belfast Lough, dropping past the Holywood hills toward the main strip at Harbor airport on the northern edge of the city. Brian Forbes could see the great cranes of Harland and Wolff, the shipbuilders, and the web of channels where the River Lagan emptied into the lough. Off to his right was the world's biggest drydock. The *Titanic* had been built in Belfast, Forbes always remembered.

The Harbor field, fog permitting, was much more convenient than the international airport at Aldergrove, fifteen miles west of Belfast on the other side of Black Mountain. From Harbor it was a straight run along Newtownards Road past the headquarters of the paramilitary Ulster Defense Association on Gawn Street, through Strandtown and Belmont to Stormont. The UDA's commander had once said that he frankly didn't care if the Brits left. He wanted an independent Ulster. "I'd rather be a first-class Ulsterman than a second-class Englishman," he said. "The Provos want the Brits out, but they also want a thirty-two-county nation. They ought to wise up. Ireland was never united except under the Brits."

Still, Union Jacks flew. In the working-class districts closest to the port area, the curbs were all red, white and blue. But farther out, as neighborhoods became visibly more affluent, these displays disappeared, as if they were an affront to middle-class dignity. He could just as well be going through any midland British town, Forbes thought idly, and then realized with a start that he *was* in the United Kingdom, wasn't he? He'd been away for three years now, and Northern Ireland had taken on the aspect of an alien entity.

At Stormont Castle, he went directly to the office of Graham Crankshaw, the new security coordinator. Not only was this Crankshaw's domain, but he also was a future rival to be reckoned with. Forbes had seen him twice at conferences in London. Crankshaw was a tall, gangly man, two years older than Forbes, with thinning blond hair. He was a Cambridge graduate and said to be an accomplished harpsichordist. The service seemed to value this sort of quirk, certainly more than Forbes's amateur boxing. Crankshaw's previous posting was something to worry about as well. He'd been chief of the section in "C" branch that drew up contingency plans against domestic sabotage and terrorism—like the seizure of a nuclear power plant, or the occupation of an embassy—and then ran exercises with Special Air Service commandos and elite police units.

"I've reserved a private room for lunch," Crankshaw said, without bothering to ask if Forbes was free.

"Very thoughtful of you, Graham," Forbes said.

They'd be lunching at Stormont House, a handsome Georgian structure about a minute's walk or so from the castle that had been the speaker's residence until the facade of Northern Ireland began to crumble and the Stormont parliament was dissolved by London. Forbes had never been in it before. The ground floor was used for formal receptions. Senior civil servants ate in dining rooms on the second floor. As they walked across the sloping greensward, Forbes gazed at the line of dormer windows on the third floor, where rooms were maintained for visiting dignitaries, one of which he would be occupying overnight.

Hidden in the surrounding foliage were rolls of heavy razor wire, shaped in an endless series of S's. You had to be specially trained and equipped to handle it. Even so, Forbes had seen a soldier who had been working on a section of it at an army compound covered with minute bleeding nicks on his arms, hands and face when he finished. Once he'd seen two birds caught in the wire at the Crumlin Road jail tearing themselves apart trying to get free.

The dining room was one of the smaller ones. Prints of celebrated Irish stallions adorned the walls. A waiter—was that the proper word for him? Forbes wondered—in a starched white jacket stood in attendance. Crankshaw nodded familiarly at him, saying, "Good day, Peter," and led Forbes directly to a Chippendale sideboard with four crystal decanters on it. "Let's see, what do we have here?" he said. "Right you are, gin, vodka, whiskey and sherry. Your pleasure?"

"Whiskey, thank you."

"I'll take the same," Crankshaw said, pouring into two crystal stem glasses. The windows faced east. In the distance Forbes could see the line of purplish hills marking the coast. "Where do you live?" he asked.

"Donaghadee," Crankshaw said. Forbes knew where it was, a village a half hour's drive away on the straits between Northern Ireland and Scotland. "Quite pleasant indeed, peaceful," said Crankshaw. "The sea air, however bracing, does play havoc with my harpsichord."

"I understand you're quite good at it."

"Kind of you. I muddle through. It's important to relax, don't you think? Get away from it all. I'm told you used to box. A bit ferocious for me, I must say."

"A misspent youth. I've taken up chess," Forbes lied.

"Jolly good. We must play sometime," Crankshaw said. "Now, then, Peter," he said, "what does the kitchen offer us today?"

"Salmon's excellent, sir. Trout as well. A nice Ulster ham, baked in Guinness?"

This was how it must have been all over the world in the old days, Forbes thought, declining another whiskey. Everything unpleasant out of sight, like the razor wire. Both ordered the salmon. They began with pea soup with croutons and slivers of Irish bacon. The service on white linen was Irish Georgian silver. A bottle of wine was presented for Crankshaw's taste. "Ah, Puligny Montrachet 'seventy-nine," he said. "Many people didn't think much of the 'seventy-nines at first, but see how well this one turned out."

Forbes tried to quell his rising irritation at Crankshaw's drawing-room manner. Then, digging into the deep pink salmon flesh, Crankshaw said, "Well, now, I trust this Clara bloke is worth all the trouble. He's really been rather an annoyance."

"Has he?"

"Yes, we received word of a convoy ambush, but because your Clara was involved we had to cancel an operation that would have netted the whole bunch. Instead, we were forced to reroute the convoy. We had word of a meeting to plan a mortar attack, but we had to allow half the participants, including Clara, to escape. It's all quite irregular, I must say."

"Too bad you didn't receive prior word of the Provo convention. That would have been quite a haul," Forbes said.

Crankshaw colored slightly. "Yes, and Clara might have been of considerble aid in that regard."

"Clara's a sleeper, you know. Not to be awakened until he's tickled."

Forbes felt more comfortable now, away from harpsichords and Montrachets. Crankshaw was a desk man, pure and simple. He'd wager that Crankshaw had never been in the field, never been privy to a kneecapping. His instincts were not honed. That was the edge Forbes had. Sometimes you had to sniff the air, and all Crankshaw sniffed were wine bouquets. That was Cambridge for you! And Crankshaw, when you got down to it, really had nowhere to go to complain. It was well known within the service that MI5's current director general was reclusive, content to have everything pass through his deputy, Roger Gravesend, and Gravesend had approved the Clara arrangement. Forbes did not have command authority, as Crankshaw did, but Forbes was Gravesend's man. Gravesend was the only person Forbes had to concern himself about.

Forbes tightened the screws a little. "Anything more on the convention?"

"Not beyond what we've reported. It was across the border, in a monastery apparently, although we're not certain yet which one. Just a matter of time, that. It was a changing of the guard. We're aware of some of the names. Young Turks taking over. More power to the Northern Command. More nationalistic, less Marxist. A natural sequence, I'd say. *Is* there something more?"

Clearly he had Crankshaw on the defensive. Crankshaw had to be wondering if Forbes was reflecting the talk on Curzon Street. Forbes decided not to confide in Crankshaw, not now at any rate. At this stage it was still not much more than a hunch. Forbes had analyzed all the arms seizures for the past six months. All small consignments, all unremarkable. Typical were suitcases in the name of a fictitious passenger that had landed at Cobh off the *Queen Elizabeth II*, containing eight Armalites and four .357 Magnum Colt revolvers plus ammunition. Obviously other shipments had gotten through. But statistically over the years such intercepts provided accurate guides to what was going on. And there had been no sign of dramatic new weaponry since six M60 heavy machine guns and twenty Soviet-made anti-tank RPG47 rocket launchers were introduced into the fighting. Five of the former from the States and fifteen of the latter, purchased in Libya, had been recovered.

Now though, in the past two months, even the small deliveries had dwindled. Something major had to be in progress, something that could upset the delicate balance so vital to preserve. From Libya? Perhaps. But there were only two usable ports, Tripoli and Benghazi, and watchers were in place in both. And in Malta as well, where a transshipment could occur.

It had to be the States. He though balefully of U.S. customs. Not all of customs, of course. He had cultivated several agents during his Washington tour who were straight-on law and order, like the one who first tipped him off about Daniel P. Daugherty. And before coming to Belfast, he had made private inquiries to them, to no avail. Still, he was sure he was on the right track.

"I don't know," he told Crankshaw in answer to his question, "that's what I'm going to attempt to find out." He held up a forkful of salmon, examining it. "Delicious," he said. "Graham, you're very fortunate having grub like this."

Crankshaw made a last defiant stand. "If it involves anything within the province, I expect to be informed immediately."

"That goes without saying," Forbes said, pleased with himself. "We're all in this together, aren't we?"

After lunch he went to his room. He removed his tie and changed from his suit to khaki slacks and a rumpled safari jacket. He told his driver to take him to the British military command in Lisburn. This was the day Clara was to make his weekly afternoon call. Forbes had dispatched orders that if the call came before his arrival, Clara was to ring again in an hour. "Brian" desired to speak with him.

The car turned left onto Knock Road and went past the headquarters of the Royal Ulster Constabulary. Before the partition, north and south, it had been called the Royal Irish Constabulary. When you entered the administration building, you saw a lighted glass display case, almost like a shrine. Inside was a tattered Union Jack. An inscription beneath the flag noted that it had flown over the main barracks of the Royal Irish Constabulary in Dublin until "3:15 P.M., 1 March 1922, when the barracks was handed over to the Provisional Government of the Irish Free State." Forbes had been quite moved when he first viewed it. Then, with all the charges that the RUC was less than evenhanded in its treatment of nationalists and loyalists, he wondered if the correct public relations image was being conveyed. On the other hand, considering the flag's present location, not too many hostile visitors would have a chance to see it.

They swept around the southeast quadrant of the city along Upper Knockbreda Road toward Lisburn. Although it was unthinkable that the IRA would dare mount an attack there, the command bristled with razor wire, pillboxes and sentry posts and car barriers. A forest of antennas reached skyward. A helicopter was taking off when Forbes arrived.

In MI5's security facility, Forbes finally felt at home. This was where the action was, not in the stuffy confines of Stormont. One of the handlers addressed him as "governor." On Curzon Street only the branch chiefs were called that. In the file room, he was given Clara's folder. There was no mention of his real name, which was kept separate, appropriately coded, in a safe. But Billy Dugan had advanced in

Provo ranks and was now attached to the quarter-master general's staff. Just what Forbes had hoped for. The file showed that he had been reporting in regularly, missing only two calls because of illness. There was a check-off for the two hundred pounds that Dugan picked up on the first of each month at a dead drop in a tobacconist's shop run by MI5 on Bradbury Place near Queen's University. Forbes observed that Dugan had never skipped this particular item.

At four-thirty, right on schedule, Dugan phoned the special number provided him. A handler passed the receiver. "This is Brian," Forbes said. "The Crown Bar, seven o'clock sharp."

"Seven?"

"Yes. Any problem?"

"No, I suppose not."

After all this time, Forbes had wondered if Dugan had begun to believe that nothing would ever come of the compact they had struck in the Castlereagh interrogation center. Of course, there were the weekly calls and the monthly cash payments, but in his mind they could have become unthinking habit. When Dugan heard his voice, though, he hadn't exhibited the slightest hint of surprise. If anything, there'd been a note of resignation, and that was all to the good.

The RUC's Special Branch would not have approved of the Crown Bar. Special Branch cops favored deserted car parks at night for informant meetings, the deserted corner of a golf course, a dark side street. That was fine as long as nobody was around to notice, but if there was, you might as well be carrying a leper's bell. Forbes preferred populated places where you'd get lost in the crowd. And the Crown Bar was perfect for his purposes. Good enough to make the tourist guides, it was a large renovated nineteenth-century pub on Great Victoria Street, which paralleled the multilane motorway dividing East and West Belfast.

The bar was next to a busy bookmaking parlor. Nothing like a pub and bookmaker to spark urban renewal, Forbes thought. He had come early and was standing diagonally across the street in the shadow of a control shack through which those entering and leaving the Forum Hotel had to pass. The gates to the circular drive leading to the hotel's entrance were locked. But security was much less stringent than during the years when downtown bombings were an everyday event.

The twelve-story Forum, the city's biggest, was classified as "deluxe." But it reminded Forbes of the bargain-rate chain accommodations he had seen all over the States. Behind the hotel was a huge parking lot where the main railroad terminal used to be. It had been blown up, however, and a new one was built on the other side of central Belfast, by the River Lagan, as part of what was euphemistically called a master plan to redevelop the city.

From the Forum's west windows, overlooking the parking lot, you could see the open grassy space, kind of a DMZ, where the motorway cut through, and on the far side the rise of hills toward the Falls Road. The foreign press corps stayed at the hotel, congregating in a bar on the second floor to exchange witticisms. The Special Branch usually had an operative lurking about to gather tidbits of gossip.

But the only memorable story Forbes could recall was about a newly arrived American magazine journalist. Thinking to take the pulse of the people, the journalist decided to ride in a black taxi up the Falls Road. When the city fathers drastically reduced bus service to the republican communities in West Belfast, the Provos had formed the black taxi association. These taxis, ancient models from London, stopped for anyone who hailed them. A ride cost thirty-five pence. The IRA took twenty percent. Downtown, the taxis lined up for passengers on Castle Street, a few blocks from the Forum. The scheme was so successful that the Protestant paramilitaries started their own routes up the Shankill from North Street, just beyond Castle. The journalist, unfamiliar with Belfast, somehow wandered past Castle Street to North. To the naked eye, all the black taxis looked the same. He approached a group of drivers and asked which one might be going by 51/53 Falls Road, the address for the *Sinn Fein* headquarters. At first the drivers stared at him, speechless. Finally one of them snarled, "Oh, 'tis the Falls you're wantin', is it? Well, step in, laddie, I'll get you there." He grabbed the journalist and tried to push him inside his taxi. Other drivers crowded around. Just then, two RUC cops on patrol showed up and the journalist managed to escape, taunts and jeers ringing in his ears. There were a lot of guffaws after the story circulated, and a lot of speculation about what could have happened to the journalist, none of it salutary.

Billy Dugan must have come in by taxi. Forbes

spotted him a block away walking by a bank from the direction of Castle Street. He was wearing dungarees and a blue cotton turtleneck. He turned into the Crown Bar with a quick side look back. Forbes stayed where he was for five minutes or so, surveying Great Victoria Street. No one appeared to have been following Dugan.

Forbes crossed over. As you entered the Crown, the bar proper, mahogany with copper insets and about sixty feet long, was on the left. Tables ran down the center. And along the right wall were a series of stalls called "snugs." Each snug had a wooden door that could be latched on the inside for privacy.

Forbes loved the feel of the place. They'd done a marvelous job. Nothing fake had been utilized in refurbishing it, which happened so often with what they called gentrification in the States.

A scattering of drinkers hugged the bar. Dugan was a third of the way down, hunched over a Guinness. Forbes touched him on the shoulder. He turned slowly, his face expressionless, his eyes as dead as the day Forbes had first seen him.

Forbes ordered a Harp. "You're looking well," he said.

"I am?"

"Yes. Put on some weight, I'd say. Good thing. You needed it. You looked a bit peaked the last time we were together."

"Had nothin' to do with me weight."

"Yes," Forbes said cheerily. "Probably so. Let's retire to one of the snugs, shall we? Have you had supper?"

"No."

Forbes gave a waitress fifty pence in case the pub

started filling up. "We don't want to be disturbed," he said. He glanced at the chalkboard menu and ordered a dozen Strangford oysters for each of them. After that, he said, they'd have sausages and chips. "And another Harp and a Guinness for my friend."

They sat facing one another on benches across an oak table. When the tiny succulent oysters, glistening in their shells, were brought, he latched the door. Forbes especially prized them. While Crankshaw was prattling on about wine at lunch, he had meant to ask if they ever served Strangfords at Stormont. But the answer undoubtedly would have been yes.

"How's the family?" he said.

"Fine."

"Talkative, aren't you? Well, we're here to talk, Billy," he said. He decided that a little reminder of how things were was in order. "No problems with the two hundred quid?"

"No, you's know that."

"Only wanted to make sure. Why didn't you tell us about the convention?"

"Because nobody asked, and besides the deal was I was only to speak to you. Anyways, it happened so fast there wasn't time. The delegates was picked weeks ago. But that's happened before, and nothin' ever happened. I wasn't a delegate," he said.

"Why *now*? Simply to twist the lion's tail?"

"That was part of it. But the convention had to vote its approval so *Sinn Fein* could sit in parliament in Dublin."

It was amazing, Forbes thought, that in the midst of all this carnage, the Provos were such sticklers for rules and regulations. But it was precisely this adherence to tradition that gave the IRA its staying power, its call on ghosts past for its historical imperative.

"We was told some of the lads been in place too long," Dugan said. "A change was in order. To get in better fightin' shape. There was equipment needed we didn't have."

"Who's the new northern commander?"

Dugan whispered, "Denis Dillon."

That was a test, and Dugan had passed. MI5 already had learned about Dillon's ascension. Nothing would be done about it, at least not for the time being. Better to know your devil than to contend with one in the dark.

"And the new quartermaster general?"

"That'd be Paul O'Rourke. He's in the Southern Command. Never crosses the border. He's a Kerryman, from around Tralee."

"Ah, the 'lovely and fair' Rose of Tralee," Forbes said. "Where's the quartermaster headquarters?"

"Down below. I don't know. It moves around. You's know that. We just send our requests up the line, and we get it or we don't."

There was a knock on the stall door. And for once Dugan jumped. But it was only the girl bringing the sausages and chips.

"Who's the O.C. for the Belfast Brigade?"

"It's been Terrance McBride."

This was another test. Just before leaving London, Forbes had learned that McBride indeed was terminally ill and out of the picture. "Come off it, Billy. You and I both know McBride's on his last legs from cancer."

"Yes, all right, I heard that. But I'm not messin'

you. It's fookin' incredible. Nobody knows who the man is. The crack is he's under wraps to handle the new equipment."

"What equipment?" Forbes said. He edged forward on his bench. "There's a great deal more in this for you than two hundred quid a month." Forbes did not mention the taped statement and the transcript signed by Dugan in MI5's possession. They both were aware of that.

Dugan hesitated. "The Redeye missiles," he said. "To knock out the whirlybirds."

Redeye missiles, Forbes thought. He'd been so right. The new equation.

"They're part of a big shipment."

"When's it due?"

"I don't know. Soon, I'm thinkin'."

"Where?"

"Don't know. I tell you, I'm not messin'. I'm just liaison. They don't call me in and say, 'Billy, you think we should do this, do that?' They tell me what they want."

"I'm going to fix that up for you, Billy," Forbes said. "I'm going to fix it so that they'll tell you just about anything you want to ask. You know the Corrigan dump, the one in the Poleglass Estate?"

Dugan looked as if he were about to bless himself. "Holy Mother of God," he said. "You're on to the Corrigan dump?"

"We are, yes," Forbes said.

"But how? He volunteered the dump himself."

"Our little secret. *We* volunteered the dump. He was arrested for a traffic violation, and the computer turned up any number of previous violations with unpaid fines, several hundred pounds. He was taken to the Woodbourne Barracks, where he said, and I believe I'm quoting him accurately, 'Isn't there a way out of this?' And, of course, there was. A light-sensitive bug was placed in the dump that transmitted a signal to the barracks whenever it was opened."

"His wife was in on it, too?"

"Yes, quite enthusiastically."

The operation had been conducted for almost nine months with admirable restraint, Forbes thought. Rifles had been doctored randomly so they would jam or misfire. From time to time defective remote detonators were introduced. Once, the Corrigans reported an assassination plot against an RUC sergeant. The sergeant and his family were removed from their home and plainclothes troops were brought in. One of the attacking Provisionals had been shot dead.

"Jesus, the Corrigans," Dugan said. "That explains plenty."

"Yes, I suppose it does," Forbes said agreeably, slicing into a sausage. "You'll be a hero after you reveal what they've been up to."

"What am I supposed to do? Walk in and tell the lads, 'Guess what, the Corrigans are workin' for the Brits,' and how do I know that? 'Oh, a little bird told me,' I says."

Forbes regretted having to give up the Corrigans. But that was the way it would have to be. He comforted himself with the thought that it was only a matter of time in any event before they'd be found out.

"No," he said, "you said it yourself. Too many things have been going wrong. You've been analyzing it. Something fishy about that dump. They ought to take a hard look. Now the bug's in the first crossbeam in the garage. Additionally, there's a radio beeper attached to the underside of a table by the bed in the house, which the Corrigans also used to alert us. Two beeps if weapons were being removed. A steady beep if they were in trouble.

"If your chaps can't find them on their own, you'll have to do it. 'My, what do we have here?' you'll say. Then you start finding out more about the new shipment. Some of that shipment could have ended up in the dump if it weren't for you. You remind them of that. You get right on this, Billy," Forbes said. "We'll meet here, same time, in a week. If something comes up before then, you ring in and say you have to speak to Brian. I'll get the message straight off. And, by the way, I believe we'll be able to manage ten thousand quid for this one."

Dugan stared at Forbes. "I'm thinkin', the same thing could happen to me as the Corrigans."

"No, Billy, I'm the difference, don't you know?" Forbes said, smiling. "The Corrigans aren't mine. But you are."

There were three hundred fifty black taxis in the Falls Road association. Gerry McMahon drove one of them. Officers in charge of the Belfast Brigade traditionally occupied themselves solely with their command, but McMahon had insisted on keeping his job. You couldn't come up with a better cover, he had argued. Instead of a headquarters that was shifted from safe house to safe house, his command post would be continually on the move. And driving up and down the Falls Road, listening to the talk of his passengers, gave him a feel for community mood shifts that he never could have gotten in the normal remoteness of his position.

In the black taxis, the space for baggage and the meter that you found in London was replaced with an extra front seat, and anyone delivering intelligence to the O.C. would simply slip in next to McMahon and pass on the information. None ever dreamed for an instant that the O.C. himself was the recipient of what was being imparted. McMahon was thought to be just another way station up the line to the fellow with the big stripes.

On the brigade staff so far, only his adjutant, his intelligence officer and his quartermaster knew who he was. He'd been lucky, and he had begun to believe that his luck would hold. He had only been imprisoned once, during the internment roundups in the early 'seventies, his photograph and prints on file, but that by itself didn't mean much. Even the Brits had acknowledged that hundreds of the internees hauled in then bore no relationship at all to the IRA. And it was in the Long Kesh cages that McMahon had perceived that he was part of a great drama being played out, that he had a sense of purpose and continuity, a destiny to fulfill, which would sustain him in his darkest moments, far beyond his immediate rage after his father's home had been firebombed.

The day always came back to him, the day Jack O'Connell, the chief of staff now, was conducting one of his discussion groups in the Kesh, and O'Connell had read from a writing and asked who did they think had written it? *"It is England who debauches and degrades you,"* O'Connell had read. *"It is England who foments and perpetuates, as far as in her lies, the spirit of religious dissension among you. . . . It is England who supports and nourishes that rotten faction among you, which, to maintain itself, is ready to sacrifice, and does daily sacrifice, your dearest rights."*

"That'd be the beautiful words of Patrick Henry Pearse," said one of the boys—and there was a murmur of approval, Pearse, the leader of the Easter uprising!—but O'Connell said, "No, listen to me, lads. It was Wolfe Tone, who led the rebellion of seventeen ninety-eight."

In the black taxi, Cathleen Cassidy sometimes rode with him. And now, five days after Forbes met Dugan in the Crown Bar, she shut the glass partition between the front and back seats and said, "I hear the Corrigans were banged last night."

"Yes, there'll be an announcement shortly, later today, the whys and wherefores."

"Serves them fookin' right."

"Yes, I suppose."

"What's that, *suppose?*"

"'Tisn't easy, executing a woman. I can't pretend to like it."

"Fundamentally you are a sexist, like all the rest," she said.

He glanced at her, so demure in her black cotton jacket and skirt, staring straight ahead, her freckled aquiline nose in profile, hands locked in her lap. Her black hair, parted in the middle, was pulled back and held at the nape of her neck with a tortoise-shell clasp. The women, he thought, in the end they were always the strongest. And maybe in the beginning as well.

"He said," McMahon said, "he didn't know why he did it. It was the wife who convinced him. They had to look after themselves, he said she said. He was on his knees for mercy. He said he'd be a double agent. Just give him another chance."

"And what did she say?"

"Nothin' really. She said we were all fools," McMahon said. "At least they had no kids. It was all there, in front of our nose, what they were doin'. The surprise was that it took Billy Dugan to find them out. Billy's a good lad, solid he is, but you wouldn't think he'd be the one to backtrack to all the little things that went wrong. 'We should take a looksee,' Billy said, and the lads went into the premises when they weren't there, and the bugs were located, actually it was Billy who located them, and he'll be rewarded."

McMahon stopped while a British foot patrol swung out of the Springfield Road. "I'm off to Derry tomorrow to see Denis Dillon," he said. "O'Houlihan's got an American writer wants to interview him."

That was the other advantage of having a commercial license. In his spare time he drove for O'Houlihan's car service. O'Houlihan was always in demand with the foreign press whenever there was a big flap going on, and when McMahon told O'Houlihan he had to get somewhere, he got the first available hire. O'Houlihan was aware that it was more than McMahon who was doing the asking.

It was a perfect foil against the roadblocks. Sometimes they just waved you through after a cursory examination. Other times, they held you until they checked your credentials by radio. A Brit squaddie, though, could suddenly decide he didn't like your looks and could plant something, like a stick of gelignite explosive, in the boot of your car and say, "What's this?" and you'd be taken to an army barracks and then worked over in a RUC interrogation center and then as likely as not it'd be the Crumlin Road jail and the Diplock court and finally some fine years in the H-Blocks. But this would not happen if you were in a white shirt and black tie, driving a foreign correspondent or a foreign television crew to an interview.

And right now, whether or not British intelligence knew that Denis Dillon was the new northern commander, he was still under constant surveillance, and anyone seen near him or in his company automatically went on the suspect list, unless you were that same chauffeur, in which case you'd hardly be noticed.

McMahon picked up the American writer at the Forum Hotel. He wanted to sit democratically in front, but McMahon said that it was against company policy. For class-conscious Brit soldiers, appearances mattered. Driver of no consequence in front, master in back.

Still, the writer, whose name was Behn, wanted to talk. As they drove northwest out of Belfast toward Derry on the M2 motorway, Behn asked, "Where do you live, Gerry?"

"In Ballymurphy, in West Belfast."

"You must be Catholic then."

"Yes, you might say that."

"I'm Jewish myself, you know. Gives me a neutral

position. I can see the Catholic side, but the way it stands, it looks insoluble to me. The Catholics want power, and the Protestants, the loyalists, the unionists, whatever you call them, have the power and they're not going to surrender it. If the British weren't here, you people would be tearing yourselves apart."

McMahon didn't say anything. Behn was parroting the Brit line. He must have been thoroughly briefed by the British foreign office. All McMahon needed was for this Behn to mention up at Stormont about a driver who had told him that the bloodletting couldn't be any worse than it was and that if the British would only leave, maybe the factions in Northern Ireland would be forced to face reality and work things out, that the working class, Protestant and Catholic, would discover they were in the same exploited boat, and somebody would say, "Oh, really? Who was that driver? Do you recall his name?"

"I'll say one thing," Behn said. "The problem with the loyalists, you want to call them that, is they're only *against* things. Against power sharing. Against a united Ireland. Against the British leaving. I was interviewing this loyalist guy down at the shipyards. I said, 'Well, what are you for?' and he said, 'If it comes to it, I'm for repartition, the three western counties,' and I said, 'You can't be serious,' and he said, 'I am, I'll never submit to the pope's rule.' "

Behn appeared sunk in deep thought. "But I can't go along with IRA violence," he said. "Won't get them anywhere. Turns people off."

Since Behn was Jewish, McMahon ventured, "Some say the IRA's like the Haganah and the Irgun was, fightin' for the state of Israel. They say the Brits never left anywhere on their own."

"Yeah, yeah, well maybe," Behn said.

They hit the roadblock after climbing over the Sperrin mountains. The roadblock was a major one, traffic stopped in both directions. McMahon saw the backup paratroopers lining the slopes on each side of the highway.

A paratrooper with an automatic rifle suddenly came up behind them. He stuck his head partway through the open window by Behn. "What's that you're writin' down," he said, reaching for his notebook.

Behn pulled it away. "Hey, what the hell do you think you're doing?"

The paratrooper stepped back, bringing up his rifle. "Out of the car," he said.

A lieutenant in his red beret, barely out of his teens, hurried up.

"Listen," Behn said to him. "I'm a reporter. From America." The lieutenant examined Behn's credentials. Now there was a paratrooper on the other side of the car. The lieutenant looked for a moment as though he was going to radio in for a confirmation, but then he said, "All right, move on. The boys are a bit jumpy. There was an incident down the road."

"An incident, what incident?" Behn said.

The lieutenant ignored him. "Off you go," he said to McMahon. It was the first time anyone seemed to acknowledge McMahon's presence.

"That was one mean mother," Behn said. There was a shaky edge to his voice. "They all like that?"

"On the rough side, the paras are," McMahon said.

A few miles farther, out of the mountains, they came down an incline into Derry, past well-kept houses with tiny neat lawns. "What's this, where are we?" Behn said.

"Waterside. Loyalist territory."

They turned onto Craigavon Bridge over the River Foyle and headed up to the old inner city with its twisting cobblestone streets and twenty-foot-high ramparts, ancient cannons still in place. McMahon took Behn to the west wall. There was a steep drop below to narrow flats, almost a gorge, before a hill opposite them rose sharply. In the late afternoon sunlight, the hill was cloaked in a blue haze from thousands of kitchen chimney pots.

"What's that?" Behn asked.

"That'd be the Bogside, sir, where Mr. Dillon resides," McMahon said. "Down there was where Bloody Sunday was, where the paras opened fire on the civil rights marchers."

Dillon lived in a row house. On the corner, McMahon spotted the unmarked Special Branch car parked so that everybody entering and leaving could be observed and photographed. He pulled his cap low over his face, got out and opened the door for Behn. He took Behn's attaché case and ushered him up the steps and rang the bell. "I'll go in for a cup of tea, you don't mind," he said.

"You think it'll be okay?"

"I'm certain. Mr. Dillon is most hospitable, they say."

A dark-eyed girl about sixteen, one of Dillon's daughters, opened the door. After Behn identified himself, she said, "My father's expecting you. Come in, please. He'll be with you shortly." She led him to the parlor. McMahon went directly to the kitchen, where Dillon was waiting.

"Gerry," he said. "Not good, the Corrigans."

"They got what they deserved," McMahon said. He sounded like Cathleen, he thought.

"Just in the nick. Part of the shipment could've landed there."

"Yes."

"The Redeyes have been accomplished. Sean Walsh reports the shipment will be coming within a month's time. Jack O'Connell says Paul O'Rourke down at Tralee will be handling it personally. The trawler won't come in directly. A fishing boat from Fenit, by Tralee, will meet her out in the Atlantic and the transfer will be made at sea. The equipment will be stashed south of the border. The launchers and the rockets will be brought up separately."

"I'm concerned about this Ahearn fellow," McMahon said. "Sean says he's a real gangster, a dope dealer. Out for himself."

"Gerry, we have no choice. We do what we have to."

"Yes, you're right."

"What's this journalist like?"

McMahon told him about the roadblock. "You'll have no problem."

"Thanks for your vote of confidence," he said, smiling.

"Where's me tea?" McMahon said.

"Tea, hell. This calls for Black Bush." Dillon poured out two measures of the Irish whiskey. They clinked glasses. "To the shipment," Dillon said.

Chapter

11

Jamie took a bus from Boston to New Bedford.

The *Sea King*'s two runs for Tommy Ahearn were done, and Kevin Dowd had said, "How's that captain, what's his name, workin' out?"

"Foncecas," Jamie said. "Manuel Foncecas. He's okay. Knows the boat. Knows how to handle her. But for the big trip over there, the boat needs a lot of work."

"The time's near. Make me a list, Jamie boy. Get right to it. Tomorrow, if you can."

There must have been four tons in the first load and six the next time, Jamie figured, and now that it was over, the tension between him and Ingrid had eased.

"Look," he'd argued, "this stuff is coming in all the time. Everybody's smoking it. You can get high just walking around Harvard Square. At least the money's going for the cause. These guys aren't in it for themselves. They wouldn't be doing it if there was any other way."

"I don't care. They have no right to ask you to jeopardize yourself like this. You could go to jail. You think a judge is going to say, 'Oh, now I understand. You were just helping to import marijuana here so the IRA could get weapons to drive out the British.' You think that will make any difference?"

"*Liebchen*," he said. "Nothing's going to happen. Kevin told me that it's been fixed. I don't know how, but I believe him. This is the first time I've ever had a chance to do something. I don't want to always hear about what other people are doing. Or read about it. I want to be a player. Look at Sean Walsh, what he went through, in that blanket . . . in that cell."

He did not tell her of the excitement that pulsed through him, the danger of it all, to be on the edge of life, not just carrying on like most of the guys in school he knew, all wrapped up in how much money they were going to make, their status, their future prominence. And nothing *had* happened. Those two runs had gone off without a hitch.

Each time, the mother ship, a Panamanian-registered freighter, had come up the Atlantic seaboard with Colombian marijuana taken on in the Turks and Caicos Islands in the Caribbean.

The *Sea King* would leave New Bedford, sail past Gay Head on Martha's Vineyard and Nantucket and hook up with the freighter two hundred miles in the Atlantic southeast of Montauk Point on Long Island, where she would receive the bales tightly wrapped in sheets of heavy green plastic. She'd then sail north around Cape Cod across Massachusetts Bay into Boston harbor to a pier by the New England Fish Exchange, where a couple of customs agents came on board, barely glanced around and gave the trawler a clean bill of health.

Jamie did not know that they were from a squad of "Danny's Boys," nor that after he left the trawler, the cargo was trucked to a warehouse that Ahearn had on D Street in South Boston for weighing and repackaging, and that what wasn't allocated for immediate distribution was stashed in an isolated farmhouse Ahearn had leased in the cranberry bogs around Middleboro. He did not know that all the profits were going to Ahearn, that all the cause was getting in return was the use of the trawler. "There's no gain fillin' his head with that, is there now?" Dowd had said to Walsh.

In New Bedford, as he walked along the wharf toward the *Sea King,* gulls soared in the sparkling sunlight, the air heavy with the smell of fish and the sea. A crewman on another trawler waved to him. God, how he loved the sea, Jamie thought. That was Ingrid's new concern, the trip across the Atlantic. "It'll be fun," he told her. "I've always wanted to do it."

The thing now was to go over the *Sea King* from top to bottom, to review every potential trouble spot he'd noted thus far. For sure there had to be better navigation equipment for a pinpoint rendezvous off the Irish coast.

To his surprise, the trawler was getting ready to cast off. "So you're coming?" Manuel Foncecas said.

"Where?"

"We're making another run, man. You don't know?"

"I thought it was just two runs, not three."

Foncecas shrugged. "I got a call. I just do what they tell me. It's for tonight."

Dowd hadn't said anything about a third run. He knew, though, that Jamie was going to New Bedford anyway. Maybe something unexpected had come up.

"So?" Foncecas said.

"So, sure," Jamie said. "Hey, let's go."

But when they got under way, Foncecas said it was going to be the same as before, the same location, the same old beat-up coastal tramp, the *Rosa*, the "Colon, Panama" on her fantail so badly chipped you could hardly make it out. When he first saw her, Jamie had the feeling that at any moment she would disintegrate in a great cloud of rust.

The sun was almost down when they met, the ocean as glassy as it would ever get, so the *Sea King* came alongside without difficulty. The transfer of the bales took no more than fifteen minutes. Afterward, Foncecas said, "I am going for a farewell drink with the captain. See, he's waving to me. It's only polite."

"Okay, but make it quick."

Half an hour later, Jamie was saying, "Come on, come on," when he heard it, first a far-off drone, and then it got louder, so that the noise seemed to fill the whole sky, and then Jamie saw the coast guard patrol plane swooping in low, headed directly toward them. The plane circled overhead twice. He could practically hear the cameras clicking, recording the *Sea King*'s name and home port. Now Foncecas was scrambling down the Jacob's ladder clutching a package.

As the plane turned west, away from them, the *Sea King* moved off. When they were sure the plane was gone, they started dumping the bales. "That package you had, too," Jamie said to Foncecas.

"Package?"

"Listen, Manny, I don't know what's in it, and I don't want to. Just dump it, like right now," and with the two of them standing head-to-head in the wheelhouse, Foncecas finally said, "Yes, you are correct," and Jamie, in recounting it to Ingrid, would remember that it was kind of a test, and he had passed.

Pushing north, they picked up the radio traffic from an oncoming cutter, but she was at least two hours away. Then it became evident the cutter was trying for the mother ship, so they had some breathing room. There could be intercepts up ahead, but the coast guard was stretched thin, Foncecas said, especially in the summer with so many pleasure boats getting messed up.

They got lucky the next morning when they rounded the cape on a course for Boston. A fleet of trawlers was returning from fishing the Grand Banks, and Foncecas maneuvered into the middle of them to escape any radar surveillance. And as soon as they were within range, Jamie got on the marine phone to the Excelsior Yacht Club and asked for "Patrick O'Malley." It was urgent, he said.

An hour later, Dowd called back. They spoke in prearranged code that had been set up for the first run in case anything went wrong. "We've had engine problems," Jamie said. "Make the necessary arrangements."

Stunned, Dowd called Ahearn. That was when he learned about the third run. Then he got in touch with Daniel P. Daugherty, who started cursing at once. "Can we go into that at another time, Dan?" he said as calmly as he could. "First things first."

The Drug Enforcement Administration had copied the original coast guard report of the sighting. It took a while to obtain the necessary search warrant. When the trawler could not be found in New Bedford, the net widened. Then an alert employee in the Boston harbormaster's office noticed the *Sea King* chugging in. But by the time DEA agents arrived, one of Danny's Boys, Gerald Cummins, and another customs agent already had boarded her.

Kevin Dowd, slipping behind gawkers on the pier, watched a Boston police car, siren whining, screech to a stop. On the *Sea King*, there was a lot of finger pointing and raised voices.

When Jamie came off the trawler, Dowd followed him down the pier, waiting until Northern Avenue to fall in beside him. "What happened?" Dowd said.

Jamie glared at Dowd. "That's what I'd like to know."

"Easy, lad. I mean just now, on the boat."

"There were some DEA agents, and one of them started yelling that they had a warrant, and a customs guy said, well, that was tough. Customs got there first, and it was their case and it was a false alarm and that was the end of it. The customs guy said customs didn't need a warrant for probable cause. He said the DEA guy could look it up. The customs guy said he was sick and tired of the DEA always trying to move in, like customs didn't know what they were doing. The cops didn't say much of anything," Jamie said. "So what did happen? You told me everything was arranged."

"Why didn't you tell me about this run?" Dowd said.

"Tell you what? I thought you knew. Another thing, Foncecas came off the tramp with a package. I made him toss it. I'm sure it was coke. You never said anything about coke."

"It was a mistake. It won't happen again. Unfortunately, it's an imperfect world. The next time the *Sea King* sails, it's all the way. We must concentrate on that, Jamie. Trust me," Dowd said.

That wasn't quite the end of it, though.

A DEA agent was sore enough to tip a Boston *Herald* reporter that one of the crew members on the suspect trawler was a Harvard student named Jamie McGuire. It made for a small item, picked up subsequently for two replays on an all-news radio station, in which customs agent Gerald Cummins, asked to comment, declared that the *Sea King*'s skipper, identified as Manuel Foncecas of New Bedford, had explained that his trawler experienced engine failure on the high seas and that the freighter in question kindly came to his aid. There was no evidence, Cummins was quoted as saying, to indicate otherwise. There wasn't a trace of narcotics, or anything else illegal for that matter, to be found on the boat.

Left dangling was a quote from the manager of the New England Fish Exchange. "I never bought a pound of anything off the *Sea King*," he said.

• • •

In the study of Tommy Ahearn's country place in New Hampshire near Nashua, just over the Massachusetts line, Daniel P. Daugherty was livid. "Two fuckin' loads was the deal," he screamed. "*Two*! One, two—not three, goddammit!"

Kevin Dowd said nothing. He was as angry himself. Ahearn, with all his greed, had ordered the third marijuana run on his own. Daugherty kept it up. "The whole fuckin' thing could a gone down 'count a you. I'll have your ass for this."

Ahearn sneered at him, Savonarola eyes protruding over pinched cheeks. "You'll have nothin'. You're in this deep as me, and don't forget it."

Some of the bombast went out of Daugherty. The crimson splotches receded. "What's that supposed to mean?" he said.

Both of them appeared to have forgotten Dowd's presence—Kevin Dowd, always obeisant to Ahearn, forever deferring to Daugherty. "That'll be enough," he said.

Startled, they turned toward him.

"I speak for the IRA council," Dowd said, instantly conjuring up, as he was certain it would, a cabal of shadowy figures looming over them, judging them, faceless, remorseless, hard men, men suddenly removed from their experience, unknown, to be feared.

"Dan here's right," he said, "and there'll be no more of this. But what's done's done. We have to get on with it. Tommy, the trawler's got to go into drydock. The McGuire lad says the engine needs an overhaul, new cables for the hoist. New navigation equipment for the voyage over there."

"He's just a kid, what's he know?" Ahearn said.

"He knows."

"How much?"

"Thirty thousand, give or take."

"We'll split it, me and you."

"Hah," said Daugherty. "You're really hurtin', you are, gettin' one twenty-five an ounce."

"That's on the street. There's the overhead. The boat, the crew, the warehouses, the distribution, the sweeteners. Fuckin' everyone's got hands out everywhere. And we lost the last load."

"There'll be no split," Dowd said. "That was the bargain. The boat must be seaworthy in every regard."

Ahearn had no choice. He knew it, and they knew it. "Just make sure you don't go overboard; it's my money," he said.

They walked to a barn about fifty yards from the house. The Redeyes were there, and the Composition 4 plastic explosive, rifles and handguns, boxes of ammunition and grenades. Ahearn pointed to a pile of packages in clear plastic in the corner. "Bulletproof vests," he said. "Fifteen. Police ones, the best. Compliments a couple Somerville cops, couple downtown. Passed the word what they're for, boys in blue happy to help out. No charge. My contribution."

"Oh, you're a prince," Daugherty said.

Dowd cut him off. "Very thoughtful of you, Tommy," he said. "There's more stuff comin' into the yacht club I'll be bringin' up. And we'll be hittin' the armory Saturday after this."

• • •

On Long Island, at the beach, Michael McGuire couldn't help smiling as he read an account in the local paper about a bale of marijuana that had washed ashore not a mile away. According to the story, a considerable portion of the bale was missing. The night before, the police said, a bunch of students had gotten together for a cookout preparatory to returning to college right where the bale had landed. One of the students had said, "We didn't see anything. Who needs grass to get high? This great sea air is all we need."

On Tuesday morning in his office he opened an envelope with the return address of the agency's Boston branch. There was no indication of the sender's name. Inside was a Xerox of a five-paragraph *Herald* article, headlined:

HARVARD STUDENT
IN DRUG PROBE

He flew to Boston that evening without telephoning.

Jamie and Ingrid lived on Putnam Avenue in Cambridge, about midway between Harvard and Massachusetts General on the other side of the Charles River. Putnam was lined with large formerly one-family woodframes that had been converted into multiple residences.

It was a garden apartment, in the rear. He walked in the dark toward a light at the end of a path between houses. Flagstone steps curved through a profusion of white and orange impatiens at the peak of flowering.

He could see Jamie and Ingrid through the sliding glass doors. Jamie, barefooted and bare-chested, in shorts with a swirling floral design, sat on a sofa against the far wall bent over his guitar. Ingrid was on the floor next to him, legs curled under her. She was in cutoffs and a blue halter, her head resting on Jamie's knee.

In his anger, he hesitated for a moment to take in the scene. They looked like an ad layout that held forth all the youthful, carefree promise of life, he thought. The only thing missing was a bottle of the latest California wine cooler to hit the market.

He rapped sharply on the glass. And again. Finally Jamie looked up and came toward the doors. Michael McGuire saw Ingrid looking up quizzically.

"Dad!" Jamie said. "What are you doing here?"

Michael McGuire stepped inside. There was a slight whir from the air conditioner. He could taste the sudden tension in the room. The kitchen, separated from the rest of the room by a counter, was on his left. The end of a bed showed through an open door. On the right wall there was a huge poster of a masked IRA volunteer holding up an automatic rifle with both hands. Underneath, it said, "We Mean to Be Free." Another poster, for the movie *Casablanca*, was over the sofa. It showed tinted heads of Humphrey Bogart and Ingrid Bergman. A Hal B. Wallis production, it said.

"This," Michael McGuire said, thrusting the Xerox of the Boston *Herald* article at him.

"Oh, Dad, come on, it was just grass."

Michael McGuire was left momentarily speechless. Jamie hadn't even bothered to deny it. Ingrid was sitting upright now on the sofa. "My son, the dope dealer," Michael McGuire said.

Jamie flushed under his deeply tanned face, except for the tip of his nose which remained slightly red and peeling. It was always like that, Michael McGuire remembered, during summers at the beach. Jamie's voice rose a notch. "I'm not a dope dealer," he said. "It was to get money for the movement, for the Provos."

"That makes a difference, makes it all okay?"

"Yes, it does!" Jamie was leaning forward on the balls of his feet, hands clenched. Michael McGuire remembered another confrontation, in the middle of the bay, the time Jamie in his endless despair after Mary Alice died had swum across the boat channel. They were head to head on that, and Michael McGuire had had this terrible vision that one day they could be in a physical fight, and it seemed that moment had come, except, he thought, looking at Jamie's muscular frame, it probably wouldn't be much of a fight.

But then Jamie abruptly walked a few feet away before he whirled and said, "Yes, it makes a difference. I believe in it. What do you believe in, what did you ever believe in?"

Michael McGuire wanted to say, Once I believed in your mother, and me, and you, and that we would be happy in our lives together, and what was wrong with that?

Ingrid was standing now, and Jamie walked to her and stood beside her, his face contorted. "You wanted me to be educated, and I was," he shouted.

"Where do you get off being so high and mighty? What were *you* doing in the fucking Counterintelligence Corps? Helping fucking Nazi war criminals escape, that's what! So they could help us make rockets, help us spy on the fucking Commies. Jesus Christ, that was some excuse, wasn't it? Must make you feel real proud. You don't even have to go to Harvard to know that. It's in the goddamn fucking papers every day, some fucking Nazi with blood all over his hands living it up in Wisconsin, in California somewhere, on Long Island, in Florida."

He said, "I'll never forget that limey you brought to the apartment after Mom died, that Brit intelligence stiff—'I say, Anthony Seth-Jones at your pleasure,'" Jamie said, mimicking an English accent. "'No dirty work's too dirty for us. And I know you will give your father the support he needs.' What crap! Him and his fucking Guards mustache. He probably led you around like you had a ring in your nose."

Michael McGuire struggled to keep his composure. *Hamburg!* And in his head, Seth-Jones was saying again, "Well, now, Michael, perhaps you can give us a hand. This chap, Otto Ellersieck, unhappily wandered into your zone and is being held for the Frenchies. They're after him hammer and tongs. Throwing in all sorts of paper. Naughty boy, Ellersieck. Ex-SS. Seems he ran a bit amok around Dijon. Saw to the transport of a number of our Jewish brethren to the fatherland. On the old French Resistance list. The Russians want him, too, for some transgressions in, I believe, Lithuania, but that's out of the question, of course. The point is that he's put together quite a network for us, and we'd like him back, on the lowest-level transfer, of course. He's rather like your Klaus Barbie, although really minor in comparison, I must say, and we did help your chaps on him, after all."

And Michael McGuire had done it. He never heard of Ellersieck after that. But he remembered him when he read about Barbie being found in Bolivia after so many years and extradited for trial in France. Remembered and quickly cast it out of his mind. Until now.

He wanted to say, Can't you understand? It was different then. "Yes, it makes a difference," Jamie had just said.

Ingrid spoke for the first time. "It was terrible to let those people go unpunished, to reward them even," she said. "As someone of German ancestry, I am deeply ashamed."

That's tough, he thought. He didn't need this.

"Listen to me," Michael McGuire said. "Everybody makes mistakes, and I'm right up there. But that doesn't mean you have to follow in my footsteps. This is crazy what you're doing. Take it from an expert. You're asking for trouble. Okay, I'll buy what you've been saying. The Brits don't belong in Northern Ireland and so forth, and I won't make any more wisecracks. But for Christ's sake, Jamie, there's got to be a better way. Sing at some goddamn fund-raiser, I don't know, something."

"It's almost over anyway. There's only one more delivery left."

"Jamie, please."

"It's not what you think, Dad. It's not grass. It's

what this is all about. We have to bring some material over, and it'll be legal. I mean, we won't be entering any territorial waters or anything like that. It was set up that way, and I can't back out now. They're counting on me."

"What material?"

"Arms, for the war. They need help. Things are really tough there now. You meet some of these people, you'd understand."

"My God, arms! So more people can die?"

"They're dying plenty, as it is, and they're never going to give up."

"Jamie, even a majority of Catholics there aren't for the IRA."

"You took a vote on the American Revolution, there wouldn't have been one then, either. The thing is the older people are afraid. It's the young, alienated people who say fight. It's their only hope, either that or leave, which a lot of them are doing. But the Provos couldn't exist without community support. That's the simple truth."

"It's not your fight."

"What about Vietnam?"

"What about it?"

"How come nobody ever told those fifty thousand dead guys on that wall in Washington it wasn't their fight? I read about it, the big domino theory. If we don't go in, China takes over. So we lose, and then Vietnam tells the Chinese to go fuck themselves, and now we're pals with China. Those guys died for no reason. At least there's a reason for this. In Northern Ireland, nothing changes. Only it's not important enough for the world to give a damn."

"You're so full of shit it isn't funny," Michael McGuire said.

"Thanks a lot, Dad, and fuck you, too! Why don't you call the cops and have me arrested?"

Michael McGuire stared at his son. Then he turned quickly and went out through the sliding glass doors. On the path, in his rage, he stumbled and fell into the impatiens. He staggered up and got to the street, his breath coming in short, erratic bursts. He walked he didn't know how far until he found a cab to take him to the airport. He barely made the last shuttle. In his seat, his brain felt as if it were going to explode inside his skull. His pulse beat against his temples. He kept pressing his fingers against them to relieve the pressure. Gradually the anger subsided and the pain started. He tried to focus. That fucking Nazi business had thrown him completely. Talk about being mugged. And it was so unfair. But to try to explain it, even now to himself in the darkness of the plane, sounded like such a pathetic rationale. He thought about calling Jamie as soon as he got back to New York. Get this back on the track. Then he knew that he was just going to have to ride it out.

That's what Harry Hollander said also, the next night. He had gone to the poker game to try to distract himself, but it was really to talk to someone, namely Hollander.

On the street, after the game, Hollander said, "Michael, I've never seen you play so badly."

"I've got a lot on my mind. It's my son."

"What's wrong," Hollander said, getting right to it, "is he a junkie? Seems like half the people I know have offspring hooked on heroin or something."

"No, if you can believe it, he's gotten mixed up with the IRA. You know, Ireland. It's serious."

They were on Park Avenue, passing the Regency bar. "Come on, let me buy you a drink," Hollander said.

Michael McGuire gulped a double vodka. He told Hollander about seeing Jamie in Cambridge. He left out the Nazi part.

"How old's Jamie now?" Hollander said.

"Nineteen."

"Listen, Michael, I got to tell you something. I was around nineteen and in college, too, when the Six Day War broke out in Israel, except I didn't know it was only going to be six days. I flew right over. It was practically finished when I got there, but I figured maybe it wasn't, you know. So I joined the Israeli army. I spent two fucking years in a fucking tank. My parents went nuts. I could have lost my citizenship. I didn't care."

Hollander said, "I got a friend, Hungarian. And when the Russian army rolled into Budapest after that uprising—when was it, 'fifty-six, whatever?—he went there like a shot. I mean, he was there in the streets fighting, and he got out okay. He had to do it. You tell me Jamie brought up Vietnam. Well, he's right," said Hollander. "But don't forget, some kids went because they wanted to. Nineteen, twenty, twenty-one, they had to find out what it was like, being on the line, prove something to themselves. Maybe it was the quickest way to grow up. Maybe it wasn't a problem for you."

Hollander shrugged. "Sons," he said, "what can I say?"

"I can't help thinking," Michael McGuire said, "that none of this would be happening if his mother were still alive."

At the Excelsior Yacht Club Kevin Dowd signed a United Parcel receipt for a crate of twelve .223 Colt AR-15 model SP-1 semi-automatic rifles from a gun dealer in Colorado. He got a dock hand to help him wrestle the crate into the Ford van.

For months Dowd had been thumbing through the *Shotgun News,* pondering, selecting and ordering weapons and ammunition from dealers in California, Colorado, Wisconsin, Georgia and Maryland.

The *Shotgun News* was a thick tabloid published three times a month on newspaper stock that correctly trumpeted that it was "The Trading Post for anything that shoots." Its two hundred fifty pages were crammed with ads and news about every conceivable pistol, rifle, submachine gun and machine gun except restricted U.S. military items. In the last issue a columnist was railing against congressional efforts to restrict the sale of newly manufactured machine guns to private citizens. It would, the columnist wrote, "obliterate whatever is left of the Second Amendment" to keep and bear arms.

For deliveries that crossed state lines, most of the ads required a copy of a commercial federal firearms license signed in ink. These licenses were issued by the Bureau of Alchohol, Tobacco and Firearms for three dollars once it was determined that the applicant did not have a criminal record or had not been a patient in a mental institution.

Obtaining a fake license wasn't hard. Tommy Ahearn had a friendly gunshop owner in Maine and another near Worcester, Massachusetts. He got photocopies of their licenses. Kevin Dowd whited out the original name and address and two or three digits in the license number, ran off dozens of now blank licenses, typed in new digits and the name "Patrick O'Malley, c/o the Excelsior Yacht Club" and forwarded the doctored licenses together with money orders for his purchases. Gun merchants were glad to oblige. While sales records were kept, they remained on file, and you could count on nothing more happening unless one of the weapons was involved in a crime. If that occurred, federal firearms agents would go to the manufacturer and trace the weapon through its serial number, assuming it was still ascertainable, to a wholesaler or wholesalers and finally to the retail outlet and buyer. By then Dowd would be long gone. And officials at the yacht club could truthfully say that they didn't know anything about any gun shipments, that yes, they recalled a Patrick O'Malley, but had no idea of his present whereabouts.

After the crate of AR-15s was in the van, Dowd went into the club bar for a beer. He listened to two men talking a few feet away. One of the men was saying that it had gotten too rough for his wife, that this summer was the last time. For the past three years, he said, they had taken two young kids from Belfast, one Catholic and one Protestant, for a vacation through the auspices of an international organization promoting peace and understanding. The kids had arrived, of course, despising one another, but after a while, tasting American life, they would become close and then the time for them to return came and a pall would settle over the house, and you knew that they were thinking about what they were going back to. It was too heartwrenching, he said his wife had said.

The pair this summer looked to be the worst at first, the man said. Wouldn't talk at all. "It was weird how they got together," he said. "We took them to the park for the fireworks on the Fourth and we had a picnic, you know, and the two of them staying as far apart as possible, and then after dark the Roman candles started going up, and the silver chrysanthemums and the whistlers and the peonies—I mean it was some show, were you there?—and right at the first boom, they dove under the car, and I bent down to look and there they were, shaking and clutching each other tight as ticks, and I said, 'Hey, come on out, it's just fireworks,' and one of them, I forget which, said, 'Yeah, sure, we know,' and they just didn't move an inch."

Dowd finished his beer and got up and went to the van and drove to the barn at Ahearn's place in New Hampshire to open the crate and check out the merchandise.

In New Bedford, the *Sea King* went into drydock. With this new equipment, the captain, Manuel Foncecas, boasted to other crews, his boat would sweep the Grand Banks clean. He already knew that he would be getting a $20,000 bonus for his trip across the Atlantic.

Chapter

12

In Belfast, Billy Dugan slipped into a stall at the Crown Bar and stared at Forbes and said, "It was terrible what happened to the Corrigans."

"Yes, could happen to any of us, you or me. Not a pleasant prospect."

"Usually they don't execute women," Dugan said, as if he hadn't heard Forbes. "Usually they tell her she has twenty-four hours to get out. 'Run to your masters,' they'd say. But this was too serious, they said. She was directly responsible for the death of an active service volunteer."

"They must have been pleased with your insights."

"Yes, I was complimented. They said it was fortunate that I had recognized the obvious. I'm to be promoted."

"Wonderful, Billy. You deserve it. Now what about the shipment?"

"The security's very tight."

"*Billy.*"

"It'll be comin' from America, I don't know where from. But the boat won't land in Ireland. A fishin' vessel will meet it and the transfer will be at sea."

"What vessel? Where? Out with it, Billy."

"I don't know the name. It'll be a Fenit vessel, though, they say."

"Fenit? I'm afraid my geography isn't quite what it should be."

"Fenit's by Tralee on the coast. A wee fishin' village. The quartermaster general himself is personally in charge, Paul O'Rourke. Wherever Paul O'Rourke goes, you're sure to find the vessel."

"When, Billy, when?"

"Less than a month's time, they say. Around the end of September. First week of October. They're not sure exactly themselves yet."

"Very good. You see if you can't do better on the dates, any more details. You can reach me the same way. And after it's done, there's that bonus I promised."

Forbes unlatched the stall door and ordered another Harp and a Guinness and two dozen Strangford oysters. He smiled at Dugan, savoring the thought of the oysters he'd be shortly devouring, savoring this moment, knowing that he had arrived at a dramatic turning point in his MI5 career, the kind he had always fantasized about.

In the morning he returned to London and reported the news to Roger Gravesend, who managed quite well to play the office game of superior to subordinate, as if Forbes had told him nothing more than that he thought it was going to rain tomorrow.

"Ah, yes, interesting," Gravesend said. But Gravesend had betrayed himself, reaching instantly for a Marlboro once he realized the import of what Forbes was saying, fumbling twice to light it. Forbes could see that he could barely contain his excitement.

And that afternoon Gravesend summoned him. "I have taken this up with the director general and we've seen the home secretary. First time I've accompanied him," he said with uncommon candor, almost as an aside. "You're to be commended, Brian. We're all very appreciative, and it won't be forgotten. Arrangements are being made at the cabinet level for you to go to Dublin."

Three days later he flew in for an appointment with the republic's minister of justice, the home secretary's opposite number. The *Garda* commissioner also was present. Beneath the surface civility, Forbes could sense the wariness. Ah, English and Irish, he thought. That was the maddening aspect of the IRA. It was an open secret that given its domestic economic woes, the last thing the republic's leadership wanted was to take on the burden of the six northern counties. Yet it was political suicide to say this out loud. It was right there in the Irish constitution, that the "national territory" consisted of the whole of Ireland. The way out for them was to decry violence as a solution.

He was to use his own discretion, Gravesend had said. And in his briefing, Forbes did not go beyond his possession of unspecified, reliable information. "The key," he said, "is this man O'Rourke. He must be monitored continually, with the utmost care taken that he's not warned off."

"I do believe we have that capability," the *Garda* commissioner said in a cool tone.

"I haven't the slightest doubt," Forbes said. "It's of paramount importance that the seizure be made to appear a fortunate accident. I can't emphasize this enough, and I'd welcome your thoughts."

"Easy enough, that," said the minister, anxious to intervene. "Illicit salmon fishing is greatly on the increase. Our patrol craft routinely conduct boardings."

"Excellent," Forbes said, smiling broadly.

"They're such supercilious bastards," the minister of justice said after Forbes left. "Hands across the Irish Sea, hah! Look how they bought that file clerk of yours to feed them Lord knows what."

"That was MI Six," the commissioner said. "I'm certain this fellow's Five."

"It doesn't matter. They're all alike. You know, my da, God rest his soul, was with Patrick Pearse. Inside the post office in 'sixteen, he was. He took me on a walk once, when I was a lad, through Saint Stephen's Green. He showed me where the volunteers had dug their trenches. And he took me over to the Boer War memorial, and I saw all the names inscribed. 'Look at it well, it's the traitor's gate,' he said, and I said, 'Why do you call it that?' and he said, 'Because they died fighting for the Brits.' If my da could see me now."

"It's a dream gone out of style," the commissioner said. "A dark and tragic past without relevance today."

"I wonder," the minister said. He'd heard that the

taoiseach—the Irish prime minister—had been told recently by Mrs. Thatcher, "All we need is a little time and patience," and the *taoiseach* had said, "Time? But it's been more than eight hundred years," and Mrs. Thatcher said, "Oh, I thought it was only three hundred."

"The IRA are outlaws, renegades to their own people," the commissioner said.

"Yes, of course, that's not what I was saying," the minister said, annoyed at the implication. "Now, then, there must be no slip-ups. That'd be all we need. Put your best security branch man on this."

"Neil Meehan," the commissioner said. "He's the one turned up that clerk."

Detective Sergeant Neil Meehan headed one of two special squads engaged in counterintelligence, which for any practical purpose meant the British and the Provos. And from his window in the new *Garda* headquarters on Harcourt Street, he now looked down with satisfaction at the sun-dappled expanse of St. Stephen's Green, happily ages away from its former dank, cramped offices in Dublin Castle, where England once held sway.

Imposing physically, with a square jaw, Meehan liked to think of himself as part of a new entrepreneurial Ireland. His sense of well-being went beyond the physical and spiritual to the financial, tangibly evidenced by the one-third share he held in a pub located conveniently around the corner. His own investment had been information. Before word got out that the *Gardai* would be moving to an office building on the west side of St. Stephen's Green, he had contacted two Dublin businessmen of means about purchasing and refurbishing a failed pub for sale in the then dormant neighborhood. The new enterprise, with its core clientele made up of *Garda* cops, was an instant success, and plans were afoot to acquire an adjacent structure and convert it into a small hotel.

It amused Meehan that in America, where he traveled now and again to consult with various counterparts, his actions would be viewed as scandalous, at the very least career threatening. But wasn't obtaining and acting upon inside information the essence of his job? To say nothing of life itself ?

Just this past summer during racing week at the Ballybrit track outside Galway City, he'd gotten a wonderful tip on a horse from an old friend, a canny trainer, at the bar of Sweeney's Hotel that paid all his expenses. Although he was contentedly married, with three sons, the eldest of whom had been admitted to Trinity College, Meehan always took that week, which featured the Galway Plate, a steeplechase dating to 1869, for himself alone. And this last time had been especially grand, the streets alive with fiddlers and guitarists, then his big win, scooping up a bit more cash at the card table and, to top it off, consorting successfully with a comely local girl. Meehan had met the trainer during his first visit ten years ago. What was the secret of his enviable string of winners? he'd asked, and the trainer said, "Oh, I just tell the boy to jump out front, right at the start, and keep improving his position." Meehan had smiled appreciatively, but then he thought, upon reflection, that it really was quite good all-around advice.

Meehan's normal squad consisted of seven men, which he could expand selectively as the need arose. He was pleased to have been chosen for this most critical assignment, but it galled him to have Brit intelligence pinpoint Paul O'Rourke as the new IRA quartermaster general.

He didn't trust the British, in fact didn't like them at all, with their superior manner and persistent efforts to penetrate the *Gardai*. Besides unearthing the betrayal of the *Garda* file clerk, he also had apprehended two senior *Garda* officials, in British pay, who leaked a trumped-up story printed around the world that a Soviet submarine was landing arms on the Donegal coast. The idea had been to give the IRA a suitably Marxist tinge, especially for American consumption, but in the interests of Anglo-Irish relations the affair was hushed up, the two officials, both inspectors, simply dismissed.

Meehan believed in a united Ireland, but it was an emotion that usually came late in the evening after a few drinks and some songs like "The Risin' of the Moon." Having stuck a toe in the private sector, his head counseled caution. He also believed that in this he represented the majority opinion in the free state. They had enough problems of their own. Absorbing the six northern counties would cause enormous burdens to an economy already saddled with high unemployment and onerous taxation.

The Provos, though, were another matter. The Irish Republican Army might have brought the free state into being, but the IRA, refusing to accept the half loaf of partition, had entered into a civil conflict in the 1920s as bloody and savage as could be imagined. The Provos were the direct descendants of those men forced to go underground beyond the law, and for Neil Meehan that was the bottom line. He was a cop.

There was nothing in the central file on O'Rourke, which was irritating. He called the *Garda* station in Tralee and spoke to the superintendent. Yes, the superintendent said, O'Rourke was quite well known. He had a machine repair shop, serviced automotive engines and boats as well. Meehan made a note of that. After this was over, they'd take a look at what else O'Rourke might be servicing.

"He has a share in a trawler at Fenit," the superintendent said.

"Does he now?" Meehan said. He asked him to have someone keep a discreet eye on O'Rourke, just his movements, nothing more than that. He'd be sending a man from Dublin headquarters named Bill Daley, Meehan said. He'd appreciate the superintendent showing him about.

"Salmon poachin', is it?"

"Something like that," Meehan said.

Daley phoned Dublin at four o'clock every afternoon. And at five the commissioner himself, bypassing the chain of command, was on the line wanting to know what was happening. For a week, Daley reported O'Rourke's unvarying daily routine, from home to shop and back. Meehan sensed the commissioner's frustration. "Sir, it's a waiting game," he said. "That's all we can do."

"I know, I know, but that Brit's on my back every second. Ever since that IRA convention, they think we're either incompetent or looking the other way."

"Well, that's not so, sir."

"Thank you, Meehan."

Daley reported that O'Rourke had spent the afternoon on the trawler in Fenit. The trawler was named *Valerie*. O'Rourke had talked to some men who appeared to be crew members. After he departed, though, the *Valerie* had remained in her berth alongside the Fenit breakwater.

Then, two days later, Daley called early in the morning from Adare on the N21 road to Limerick. O'Rourke had left Tralee and had just stopped for tea. He was driving alone in a maroon Toyota, Daley said, and gave the license number.

"I'll call Limerick and have another car pick him up," Meehan said. "You trail behind. I'll have them radio you a description of their car."

That evening Daley called from Carrick-on-Shannon in County Leitrim. O'Rourke had gone to an isolated farmhouse not far from the border. Several vehicles had been observed entering and exiting the farm. According to the local *Garda* station, the owner was known to be an outspoken supporter of *Sinn Fein*.

The next morning, Daley's voice was subdued. While the Toyota O'Rourke had arrived in remained parked at the farmhouse, the farmhouse itself appeared to be deserted. O'Rourke must have taken off during the night. "All right, return to Tralee," Meehan said.

"My God, you mean he's slipped through our fingers?" the commissioner said.

"No, sir. Him disappearing like that means something is imminent. Probably he went to a meeting, with the Northern Command no doubt, for final instructions. If the Brits are right, he'll be back in Tralee in short order. I've already checked. The *Valerie* hasn't moved, and it has to be the *Valerie*.

And then Daley called again. O'Rourke was back and had gone directly to Fenit, to the *Valerie,* spending the better part of an hour on board. Meehan told Daley to rent a cottage that had a view of the trawler. After that he and a photographer attached to his squad drove across Ireland to Tralee. On one count at least, they were in luck. It was a resort town where strange faces caused no stir, and although the August sky had been perversely low, bringing with it a chilled rain, September had turned unseasonably warm, just in time for the crowds attending the annual Rose of Tralee festival.

Along with other trawlers and sports fishing boats, the *Valerie* nestled on the land side of the Fenit breakwater. The massive concrete sea wall, wide enough for cars and trucks, extended for about three hundred yards into the bay before hooking back almost at a right angle. On the left, just as you came upon the breakwater, there was a small restaurant and bar. Meehan and Daley entered the bar side. They ordered pints of Harp. On the wall at the end of the bar was a bulletin board covered with color snapshots of happy anglers holding up their prizes. Meehan told the barkeep that he'd like to do a bit of sea trout fishing. Was there a good captain he could recommend?

There was one right over there, the barkeep said. Meehan introduced himself, and they went along with him on the breakwater to see his boat. Across the bay the mountains of the Dingle peninsula, purple and green and laced with gray granite, caught the late afternoon sun. They passed the *Valerie*, twin masted, some sixty feet long, the pilothouse aft, rather decrepit, Meehan thought. Meehan stopped, pointing at her, and asked, "How far out does a trawler like that venture?"

"Two, three hundred miles. Quite sturdy, they are."

"Out for salmon?"

"Yes, but it's not what it was. The government's very strict about the monofilament nets. The navy patrol boats are out night and day."

As they returned, Meehan recognized O'Rourke from his photographs, a sturdy body, unsmiling bearded face, striding toward them. Meehan and Daley drove at once to the cottage on the bay, three-quarters of a mile from the breakwater, that the Tralee *Gardai* had found for them.

The photographer was peering through a telescopic sight. As Meehan started to tell him which boat the *Valerie* was, he heard him say, "Don't worry, I've got her. I saw you pointing. O'Rourke's still on board, clear as a bell, talking to the crew."

The next two days Meehan went fishing at the mouth of the bay where the *Valerie* would have to pass if she left suddenly. The second evening, leaving Daley stationed in the bar, Meehan strolled across the road toward the beach. Coming to a rise, he saw a gaunt, weatherbeaten man in rubber waders laying out a species of seaweed called "Irish moss" to dry on the dune. There was an absolute stillness in the air, broken only by the cries of storm petrels skimming over a lagoon on his right that had a cut to the sea.

Another Ireland, no IRA, no Brits, Meehan thought as he watched the man bent over his labor. "What do you do with the seaweed?" he asked finally.

The man, never pausing, said, "It's for the perfume fellow, comes once a month."

"Perfume? What's seaweed got to do with perfume?"

"Don't know," the man said. "I just sell it."

Standing on the dune, the irony of his situation did not escape Meehan. Only a few miles up the coast, at Ballyheigue in 1916, a German U-boat had surfaced carrying Sir Roger Casement in advance of a shipment of arms to be used in conjunction with the Easter revolt. The shipment had been intercepted by the British and Casement was hanged. At Ballyheigue there was a statue of Casement that had been dedicated with great fanfare, honoring him as one of the heroes of the Irish Republic, and now Meehan was trying to thwart the same sort of shipment. He wondered if the Provos were planning to come in at the same spot. It would be just like them, he thought.

The third evening a van parked on the breakwater by the *Valerie* and three men got out. O'Rourke showed up and boarded her. At eleven o'clock that moonless night, using an infrared scope, Daley announced that the trawler was at last under way. Meehan watched her round the breakwater and head seaward. Then he called the duty officer at *Garda* headquarters in Dublin and asked to be patched through to the commissioner at home.

The news was relayed to the minister of justice.

The plan had already been decided at the cabinet level. "We must go all out on this," the minister had said. "If we botch this, if the shipment somehow passes through, we'll never hear the end of it from London," and everyone agreed.

At that time the Irish navy consisted of seven main vessels—two mine sweepers and five offshore patrol boats, the largest nineteen hundred tons, the other four nine hundred tons. Three of the latter, on standby throughout the week, were ordered out of the Haulbowline naval base at Cork and directed to proceed to the southwest coast, where they were to remain off the Iveragh peninsula for further instructions. Ten *Garda* officers from the Cork station under the command of an inspector, armed with Uzi submachine guns, were on the lead ship, the *Deirdre*, ten more on one of the two backups. The potential for violence, they were told, was high.

After the overhaul of the *Sea King* had been completed, Ingrid drove Jamie to New Bedford in her Honda.

Silent tears slid down her cheeks. It had been like that the night before, in bed when they were making love. He was holding her close to him when he felt the sudden wetness on his shoulder. No sobs, no convulsive shakes, no cries. Just the tears, as silent as falling snow.

Now he reached over and ran a finger along the nape of her neck and said, "Come on."

"I don't want to lose you," she said.

"You won't. I keep telling you. It's nothing. Nobody stops you taking stuff out. And when we're there, we transfer everything where nobody can do anything about it, on the high seas."

He'd said it so many times, he didn't know what else to say. "Look," he said, "the boat's in great shape.

It's an ocean-going trawler! People sail across the Atlantic in twelve-foot dinghies, practically, for God's sake."

Still the tears came.

"Hey, I thought you krauts were tough."

"Please."

"I can't stand you crying like this," he said. He told her to pull off the road, and when she did he took her face in both hands and tried to kiss away the tears. "I love you," he said. "It's just that I'm committed to this. They're depending on me. It's right, and I can't back out. After this trip is over, that's it. No more, I promise. *Finito.*"

"You swear to it?"

"Yes. Scout's honor."

"What's that?"

"It's an expression. Better than the Bible."

After that she drove in silence. He put a cassette of old songs by the Beatles in the tape deck. He had brought the cassette on purpose, and they listened to "Love Me Do" and "She Loves Me" and "I Want to Hold Your Hand."

Because of the trip, he would have to skip the fall semester. "I forgot to tell you. When I was over at the administrative office, I bumped into Mark Briggs. His family has a place in Aspen, and he invited us for the Christmas break. I said yes. You'd like skiing in Colorado, wouldn't you?"

"You never called your father."

"Ingrid, I can't do that now. It'd be the same story again. It'll be different when I'm back. When it's finished."

"I took your side, but you were very hard on him."

"I know. Sometimes we start shouting at each other and say things we don't mean. You'll see. We'll work it out. We always have."

"I can't help it," she said. "I have this terrible feeling."

"The only thing you have to worry about is that I don't end up in a cast again in Colorado."

She parked at the port by the wharves, and they walked toward the *Sea King*. She was wearing cutoffs and a tank top. Some of the men on the other trawlers started whistling and groaning theatrically.

"Hey, I forgot that. Better behave yourself while I'm gone," he said, grinning.

Finally he got a half smile. "That's something for you to worry about, mister," she said.

In full view of onlookers, the *Sea King* had taken on thirty tons of ice and seven thousand pounds of mackerel bait. "What you after?" Jamie heard someone shout to Manuel Foncecas.

"Broadbills, what you think?"

"How long you go?"

"A month. To the Grand Banks. Maybe to the Flemish Cap."

"That's halfway to Ireland."

Foncecas flashed a big smile that displayed his gold front tooth. "I want to try out all my new gear," he said.

"I hear the weather could be bad," someone else said, and Foncecas just shrugged.

"Jamie, you come?" he said. "Kiss that beautiful lady goodbye for now."

"Is that true about the weather?" Ingrid said.

"No, it's only talk. Somebody always says something

like that. Okay, see you. No more tears. Back before you know it," he said, holding her close.

On board, though, he learned that the possibility of bad weather and the length of the trip had made two of the three regular Portuguese crewmen beg off at the last minute despite guarantees of fifty dollars a day. "Well, for what we're doing, we won't need them," Jamie said.

From the deck, as they cast off, he waved at Ingrid and then saw her walk away, head down. He was sure she was crying again. "Hey," he whispered, "it's going to be all right."

The *Sea King*, eighty-seven feet long, with her newly painted black hull and white superstructure, eased out of the harbor, cruised past the Vineyard and Nantucket, and after Cape Cod, instead of heading for Nova Scotia, cut across Massachusetts Bay toward Gloucester. Along the way, they began dumping the ice and mackerel.

They arrived in Gloucester after dark and tied up at a pier containing sheds of the S & J Trading Co., a fish-processing facility that Thomas Ahearn had leased as a second warehouse for his operations. As they came in, Jamie saw Kevin Dowd waiting for them.

For three days, Dowd, Bernie Quinn and another Ahearn stalwart had been moving the material from the barn in Nashua to the S & J sheds in the Ford van and a rented truck. Carting the M16 rifles and machine guns, Dowd had driven right past the armory he had broken into three weeks before. According to an investigative update in the *Globe* that morning, the theft, described as the "work of professional burglars, undoubtedly with links to organized crime," remained without firm leads.

In all, along with the Redeyes, which weighed almost nothing, there were nearly nine tons of arms, ammunition and electronic equipment. Dowd was tenser than Jamie had ever seen him. He said that there was a slight change in plans. He would be going with them to make sure everything got to where it was supposed to go and to replace the missing crewmen. He was depending upon Jamie to show him what to do.

Jamie saw a skinny man pacing back and forth apart from them on the pier, with fierce black eyes darting every which way. He was carrying a MAC-10 submachine gun. "Who's that?" Jamie asked, and Dowd said that he was a friend, and when Jamie looked curiously at Dowd, Dowd said, "All right, his name is Tommy Ahearn. He's arranged all this for us, he has. Don't be askin' so many fookin' questions."

It took nearly three hours to load the trawler. In one of the sheds, Jamie passed a young woman with frizzy red hair standing beside a man who had a canvas carryall. "You must be Jamie," she said in a Belfast accent. "I'm Rita. I've heard about you, and I want to thank you." She did not introduce the man, and when Jamie turned toward him, he just nodded curtly. He had a slight build, curly black hair and a neatly trimmed beard that ran up to his sideburns.

They left about two A.M., slipping out of the harbor behind some lobster boats. Moments before they left the pier, the man jumped onto the deck. Jamie watched him go to the stern. On the pier the girl,

Rita, waved, and the man raised a clenched fist. Then she, too, clenched her fist.

As soon as they reached the open ocean, even though there was only a moderate swell, the man with the beard almost immediately became seasick and Dowd took him to one of the crew cabins aft of the pilothouse.

At a pay phone in Gloucester, Rita Carroll, having taken a few days off from her au pair job with Mr. and Mrs. Moses Weinstein of Glen Cove, Long Island —to visit, as she put it, "some acquaintances in Boston"—placed a call to Jake Mooney in Queens. "They're just off, not an hour ago," she said.

Despite the time, he'd been up and waiting. "Oh, that's grand," Mooney said. He then dialed a number in Belfast. He asked after several fictitious relatives. He inquired about the Belfast weather and spoke of how hot the summer had been in New York. He said he'd been so busy at work that he had been unable to enjoy his usual vacation. Now, worse yet, he could not even accompany some friends on a long-planned fishing excursion. They had left already, indeed this very day.

"I expect the trip will last about thirteen days," Mooney said.

"Thirteen, is it?" the voice in Belfast said.

"Yes. That's what they told me."

The man with the beard remained in his cabin.

"That guy's not very friendly," Jamie said to Dowd.

"Mick? Ah, he's a good lad at heart. Explosives men are like that, don't ye know? Loners, a little edgy by nature. And he's the best, Mick is. The Brits would dearly love to get their hands on him."

"More than you?"

"Oh, yes. No comparison."

"How come?"

"Sweet Jesus, Jamie, let well enough be."

"I thought we were all in this together."

Dowd contemplated him and then he said, "Sometimes, there's knowin' too much. But there's no gainsayin' it. You're right, we're in this together and there's no turnin' back, is there? That'd be Mick Connally back there. He did the Brighton bombing, the only one hasn't been caught."

"Brighton?"

"Yes, the hotel where the Thatcher bitch was."

Now he remembered. It had been big news at the time. An explosion had rocked the Grand Hotel in the resort city of Brighton on the English coast southwest of London, at the annual Tory conference attended by the prime minister and her senior cabinet members, but they miraculously survived the attack.

"A lot of innocent people got killed and hurt," Jamie said. "I mean, how could you do that?"

"Listen to me, so were innocents when the Jews, the Zionists, bombed Brit army headquarters in the King David Hotel in Jerusalem, which they did fightin' for independence, and I'm not hearin' too many complaints about that these days. That's what really got the Brits on the road to gettin' out of Palestine, and it's right there in the history books. This is war, lad, and if that bomb went off the way it was supposed to, maybe we wouldn't be wallowin' around here in the middle of nowhere. Troubles you, does it?"

He had said nothing, but it did affect him to be suddenly confronted with this reality. He couldn't help it. He began to feel glad that it, his part, would soon be over.

And he felt this even more days later when Connally finally emerged on deck.

"Can I get you a cup of tea?" Jamie said.

"Yes."

Then afterward he asked, "What's it like, setting a bomb? What do you feel?"

"I don't feel nothin'," Connally said.

Sometimes Jamie sat by himself on the foredeck, getting drenched by the spray as the *Sea King* rose up and down through the mid-Atlantic swells. It wasn't a lake out here, but there wasn't a hint yet of the heavy weather that had been predicted. He liked the motion, like a constant miniature roller coaster that you'd pay money to ride in an amusement park. He had never been seasick, so it was hard for him to imagine how anyone else could be. It was like not really understanding how anyone could be tone deaf or unable to carry a tune, he thought. Like his father. Although he always called him "Dad," in his head he thought of him as "Father."

That was funny. He thought of his mother only as "Mom." He guessed he'd got his sense of music from her. The truth was that now he could only remember snatches of her, the warmth of her body, the way she sang to him when he was having supper or sitting beside her at the piano, how she giggled with him when he confessed that he wanted to marry Marie Tynan in the third grade, and she asked why, and he said because Marie's mother made such good brownies, and she said, "That's the best reason I ever heard of."

He wondered what he had lost, having lost her. But that was something *he* would never know, and there was no point brooding about it. Once, that Ray Bendicks down the block was complaining about his parents being divorced and how he couldn't stand what they were saying to him about one another. "What would you do?" Bendicks asked, and when he said, "I don't know, my mom died," Bendicks said, "You're lucky," and, crying all through it, he'd beaten Bendicks up.

He loved his father, and he knew his father loved him. He knew his father had been devastated by her death. For a while he'd had bad dreams that his father really didn't want him anymore, but he had come to realize that wasn't so. Still, it was hard to talk to his father about his innermost feelings. He had wanted to say that he would do his very best to help make up for the loss, but the right opportunity never seemed to arrive.

Actually, he thought that things were getting pretty good between them. Ingrid, the way he had accepted her, was a perfect example. The problem, though, was that deep down his father continued to think of him as a kid. He winced whenever he thought of the explosion that night in Cambridge about what he was doing. It had happened so fast. He knew his father had been stung by that crack he made about the Nazis. Surely he must know that he wasn't being serious. But he regretted it anyway. He had been positive his father would reach out to him afterward. Before, when they had fights, that's what always happened. By the time he realized that this one was different, it was too late. It would just deteriorate into an angry replay. He'd wait until he got back. Like he told Ingrid, he thought they'd work it out so everything would be okay between them. Better even.

In the wheelhouse, Manuel Foncecas bent over charts displaying the eastern Atlantic off Ireland.

Gazing at the endless swells, Dowd said, "How are we ever to find her?"

"That's no problem if she's where she's supposed to be," Jamie had said. "That's why we put in the new navigation gear. And she's supposed to be moving along that bank there, the Porcupine Bank. See where it's marked?" he said, fingering a spot a hundred fifty miles due west of the Dingle peninsula on the Irish coast. "If worse comes to worst, we'll put out a radio call. Fishing trawlers are always talking to each other."

Jamie was the first to spot the *Valerie* in the afternoon three days after she had left Fenit. The sighting was confirmed when the *Sea King* drew closer and a large piece of canvas was draped over the *Valerie*'s port gunwale with the letters "IRA."

There was a moderate sea. Foncecas maneuvered so that the two trawlers were moving parallel, about two hundred feet separating them. Jamie began winching up the crates and steamer trunks stored in the hold. The *Valerie*'s seventeen-foot dory with an

outboard motor was lowered. Two crewmen ran the
dory to the *Sea King,* threw lines to lash it alongside
and took on the first load. The work, involving all
hands, was backbreaking and maddeningly slow, the
possibility of a mishap hovering about them like an
evil genie. Hardly anyone spoke, save to utter a warning or a curse.

Time ticked by when Dowd decided to repackage
the Redeyes into two parts. "We dare not chance it,"
he said. In all, the transfer required nearly six hours.
It got dark, and the final two trips were completed
under lights beamed from both trawlers. At last,
though, it was done, not an item lost. The dory returned to get Connally. He jumped in without a
word, turned and simply brought up a clenched fist
as he had in Gloucester.

"Wait!" Dowd said unexpectedly. "I must go meself. I can't miss this one." He embraced Jamie.
"Luck, lad, and thanks. I'm doin' this because I have
to. You did it because you wanted to. I won't forget.
Be in touch."

Then he also dropped into the dory. Jamie
watched him climb aboard the Irish trawler. As the
Valerie moved off, Dowd raised two triumphant
thumbs up. That was the last Jamie saw of him.

High in the sky, when they had begun the transfer,
a plane had passed overhead. Jamie didn't give it a
second's thought. Throughout the voyage the con-
trails of jets flying to and from Europe had been an
everyday event.

Now, in the night, Jamie heard the far-off sound
of jet engines. It never occurred to him, nor to any-

one else on the two trawlers, that it was the same plane.

It was a Royal Air Force Nimrod early-warning plane crammed with an integrated state-of-the-art electronic surveillance system. With its twelve-man crew, it had been brought into the RAF facility at Belfast's Aldergrove airport.

Four hours after Detective Sergeant Neil Meehan alerted Dublin that the *Valerie* had departed Fenit, the Nimrod lifted off. Powered by four Rolls-Royce engines, it climbed within minutes out over the Atlantic to forty thousand feet, banked south and, throttling back to two hundred knots, made its first pass above the *Valerie*.

The Nimrod's detection radar coupled to a data processing program fed into a digital computer that produced startlingly clear, clutter-free pictures, at night and through cloud cover. Even at that altitude, it could pick up and isolate a submarine periscope breaking the surface fifteen miles away.

Locking on to the *Valerie*, tracking her speed and course, was a breeze.

Actually, Meehan's musings about the possibility of the shipment being brought ashore at Ballyheigue, near the statue honoring Roger Casement, wasn't far off the mark. It had been given serious consideration, the dramatic link to Casement almost irresistible. But in the end, caution won out. The arms would be landed in a cove by Bantry Bay, as far from Northern Ireland as you could get, south of the Ring of Kerry.

The three patrol boats of the Irish navy, dispatched from their base at Cork, were stationed off the southwest coast, circling behind three uninhabited craggy islands, really rocks, just inside the free state's three-mile territorial limit. When the Nimrod relayed the *Valerie*'s returning course, it would take her precisely toward them.

The presence of armed *Garda* police electrified the patrol boat crews. Word had spread swiftly. It was an IRA operation. An IRA gun runner! After months of routine fishery enforcement, Brendan Muldoon, a sublieutenant on the bridge manning the *Deirdre*'s forward radar, quivered with excitement. The bridge was packed with the captain, the executive officer, the gunnery officer and a *Garda* inspector. Muldoon could sense their excitement, too.

At ten P.M., almost twenty-four hours to the minute after the *Valerie* had parted company with the *Sea King*, Muldoon picked her up on the radar screen, nine miles distant. The *Valerie* kept coming steadily on, course unchanged, headed between the rocks and the mainland. When she was about a mile inside the territorial limit, the *Deirdre* dashed from her hiding place, the two other patrol boats, *De Valera* and *Parnell*, fanning out east and west.

In the night mist, the *Valerie*'s running lights could be seen dimly from the bridge. Over the marine radio, the *Deirdre*'s captain identified himself and ordered, "Halt your vessel." Her signal lamp flashed, "Stop, I wish to board you." Searchlights caught the trawler as she tried to turn back to the open sea. An awed Muldoon, having abandoned his radar screen, watched as a burst of 40-mm Bofors tracer shells arched over the *Valerie*'s bow. After that she hove to.

Muldoon heard someone shouting at them through a megaphone, "We have no salmon!"

Two boarding parties in rubber dinghies were ferried to the trawler. Below decks, the *Garda* inspector, in the twitching beams of flashlights, pried open a crate and gazed down at the glistening M16s. The men on the trawler were separated. Placed in custody on two of the patrol boats, they were briefly questioned.

Kevin Dowd identified himself. But Mick Connally gave a false name and address and like the others refused to answer any more questions without the counsel of a solicitor.

Chapter

14

Two hours later in London, in his Curzon Street office, Brian Forbes's adoring secretary, Pamela Price-Smith, rushed in with the teletype message from Dublin. It read, "Intercept successful. Details follow."

Forbes came up out of his chair. A dizzying elation rushed through him. Light-headed, he walked in a tight circle behind his desk, fist slamming into palm. By God, they'd done it!

He grabbed hold of Pamela, lifted her and swung her around him. He put her down and kissed her soft, full mouth. "We did it!" he cried.

"Oh, Brian," she said. "I'm so happy for you." She had, of course, volunteered to stay with him in the office until the results of the operation were known. She had a flawless classically English rosy-cheeked complexion, the kind poems were written about, Forbes thought.

He had a sudden urge to celebrate. "What are you doing tonight?" he demanded inanely.

"Brian, it's already morning."

"I don't care."

He wondered where they could go at this time. He didn't belong to any of the fashionable clubs that were still open. Then he remembered one of the chaps monitoring the Middle East who had joked about the new Lebanese establishments that had opened on Edgware Road and how they typically managed to evade the regulations governing closing hours. Best of all, it was practically on the way to Pamela's flat in Notting Hill, just beyond Bayswater.

They stopped at a place called Cedars of Lebanon. It was sleek and dark inside, rather like the clientele, Forbes thought. They sat in a black leather banquette holding hands. Forbes, who ordinarily drank sparingly, ordered a double whiskey. She asked for a kir royale.

"What's that?"

"I'm not sure. But it's got champagne in it and it's quite bubbly."

He laughed, and when they clinked glasses, he said, "Up the IRA's you know what."

In her parlor, she kissed him and said, "Wait here a sec till I tidy up. The bed's such a mess."

What difference does it make? he thought. It's going to be a mess again straight off. He sat on the sofa. She actually had his photograph, in an oval silver frame, on an end table. Throughout their affair, although he'd been with her many times before, it was the first time he could remember ever being away from home for an entire night when he wasn't working.

Then he thought about the message from Dublin once more, and then about Billy Dugan. *Clara!* He'd nearly forgotten. Immediately in the morning he would arrange for the ten-thousand-pound payment. It was just the beginning. He expected many more great things from Clara. After the disaster of the arms seizure, there'd be a huge shakeup in the Provo quartermaster's staff, which would only benefit Billy. It would be as if he, Brian Forbes, had a seat on the IRA Army Council.

And then Pamela called to him from the bedroom.

At daybreak, out of habit, while Pamela was attending to tea, he switched on the BBC's "Breakfast Time" program. A minute later, aghast, Forbes could not believe what he was hearing and seeing. A news reader was reporting dramatic events in Ireland.

"The Irish government," he said, "announced early this morning that three patrol craft of the naval service have seized a fishing trawler carrying a large shipment of arms destined for the IRA. Apparently forewarned, the three patrol craft had been lying in wait off the southwest coast of Ireland for several days. There were no casualties, the trawler's crew having been taken by complete surprise. A government spokesman in Dublin hailed the alertness and efficiency of the naval service."

Three patrol craft. The words ricocheted in Forbes's head.

"This simply was," the spokesman was further quoted as saying, "another example of the Irish gov-

ernment's determination not to countenance IRA
terrorism and violence."

Three! Apparently forewarned! Forbes recalled his
meeting with the minister of justice. *It's of paramount
importance,* he had said, *that the seizure be made to appear
a fortunate accident.*

The news reader continued. "Preliminary reports
indicate that the amount of weapons on board the
trawler was one of the largest in the current conflict
in Northern Ireland, perhaps even larger than the
five tons intercepted on the German-owned vessel the
Claudia off Dublin in 1973. It is considered a major,
if not catastrophic, setback to Provisional IRA plans
to escalate their terrorist campaign in the coming
months."

But Forbes wasn't listening. On his feet, he was
screaming at the television set, "Bloody, stupid
fools!" Pamela Price-Smith, modestly attired in a
robe, her face still aglow from whispered remarks
during the night of a more permanent relationship,
turning now to bring Forbes his tea, promptly
dropped the cup, gaping at him in bewildered astonishment.

Forbes ignored her. Suddenly the television screen
was displaying film. It was footage received only moments before, the news reader said, voice over. And
Forbes saw the *Valerie* at the other end of a hawser
being towed by a corvette-type patrol boat, two additional patrol boats running escort.

It looked like a bloody goddamn armada, he
thought. This same program was being aired in Belfast, Derry, all over Northern Ireland.

The trawler was being towed, the news reader said,

because of engine trouble. As a result, arrival at the Haulbowline naval base was not expected until this evening. The investigation, meanwhile, was continuing. There would be further reports.

It was the end of Clara, Forbes thought. The end of his meticulous design to put a super mole high inside the IRA. *Why* the patrol boats, three of them, were there, *how* they had been forewarned, had yet to be addressed in any of the news reports. They would be, though. Sooner or later, the Provos would winnow out this fellow and that, and eventually they would come to Billy Dugan, the newest, the latest, to be on the inside, and at the first question, fragile Billy would crack wide open, like the teacup Pamela had just dropped.

At Curzon Street, Forbes went directly to Roger Gravesend's office.

"Well done, Brian," said Gravesend, basking in the morning's triumphant news, seemingly unaware of all the consequences, actually rising to shake Forbes's hand.

"Not so well done, sir," Forbes said and pointed out the fate that currently awaited Billy Dugan, to say nothing of their own plans for him. "This is a major blow to the Provos, materially and spiritually, but as you certainly know, it's not going to crush them by any means," he said. "We must keep our foot on their throats. They're in a certain amount of disarray now, but to discover an informer, *this* informer, will restore their credibility and morale unless we act quickly."

"Yes, you're right, of course." Gravesend appeared a bit crestfallen, like a sticky-fingered child deprived of a stolen sweet. "What do you suggest?"

"Immediate damage control, as the Americans say." He requested permission to call the justice minister in Dublin.

"All right. After all, you two were in it together from the beginning," Gravesend said, not too subtly distancing himself, Forbes thought.

The call went right through. "Minister," Forbes said, "I'm in the deputy director general's office. I'm speaking on a secure phone."

"As am I."

"Congratulations on the events of last night."

"Yes, thank you. It went quite well, I thought."

"It's unfortunate, however, about the three boats, half your fleet, I'm advised. You'll recall it was to be an accidental encounter while on fishery protection."

"Considering the gravity of the situation, we deemed it best not to chance a slip-up. Think of what would have occurred if that trawler had got through, the innocent lives that have been spared."

"Yes, but was it all really necessary to mention the fact publicly?"

"An overzealous press person, spurred by patriotic fervor. He's been talked to."

Forbes visualized the crafty porcine politician face, eyes buried in pouches of fat, at the other end of the line, could hear him ordering the hapless spokesman to get the news out on the double, show them what stuff the *Gardai* and the Irish navy were made of.

"We'd appreciate it if no more specifics were revealed. For security."

"Done."

And why not? Forbes thought. You've got all you needed.

"Oh, by the by, we believe that one of the men taken from the trawler was Mick Connally, your long-sought Brighton bomber."

Gravesend was listening on an extension. Forbes saw his eyes widen. The sly Fenian bastard, Forbes thought, saving the best for last, changing the whole tenor of the call.

"Are you certain?"

"The *Garda* inspector on the scene recognized him from a photograph, and he's admitted it. Obviously, we don't have fingerprints yet."

After Forbes hung up, Gravesend said, "Good lord, *Connally!* I must see the director general at once. Scotland Yard will be absolutely fuming. He'll like that. They've been turning the world upside down for him without success."

"And Clara?"

"Yes, yes, do what you have to do," Gravesend said, already on his way out the door.

When Forbes arrived at his own desk, Pamela handed him several message slips. "Your wife's been phoning," she said. "She called the duty officer twice last night."

She had an expression on her face Forbes had never seen before. After a second, he realized what it was. A smirk, a bloody smirk. "Thank you," he said, and had to say it again before she left and he dialed home.

"Where have you been?" his wife said. He could tell from the slur in her speech that she'd already been at the bottle. "I've been frantic. I would have called the police, but I was afraid to because of what you do."

"I was busy all night. It was that IRA trawler business. You must have heard about it."

"You could have rung me at least."

"Yes, you're quite right. I should have rung you."

That afternoon and the next morning, media attention focused on the apprehension of Mick Connally. "Inhuman Bomber Held," a London evening tabloid trumpeted. Another said, "IRA Monster in Police Custody."

There were lengthy rehashes of the attempt on the prime minister's life, how the police had interviewed more than eight hundred people from fifty nations who had been guests at the decimated Brighton hotel in the weeks preceding the explosion, how all the conspirators save Connally, the subject of a worldwide manhunt by Scotland Yard, had been arrested and sentenced to a minimum of thirty-five years in prison.

Forbes liked that. Then, as he feared, the press emphasis began to shift after the trawler was towed into Cork harbor late in the evening. A swarm of reporters and photographers were kept away from the captured men and the officers and ratings on the lead patrol boat *Deirdre*. The forty-five-man crew was instructed not to speak to reporters under any circumstances, and none did. But the Cork correspondent of the *Irish Times,* acquainted, as it happened, with the family of young Brendan Muldoon, the sublieutenant manning the *Deirdre*'s forward radar, sought out the father in a neighborhood pub where he was regaling one and all with the exploits of his son.

According to his son, Muldoon elder said, accepting the offer of a pint from the correspondent, the patrol boat had lain in wait for three days for the *Valerie*, the trawler's name and configuration known, her oncoming course relayed continually by an RAF Nimrod surveillance plane. "Then Brendan spied her on his radar," he said with pride, "and it was touch and go for a time, it was, so Brendan said." The trawler, he went on, had been taken by surprise and desperately tried to flee, only to be halted by shots fired across her bow.

"Yes, I'll have another, thank you. This is all on the quiet, mind you," the father told the correspondent.

"Of course," said the correspondent. "Say no more."

His page-one account led to a new round of headlines and, especially in London, to speculation about a British hand in the seizure. A spokesman in Dublin declined further comment. "I'm not at liberty to discuss that," he said, immediately confirming it in everyone's mind.

As befitted an officially nonexistent arm of Her Majesty's government, MI5 had no press office to respond to questions. It did have, however, a coterie of favored journalists to whom it passed, when the occasion demanded, information helpful to its interests or injurious to its enemies, real or perceived.

And Forbes, under the aegis of the deputy director general, briefed the security officers charged with cultivating these contacts to provide various pieces of what was called the "story behind the story" with just enough elements of truth to make it all plausible.

"It's to be pointed out," he said, "that this is the largest interception of IRA arms to date. The presence of Redeye missiles alone, a grave threat against British helicopters, makes it the most important seizure in the lamentable history of Northern Ireland, demonstrating that the IRA will stop at nothing to gain its goals."

Forbes gazed at their bored faces as they listened to this humdrum fare, so their startled looks were all the more satisfying when he said, "You also are authorized to reveal that these weapons were transported from America and transferred at sea to the Fenit trawler *Valerie*. From the first, however, federal law enforcement agencies in the United States, principally the FBI, learned of the shipment. A U.S. spy satellite had tracked the mother ship across the Atlantic as she sailed toward her rendezvous with *Valerie*. This intelligence was then passed on for use by British surveillance aircraft. The name of the mother ship is known and an international search is being conducted for her whereabouts. Beyond this, you may not go."

He paused, enjoying being the center of rapt attention now. "Ah, yes, do say that this success exemplifies Anglo-American cooperation against terrorist activities," Forbes said, and then, reluctantly, "Best to add Irish as well."

The following morning Roger Gravesend appeared to be in a state of shock behind swirls of cigarette smoke. "The prime minister called the director general directly," he blurted. "She never does that.

She always calls the home secretary, who calls the director general. She called to compliment the director general on the capture of Mick Connally. She was especially gratified that such a large amount of plastic explosive was prevented from falling into the IRA's hands. She wanted to know who was responsible." Gravesend stared at Forbes. "The queen will personally present you with a commendation. It'll be secret, naturally, but it will be included in your record of service."

It was unnerving the way Gravesend kept staring at him, and Forbes wondered if he was thinking what *he* was thinking. All this time Forbes had tied his future to Gravesend, and now, perhaps, it had all turned around. It was a moment for delicate diplomacy. "I could have accomplished none of it without your support and counsel," Forbes said.

"Yes, well, thank you." Gravesend rearranged the news clips on his desk describing the "sophisticated international tracking operation," all of them based on "reliable" or "informed" sources, that had resulted in the *Valerie*'s capture. "This will do it quite nicely, I should think," he said.

"Not entirely, sir. There are still some holes. Why the mother ship wasn't seized before leaving America can be explained away. Because we wanted to see exactly where and to whom she was going. But for the benefit of the Provos, we must more precisely pinpoint the original source of our intelligence to safeguard Clara. As it is, it remains dangerously up in the air."

Fumbling for another cigarette, Gravesend said, "What do you propose?" and Forbes said, "We must create another informant." When he finished outlining his plan, Gravesend blanched.

"But that would involve the American ambassador. And the foreign office. You know we don't like to go outside. Perilous. Always due bills down the road." He peered at Forbes. "And leaks!"

"Considering the prime minister's keen appreciation of what we have accomplished so far, perhaps we could bypass the usual channels with her authority. Might not the home secretary speak privately to the ambassador about this?"

Gravesend wriggled uncomfortably. "Perhaps. I'll discuss it with the director general. Best I can do. By the way, were the Americans made aware of their vital cooperation in the seizure?"

"No, that's another part of the plan. To make it irresistible." Almost gaily, Forbes returned to his desk and Pamela Price-Smith.

"Am I to see you tonight?" she said.

She'd never been so forward. He rather liked it. Showed a hidden spunk. "Yes," he said, "but I can't stay over, I'm afraid. I have, regrettably, other responsibilities, you know."

Blushing, she handed him a package.

"What's this?"

"A new shirt," she said. "I got it at Harrods. Blue, like the one you're wearing, so no one will be the wiser."

Then he phoned home. The cleaning woman, who came once a week, answered. His wife was, as she put it, resting. Forbes could imagine. "Tell Mrs. Forbes I shan't be home till after dinner. Late."

He thought about Pamela's pliant ardor. And the

prime minister's call. His career ambitions had always precluded divorce. Or so he had believed. Maybe it wasn't so important anymore.

In Washington, the FBI's chief of public affairs, at the J. Edgar Hoover Building, didn't know what to think. While there'd been immense changes since Hoover's autocratic reign, one principle remained inviolate. No matter what, you covered your ass—everything recorded, triplicated, every case bucked up the line for authorization, every "i" and "t" dotted and crossed, free-lancing the most heinous of sins.

And the public affairs chief, a veteran Washington reporter named Terry McDonell, hadn't heard a word about a huge arms shipment headed by boat for the IRA that had been foiled in large measure by the FBI. What was worse, he couldn't find anyone else in the bureau who knew about it either.

The first two overseas calls for details had come in from London newspapers, the next from Dublin, and then two others from local British correspondents. And McDonell sensed there would be plenty more.

He had been brought in by the new director, a former judge, with only one admonition. They were going into an entrenched, foxy bureaucracy, as good as there was in the capital, the judge had said. "Just make sure I'm not blindsided." And now it was happening.

McDonell had even bit a humiliating bullet, phoning the FBI's New York office to see if the foreign intelligence squad there was into an operation that hadn't been reported yet to headquarters. Nothing.

He sent out feelers to learn if the CIA, or Alcohol, Tobacco and Firearms, or the customs service, had something to do with this. Zero.

He put in an urgent call to the director.

"Make it snappy, Terry. Remember, I've got that doubles match with those network news guys."

Five minutes later two assistant executive directors and an assistant director were lined up nervously in the director's office. All swore ignorance.

"Okay," McDonell said. "I'll say that any information right now has to come from the British and Irish governments. That we're not in a position to confirm anything one way or another. That'll make us sound discreet and gracious."

"You do that, Terry," the director said, grabbing his racquet. "And find out why we're being credited with something we don't know anything about."

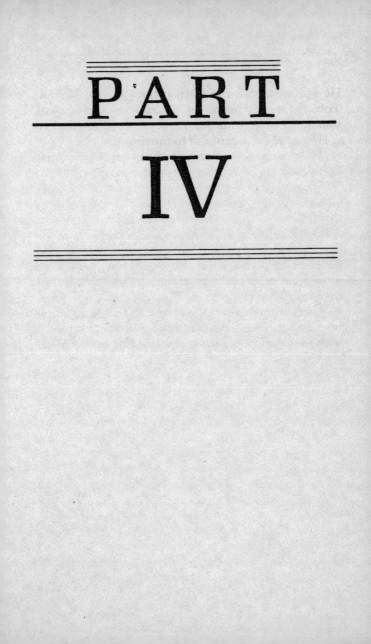

PART
IV

PART

IV

Chapter

15

Midway through the *Sea King*'s return across the Atlantic, the bad weather that had been predicted finally hit. And despite being lightened nine tons once the arms cargo was transferred, plus another twenty tons of fuel already consumed, more than a day was lost in the storm. The one time in his life when he should have been seasick, Jamie thought, he was too scared.

The storm had been awesome in its ferocity. Giant combers roared at the trawler. One moment he was plunging down into the chasm of a trough, sure that would be the end of him, and then somehow the *Sea King* was miraculously rising through the next great wave, decks awash, the whole boat shuddering, over and over again, the wind howling so you couldn't hear yourself think, tearing off a lot of the rigging. Once a wall of foam-flecked water surged over them with such force that it smashed the windows on the

302 // PETER MAAS

port side of the wheelhouse, flooding them knee-deep in the ocean and threatening to wash them to kingdom come. But the captain, Foncecas, had been marvelous, much better than Jamie had believed possible, laughing even, his gold tooth bared, and then bellowing wildly as he kept the *Sea King* headed into the wind and waves. It lasted sixteen hours, and all at once it was over, the glowering black sky gone, the sunlight dancing on long, peaceful blue swells.

They limped into Boston harbor without further incident and docked where they usually did, by the fish pier, for repairs. That way, Foncecas said, they didn't have to explain in New Bedford why they hadn't returned with a catch.

He took a cab to the Putnam Avenue apartment. Ingrid's Honda was parked in front. He quietly let himself in through the glass sliding doors and yelled, "Hey, the wandering seafarer has returned."

She flew out of the bedroom and threw her arms around his neck. She started to sob uncontrollably. "Oh, God, oh, God," she cried, "you're safe! I've been frantic with worry since I heard about it."

"Heard about what?"

"You don't know?"

"What are you talking about? I've been in the middle of the Atlantic, in the middle of the biggest goddamn storm I ever saw."

"Jamie, it was in the paper and on TV. About a trawler carrying arms to the IRA that was stopped by the Irish navy."

"Are you serious?"

"Yes, my God, yes. It said the British knew all about it, from the FBI, I think. It said that the shipment came from America on another boat, and they know the name and everything."

"You mean Kevin Dowd was caught?"

"Yes, yes. It said that he was an illegal resident in Boston for many years, that he was wanted by the British. It said that another man was captured, too, who tried to bomb the prime minister, the whole British cabinet."

"Jesus, I can't believe it. Kevin!"

"It's true. I'll show it to you."

He sat down and tried to focus. "My dad," he said, "have you talked to him?"

"No, yes. I mean, I haven't spoken to him since the story. I tried to call him, and his secretary said he was unreachable. He was fishing in Alaska with a client. But I talked to him before that. He called right after you left. I had to tell him the truth."

"What did he say?"

"He didn't say anything. He just slammed down the receiver."

"Oh, boy, I better call him," and on the phone to Michael McGuire's secretary, he said, "This is Jamie. Is my dad around?"

"No, he's been in Alaska, but he stopped off at the L.A. office for some meetings. He isn't due in the city till next week. If you need him, here's the number."

He phoned at once and said, "Dad, I'm back in Boston."

"Good," Michael McGuire said, his voice icy.

"Look, Dad, I'm sorry, I'm really sorry about what happened, some of the things I said. I didn't explain myself too well, and I'd like another chance. But the main thing is, I wasn't kidding. I did what I had to do, but that's it. It's over."

There was a long pause. "You mean that?"

"Yes."

Michael McGuire said. "Okay, tell you what. Soon as I get to New York, I'll call you and we'll get together."

"Thanks, Dad," and after Jamie had hung up, he said to Ingrid, "I'm sure he hasn't heard what happened. He would have said something."

"Jamie," she said, "if they are aware of the *Sea King*, why are they still looking for her? It doesn't make any sense."

"I don't know," Jamie said.

In Washington, Alan Nyquist, commissioner of the U.S. Customs Service, took the overseas call from Brian Forbes. "Nice hearing from you again," he said. "Been too long. What can I do for you?"

"Sir," said Forbes, "I'm calling about that arms seizure off the Irish coast."

"Ah, yes. There's considerable buzzing in some circles around here about what we did to help, since nobody seems to know."

"Exigencies of the moment, I'm afraid," Forbes said. "There was literally no time to alert anyone. I hope to be in Washington shortly to explain in person. I trust there's not too much unhappiness."

"I can only speak for myself, but I doubt it. As we say, you don't look a gift horse in the mouth."

"Quite so, sir, and well put, I might add. In any event, there is an immediate problem. Our surveillance aircraft shows that the mother ship was another trawler called *Sea King*. I am dispatching photos by courier. We were unable to determine her home port, however. Even more unfortunate," Forbes said, "the Nimrod was returned immediately to normal NATO duty and failed to track *Sea King* following the transfer. She could have come from Canada. We think not. Our assumption is New England. We ask your aid. Extreme discretion is advised. Past history indicates that our old friend Daniel P. Daugherty must be involved somehow."

"Daugherty, huh?"

"Yes, sir."

"I'll get back to you," Nyquist said. He got on the phone to his northeastern regional chief, Barry Goldfarb, a Jew who had worked his way up the promotional ladder on merit in what essentially was an Irish-dominated hierarchy and who had often expressed annoyance at the way Daugherty used his political connections to operate as if he were running an independent barony.

"Where's Daugherty?" Nyquist said.

"Let's see. Yes. He's on tour. In Buffalo as we speak. Next stop, Philadelphia. The semi-annual traveling reunion of 'Danny's Boys,' featuring wine, women and laments for old Ireland. Won't return for a week."

"Good," Nyquist said.

Like other regions around the country, the northeast had a commissioner and two assistant commissioners, one who ran the inspectional services, everything from administration to examining baggage, and the other, Daugherty, for law enforcement.

Under him in each district office the law enforcement squads were led by a special agent in charge who was called a "SAC."

"How does Daughtery play with the Boston SAC?"

"It's not a marriage made in heaven, I can say that. Half the squads breeze right by him to Danny boy."

Then Nyquist told Goldfarb about the *Sea King*.

Two hours later, Goldfarb was saying, "She's out of New Bedford. Not in her berth, though. She's supposed to have left about a month ago for the Grand Banks. But when you gave me the name, it rang a bell, and I did some checking. There was a coast guard narcotics trafficking alert out on her a while back. Some of Daugherty's guys beat everyone to the scene. Couldn't find a thing on board. Drug enforcement and the Boston narcs bitched like hell."

"That cinches it," Nyquist said. "I want that trawler located. Scour the docks. And I don't want Daugherty to know about this."

"He'll find out eventually."

"Good. I hope he reads it in the papers."

"Speaking about the papers, there's one other funny thing about what I was telling you before. Funny enough to get a write-up. A Harvard kid named Jamie McGuire was in the crew. I got the clip right here."

It took three days before two customs agents in a routine patrol stumbled on the *Sea King*, still at the Boston pier. Jamie read about it in the *Globe*. The story said that the trawler was suspected of transporting a huge weapons cache across the Atlantic in a botched conspiracy to aid the IRA. According to the *Globe*, the Portuguese captain, found supervising repairs when the agents boarded the trawler, was detained and later released. He was said to have insisted that he knew nothing about drug or arms smuggling. All he had ever smuggled was Canadian swordfish.

In Washington, the commissioner of customs was quoted as declaring, "The *Sea King* may hold the key to secret arms deliveries from the United States to the Provisional Irish Republican Army." Although no charges had been formally filed, he said, the investigation was continuing.

"Jamie," Ingrid said, "what are you going to do?"

"Nothing," he said. "Hang tight, I guess. What else?"

The discovery of the *Sea King* was big news in London. The story broke just as Forbes was preparing to leave for Washington.

Roger Gravesend summoned Forbes to tell him that the trip had been authorized. "The prime minister did not, as you originally suggested, use the home secretary to circumvent the foreign secretary. She rang up the American ambassador herself," Gravesend said, his face wreathed in what now appeared to be perpetual astonishment. "I am told she said that with these mad bombers running about, it was a matter of great personal concern to her, and the ambassador was pleased to oblige. Not only is he making the arrangements for the meeting you requested, but will accompany you, if desired. He's due back for consultations, as it happens. The prime minister said that his presence would be most appreciated. So there you have it," said Gravesend, his voice trailing off. "Amazing, simply amazing."

Except for his accent, however cultivated, Forbes thought, the ambassador, Winston Taylor Groome III, could have easily passed as establishment English, in his late forties, medium height, thinning light brown hair, somewhat pudgy, tailored by Huntsman.

They sat together on the flight. In checking Groome's background, Forbes found it quite impressive for an American. He was the scion of a wealthy Main Line Philadelphia family that prided itself on government service. The family fortune came from early railway interests. Although Forbes already knew the answers, he asked anyway to build a bridge of cordiality. "Have you been in the diplomatic corps very long?"

"Only since the last election," Groome said, lighting up a filtered Dunhill. "But we were always taught to answer our country's call. My grandfather was at the war department under President Coolidge."

"Really?"

"Yes, and my father was a roving ambassador for President Eisenhower."

"Splendid," Forbes said. "We can't thank you enough."

"Only too happy to help. Anglo-American cooperation is what we're all about. The world would be in a pretty fix without it," Groome said. "Actually, I'm rather looking forward to this. You don't know how boring an ambassadorship can be, even at the Court of Saint James."

The meeting was held in Nyquist's office. Forbes

and Groome were the first to arrive. Nyquist had brought in Goldfarb, and after introductions Groome said to Nyquist, "I thought you'd be in some embassy by now," and Nyquist said, "They offered me Reykjavik, can you beat that? After what my mother's kicked into the party coffers. I'm holding out for Stockholm. I hear I have a pretty good shot."

"I, for one," Forbes said, "am delighted that you're right where you are."

"Coming from a professional, I appreciate that, Forbes. Means a lot to me."

Also at the meeting were the directors of the Bureau of Alcohol, Tobacco and Firearms and the FBI. The presence of the new FBI director, Judge William Tallman, had caused a stir. To a man, all of his assistant directors were dumbfounded. It was unheard of for the director to venture forth in official Washington other than to the White House, and then only in answer to a summons from the Oval Office, and to the office of the attorney general, his nominal superior. It would set the worst kind of precedent, he was told. A real downer for bureau morale, if word got around. Even Terry McDonell, who came with him, had doubts.

But he had insisted. He wasn't going to make a habit of it, he said. It was just a one-time gesture to show that the FBI's old rigidity was a thing of the past. "Hands across the agencies" was how he put it. That wasn't the reason at all, however. Tallman was an avid collector of Early American furniture. He despised the sterile, heavy-handed look of the J. Edgar Hoover Building. He'd heard about the elegance of Nyquist's office in the customs service headquarters on Constitution Avenue, once the home of the Department of Commerce, with its vaulted hallways and marble floors and cobbled courtyard, and this was the best excuse he could think of to take a quick look at it.

And it was as advertised, an office sixty feet long, with sixteen-foot ceilings and a huge fireplace you could almost walk into. He wondered if it worked. By God, he thought, if he were in residence it damn well would! But what caught his eye was Nyquist's desk, a massive mahogany partner's desk, circa 1850. He recognized its maker immediately, a Rhode Island craftsman whose homegrown genius had made his rare English copies in fact sought-after originals. This boob Nyquist probably had no conception of what he had here. What a waste, Tallman thought.

"Judge, I want to thank you for your courtesy in coming," Nyquist said.

"My pleasure," Tallman said.

Forbes had something for everybody. For the ATF, he brought a list of the serial numbers of the weapons taken from the *Valerie*, most of which had not yet been obliterated. And for the FBI he announced that the British security service had developed an informant within the IRA who had revealed the shipment initally and was shortly expected to provide the names of key figures in the American end of the ongoing conspiracy.

Judge Tallman couldn't keep his eyes off the desk. As if conferring with McDonell, he whispered, "You see that beauty? Get general services on the ball. Find out if they've got another one stashed away in a warehouse."

Distracted, McDonell told Forbes, "That's terrific," and then looked questioningly at Tallman.

"The desk, goddammit," Tallman whispered.

"I want to thank you for coming today on such short notice," Forbes said. "What I'm about to say has our highest official secrecy classification. As I have already noted, Her Majesty's government has developed an informant within the IRA, and not just any informant. For years, we have been attempting to insert a source—a 'mole' as he's popularly called these days—in the highest circles of the IRA. We are now on the verge of success. The seizure of the arms trawler off the Irish coast is a testament to it."

Forbes gazed around the table. He had everyone's attention, even Judge Tallman's. "When fully realized, this endeavor will have enormous law enforcement impact as regards the IRA on both sides of the Atlantic. The source's identity has to be protected at all costs. Alas, with success has come danger. Certain events beyond our control surrounding the interception of the recent arms shipment threaten to expose him," Forbes said.

"By the process of elimination, if nothing else, we believe it will be only a matter of time before the Provisionals begin to close in on him, and all our efforts will be for naught. That was why stories were hastily passed on to friendly journalists in London speculating that the tip might have come from information supplied by U.S. agencies."

"I'd say they were a little more than speculative," Tallman said.

"Yes, well, we had no choice. It was a stopgap measure," Forbes said, "and we apologize for any inconvenience if, indeed, there was any."

He waited for a challenge to that. There was none, so he said, "It's imperative that the IRA be completely deceived. It is the reason for this meeting. The shipment came from America. Therefore, why not offer convincing evidence that the source, the betrayer if you will, was beyond doubt American? It is the hope of Her Majesty's government that you agree to participate in a more definitive creation of this legend."

"You mean," Judge Tallman said, "you want us to have someone else take the fall for you? I don't exactly get that. Okay, the IRA are terrorists and so forth, but they're not blowing up anything here, or taking American hostages. I'd say it was your problem, not ours. That's pretty dicey, what you're asking."

"Sir," Forbes said, "we are allies."

"I agree with that," Ambassador Groome said. "What are allies for?"

"Count me in a hundred percent," Nyquist said. "I've been listening to Forbes, and unless somebody has a better idea, I think customs has a way to do it. What I have in mind is—"

"Tell you what," Tallman said. "That's fine with me, whatever you come up with. We'll support it, within reason." He got up and motioned McDonell to follow him. "Nice meeting you," he said to Forbes. The director of the ATF, not certain why, tagged behind to find out.

In the corridor Tallman said, "I don't think we should know the details, if something screws up. Terry, be helpful. To a point."

In Nyquist's office, Forbes said, "They left rather abruptly. I trust there's nothing amiss."

"No, no," Nyquist said. "The judge is just being careful. He's still contending with all kinds of inherited headaches. Crazy surveillance operations. Racial discrimination in the bureau. He doesn't want some congressional committee on his ass for something that happened *after* he took over."

Nyquist said, "Will you excuse me and Barry for a minute?" Then he walked Goldfarb to the far end of the office. "You know, Barry," he said, "one way or another, I'm leaving soon, and I think I ought to be replaced by a career man. Like you. We pull this off, the old guy in the Oval Office is going to be very pleased, when he hears about it. He's dotty about the prime minister. Now listen, that kid from Harvard you told me about might be the key. You have someone up in Boston who could lean on him, on a weekend, say, without Daugherty getting wise?"

"Bertelli. Angelo Bertelli. He's a group supervisor and he's good, and he doesn't go for Daugherty's Irish bullshit."

"What'd we get off that trawler, what was the name?"

"*Sea King.* What we got was all circumstantial. A fully loaded nine millimeter Browning automatic with the numbers etched off with acid. Impossible to bring them up. And marked charts showing the Irish coast."

"And no fish."

"No fish. Least that's what they said at the fish pier."

"Who owns the trawler?"

"On the record, a couple a regular businessmen. Bought her as an investment. They're clean as far as we can tell. But a dummy corporation leased her. There's some talk it's one of Tommy Ahearn's fronts."

"Who's he?"

"A big-time hood. Runs the Irish mob in Boston."

"Hell, I always thought organized crime was mixed up in this, but I figured it was the Mafia."

"That's what drives Bertelli nuts. Mafia this, Mafia that."

"All right, you light a fire under this Bertelli's tail."

Nyquist walked back to Forbes and Groome. "Well, I think we've worked something out," he said.

Even though it was Saturday, Ingrid had a duty turn at the hospital, so Jamie was alone when the knock on the glass doors came. Standing outside was a hawk-nosed man, slender, with olive skin.

"Yes?" Jamie said.

"Bertelli, Angelo Bertelli," he said, fishing out his identification. "U.S. Customs Service. Law enforcement."

"What can I do for you?"

"I'd like to talk to you."

"About?"

"About a trawler called the *Sea King*."

"What makes you think I know anything about a trawler with that name, or any trawler?"

"Come on, kid. We've got eyewitnesses in New Bedford saw you on her all summer. Don't jerk me around. Like I said, I want to talk to you. Can I come in?"

"I don't know."

"Listen, this isn't an arrest. I can make it an arrest, if that's your heart's desire. And you're welcome to call a lawyer. But let me tell you something," Bertelli said. "It's Saturday afternoon, and the federal magistrate's office is closed. Since twelve on the dot. Which means even if you get a lawyer, you're locked up till Monday, nine A.M. So why don't we make it easy on everybody?"

"All right, come in," Jamie said. It was happening, he thought, but *what* precisely?

"Nice place you got. Live alone?" Bertelli glanced around and saw Ingrid's panty hose draped over a chair. "I guess not, less you dress different than I think. I was in college, I didn't have a layout like this."

"Is that what I could be arrested for?"

"Cute. Real cute. You go to Harvard to learn comedy routines? I'll tell you what you could be arrested for, smartass. For smuggling dope. Grass. You were on that trawler, the *Sea King*, last summer. Remember?"

"They didn't find anything. Your own customs people said it was a mistake. They were there."

"Yeah, but the DEA and the cops didn't buy it, and they were there, too. So we've come up with more evidence. You could save yourself a lot of grief, you unburden yourself a little."

Jamie wondered whether to believe him. No, he decided. If this Bertelli had anything, he wouldn't be going through all this. He'd be under arrest, forget about Saturday. "I don't know what it could be," he said. "Okay, I worked on the *Sea King*, but I don't know about any dope. I was a college student earning money."

"Is that right?" Bertelli said. "Well, try this on for size then, mister college student. How would you like ten years in the slammer, get your ass reamed out good in there I hear, for smuggling guns, plastic explosives, missiles?"

"Into Boston? You've got to be kidding."

"Not here. There. To Ireland. To terrorists. Conspiracy to violate the Neutrality Act. Conspiracy to export arms without a U.S. Department of State license. Failure to register said cargo with the U.S. Customs Service."

Jesus, Jamie thought, had Foncecas talked? But that couldn't be. If Foncecas had talked, why didn't Bertelli get it over with and pull out the handcuffs? For sure, Bertelli knew something, though. *How?*

Bertelli said, "The *Sea King* left New Bedford last month, and you were seen on her."

"Look, I was just a hired hand. I don't know anything."

"You admit you were on the crew?"

"Yes, so what?"

"You're in deep shit, is what. This isn't the end of it. I'll be back. I was you, I wouldn't be going anyplace soon. Stick around. Here's my card, your memory starts improving. For your sake, I hope it does. See you."

After Bertelli left, Jamie sat sipping a beer, trying to think. Should he call someone? But who? Kevin was the only person he knew, and Kevin was in some jail in Ireland.

When Ingrid came home, he told her about Bertelli's visit.

She clasped a hand to her mouth and said, "Oh, my God. Have you spoken to your father?"

"No, I can't do that. Not now."

On Sunday morning Goldfarb called Bertelli at home. "You see him?"

"Just like you said."

"So, how'd it go?"

"He hung tough."

"What's that mean?"

"It means he didn't say much, is what."

"Did he admit he was on her?"

"Yeah, finally. Said he was only a hired hand. Nobody ever told him nothin'."

"What'd you tell him?"

"That he was in big trouble. He just let it go."

"You think he knows anything important?"

"Probably. I could only push him so far based on what you gave me."

"Did he say he was getting a lawyer?"

"No."

"Tell you what. You give him a CI number and write him up."

"How do I do that?" Bertelli said. "CI" was the symbol for confidential informant.

"Last I heard, you use a typewriter. Listen good, Angie. There's a lot a heat on this one from Washington. I can't go into it too much, but this pans out, there's a big vacancy where Dan Daugherty's butt sits, you get my meaning, Angie? And don't worry. You got my authorization."

Bertelli didn't respond. Goldfarb could hear the

clicks working in Bertelli's head. Bertelli was thinking, Should I ask for it in writing? Well, *he* hadn't asked Nyquist for that. Sometimes, at a crossroads in a man's career, Goldfarb thought, you had to grab for the brass ring, couldn't play it safe. He pondered what he would say if Bertelli asked for a written authorization, but he didn't have to face that.

"When do you want me to do it?" Bertelli said at last.

"Tomorrow. First thing. Just put in what we already know. That the source was on the trawler. Was present at the transfer. That further information is being developed. Make it, you know, positive. And make sure you copy Daugherty."

"He hardly reads any of this stuff."

"This one he'll read," Goldfarb said. "Bet the farm on it."

Daniel P. Daugherty shuddered. It was like the goddamn domino theory in action.

First the seizure off Ireland. Then the stories in the *Globe* about the FBI knowing everything. Then the *Sea King* being found without him knowing anything ahead of time. And now this.

He read the Bertelli memo again. *What* was the memo saying? He thought about talking to Bertelli, but maybe that wasn't such a wonderful idea, him being suddenly so interested. That fuckin' guinea bastard!

An hour later Daugherty was seated in the rear of the Liffey saloon by the Boston Garden, near the

Thomas P. O'Neill Building, staring into Tommy Ahearn's bituminous eyes.

"Who is he, this source?" Ahearn said.

"I don't know. S-983-BO, is all. S stands for 'source.' The number's his number. BO is Boston."

"There's got to be a name goes with it. You tellin' me the fuckin' agent drops dead, the informant dies with him?"

"No. There's a safe for that, where the names match up."

"Who's got the combination?"

"The SAC, the special agent in charge."

"That's it?"

"And, uh, me."

"So get the name."

"I can't take a chance. It's too dangerous. You got to sign in and out, everybody."

"You find a way. I go down on this, Danny boy, you're goin' with me. I seen this comin'. I can read the papers. You know what them crazies over in Belfast got to be thinkin', they get around to it. Tommy Ahearn, is what. And I'm not sittin' around waitin' for them, they start thinkin' that. I'll be up in Nashua tonight. You got the number, right?"

"Yes."

"You call me, Danny. Else you're dead meat."

At ten P.M., only the duty agent was left in the office. Out front. Daugherty let himself into the secure room and, cursing his fumbling fingers, opened the safe on his second try.

On the street afterward, three blocks away, he dialed Ahearn from a pay phone.

"It's the McGuire kid," he said and hung up.

Chapter

16

Jamie said, "Could I borrow the Honda for a few days?"

"Yes, of course," Ingrid said. "Is something the matter?"

"I, uh, look, I'm sure it's nothing. It's hard to explain. I just have this feeling I'm being followed, *watched*. Two or three times I've seen this same guy around, a big guy, kind of burly, like once I saw him when I was in a coffee shop staring at me, then when I was going into the library, and then walking back here."

"Who could it be?"

"That's what I don't know. Maybe a customs agent. Or maybe somebody else. But I can't think who. Hey, maybe I'm getting paranoid. I just want to drop out of sight for a while. Go to Dad's place at the beach. See what happens."

"I'm going with you."

"No, I don't want you involved. If someone comes

asking for me, that's how we'll find out. You can just say I took off."

"Jamie, I don't want to be alone again."

"It'll only be for a little while. I'll call you as soon as I get there."

But he did not call.

Not that night, nor the next day. Thinking that he might have taken a roundabout route to throw off anyone following him, she waited until the evening of the second day before she started calling herself. She called every hour. The phone rang endlessly.

In the morning, finally, she called Michael McGuire.

The moment she said, "Mr. McGuire?" on the phone, her voice so small, he sensed something was wrong.

"Ingrid, what is it?"

"Has Jamie spoken to you?"

"He called me last week, in L.A. I just flew in. I was going to call myself. He said that he was back, and all this craziness was over. We were going to get together."

"He's disappeared," she said. "This is the third day now I haven't heard from him. I don't know what to do."

He heard her begin to weep.

"Ingrid!"

"Yes, I'm sorry," she said. "Forgive me, please. I'm so worried."

It was completely unlike her usual cool, composed, efficient manner. Michael felt the apprehension rising in him. He began to hope without hope that they'd had some sort of a lovers' quarrel.

"Do you know about the *Sea King*?" she said. "It was all in the *Globe*."

"Big news in Boston isn't necessarily so in L.A. What's the *Sea King*?"

"The trawler Jamie went to Ireland on. The authorities know about it. A man questioned Jamie. A man from customs. I have his name. Then Jamie said he thought someone might be following him. It wasn't the same man. He didn't know who it was. That's why he went to your house at the beach."

"He's at the beach?"

"That's where he said he was going. But he hasn't called. I've tried and tried to reach him, but there was no answer."

"Ingrid, I'll get back to you." He left a message with the wife of the house watcher he used at the beach. But when the house watcher returned the call, he said he'd been by the house every day and hadn't seen Jamie around at all. He'd missed Jamie during the summer, he said. "That's a nice boy you have, Mr. McGuire. Is everything okay?"

"Thank you, I don't know. If you do see Jamie, please have him phone me at once. Put a note on the front door."

He phoned Ingrid and told her that Jamie hadn't shown up. "Have you said anything about this to the police?"

"I called the police," she said, "and the state police to see if there had been, you know, an accident. There was nothing." She started to cry again.

"I'll get there as soon as I can," Michael McGuire said.

A storm moving through New York caused massive

flight delays, and it was nearly six P.M. before he landed in Boston. Then, as he was getting out of the cab, he saw the Honda parked in front of the house on Putnam Avenue. Thank God, he thought, and hurried down the pathway to the rear and pounded on the plate-glass door. He could see her inside, hunched over on the sofa. No sign of Jamie. Later he would remember how tight and ashen her face was, eyes swollen and red-rimmed, but right then he saw none of this. "Where's Jamie?" he said.

She looked at him in astonishment. "What do you mean?"

"Come on, he's here, isn't he? He's got to be. Your car's outside. You told me Jamie took your car."

She tore past him out the door. He ran after her to where she was standing on the sidewalk next to the Honda. She stifled a scream. "It wasn't there before," she said, holding her hands to her mouth. "Look, the keys are in the ignition. Who has done this?"

She was sobbing uncontrollably as he led her back to the apartment.

Finally he got her calmed down. It was then that she told him everything Jamie had said about the voyage, how they'd first gone from New Bedford to Gloucester, about a man named Tommy Ahearn who was pacing back and forth on the dock holding a submachine gun and had arranged everything, about Mick Connally, and how while he could understand where Connally was coming from, it was too tough and Jamie was happy he would be out of it, and how at the last second, to his surprise, Kevin Dowd had suddenly gone with the Irish trawler.

Then she said, "The car, it's like a warning. And I

still don't understand why it took so long to find the *Sea King*, if they knew about her all along."

"You say that Connally and Dowd were captured by the Irish navy?"

"Yes, that's what the paper said. When you were in Alaska."

"What about this fellow Ahearn? Was he on the trawler, too?"

"No, I don't think so. Jamie just said he saw him on the dock in Gloucester, with the gun. Jamie said Kevin Dowd said that he was the one who had arranged everything and not to ask so many questions."

Michael McGuire looked at his watch and said, "It's late. Can I take you somewhere to eat?"

"I can't. I can't eat anything. But I'll fix you something. You can stay here. That's a pull-out sofa."

"No, I have a reservation at the Copley. You try to get some rest."

"You blame me for this, don't you?" she said. "You think it's my fault. That I should have stopped him."

He looked at her drained face, the purplish smudges like bruises under her eyes, and he took both of her hands and kissed her on the cheek. "No, I don't blame you," he said. "If it's anybody's fault, it's mine. Jamie just got in over his head, but let's see. Maybe we're letting our imaginations get the best of us."

Michael McGuire counted fourteen rings the next morning before a switchboard operator finally answered and said, "Boston Police Department."

"I want to report a missing person."

"You'll have to go to a district station for that, sir. Where are you?"

"The Copley Plaza hotel."

"That'd be District Four."

"Where's that?"

"Warren Street, sir. Warren and Berkeley. Just a short cab ride." The operator got very chatty. "It's really Area D now, after all the districts got consolidated, but everybody still calls it District Four. You just tell the cabbie you want to go to the District Four station."

District Four was below the Boston Common. The cab driver said, "Cops love working District Four. 'Cause of all the clubs and bars. A cop pulls down twenty-one dollars an hour workin' off-duty details standin' around some nightclub. My cousin's a cop. He says you pay the rent with your salary, but you make a livin' doin' details."

Behind the station house's chest-high desk, a pasty-faced middle-aged woman with an old-fashioned peroxide beehive hairdo was leafing through the tabloid Boston *Herald*. A chunky sergeant peered at some paperwork through half-lenses.

Off to Michael McGuire's right, a black man with a rope for a belt and torn trousers was walking in tight little circles muttering, "Nobody gives a fuck."

"I'd like to report a missing person."

The woman, intent on an item in the *Herald*, jerked her thumb in the sergeant's direction.

"The missing persons unit is up at headquarters," the sergeant said.

"But I called them on the phone, and they said to come here."

"Yeah, well, it ain't here."

Michael McGuire tried to keep calm. The important thing, he told himself, was to get something going on Jamie, not to get into an argument with some obtuse desk sergeant.

"Look, mister, it's no big deal," the sergeant said, as if reading his mind. "Headquarters is just three blocks up Berkeley. You can walk it."

Michael McGuire passed narrow cross streets with rows of graceful, gentrified brownstones. Beyond Columbus Avenue, he saw a blue and white sign jutting out from a white granite building that said "Boston Police Headquarters."

He went up the steps to the lobby, where a uniformed police officer, glistening black hair slicked back as though he had just emerged from a shower, sat at a desk in front of two elevators.

"I want to report a missing person."

"You have to do that at a district, sir."

"Listen, I was just at a district, District Four, and they said to go to headquarters."

"Did you fill out a report there?"

"No, they said the missing persons bureau, whatever, was here."

"Sir, it isn't. It was moved. It's at the District Six station in Southie, uh, South Boston. Homicide was moved there, too," he said, apparently wishing to be as helpful as possible.

There was some sort of a jam snarling the central artery connecting the highways north and south of the city, and the traffic inched painfully forward. Oh, Christ, Michael McGuire thought, what else? Finally the cab crossed the Broadway bridge into South Boston and passed the spires of Sts. Peter and Paul's church, the first station of worship for the waves of Irish immigrants that began pouring into the city after the great famine.

Although he would never know it, the District Six house, on D Street, was just around the corner from where Kevin Dowd had lived and plotted. The lobby floor was crusty, peeling brown and white checkered linoleum with patches of exposed warped floor. A fat, balding cop manned the desk. He was wearing a big Claddagh ring. The ring had originated in County Galway and with its gold heart often served as a wedding band if worn on the correct finger. Otherwise it announced your romantic situation. If the tip of the heart pointed toward you, you were taken. If it pointed away, you were available.

The cop's ring proclaimed marital status. "Yes?" he said.

"I want to see someone in missing persons."

"You been to your district, you fill out a one-one?"

"No. District Four sent me to headquarters, and headquarters sent me here."

The cop shook his head. "They don't want people upstairs. I'm not supposed to let anyone up. If the captain was here, you could ask him, but the captain, he ain't in."

"Listen, I'm getting fed up with this runaround," Michael McGuire said. Then he noticed a young black woman off to the side surveying him, his gabardine suit, blue button-down shirt, rep tie and cordovan loafers. She was wearing jeans, white leather sneakers, a white pullover and a navy blue beret. Neatly braided Rastalocks cascaded down from under the beret. She was holding a copy of *People* magazine in one hand and a chocolate-covered ice cream bar in the other.

"I'll take him up, Tim," she said.

"Sure, okay, Marylou, you want to."

Michael McGuire followed her behind the desk. She punched buttons in a lock. A buzzer sounded and she opened the door and started up a flight of stairs. A long, grimy corridor led off the landing. There was a printed sign marked "Homicide," the next one was "General Investigations." Around a corner another sign said "Warrants." This one, though, was handwritten and tacked to the wall on a piece of yellow posterboard. Obviously there was a pecking order at work here. The farther an office was from the landing, the less important it was. Michael McGuire glanced inside the warrants office. Two gray-haired men in plainclothes sat at walnut desks. One had his feet up, staring vacantly into space. The other was bent over a pile of index cards, shuffling through them. There were more mounds of cards on a table next to file cabinets. It looked like a library reference room in the throes of a nervous breakdown.

Finally, at the very end of the corridor, they came to a door. This one had no sign. The black woman took a last bite of the ice cream bar, unlocked the door and opened it. "This is missing persons," she said. "I'm the missing persons unit."

"You're a police officer?"

"Detective. I should be working undercover, huh?"

The office was tiny, no more than ten or twelve feet square. A desk and file cabinets took up most of the room. The walls and cabinets were taped with flyers carrying the names and faces of missing people, most of them children. One was for a pretty teenage girl from Cincinnati. Her parents were offering a $10,000 reward.

"I don't usually let anyone up here," she said. "But you didn't look like, bizarre. Usually people make out a report in their district and I get a copy. It's up to the district detectives to look for the person. I mean, I don't go out into the street lookin' for them myself. The trouble is the district detectives aren't out there either. They got murderers, rapists, junkies hitting ten places a day. You think they going to waste time on somebody just missing. They think it's mostly runaways, which mostly it is."

There wasn't any place for him to sit. Here he was, an important executive in a major advertising agency, thrust into a world he didn't know, standing before this young black woman as if she were the oracle at Delphi.

She took out a white form, with carbons and pink and blue copies, and put it in her typewriter. "Okay," she said, "what's your problem?"

"My son's missing."

"Name?"

"James John McGuire."

"Age?"

"Nineteen.

"Address?"

"Sixteen ninety and a half Putnam Avenue, Cambridge."

She stopped typing. "That's not our jurisdiction."

"Isn't Cambridge part of Boston?"

"No, it's its own city." She sighed and said, "But

you think we're bad, you ain't seen nothin', you're over there. Okay, I'll make an entry anyway, so the FBI automatically collates it for wanteds and bodies, get a nationwide bulletin out. Now I need as much information as you can give me. Has he disappeared before? You can't hide anything, because if you hold back something you think's embarrassing, it's usually the very thing I need to know. Is he married? Does he have a girl friend? Did they have a fight? Was he in some kind of trouble?"

"Uh, I believe he might have been a victim of foul play." Michael McGuire couldn't believe he was using such stilted language. He couldn't bring himself to do anything else. Somehow it made it easier.

"How's that?"

"Well, he was a student, just starting his sophomore year at Harvard, but during the summer he was on the crew of a fishing trawler, the *Sea King*, that's suspected of bringing arms to the IRA, ah, in Ireland."

"Oh, yeah, I read about that in the papers."

"Can't something be done? Can't this be investigated?"

"It's going to be investigated. I'll see to that. At least I can put the information in the right places. It's the system that's screwed up. The way the city morgue is, I got a better chance turning up a body if it's in Toledo. But I took this job because I had a relative up and leave a few years back. I don't like to talk about it, but I know how crazy it is trying to find out what happened. I know there's family left behind."

He could be reached at the Copley Plaza, he said, and then he gave her Ingrid's number, too.

She walked him back along the corridor. As she

was returning, the detective with his feet up in the office decorated with outstanding warrants said, "Hey, Marylou, big day. A visitor." He had heavy-lidded eyes, like a lizard on a rock waiting for a fly to drop by.

"You're very alert, Sullivan. Listen, you got all the right tribal connections. Guy's name was McGuire. His son's missing. He was on that trawler customs found down at the fish pier, the one in that IRA delivery. You know anything about that?"

"Forget it, Marylou. Word's around. The kid was a snitch."

"That's past tense on purpose?"

"Hey, Marylou, you're a real kidder."

Right afterward, she punched in her computer hookup to the FBI re James John McGuire, his age, description, last known address. Possible kidnap. Possible homicide. Possible violation multiple federal statutes.

At a Howard Johnson's near the Putnam Avenue apartment, Michael McGuire told Ingrid about his day with the police. Plates of fried clams they had ordered lay untouched in front of them. He finished his second bourbon on the rocks and was about to ask for a third. "You ought to eat," he said. "You're not eating."

"Neither are you."

"No," he said. He did not order the third drink.

"What are we going to do now?"

He rubbed his chin, feeling the stubble. "I'm going to see that customs guy tomorrow. What was his name, Bertelli?"

"Yes, Angelo Bertelli."

"I'm going to tell him everything. It's the only way we can get anything done. I learned that much from that girl, the detective in missing persons."

"Can I go with you?"

"I think it's better not to." He told her that the first thing Marylou Robinson had raised was the possibility of a lovers' quarrel. "I don't want to give him a chance to even suggest that."

She stared at him. "Would you stay at the apartment tonight? It's just—Oh, I don't know what it is. It's silly, but I would feel better if you were there." Tears filled her eyes. "The sofa has a pull-out bed," she said.

"Yes, you said so. Of course."

She drove him to the hotel and waited while he got his things. He should not have left her alone to begin with, he thought. Despite what he had said, he wondered if subconsciously he was blaming her for all of this, for not stopping Jamie before it was too late.

At the apartment while she was making up the bed, he gazed at the IRA poster, hating it. Abruptly he walked over and ripped it off the wall. She looked at him, startled, but she did not say anything.

In bed, he could hear her moving around in the bedroom. Then there was silence, and then he could hear her sobbing. There was silence again, and then in darkness he heard her crying out, "Jamie!" He felt his own eyes fill. And then it was silent once more.

He finally drifted into fitful sleep. He dreamed of Jamie, of fishing with him that first time so long ago, of Jamie's excitement when he hooked the blue, shouting, "I've got something!" and of himself, the proud father, saying, "Good work, son," and he dreamed of Mary Alice, her eyes sparkling, standing at the dock, and then she disappeared and he was calling out to her to please not leave, that he needed her so desperately. But it was no use, and then, all at once, Jamie was in the water swimming steadily away from him, and now he was calling to him to come back, "Jamie! Jamie!"

Michael McGuire came bolt upright. The overhead light in the room was on. He blinked against the glare, trying to focus. He saw Ingrid standing beside him. She was wearing a blue robe. She had a hand on his shoulder. "Are you all right?" she said, her voice anxious.

"Yes, no, who knows?" he said. "No better than you, for sure. What happened?"

"You were yelling in your sleep. You were calling out for Jamie."

"Yes, I remember now. Oh, God."

"Can I get you something, some warm milk?"

"No, I'm okay, I think, hope."

"Goodnight then. Thank you again for staying."

It was daylight when he awoke. She was gone. There was a note saying she'd gone to the hospital. If she couldn't go with him, the note said, work was all she had left to maintain her sanity. There were directions on the kitchen counter about coffee.

He suddenly felt ravenous, though, and he walked to the Howard Johnson's where they had been the night before and ordered pancakes and bacon. He never ate them. The front-page headline in the morning *Globe* he had just bought said,

Boston Informer's Tip Reportedly
Led to IRA Arms Shipment Seizure

According to the authoritative *Times* of London, the story began, the recent interception of tons of weapons and plastic explosive, including Redeye missiles, destined for the IRA was due to information that an informer in Boston gave to federal law enforcement agencies.

It said that MI5, the supersecret counterintelligence apparatus charged with Britain's domestic security, had developed evidence of a cabal within the U.S. Customs Service, part of the so-called Emerald Society, which facilitated aid to the IRA. Based on this, an informer cultivated by customs agents subsequently revealed that a huge arms hoard was being assembled for transport across the Atlantic to Ireland.

As soon as the trawler carrying the arms, the *Sea King,* left New Bedford, customs officials reportedly contacted the FBI, which in turn alerted British and Irish intelligence. A U.S. spy satellite was said to have tracked the trawler throughout her voyage.

Customs commissioner Alan Nyquist was quoted in the *Globe* as hailing this operation as an outstanding example of Anglo-American cooperation against terrorism. He said that an internal customs investigation was continuing. He also expressed his belief that organized crime figures, heavily engaged in narcotics, had played a key middleman role in the arms shipment.

An FBI spokesman announced that the bureau was probing the circumstances surrounding the shipment, but refused to elaborate. The identity of the informer, the story concluded, remained unknown.

• • •

Michael McGuire took a cab to the Thomas P. O'Neill Building. He told the receptionist in the customs offices on the eighth floor that he wanted to speak to Angelo Bertelli. No, he didn't have an appointment, he said. Just tell Bertelli that the father of James McGuire was there to see him.

Ever since he got to work, Bertelli had been brooding about the *Globe* story. He'd tried Goldfarb, but Goldfarb's secretary said that he was en route by plane from Washington. He wouldn't be available for at least another hour.

When Michael McGuire was ushered in, Bertelli could see how tense the father was. His initial thought was that he had come to make some sort of a deal for his son.

But the first thing he said was, "What did my son say to you?"

"You don't know?"

"I thought I did. Now I'm not so sure. Did you read the story in the paper this morning?"

"Yes."

"Well, do you know my son's been missing practically since the moment you had him in for questioning?"

"Missing!" Bertelli couldn't keep the surprise out of his voice. "What do you mean, missing? He take off, or something?"

"He was planning to. He told his girl friend that he thought he was being followed. Maybe by your people. He wasn't certain. He was going to go to a beach house I have on Long Island. But he never got there.

He borrowed his girl friend's car, and three days after he disappeared the car was back, parked in front of her place. No sign of him. I think your interrogation has something to do with all this. What did he tell you? I've got to know. Was he the person they were writing about, the informant?"

"Mr. McGuire, I didn't know your son was missing. This is the first I heard of it." Bertelli wrestled with himself. He thought about Goldfarb, what Goldfarb had said, the write-up Goldfarb wanted. This McGuire looked like a good guy. He sympathized with him, could see the anguish in his face, could see him trying to maintain some kind of control. "To tell the truth," he said, "I figured you were coming in for your son, tell me what was going on, and maybe now you should. But your son wasn't an informer, least I know, that's what's worrying you."

Then Michael McGuire told Bertelli everything he could recall, beginning with Jamie's encounter with Kevin Dowd at The Crooked Plough. "He's a wonderful, caring boy," he said. "I got into this, found out about it, late. Just before the shipment. But that's no excuse. I should have put my foot down. Come to you then, I guess. How, though? Christ, it's so complicated. He was committed to Irish freedom, I can tell you that. This was going to be it, this one trip. You've got to find him. *Who* is this informer? Doesn't he know something?"

"That's confidential, Mr. McGuire." Bertelli chose his words carefully. "But I guarantee, I'll do what I can."

"I forgot one thing. Have you ever heard of a man named Ahearn, Tommy Ahearn?"

"If it's the same Ahearn, he runs the Irish mob

here. Real tough wiseguy. Nobody to fool around with. Why? Your son say he was mixed up in this?"

"I'm not completely sure. My son told his girl friend that he was at the dock in Gloucester before the trawler left. Carrying a gun. Jamie said Kevin Dowd said Ahearn had arranged everything."

"That'd be unusual. A boss like Ahearn isn't usually on the scene himself."

Then he gave Bertelli his hotel number and Ingrid's number, and his home and office numbers in New York.

As soon as Michael McGuire had left, Bertelli tried Goldfarb again, and this time he got him. At last Goldfarb was back from Washington. He couldn't remember Goldfarb being in Washington so much. Why hadn't he demanded authorization in writing from Goldfarb about the write-up? Because Goldfarb had dangled Daugherty's job in front of him, was why. He was up for sucker of the year, Bertelli thought. You think about it one second, Daugherty had Congressman Corny Gallagher in his hip pocket. Everyone knew that. What a fool he was!

"I got to see you," Bertelli said.

"So see me. I'm here."

Face to face with Goldfarb, Bertelli said, "That McGuire kid's father was just in to see me."

"Yeah?"

"He said the kid's missing."

"Really?"

"Yeah, really. I wouldn't want to think me talking to him had anything to do with it."

"Don't worry about it. Anybody around here's got anything to worry about, it's Mr. Daniel P. Daugherty."

"What the hell's going on?"

"What's going on, you got to know so much, is this is a Brit operation, MI Five. That satisfy you? We're playing catch up, is all, so Washington can show them we're not complete assholes. Washington's real interested in that. Look, start acting like the new assistant regional commissioner for law enforcement, which you're going to be, you don't fuck up."

After leaving Bertelli, Michael McGuire went to the Boston field office of the FBI in the John F. Kennedy Federal Building. He asked to see the special agent in charge. Mr. Crosson was tied up in a meeting, he was told. What was the nature of his business?

He identified himself. He was, he said, the father of a member of the crew of the *Sea King*, the boat that was involved in an IRA arms shipment. "It was in the paper this morning," he said. "You must have seen it."

"Please take a seat."

He saw the man at the desk make a call, and then another. On the wall was a wooden plaque with names in gold honoring agents in the Boston office who had died in the line of duty. There were a number of slots on the plaque yet to be filled.

About twenty minutes later, a youthful agent appeared. He said his name was Corcoran. "What can I do for you, sir? You say you're the father of James John McGuire?"

"Yes, I want to report my son missing."

"We know that, sir. It came over the computer from the Boston police."

"Oh," Michael McGuire said, offering silent thanks to Detective Marylou Robinson.

"Rest assured, the FBI is doing everything possible to locate your son. Is there anything more you can tell us?"

Michael McGuire followed him into a cubicle off the reception area.

"What business are you engaged in, Mr. McGuire?"

"Advertising. What's that got to do with it?"

"We like to have as complete a picture as we can, sir."

Then Michael McGuire recounted the same story he had told Bertelli. He watched Corcoran write it all down.

"And you say," Corcoran said, "that your son said he saw a man who was identified to him as Ahearn holding a submachine gun on the dock in Gloucester?"

"Yes. Shouldn't Ahearn be questioned? He could be the key to all of this."

"Sir, all I can tell you is that this matter is being handled with the highest priority. I want to thank you, you've been very helpful," Corcoran said. "We'll be in contact with you, rest assured."

"Stop saying that. I'm not resting assured. Goddammit, my son's missing. I want him found."

"We will do our best," Corcoran said, and like Bertelli, he asked how Michael McGuire could be reached.

Afterward Corcoran went in to his supervisor, who

had already been informed of Michael McGuire's presence. "Jesus," Corcoran said, "he laid out everything about the shipment, the whole bit."

"Write it up," the supervisor said. "This is Washington's baby, is all I know. Airtel it attention Terry McDonell, that's one 'n,' SOG." SOG meant Seat of Government, FBI headquarters in Washington.

"He mentioned Tommy Ahearn maybe being in it. He said he wants Ahearn questioned."

"That's nice. We'll invite him right down. Mr. Ahearn, hate to bother you, but you mind telling us about shipping some illegal weapons to the Provisional Irish Republican Army? We need your testimony because we don't have any evidence."

Michael McGuire took a cab to Ingrid's apartment. She hadn't returned from the hospital. He found a beer in the refrigerator.

The phone rang. It was a woman's voice. "Mr. McGuire?"

"Yes."

"This is Detective Robinson, from missing persons. Listen, I don't want to upset you, but I think something bad may be happening to your son."

"Have you heard something? Tell me!"

"Nothing specific, you know. A feeling I have. But I'd go to the FBI, I were you."

"I have."

"Good. And I'm pushing the department on this. Do what I can."

"I want to thank you for getting the bulletin out fast."

"That's my job."

When Ingrid got home, he didn't mention Robinson's call. He told her what he'd learned. Jamie had been reported missing by the police. The FBI had told him it was a top priority case. Bertelli at customs claimed he had no idea Jamie was missing.

"It's the car that frightens me so," she said. "I keep praying that Jamie brought the car back so I wouldn't be involved. But that doesn't make any sense. He would have told me. Maybe he did not have time. I thought about the car all last night. And if it wasn't Jamie, why would anyone do something that cruel?"

"I just don't know. I thought about using my agency to help with the media," he said. "Getting Jamie's picture out and so on. But that could cause him more harm. It's like a house with secret passages. The FBI guy said all the right things, but he was stroking me. You could see that. Like there's something else involved here. Bertelli wasn't much better. He seemed awfully jumpy."

Michael McGuire looked at Ingrid. "I'm going to take another shot at Bertelli. It's the only thing I can think of."

He underlined portions of the *Globe* story, and in the morning returned to see Bertelli without calling first.

"Tell him I'm not here," Bertelli said. Then he thought better of it. See him, talk to him, be his pal, that was the smart thing. Else who knows what the father might do. Maybe start talking to reporters, make unforeseen waves. Bertelli winced at the possibility. Why the hell had he ever written up that CI

report Goldfarb had wanted? He had to start covering himself. "No," he said on the intercom. "Check
that. Bring him in."

"Mr. McGuire," he said, rising to his feet, extending his hand.

Michael McGuire sensed again Bertelli's edginess.
"I'm sorry to barge in like this."

"No problem."

Behind Bertelli, there was a splendid vista of Boston harbor, the bay, the ocean. "That's a fabulous
view you have."

"What? Oh yeah. It gets so you hardly notice it,
though. What can I do for you?"

"Any word on my son?"

"I was hoping you heard something. I want to be
all the help I can, but we're not exactly in the missing
persons business. That's for the local police and the
FBI, if it's a federal matter, which probably it is."

"Yes, I know. But you're the only person I've
talked to that I have any confidence in."

"I wish I could do more."

Michael McGuire took out the *Globe* clipping.
"Where do you think a story like this came from? I
mean, did it come from you, from the customs service?"

"Believe me, I don't talk to reporters ever, Mr.
McGuire. It isn't my job. Maybe it was Washington. I
don't know where these guys get half their stuff."

"I can't help wondering if your interrogation of my
son doesn't have some connection with this, all of it."

"I don't see how."

"Well, why did you question him in the first place?"

"Uh, I can't go into our procedures," Bertelli said.

"But I can figure what you're going through. It was a tip that came from upstairs is all I can say."

Michael McGuire watched as Bertelli nervously shuffled the papers on his desk. "Now, if you'd excuse me," Bertelli said.

"One more thing. I noticed in the story that the British secret security service, MI Five, played some role in this. I used to work with MI Five."

"You did?"

"Yes, I was in army counterintelligence, in Europe after World War Two."

"No kidding," Bertelli said. He leaned back in his chair. He seemed suddenly to relax at the news, as if a great burden had been lifted from his shoulders. After a moment he bent forward conspiratorially, almost in relief, as though he had forgotten who Michael McGuire was and why he was there. "Then you'll understand. You get orders, you know, and you just do them, right? That's how those spooks operate. Between you and I, the way I get it, this is all, uh, an MI Five deal, which is how come I don't know any more myself."

"I appreciate you telling me."

"Like I said, I'm sorry I can't be more help. Soon as something turns up on your son, I'll call you. I still have your numbers."

"Yes, thank you," Michael McGuire said.

At Logan airport, he phoned Ingrid. "I'm going to New York, and then to London. I've got a lead, I think. I'll only be gone a couple of days. I'll call you."

"That's what Jamie said."

"Ingrid, please. I know it's hard, but you have to hang in there."

• • •

In his apartment, Michael McGuire found the up-to-date home telephone number and address of Anthony Seth-Jones. It was Seth-Jones's conceit to send cards annually in celebration of November 5, Guy Fawkes Day, the day in 1605 that English Catholics, chafing under religious oppression, were foiled in an attempt to blow up the houses of Parliament along with King James I.

Michael McGuire would always respond at Christmas. But while Seth-Jones had called twice to say hello from Washington, presumably there on MI5 affairs, they had not seen each other since the Englishman visited him and Jamie after the death of Mary Alice.

"Michael, how pleasant to hear from you," Seth-Jones said on the overseas line. "I trust it means I'll be seeing you soon."

"Yes, something unexpected has come up. I'm planning to be in London in the morning. You're still at the same old shop?"

"Barely. I'm to be pensioned off shortly, I'm afraid. I'll be doing some private consulting. That's why I've taken this place in West Sussex. Quite lovely. Roses, that sort of thing. Quick hop into London by train."

"I'll be staying at Brown's. Can we meet there for lunch? Say one o'clock tomorrow."

"Perfect. Five minutes from the office. We're on Curzon Street now, you know. Looking forward to it. Well, cheerio."

Yes, Michael McGuire thought. *Cheerio.*

Chapter

17

On the flight that night to London, Michael McGuire picked at his dinner and afterward had three cognacs in an effort to get some sleep. Finally he dozed off and had the same dream he'd had at Ingrid's, fishing with Jamie, the magic of their connection, and then of Jamie swimming off while he cried out helplessly after him. Awake, shaking, coated with clammy sweat, he must have said something out loud. A flight attendant had her hand on his shoulder. "Are you all right, sir?" she said.

For a moment in the darkened cabin, he did not know where he was. He was startled by flickering images in front of him before he realized it was a movie. "Yes, I guess I was having a bad dream," he said. He asked for a glass of water. He had to get some rest, he thought. And when the attendant brought the water, he swallowed a Valium with it. The last thing he remembered thinking about was

Mary Alice. Suddenly he was glad that she wasn't there to bear witness to the terrible failure he felt as a man, a father.

The Valium left him groggy when he was awakened again to fasten his seat belt for the landing approach. But at least he'd slept, and without dreams. He had a cup of coffee and began to feel better.

A driver was waiting at the baggage console, holding up a sign with "Mr. McGuire" on it. "Anything to declare, sir?"

"Nothing."

"Right you are, then," he said, and carried his suitcase with a cheery wave past a customs inspector.

In the car for him was a London *Times*. On the third page, under the heading "Northern Ireland," as if that was all that had to be said, there was a brief article that began, "A young Catholic man was shot dead in front of his family in his north Belfast home last night in an apparent sectarian murder by a Loyalist gunman." Without skipping a beat, the story went on to report, "A part-time member of the Ulster Defense Regiment remained grievously ill in a hospital following a shooting incident yesterday in Coalisland, County Tyrone, where he was set upon by masked gunmen."

At Brown's Hotel, his room was large and gloomily Edwardian, on the second floor overlooking Dover Street. He ordered a pot of coffee and showered and shaved. He went downstairs early and arranged with the maitre d' for a quiet table in the restaurant. He still had nearly an hour to kill, so he went out the Albemarle Street entrance and walked a short block to the Burlington Arcade. Years before, he'd bought a Victorian garnet necklace in one of the shops there for Mary Alice. She loved garnets, and he remembered how she'd held the necklace up and smiled with such delight at the shifting dark red luminescence of the stones and said, "Oh, Michael, I love it. It's beautiful." He thought about Tony Seth-Jones and how to approach him. He decided, finally, that he would just have to play it by ear.

He was already seated when Seth-Jones arrived punctually at one, portly, ruddy faced, mustache almost completely gray now, eyes, well, piggy, Michael McGuire thought. He was, he realized, seeing him the way Jamie would have.

"Michael, old chap, you haven't changed a bit," he said. "Wish I could say the same, but I do have some years on you. Good Lord, that's not Perrier you're drinking, is it?" He ordered a whiskey and water. "Days are numbered at the office," he said. "Not that much need for a clear head in the afternoon."

Michael McGuire was hardly able to return a greeting before Seth-Jones began rambling on about his forthcoming retirement. One didn't think it would ever happen, and abruptly one awoke one morning and it had. "One's time always comes," he said, as if stumbling upon a profound philosophical tenet.

"Have to have new blood in the office, a constant process of reinvigoration is required. That's what they said," he said. He ordered another whiskey. "Best to exit gracefully, don't you think? I still have my health, thank God. And my pension. Nothing grandiose, mind you. But with my consultancy, I'll be able to manage quite adequately."

Seth-Jones gestured at a waiter. "I'll have another,"

he said, handing him his glass. "I wonder what the last day will be like. I'll be requested to open my safe and turn over my files. Cards, hundreds of them, all those years. Old-fashioned now, you know. It's all satellite transmissions and computers these days. I'll be asked for my diaries, so they can be burned. I shall have to sign off my access chits. There'll be a fare-well gathering, I suppose. Someone will raise his glass and say, 'Three hurrahs for old Tony!' "

The Sussex cottage was just what he'd been search-ing for. "Didn't know I was interested in gardening, did you?" Seth-Jones said. His former wife had got-ten him into it. She was in Australia somewhere, hadn't heard from her in years. "The truth is she ran off with some other chap," he said. "Not from the office, nothing scandalous like that. A civil engineer. Outdoorsy."

He'd miss being in the thick of things, no two ways about it. "I have my memories, though," he said. He looked at Michael McGuire like a penitent seek-ing absolution. "The stories I could tell, the book I could write. But I can't. The Official Secrets Act, you know."

He peered glumly at his empty plate. Still, there was a need for him, he said. The private firm he would be associated with enjoyed numerous military contracts, highly classified. He couldn't go into the particulars, of course, but he'd be advising them on vital matters of security. His voice trailed off.

Michael McGuire did not know exactly how to begin. Seth-Jones saved him the trouble. "Forgive me, I didn't mean to rattle on like this," he said. "What about you? Still in advertising, are you? Heard you remarried. Someone said that, I can't think who. And your son, how's that boy of yours? Must be quite a strapping young man by now."

So he told him. "Jamie's disappeared," Michael McGuire said. "He got caught up in the Irish republican movement, the IRA. It's a long story. But he was on a trawler called the *Sea King* that brought over an arms shipment that was seized off the Irish coast last month."

All the forced joviality in Seth-Jones vanished. "Your son was involved in *that*?"

"You heard me. But that's not the point. The point is that my son's missing. Mysteriously. I want you to do me a favor. I know for a fact that the office, your office, MI Five, had a big hand in this. I want to know what it was. Find out for me. You hear me, Tony?"

"Impossible," Seth-Jones said, sputtering. "What you're asking is unthinkable. I'm sorry, I must be getting back."

Earlier, walking through the Burlington Arcade, Michael McGuire had considered pleading for Seth-Jones's help, begging for it if he had to. He said, "Listen, Tony, I regret putting it like this, but you aren't giving me any choice. A minute ago, you told me all about those stories you could tell. Hey, I've got a story, too. Remember Otto Ellersieck, Tony, that fucking Nazi butcher you got me to help save in the good old days? That's hot stuff right now. I'll bet old Otto's right here in merry old England. Little vine-covered cottage in Cornwall? Or maybe right next to you in, where is it? Oh, yeah, West Sussex. Plenty of headlines there. The office is really going to love that. So's your new employer with all those classified contracts. You want your face plastered all over the place? Believe me, I've got nothing more to lose," Michael McGuire said. "I don't give a flying fuck about the Official Secrets Act. Think about it. Hard."

The flush spread through the capillary network in Seth-Jones's already red face. "I'll see what I can manage," he whispered.

"You do that, Tony."

"I'm not promising anything."

"You've been there forever. You'll find a way. I have every confidence."

"I'll ring you."

"You be sure to do that. Be in my room all afternoon," Michael McGuire said. "Here's the number. You call me one way or another. The clock's ticking. For you."

He watched Seth-Jones leave. Both their coffees had remained untouched on the table. He ordered a fresh cup, brooding about what Seth-Jones would do. But in his experience, when he wasn't bluffing, the other guy usually knew it, and he was sure Seth-Jones got the message. He went to his room and lay down. He felt the jet lag, but he couldn't sleep. Pacing back and forth, he went over to the refrigerated bar and opened it. He started to reach for one of the miniature vodkas, then put it back and slammed the door.

At four-thirty the phone rang. "I will be at the American Bar at the Savoy," Seth-Jones said. "It opens at six. Be prompt. My train departs Charing Cross at half past seven. As you enter, there's a table to your right, by a bay window. I've reserved it."

When Michael McGuire arrived, two minutes late, he was there draining a glass and ordering another.

"What's that you're having?"

"Gin and tonic."

"I'll have the same," he said to the waiter. "With ice."

After they were served, Seth-Jones, avoiding eye contact, said, "I've done what you asked at great risk to myself. My name must never be mentioned."

"Don't worry, it won't."

"There's an informant of utmost importance in Northern Ireland who touted the shipment. The office is understandably keen to protect him at all cost."

"Who is he?"

"I have no idea. But he is a crucial source within the IRA, potentially the best they've ever developed. Following the intercept, authorities in America were asked to help divert any possible suspicion that might fall upon him, and they, ah, agreed to cooperate. The office had no idea of your son's existence. It was all done over there, whatever it was, on your side of the water. Your ambassador here was the go-between."

"The U.S. ambassador?"

"Yes."

"Anyone else? If I think you're holding back, the deal's off."

"I believe your chief of customs service was present. And the FBI director. There were others as well."

"You're telling me Jamie was the fall guy?"

"I don't know the details."

"Do they know what happened to Jamie? Where he is?"

"Apparently not."

"Who dreamed all this up? Someone in MI Five?"

"I've told you as much as I can. If this isn't sufficient, do what you like."

Michael McGuire swirled his gin and tonic and then swallowed half of it. "All right," he said. "Thanks."

There were no goodbyes. Jaw set, Seth-Jones rose stiffly. "Your son never should have got mixed up in this," he said, and marched out.

He remained sitting. He asked for another gin and tonic. "Make it a double," he said. The bar began filling up. Around him was a crescendo of laughing, chattering voices. He finished the drink in a single gulp. He paid and got up. Outside the bar, in the lobby, instead of going out the front of the Savoy, he turned left, without really noticing where he was going, toward the river side. He stumbled down some steps. There were more tables, more people enjoying the cocktail hour before dinner, the theater. Faces swiveled up at him. He ignored them. He continued blindly, down other steps, and then he was outside the hotel. He was in a garden. He crossed it and next the Victoria Embankment, oblivious to the traffic, the horns sounding around him, brakes squealing. Over a parapet he looked down at the dark, oily flow of the Thames.

He knew the name of the ambassador. Groome. He remembered how the Groome family had been big contributors in the last presidential campaign, that the president often stayed at the Groome estate in Palm Springs in California.

He walked along the embankment. As the river curved, he saw before him the tower of Big Ben and spires of Westminster Abbey and the Palace of Westminster and great stone lions on Westminster Bridge so artfully lighted in the night. The stomach spasms came without warning. Michael McGuire leaned over the parapet and threw up.

Three weeks after the *Valerie* had been intercepted, Kevin Dowd was incarcerated within the gray cut-stone walls of Portlaoise prison southwest of Dublin. Portlaoise had been built by the British in 1830. Conditions in it had not much improved since then.

"Mo chara," Cathleen Cassidy said to him in Gaelic. "My friend."

Two fine wire-mesh screens a foot apart, stretching from the countertop to the ceiling, separated her from Dowd in the room reserved for visitors to IRA inmates. She had come from Belfast, dispatched by Gerry McMahon.

Mick Connally had already been extradited to London for his role in the Brighton bombing. The Irish free state, however, refused to return Kevin Dowd on the grounds of insufficient evidence in the old shooting incident that left him gravely wounded in the stomach and had led to his escape to the United States from the Crumlin Road jail. An affidavit from the English undercover army sergeant who shot him, attesting that Dowd had fired a weapon first, was presented. But because of the wee lad who had found the gun in the high grass and the medical attendant in the ambulance who washed off all trace of gunpowder on Dowd's hand, it was only the sergeant's word.

Feelings in the republic also were running high

against British justice. The very week the *Valerie* had been intercepted, the British attorney general announced to the House of Commons that a long-awaited investigation into a "shoot-to-kill" policy of the Royal Ulster Constabulary allegedly master-minded by MI5 would not be made public in the interests of "national security." Those accused in a series of officially sanctioned assassinations would not be prosecuted, the attorney general said, although he assured house members that "disciplinary measures would be taken."

And it had just become public knowledge that the first British soldier in the last twenty years to be convicted and sentenced to life for murder in Northern Ireland—for shooting down a young Catholic husband and father who was simply walking along a street—had been secretly released and returned to active duty.

So Dowd would face gun-running charges in Dublin. Through his solicitor he had issued a statement emphasizing that nothing in the shipment was for use in the free state and, further, that members of the *Valerie*'s crew had no notion of the trawler's mission when she set to sea. His solicitor told him to expect a ten-year sentence. He would be eligible for remission, parole, after five.

Cathleen Cassidy, purporting to be a cousin of Dowd's, would have thirty minutes with him. At the end of the counter over which she faced him through the wire mesh, a guard sat monitoring their conversation.

"How goes it?" she said.

"I can think of other places I'd rather be. But I'm

comforted by my company, ghosts of the Young Ire-
landers and the Fenian Brotherhood and the Irish
Republic Brotherhood," he said, glancing at the
guard. "And the Invincibles and the Skirmishers and
the National Volunteers. They're all around, ye
know, from the rebellion of eighteen forty-eight and
'sixty-seven and through the eighties and to nineteen
sixteen and after. The spirit of O'Donovan Rossa visits me often. The grave of Wolfe Tone is not far off,
in Kildare. I can stand in the yard on the very spot
where Patrick Geraghty of the good old IRA, an ordinary man like me, was executed in nineteen twenty-
three."

"Aunt Florence sends love," she said.

"Is she well?"

"The rheumatism's quite bad, it is. She can't get on
without a cane."

"Ah, 'tis sad, that."

"Wee Annie has the whooping cough. Can you
imagine, in this day and age?"

"I can't, no."

"Mary has herself employment. Knittin' Aran
scarves for America. It helps."

"Good, that's good."

"It's needed, Lord knows. Tom can't find work at
all, decent or not."

"Terrible, terrible."

"Joe's funeral was a week ago today. It was the
drink. Father Murphy was most solicitous to Molly."

"I'm glad. An exceptional man, he is, Father Murphy. Gave my first communion, he did."

As this litany of familial woes continued, the guard
began to nod.

"Gerry sends best wishes," she said.

At the mention of McMahon, Dowd came alert. "How's Gerry doin'?"

"He's had to give up the taxi. Exposure to the elements grew too harsh."

"It was to be expected."

"Yes, perhaps it's as it should be. He seeks shelter where he can."

She shot a sidelong look at the guard. His eyes were closed, head tilted forward. She could hear his breathing.

"I bring good news," she whispered. "We know the informer."

"Who?"

"The American, McGuire." She saw Dowd blanch and shake his head violently. "What's that?" she said.

"It can't be," Dowd whispered back. "I know the lad. He'd never do it, *never*. I'd stake my life on it. Where did this come from?"

"The gangster you used, Ahearn."

"No! If it'd been anyone over there, I'd say it was Ahearn. There's somethin' rotten. I sniff the stink. And I hear the Brits laughin'. The answer isn't over there, it's here."

"Here?"

"Yes."

The guard awoke with a start. Probably, she thought, if they had kept on talking in a normal tone, he'd still be dozing.

"I'll tell Gerry," she said.

"You tell him to look to his own backyard. Tell him to think. Who knew about the shipment most recently? That's where the answer is."

• • •

Michael McGuire left London for Belfast from Heathrow airport. It was a forty-five minute flight, but he was advised to be on hand at least two hours before departure. He joined a long line at a special section of the terminal. Not only was there the normal security gate, but also every ticket holder was thoroughly hand-searched, each piece of luggage, every parcel, whether carry-on or checked through, was first screened, then opened and ransacked.

Questions were asked, proof of identity demanded. "What is your purpose in Northern Ireland?" an officer said.

"Sightseeing," Michael McGuire said.

The man next to him on the plane said he was a regional space salesman for a newspaper, the Belfast *Telegraph*. He lived, he said, in Portadown, southwest of the capital. He was returning from a week's vacation in Fance, which his wife had won in a contest. She was back in the smoking section. He couldn't get her to stop the cigarettes.

He was in advertising himself, Michael McGuire said. How were things in Northern Ireland?

"Not good, not at all," the man said. It was the violence. Personally, he was against it. Very bad for business. "You're American, are you?"

"Yes, I am."

"Ah, you know, some of my best friends are Catholic."

Michael McGuire refrained from saying anything. Perhaps it was a heartfelt remark. He couldn't help thinking, though, how many times he'd heard that about blacks and Jews.

"The violence, the killing," the man said, as if unable to relinquish the thought. "It's like my wife's smoking. Some people just can't stop. Where are you staying in Belfast?"

"The Forum. How is it?"

"I'm told excellent. I've never been there. Barbed wire, and so on. The foreign press favors it when trouble erupts. Used to be called the Europa. I've heard they're changing the name back. Good idea. More international sounding, don't you think?"

After registering, Michael McGuire wandered into the bar on the second floor. Almost every American brand of liquor was displayed on the shelves behind the bartender. He ordered a Jack Daniel's, and with that fell into conversation with a reporter from the Washington *Post*. "This place can be packed," the reporter said, "but right now things are pretty quiet." He was going to Derry to do a feature on Denis Dillon. "Dillon was elected to the House of Commons on the *Sinn Fein* slate, but he won't take his seat. There's talk he's also a chief of staff for the Provos, the IRA. Maybe so, maybe no."

"How do you get in touch with the IRA?"

"You don't. They contact you, they feel like it. The best bet is the *Sinn Fein* headquarters. That's up on the Falls Road. It's only five minutes by cab. Ask for the press officer, Gabriel MacStiofain. Nice guy, if you buy what he's saying."

A few feet away a plainclothes Special Branch cop, overhearing this, took note of Michael McGuire's name. He went down to the hotel management office and checked the registration. The name and address matched the passport. There was also a corporate address on Madison Avenue, New York City. The cop did not pursue the matter. Anyone asking that openly about the IRA wasn't really worth the bother. Another thrill seeker anxious to tell everyone back home that he'd actually met one of the boys.

Michael McGuire went into the adjoining dining room for a solitary dinner. He ordered salmon, scraping away enormous gobs of mayonnaise to find it. Jesus, he thought, what a cuisine! He glanced outside the restaurant window. The street, Great Victoria Street, was deserted. The only human activity he saw was in the guardhouse in front of the hotel by the circular drive nobody was allowed to use. He retired to his room. It was barely large enough for his single bed and small chest. A television and bar were under the window. He gazed out of the window at the faint lights dotting the hills of West Belfast. Usually in a city, even a small one, there was always a glow in the sky above it, a kind of manmade aurora borealis. Not this city, though. He thought about tomorrow. What would happen? Would anything happen? He opened the bar and took out two cognacs. He turned on the television. Only two channels seemed to be operating. One was showing a travelogue about Spain. The other presented what must have been the main sporting event of the evening, a snooker tournament being held in Liverpool. He poured the two cognacs in a glass and lay on the bed watching the snooker tournament, trying to figure out what the rules of the game were, and, still dressed, he fell asleep.

. . .

In the morning, famished, he devoured deliciously fresh eggs and sausage and toasted soda bread. They should stick to breakfast here, he thought. And after getting directions from the front desk, he decided to walk. "Twenty minutes at most," the room clerk said.

It was the longest walk he had ever taken.

As soon as he crossed the Divis Street bridge down from the hotel, over the motorway dividing the city, he entered another world. The transformation from the pristine respectability around the hotel he had just left was stunning. It wasn't only the immediate physical wretchedness, or the graffiti that shrieked at him—"Informers Beware!" in great jagged black letters, and "Stop the H-Block Torture!" There was a defiant wildness in the air, as real as it was intangible.

Immediately to his left was a jumble of blackened brick row houses on twisting streets that belonged in a Charles Dickens novel. Beyond rose the grime-streaked towers of the Divis flats built to replace them. It was hard to judge which were worse. Kids were playing in mounds of rubble. The sidewalk was badly cracked, in some stretches nonexistent. He passed a greengrocer and a clothing shop. Although they were open for business, the windows were all boarded up. This was the front line of battle. Street-lamps were smashed. Metal strips had been riveted over the slit of a postal box so only the slimmest of letters could be inserted. Heavy mesh and razor wire encased a welfare office, even its roof.

As he trudged up the incline of the Falls Road, the undulating humps of Divis and Black Mountain loomed ahead. Pale sunlight touched down, as warm as a mortician's smile. Traffic was sparse, mostly black taxis crammed with passengers. Suddenly he saw a column of British soldiers. There were sixteen of them, all with automatic rifles. At an intersection, the point man dropped flat and wriggled around the corner on his belly. The last soldier in the column moved backward. The soldiers in between crouched and turned edgily.

The *Sinn Fein* headquarters was on the corner of Sevastopol Street, a name bestowed on West Belfast in honor of the British army's Crimean campaign during the empire's glory days. A shabby two-story stone structure, it was surrounded by huge boulders to protect against car-bomb strikes. A heavy wire cage covered the entrance. Under the lens of a closed-circuit video camera, Michael McGuire pressed the bell.

Over the intercom, a voice said, "Yes?" and he said, "I'm here to see Gabriel MacStiofain."

A buzzer sounded. He went inside the cage and waited while a steel door was unlocked. There were two men in a cubicle. One said, "Gabriel's expectin' you?"

"Please give him this," he said, and handed him his business card. On it, he had written, "I am the father of Jamie McGuire, who was on the *Sea King*."

About ten minutes later, a chubby bespectacled young man descended the worn stairs and said, "Mr. McGuire?"

"You're Gabriel MacStiofain?"

"I am."

"You saw what I wrote. I want to see somebody in

charge, really in charge. You're the only name I have. A reporter gave it to me."

"It's rather short notice. I'm not sure I can oblige you."

"Try. I'll wait as long as necessary."

MacStiofain stared at him for a moment and then turned and spoke to one of the men in the cubicle. Then MacStiofain said, "I'll see what I can do."

The man MacStiofain had spoken to said, "Come with me," and led him along a dark, narrow corridor into what appeared to be some sort of meeting room with a number of benches. At the opposite end of the room were perhaps fifteen women, most of them holding babies or tending to small children. Three of the women were a good deal older and had no children. "Gabriel says you're to wait here," the man said.

About an hour later, the man came back and motioned to the women, who immediately began filing out past him. "Who were they?" Michael McGuire asked when the last of the women were gone, and the man said, "They're wives and mothers of some of the lads in the Kesh. We take them out in the bus."

Michael McGuire looked again at the scripted words on the wall to his right. They had suddenly taken on a new meaning. *I think how they suffer in Prison alone. Their friends unavenged and their country unfreed: "Oh, bitter," I said, "is the Patriot's mead."*

He had not smoked for ten years. All at once he desperately desired a cigarette. He felt himself grinding his teeth. Finally he took out another of his business cards and began chewing on it. Before he knew it, he had not only chewed the card, but swallowed it.

Nearly two more hours passed before a handsome

woman with black hair pulled back entered the room and approached him. "Mr. McGuire?" Cathleen Cassidy said. She did not introduce herself.

"Yes."

"Please follow me."

They went out of the building, turned left on Sevastopol and left again. They came to a street named Kashmir. There was a wall across it at least twenty feet high, topped with coils of razor wire. "What's that?" he said.

"They call it the 'Peace Wall,' " she said. "To separate the Falls and the Shankill. That other street is Bombay, where the loyalist mobs stormed in from the Shankill, in 'sixty-nine." She seemed to be speaking more to herself than him. "We had no weapons then. We were defenseless."

"Oh," he said. Now, after all the twists and turns, he had no idea where he was. He had a sense that they were being watched. The odd man on a corner. A gesture, a signal, he felt more than saw. They were going by an alley when she abruptly said, "In here," and pulled him with her.

They were behind a block of houses. She hurried him through a rear door. They were in a tiny kitchen. In the cramped front parlor a young woman in her early twenties sat on a couch watching television. A baby was crawling on the floor.

They went up a narrow staircase. She knocked on a door, opened it and ·motioned Michael McGuire inside, without going in herself.

In a chair, a rocker, sat Gerry McMahon, dressed in corduroy trousers and a gray sweatshirt. He gestured toward the bed. It was the only place left to sit.

"Who are you?" Michael McGuire said.

"A friend, I would hope. And someone you said you wanted to speak to."

"I thought you'd be older."

"Longevity is not that common in my trade, Mr. McGuire. What is it that I can do?"

"Do you know my son?"

"*Of* him, yes. A brave lad, a fine lad, I'm told."

"Yeah, well, he's disappeared, missing. You understand what I'm saying." For the first time Michael McGuire uttered what he most feared. His voice cracked slightly. "He could be dead. Because of you and your goddamn arms shipment."

McMahon's eyes narrowed. "When did this happen?"

"Last week. Only I didn't know about it right away. I've got to find him. You've got to help me."

McMahon leaned back in the rocker. There was a knock on the door and the young woman who had been watching television came in with a tray of tea and cookies. She set it down on the bed. McMahon bent forward to take a cup. He said, "I know nothing of your son's disappearance. That's not to say I won't."

"The word I was getting was he was supposed to have informed about the shipment."

"Not true."

"You don't have to tell me that. There're a lot of things I maybe didn't know about Jamie, but that's not one of them."

"We know who the informer was."

"Was?"

"Yes. He was executed and his body dumped night

before last by the main police barracks on the Knock Road. The Brits haven't announced it yet. They might not. Embarrassin' it is for them. Their prize tout. His name was Billy Dugan."

"So that's the guy they were trying so hard to protect."

"They?"

"The British, MI Five, with American help. The American ambassador, the head of customs, the FBI director. Others I don't know. They wanted to shift suspicion away from a mole they had in the IRA."

"At one time we did hear that it was your son, but Kevin Dowd set us right straight off."

"What was your source?"

McMahon bent forward and poured himself another cup of tea. He broke a cookie in half and nibbled at it. "You won't have some tea?"

"No."

"I'll only be tellin' you this because of your son, Mr. McGuire. Most of us in the struggle have no choice. Your son did, and he came forward. He will be remembered."

"Who was it?"

"A man in Boston named Ahearn."

"Thomas Ahearn?"

"You've heard of him then?"

"More than once." Michael McGuire hesitated. "Before I go, let me ask you something. You don't really think you're going to win this thing?"

"I do. If I did not, I would be in America this very moment doin' a wee bit of carpentry for a basket of dollars in one of your fine homes. It will happen. If not in me lifetime, me son's. If not in his, *his* son's.

I'm but a tick of the clock that's been runnin' over eight hundred years."

After Cathleen Cassidy put him in a black taxi, she returned to the room. "What did you tell him?"

"I told him it was Ahearn," Gerry McMahon said.

From the hotel Michael McGuire telephoned Ingrid.

"Oh, God, have you learned anything?" she said.

"Yes, I think so."

"Can you say?"

"Not really. Not on the phone. I'll be flying to New York tomorrow."

"You can't come directly to Boston?"

"I have to do something in New York first."

He caught the last flight out of Belfast for Shannon. He stayed overnight in the airport hotel and left in the morning. Once, when the cloud cover parted for a while, he pressed his forehead against the window, staring down at the vast, wrinkled Atlantic, thinking of Jamie.

But mostly only one name kept pounding in his head. Ahearn.

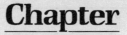
T hat afternoon, after landing at Kennedy, Michael McGuire phoned Harry Hollander from the airport.

"Michael, good to hear from you. You missed the game last week."

"Harry, I've got to see you. Can I see you now?"

"Sure, I was just going to the club, play a little backgammon. You want to meet there?"

"No, I want to talk to you alone. Can I come to the apartment? I'm at the airport."

"Hey, I'll wait."

Forty-five minutes later, sitting in Hollander's library overlooking Park Avenue, Michael McGuire said, "I need a big favor, Harry."

"Sure, name it."

"You still see that Mafia guy, Balamenti, you were in jail with?"

"All the time. I told you, we're bonded. Shame you

never got down to the restaurant to meet him. A real sweetheart."

"I need a gun, a pistol. You think he could get one for me?"

Michael McGuire had braced himself for all kinds of questions. He'd readied an explanation about a lot of break-ins at the beach and the need to have a pistol for protection. But Hollander didn't ask anything, and then he remembered that after his disastrous marriage to Allison Ashley, when he had berated Hollander for not warning him about her, Harry had just shrugged and said, "Every man to his own spinach." He felt a wave of affection for Hollander.

"I'll see what I can do."

"Time is important."

"I'll call you tomorrow."

It was unbelievable. Not four hours later, Hollander called him at home. "I'll meet you in the morning, say eleven, by the fountain in front of the Plaza."

Michael McGuire was there ten minutes early, pacing back and forth. A street band was setting up for a noon concert. Across Fifth Avenue, the toy store F A O Schwarz had moved. Waiting, he remembered all the times he'd been there with Jamie.

Then he saw Hollander strolling toward him carrying a plastic shopping bag with red and green lettering that said "Palumbo's Fruits and Vegetables."

"Sorry about that," Hollander said. "Gucci doesn't have a store downtown."

There was another bag inside, brown paper, sealed with tape.

"It's a Smith and Wesson thirty-eight Chief Special. Five shots. A lot of plainclothes cops carry them. My friend says automatics can jam on you, you're not used to them. Not much good for squirrels, but it's light and handy. You can stick it in your belt. It was lifted off a shipment on the Brooklyn docks, so you don't have to concern yourself about that."

"How much do I owe you?"

"No charge, pal. Didn't cost me anything. Take me to lunch on your expense account someday and we're even."

"Harry, I can't thank you enough."

"You going to make poker this week?"

"I'll try."

Michael McGuire hailed a cab and headed for LaGuardia. He called Ingrid and told her he'd see her in the afternoon, late.

In Boston, he went directly to the main public library on Boylston Street. In the periodical room he looked up organized crime, found the references to Ahearn, Thomas A., and read through the *Globe* stories stored on microfilm.

He was described most frequently as the kingpin of the local Irish underworld and was credited with its resurgence as a power after years of Italian dominance. He was said to be the major importer of marijuana into New England. There were allegations that his gang was responsible for numerous bank robberies, jewel thefts and hijackings, that it engaged in labor racketeering and extortion and controlled a substantial portion of bookmaking in the Boston area.

He was characterized as an outspoken supporter of

the Irish republican cause, although an anonymous source was quoted as saying, "What really makes Tommy tick is his love of money. He's Irish, and when it suits him, he brings that out, the patriot bit. It's a convenience."

He owned a Cadillac Sedan de Ville, a Mercedes Benz 420 SEL and a luxury power boat he kept at the Excelsior Yacht Club on Dorchester Bay. He had a large residence in Somerville, was married and had two daughters, although at major sporting events he was often seen in the company of young women. An article two years old noted that he had bought a home in Hillsborough County in New Hampshire, just across the state line, near Nashua, where he spent most of his spare time in the guise of a country squire. The realtor, unnamed, who sold him the property was quoted as saying, "He seemed to be a hell of a nice guy. I wish I had more buyers like him. He paid in cash."

After he had finished reading, he went to a pay phone. "Detective Robinson," he said, "this is Michael McGuire. You remember me?"

" 'Deed I do. Any word yet on your son?"

"No. I'm calling because I need some advice."

"What's that?"

"Suppose I was trying to locate someone in a rural area, somebody unlisted, how would I go about it without the kind of access you have?"

"Where?"

"Hillsborough County. In New Hampshire."

"I know where it is. You could go to the deeds office at the county seat, Manchester. That's open to the public. But I don't know if they're computerized, or what. Could be ledgers. Take a while going through them. Who you looking for?"

"Thomas Ahearn. You heard of him?"

There was a long pause before she said, "Mr. McGuire, you sure you know what you're doing?"

"I'd be very grateful."

"See what I can come up with. It's late, though. I don't know if I can do it today."

He gave her Ingrid's number. "I'll be there tonight and tomorrow."

"I'll get back to you," Marylou Robinson said.

Ingrid was waiting for him. "Oh, God," she said, "I was starting to believe I would never see you again."

"I'm sorry. I should have called more. There were times I wanted to, but I was afraid to talk on the phone."

He told her about Anthony Seth-Jones. He explained precisely the leverage he had employed. He could see her remembering the confrontation he'd had with Jamie in this same room.

"But Jamie didn't know what he was saying," she said. "He told me that, that you couldn't have taken it seriously. He was so sorry about that night."

"Well, he was right on the button, and it's something I'll always have to live with. Along with a lot more."

"How could they do such a thing," she said, "those people in London and Washington?"

"I don't know. They just do."

He told her about the meeting with the man in Belfast whose name he did not know, Gerry Mc-

Mahon. "Ahearn is the key to finding Jamie," he said.
He hesitated. "Or finding out what happened to him.
All I know is that I'm going to have to take a crack at
Ahearn myself. He has this place he goes to in New
Hampshire."

"How are you sure he will be there?"

"I'm not, but I don't know what else to do. He has
a house in Somerville, but his family is there. I don't
know where his hangouts are or what his normal
movements are. I can't go around asking too many
questions, and anyway, he's bound to have people
with him. According to the story I read in the library,
he uses New Hampshire as sort of a regular retreat.
It's my only chance to surprise him."

Then he reached into the shopping bag that said
"Palumbo's Fruit and Vegetables" and took out the
brown bag and opened it, and she saw the revolver
for the first time. Her eyes dilated slightly, but she
did not say anything. He hadn't really noticed their
color before. Brown with green flecks in them. Now
the flecks grew more pronounced. She seemed to be
appraising him. Her hands, clasped in her lap, remained absolutely motionless. She closed her eyes for
a second and nodded ever so briefly, as if to herself.

He hadn't held a gun since the army. It was, as
Hollander had said, amazingly light and it slid comfortably inside his belt. When he buttoned his jacket,
there wasn't any bulge. It was double action, which
meant that you didn't have to cock it. When you
sqeezed the trigger, the hammer worked automatically. He tried it and listened to the flat click.

An ammunition box was in the paper bag with fifty
.38-caliber bullets. Instead of steel jackets, they had

leaded hollow points, so that they would immediately expand upon impact. He opened the cylinder and loaded the revolver.

"You seem so expert," she said.

"I'm not," he said. "It's like riding a bike. You never forget."

"I am going with you," she said. "You will need me."

"That's out of the question, Ingrid. Forget it. I don't want you involved in this."

"Yes, that's what Jamie said also. He didn't want me involved when I wanted to go with him. Now you don't want me involved. Like son, like father. Jamie didn't understand, and you don't understand. I am involved already."

"We'll talk about it tomorrow," Michael McGuire said. But he knew that it was past arguing. She would be with him and, he suddenly realized, he was glad of that. He'd been alone too much. "I better try and get some sleep," he said.

He could hear sounds of her moving around in her room. She had an extraordinary inner strength. Like Mary Alice's. They were different, of course, but it was really a matter of style. He wondered if that was what Jamie had seen in her. He dreaded the prospect of more nightmares. But this time, wrung out, he fell almost at once into a dreamless sleep.

In the morning he considered phoning Corcoran at the FBI and Bertelli to see if anything had turned up on Jamie. He decided not to, not now.

About ten A.M. Marylou Robinson called. "Bingo!" she said, and gave him the directions out of Nashua for Ahearn. "There's no street number, anything like that, even a mailbox. Just where the road bends there's a gate with two white posts. You can't see the house, cedar shingles. And a red barn behind it. It's in a grove of evergreens. You be careful, hear."

They left Cambridge along Memorial Drive and picked up the interstate north through Somerville. The drive to the state line took about an hour. Immediately on the New Hampshire side, where there was no sales tax on alcohol, cars lined up in front of a liquor store the size of a supermarket. Signs proclaimed, "Open Sunday."

A mile or so farther, on the outskirts of Nashua, they turned east and crossed the Merrimack River. Following Marylou Robinson's directions, Michael McGuire told Ingrid to go left at an intersection, and they passed the last of the tract house subdivisions and were in open country on a narrow blacktop road. Then, around a bend, he spotted the two white posts on the left. "This is it," he said. "No mailbox." A gravel driveway disappeared into a thick stand of pine trees.

About three hundred yards up the road, on a treed knoll that featured towering twin copper beeches, they came to another driveway on the right with a painted sign that said "Mulford's." It was a dairy farm, the surrounding fields dotted with Holsteins, the barns and a big silo some distance off. The knoll afforded a clear view of the white posts, and they parked under the trees.

"What if somebody from the farm asks what we're doing?" Ingrid said.

"We'll just say we're picnicking, and is it all right?"

The weather was unseasonably warm, hot really. Michael McGuire removed his suit jacket. The Smith & Wesson was sticking out of his belt, so he put it inside the folds of the jacket on the rear seat. She was wearing faded jeans and a blue sweater. When she raised the sweater over her head to take it off, he could see her breasts pushing against her blouse, and he remembered how she looked in a bikini with Jamie at the beach. Now there were tiny beads of perspiration on her upper lip.

Very few cars traveled the road. They could hear the sound of one coming, and they would tense as each rounded the bend and then kept going. They got out of the Honda and walked under the trees.

"You're thinking of Jamie?" she said.

"All the time. And myself."

She looked at him, curious. "Yes?"

"Why I didn't stop him."

"You don't think what he was doing was right?"

"Of course I don't. Don't tell me you do?"

"I'm not sure."

"*Come on.*"

She sat down, plucked a blade of grass and chewed on it. Somehow that infuriated him. "Look at this hoodlum Ahearn he got mixed up with," he said.

"Jamie didn't know about him until the last minute when they were leaving. I think you are dismissing Jamie, what he was doing, too easily. If you dismiss Jamie," she said, "you are dismissing all those people before Jamie, thousands of them, tens of thousands of them, for all these years, hundreds of years, who fought and died and suffered and were imprisoned.

You must understand. He was committed. You asked me if I thought he was right. *He* thought he was right, and that is what's important, no matter what."

Tears began sliding down her face. She pulled up her knees and hunched over them, her body convulsing.

"I ook," he said as gently as he could, "he was committed because I didn't give him anything else."

Eyes glistening, she stared at him and said, "You're so stupid. He adored you."

"Stop trying to make me feel better."

"And respected you. Why do you insist on making everything so black and white? Jamie did respect you. That doesn't mean he thought you were perfect."

"After his mother died, I got totally involved in myself, and he was just a little kid. I really screwed up. You can't imagine how badly I screwed up. I can't stand thinking about it, even now."

"He didn't think of it that way. He told me. He said how lonely and confused and sad you were, and how sorry he was, and how he wished so much to be able to help you, but he didn't know what to do, or if there was anything he could do."

"He said that?"

"Yes." Then suddenly her eyes widened and she said, "Oh, my God!"

"What's wrong?"

"I've been talking about him in the past. That's not right, is it? It isn't finished. It can't be."

"I don't know," Michael McGuire said.

They stared at the white posts. There was the sound of another engine beyond the bend, but it was only a pickup truck with two workmen in it.

"Suppose he doesn't come," she said.

"We'll keep waiting. If he doesn't come today, we'll check into some motel and come back tomorrow. Sooner or later, he'll come. He has to."

"Are you hungry? Do you want me to find a store and get something for sandwiches?"

"No, I don't feel like eating. How about you, though?"

"I'm not hungry either."

"I could go for something to drink," he said. "There was a gas station a couple of miles back. Maybe you could get some sodas."

"All right, yes."

He watched her drive off in the Honda. She truly had guts, he thought. He wondered if she was telling him the truth about what Jamie had said. The two of them, he and Jamie, struggling to reach each other, crying out inside of themselves. He decided that she was too straightforward a person not to. Mary Alice would have made the difference then. Just as Ingrid had made a difference now. Why was it that men always needed women to make a difference?

When she returned, she looked at him, and he said, "No, nothing." Sipping a Coke, he gazed at the sun going down and thought of all the glorious sunsets he had witnessed with Jamie and Mary Alice at the beach. When night fell, there was a crescent moon overhead. It cast enough light so that they weren't left in total darkness. He saw the stars glittering and cursed the memory of The Crooked Plough.

At nine P.M., he said, "I guess we better pack it in."

"Let's wait another half hour. I'll go crazy sitting in some motel room."

Twenty minutes later, they saw the beam from headlights. A car came around the bend, and it slowed and swung into the driveway and stopped in front of the white posts. They saw a figure from the car approach the gate and open it. The car moved forward through the posts, stopped again and then disappeared in the pine thicket.

"There's more than one of them," Ingrid said. She was whispering. "Someone else was driving."

"Yes, at least two. I hope that's all."

"How far is the house?"

"That detective said it was just on the other side of the trees. Not far."

They waited to see if another car showed up, but none did. She started the Honda, and with the lights off, eased back down the road. About fifty feet from the driveway, there was a flat sandy break in the trees. Ingrid pulled off the road and parked there.

"If you hear something," Michael McGuire said, "or if I'm not back in an hour, go to the police in Nashua and get them out here. And listen, I'm glad you came."

"Oh, Michael, please be careful." She leaned toward him and kissed him on the cheek.

"I will," he said. He tucked the Smith & Wesson in his belt. The air was still very warm. He felt a trickle of sweat down his spine. "Okay, see you," he said, and opened the door and shut it softly behind him.

He went into the pines, turned left and crossed the driveway and went parallel to it through more trees. The pines were set on a rise. Moonlight came through gaps in the branches above him. A carpet of fallen needles muffled his steps. The fragrance of the

pines was all around him, and he remembered another time, walking alone through other pines at
night in Canada when Jamie had been in camp,
where Jamie had hit the long ball and slid into third
base and given him the thumbs-up and a big smile.

He had gone, he guessed, about fifty yards when
the rise leveled off and the trees ended, and he saw
the house, perhaps a hundred feet of lawn separating
him from it. The car, a Mercedes, was parked to his
right by the main entrance. Farther on, past the car,
on another rise, he could see the silhouette of a barn.

The house had two stories. There were lights on
the ground floor on the side facing him, and more
lights directly above on the second floor. He edged
out on the lawn.

One of the lighted screened windows was open,
and as he got closer he could hear voices. He recognized Ahearn from his photographs. Ahearn was
seated behind a desk in what appeared to be a den.
He was in shirtsleeves, tie yanked down. A girl was
standing in front of the desk, almost as if she were at
attention. Blond hair cascaded to her shoulders. Her
face was heavily made up. She had on a tight skirt
and high heels. Despite the makeup, she appeared to
be in her teens.

Ahearn was saying, "Go up and take a bath. I'll be
up. I got some calls to make."

He really likes them young, Michael McGuire
thought, and this is where he brings them. After she
had left, he watched Ahearn pick up the phone. He
had a pinched, mean look that made his eyes even
more baleful.

Michael McGuire waited to see if anybody else

came into the room. There was a rustling over his head and curtains suddenly closed off the light from the upstairs windows. He heard soft rock music. The girl must have brought cassettes of her own. He couldn't imagine Ahearn being a rock fan. Except for Ahearn on the phone, he didn't hear any sounds. Not knowing quite what to do next, he walked around to the front door.

It was partly open. There was only a screen door between him and the house. He tried the handle, and to his astonishment it wasn't locked either. He'd been reading too many stories in the papers about big-time mobsters and their cordons of bodyguards. Why should Ahearn be concerned about security in this remote unmarked place?

Inside there were stairs directly ahead of him. He heard water being run for a bath. Ahearn was clearly fussy. He not only liked them young but also clean. A room to the right was dark. He followed the light on his left to the den where Ahearn was talking and paused. He heard Ahearn say, "I'm up here tryin' to relax, Christ's sake. Okay, it's so important, I'll come in tomorrow. Three o'clock."

Michael McGuire took the .38 out of his belt, and as soon as Ahearn had hung up he stepped into the den and stopped about ten feet from the desk.

He saw Ahearn's eyes dart from him to the revolver and back again. "Who the fuck are you?" Ahearn said.

"My name's McGuire."

"So?"

"I'm Jamie McGuire's father."

"That's supposed to mean somethin'?"

"Yes."

"Well, it don't."

"Remember, he was on the *Sea King*."

Michael McGuire had to hand it to Ahearn. He had remained seated without a flicker of emotion in his face. "You sure you're in the right place, mister?" Ahearn said.

"You don't remember Kevin Dowd either?"

"Never heard of him."

"My son's disappeared, Ahearn. You tell me where he is or I'll blow you right out of that chair. You think I'm bluffing, try me."

That finally prompted what looked like a shadow of alarm in Ahearn's eyes. A muscle twitched in his right cheek. He appeared to be working out something to say. Then all at once he was as expressionless as ever.

It was, Michael McGuire would think, because he'd been concentrating so hard on Ahearn. He didn't hear, even sense, the presence of Bernie Quinn behind him until he felt the gun barrel pressing against the back of his neck and Quinn said, "Let go the piece."

He dropped the revolver. He watched it bounce on a hooked rug in front of the desk.

"Where the fuck was you?" Ahearn said to Quinn.

"Checkin' the barn."

"Christ, what I got to put up with."

Then Ahearn turned on Michael McGuire. His face contorted. "So you want to know about that scumbag rat kid of yours, do you?" he said, snarling. "He's fish bait, what's left of him. That little Harvard punk started blabbin' his fuckin' guts to the feds, and

Bernie Quinn here took him outa Gloucester for a nice boat ride, he likes boats so much, and put a bullet behind his ear, right where Bernie does it good, and he's down there somewheres with the lobsters crawling all over him, is what. You want to be with him so much, I'll have Bernie dump you in the same spot."

"He was only nineteen years old," Michael McGuire said. "Didn't you give him a chance to explain? He never said anything to anybody."

"Sure, sure."

Ahearn was actually enjoying this, Michael McGuire thought. He shut his eyes. Vertigo seized him. He was sure he was going to fall. An unutterable sadness rose through him. It was instantly followed by a surge of rage beyond any he had ever experienced. He felt himself trembling uncontrollably. He was aware that he was going to die, but he didn't care. It was *how* he died that was crucial now.

He had to die right there, before Ahearn's gloating ended. And he knew precisely what he must do. He would dive suddenly for the revolver where it lay three feet away to his left. He would grab it, rolling as he did. Taken by surprise, the man called Quinn behind him might miss the first time, or just wing him. And he might even be able to get off a shot himself, might even take Quinn down with those hollow-nose bullets. And then he would go after the real killer, Ahearn, sitting there stupefied, paralyzed.

He knew he was fantasizing, and he forced himself to stop. What was important were shots, as many as possible. Ingrid, in the car, would hear them. Better yet, maybe she was outside the car, listening, intent on nothing else except sounds from the house. He was certain of it. And she would do exactly what he had instructed. Go to Nashua and bring the police. Ahearn didn't know about Ingrid. They would take their time cleaning up the mess. Maybe they'd lug his body out right away. But there would be all that blood that had gushed out of him, and that wouldn't be so easy. Ingrid would be the avenging angel. For him and for Jamie.

Dive, grab, roll. He steeled himself. He would go on the count of five. *One*, he silently counted. *Two. Three.*

The shot was deafening. He waited for the pain that was sure to come. Then he heard the grunt behind him. He saw Ahearn staring past him, open-mouthed. There was another shot, but he did not turn around. He had only a single thought, the Smith & Wesson on the floor. He bent for it, and as he came up with it Ahearn was frantically yanking open a drawer. Michael McGuire fired. He missed Ahearn, the bullet smashing instead into the desktop, sending papers on it flying. Ahearn froze, though. He raised his hands, palms out, as if to shield himself. "Don't," he said.

Michael McGuire aimed between the hands and squeezed the trigger. A crimson stain spread down the front of Ahearn's shirt. For a fraction of a second, he remained stationary before he toppled back into the chair he had been sitting in. His head lolled to one side. His eyes were open, unblinking. They looked as fierce, cold and black in death, Michael McGuire thought, as they did when Ahearn was alive.

The other shots! He whirled and saw the massive bulk of Bernie Quinn for the first time, his bull neck

and huge arms that made the green knit polo shirt
he was wearing seem so inconsequential. Blood was
streaming down his dangling left arm. His left leg,
with more blood, stuck out at a grotesque angle. He
was slumped on the floor against the wall. But he was
still moving, straining with ferocious will toward a
gun that was inches away from his right hand.

Michael McGuire stood over him and fired again
and watched the blood spurt from Quinn's neck, and
then Quinn stopped moving.

He heard Ingrid weakly saying, "Michael, oh, Michael," and he saw her face at the window.

She had waited for two minutes after he had left the
car and gone into the pines before she followed him.
She could hear him ahead of her, and she was worried that someone else might hear him.

When she got to the edge of the lawn, she saw him
going across it to a lighted window. Someone inside,
a girl, was leaving the room, and then she saw Michael McGuire go around to the front entrance.
Right after that, still hidden in the pines, she heard
the crunch of gravel and in the moonlight saw a man
come down from the barn toward the house and go
into it.

She crept over the lawn to the window and got
there as Quinn came up behind Michael McGuire.
She had a Beretta automatic in her hand.

Jamie had given it to her before he drove off that
last time. He had gotten it from Kevin Dowd, and he
wanted her to have it for protection. Just in case, he
had said. It had nine rounds and it was loaded, so all

she had to do was pull the trigger. He showed her the safety lever, how when the red dot by the lever was covered the safety was on, and when it was exposed the Beretta was ready to be fired. He had practiced with it on the *Sea King*, with Dowd, and he showed her how to grip the Beretta with both hands and to aim it with her arms extended, elbows locked.

After Jamie had gone, she put it on a shelf in her clothes closet, and she had forgotten that it was there until the night Michael McGuire returned from New York and she had seen him with the revolver. She slipped it in her shoulder bag when they departed for New Hampshire.

And now at the window, she didn't know what to do with Quinn poised behind him. She thought of yelling, to distract Quinn. But then she heard Ahearn sneering about how Jamie had been murdered, the sadistic pleasure he took in detailing it, and she simply released the safety mechanism and aimed the Beretta the way Jamie had taught her and fired, making certain not to jerk the trigger.

Her first bullet had hit Quinn in his upper arm. He staggered against the wall from its force. But he didn't go down. She fired again, and this time Quinn's leg crumpled and he slid to the floor. She heard other shots, but she kept her eyes fastened on Quinn. And to her horror, she saw him trying to get up, trying to reach for his gun. She pulled the trigger once more, but the Beretta jammed. She was about to shout a warning. "I was praying you were all right," she told Michael McGuire, "and then I saw you go over to him."

She ran to the front door and now, standing next

to him in the den, she said, "There's someone else here. I saw someone before in this room."

"It was one of Ahearn's doxies. She's upstairs, probably hiding under the bed."

The phone began to ring, startling them both.

"Let's go," he said.

At the screen door, he wiped the handles with a handkerchief. He couldn't think of any other surface he had touched. They started down the driveway. Suddenly Ingrid pulled on his arm. "My God, the Beretta. I dropped it in the grass by the window," she said, and ran back to get it.

The phone was still ringing. And then, as they reached the Honda, there was a scream, and more screams, pitching higher and higher. "Just get on the road and wait a second," Michael McGuire said. He picked up a pine limb and brushed the sandy patch where the Honda had been parked. "Tire tracks," he said.

They did not encounter any cars until they went back over the Merrimack bridge. She wheeled the Honda onto the interstate.

"Not so fast," he said.

"Yes, right, not so fast."

They were approaching the state line when she began to shake. "Pull in there," he said. The big liquor store was still open. He went in and bought a bottle of Jack Daniel's. And an Absolut vodka. He thought she might prefer that.

She already had moved to the passenger side when he returned. In Massachusetts, he braked on the shoulder along a deserted stretch of the highway and asked her for the Beretta. She took it out of her bag and handed it to him dumbly. He wiped it clean and got out of the Honda. He waited there until there was no traffic passing in either direction and flung it into the brush as far as he could. And then he did the same with the Smith & Wesson.

She slumped in the corner of her seat against the door all the way to Cambridge, sobbing. He did not say anything. What, he thought, was there to say?

He helped her down the path to the apartment. Inside, she suddenly clasped her arms around his neck. She thrust herself against him, moaning softly. Her lips parted against his mouth. He felt her body shaking.

After a moment, without saying anything, he disengaged her arms. He led her to the sofa. She sat there gazing blankly into space. He poured himself a Jack Daniel's and a vodka for her.

She seemed to refocus when he brought the vodka to her. "No," she said. "It will make me drunk."

"You're lucky," he said. "I could drink this whole bottle and it wouldn't do a thing. Numb me, that's all I hope. Drink it."

She downed the vodka, gagging slightly. She looked at him. "Do you believe he was telling the truth about Jamie?"

"Yes."

He went up to the kitchen counter to make himself another drink. When he turned around, she was curled up, fast asleep. Despite the warm weather, he brought a light blanket from the bedroom and covered her. It seemed like the right thing to do.

He sat there trying to concentrate. But he couldn't get a clear image of anything. Flashes of Jamie, mostly as a little boy, came to him, elusive, like still jumps on film.

He had another drink. Was there redemption in slaying your son's slayer? Should he peruse Homer for the answer? Was it in Sophocles? Or Aeschylus? Euripides? The Holy Roman Catholic Church? Could Harry Hollander tell him?

Did he feel good about killing Ahearn and that thug of Ahearn's? Yes, he goddamn well did, he told himself. But had it done any good, really? What about all those other people? Groome? The customs chief? The FBI director? That MI5 guy? He didn't even know who the MI5 guy was. Could he ever find out?

He had the bottle beside him now. Easier than getting up and going to the counter. He remembered staring at the window overlooking the backyard, seeing the dawn begin to come. Ingrid, he thought, had saved his life and he had nothing to live for anymore. He must have slipped into the kind of twilight zone you couldn't exactly recall later.

When he opened his eyes, she was still asleep on the sofa. He went into the bathroom and washed his face and brushed his teeth. He put on his jacket and went out. Two blocks away on a corner he found a vending machine with copies of the morning *Globe* in it. The front-page headline said, "Mob Boss Slain." He folded it and tucked it under his arm, stopped in a bakery and bought some croissants.

The sofa was empty when he returned. He heard the shower running. He put the coffee on and set out the croissants. Ingrid emerged from the bedroom in a robe, a towel wrapped around her head. She sat on one of the counter stools.

"You better eat something," he said. "You haven't eaten since yesterday morning."

She nibbled on a croissant and sipped the coffee. They read the *Globe* together. The slaughter was graphically described, the dead men apparently victims of a carefully planned ambush, since weapons available to them had not been fired. The person who had notified the police was identified as Barbara (Babs) Burnett, sixteen, a resident of Charlestown, who, despite existing laws governing age, had been a topless dancer at a club said to be operated by Ahearn. According to Miss Burnett, she had heard no shots, having been on the second floor bathing at the time. It was only when the phone had rung incessantly that she said she had gone downstairs to investigate and discovered the blood-covered bodies of Ahearn and Quinn.

A spokesman for the New Hampshire State Police claimed that the murders were obviously Boston related. This type of occurrence, he said, was not native to New Hampshire.

Some law enforcement authorities in Boston speculated that the assassinations were the result of a struggle for control over the lucrative New England cocaine market, and that Latin American elements, principally Colombians, who had settled in Rhode Island, were responsible. There were other rumors linking Ahearn to a trawler, the *Sea King*, suspected of transporting an intercepted shipment of arms to the IRA, and rumors that IRA gunmen, blaming him, had done in Ahearn. There was a rehash of

Ahearn's rise to power, and also of the life and times of Bernie Quinn, harking back to the incident at a Salisbury beach where he bit the breast of a gang leader's mistress and triggered a bloodbath a decade ago in the Irish underworld. Quinn, not Ahearn, had been the primary target, an anonymous source maintained. "They never forget," he was quoted as saying.

Nowhere was there mention of the disappearance of Jamie McGuire.

In the District Six station house in South Boston, Marylou Robinson entered her tiny office at the end of the grimy corridor on the second floor. She opened a Styrofoam cup of coffee, unsealed the plastic wrapping from a cheese Danish and settled back to peruse the *Globe*.

"My, my," she murmured as she began reading about the gangland slayings. When she finished, she allowed herself a private grin. Her day had hardly begun, she thought, and here it was, already made.

She strolled down the corridor to warrants, where she found the veteran detective Sullivan in his customary position, feet on his desk, eyes at half mast.

"Yo, Sully," she said. "You catch the *Globe*? What's all this about brother Ahearn?"

"What's it to you, Marylou? He ain't missin', for sure." Sullivan chortled at his own wit, displaying yellow teeth. "Anyways, I don't have to read the papers. The inside word is the guineas did it, you want to know. Take it from me."

"Is *that* right?" she said.

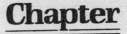
19

Late that afternoon, Michael McGuire and Ingrid Gerhard took a cab to the John W. McCormack Federal Building and sat waiting in the reception area of the United States attorney's office.

"There's still time for you to walk out of here," he said to Ingrid.

"No."

The arguing had started the moment he told her what he intended to do. It had come to him the night before. It was the only way. "I don't know what's going to happen," he had said. "I could end up in the slammer for God knows how long. There's no reason to expose you to that. It was all my idea in the first place and I'm not about to let you put your head on the block when there's no need to."

"If you won't let me go with you, I'll go myself. Suppose they don't believe you? I'm your only witness."

"They may not see it that way."

"I don't care."

Then he was occupied most of the day trying to reach Shelby Whitson, the U.S. attorney. "Look," he had said to a secretary, "I know Mr. Whitson is a busy man, but this is important." On his third call, after refusing to be transferred to an assistant attorney, he said, "Does Mr. Whitson have a deputy? I'll settle for him."

With audible relief, the secretary passed him on to another secretary, who said, "Dennison Healy's office." But Healy appeared to be as unavailable as Whitson. "Mr. Healy is in conference. May I have your number?"

"No. Tell him that I'm calling in regard to vital information about the *Sea King*, the trawler that brought tons of arms to the Irish Republican Army last month. I'm sure he knows about that. I'll hold on as long as I have to."

Finally, a voice said, "Healy."

"Mr. Healy. My name is Michael McGuire. I am a senior vice president of one of the biggest advertising agencies in New York, the Interaction Group. You must have heard of it. If you want to check me out, we have an office here in Boston. As I told your secretary, I have extremely sensitive information concerning the *Sea King* for Mr. Whitson, and I don't want to deal with any go-betweens. I know I should be arranging this through a lawyer. But any lawyer worth his salt would try to talk me out of it, and I don't want that."

"What's your connection with the *Sea King*, Mr. McGuire?"

"My son was on the crew."

There was a long pause, and then Healy put him on hold. When he came back on the line, he said, "Okay, Mr. McGuire. Four o'clock. This better be good."

Now, in the reception area, a secretary beckoned them. Michael McGuire looked pleadingly one last time at Ingrid, who stared straight ahead, jaw set. At the end of a corridor a chunky man in shirtsleeves waited, as if appraising them. "Dennison Healy," he said.

In his office, behind his desk, Shelby Whitson nodded, but did not rise. Michael McGuire recognized him from his photographs. Even in New York, Whitson's anti-corruption and racketeering cases had gotten a big play. In his early forties, he had a fine-boned, rather aesthetic face. He was usually characterized as having a bright political future, a senatorship, maybe more. He had left a thriving private practice to become, according to endless media profiles, a "relentless prosecutor." His enemies called him "self-righteous" and "Mr. Holier Than Thou."

A light-skinned black man sat on Whitson's left. Healy introduced him as Lee Tucker, chief of the criminal division.

To Michael McGuire's surprise, Whitson did not begin with the aggressive inquisition he half expected. "Well, Mr. McGuire," he said, "what can we do for you, or perhaps it's more appropriate to ask what you can do for us? We always welcome information in this office. We depend upon concerned citizens."

"I hope you'll still feel that way when you've heard

me," he said. "I don't quite know how to begin, but I do want to say that Miss Gerhard insisted on coming with me against my wishes. She is truly an innocent player in this matter, and I count on you to remember that."

He hesitated, groping for the right words.

"Denny said it had something to do with the *Sea King*."

"Yes," Michael McGuire said. "My son Jamie, age nineteen, was on the *Sea King*. He cared deeply about the troubles in Northern Ireland and he wanted desperately to do something to help drive out the British. It's a long story why, which I can explain to you later. Because of this, he did some foolish things. He not only was on the trawler during the gun-running trip, but he was on her when she carried some loads of marijuana into Boston last summer, the profits from which he believed would be used solely to raise money for the struggle he had committed himself to."

He stopped for a second, fighting off the tears. "I'm not trying to excuse any of this, but Jamie did not deserve to die, to be killed as he was. To be murdered in cold blood."

"How do you know that?"

"The man who ordered it told me."

"Who?"

"Thomas Ahearn."

Michael McGuire heard a soft whistle from Tucker.

"Maybe we should start from the beginning," Whitson said, leaning forward.

Was that significant? Michael McGuire thought.

Whitson saying "we," not "you." Then he told them about being in the Counterintelligence Corps and working with Anthony Seth-Jones. He saw tears brimming in Ingrid's eyes.

"Seth-Jones said that a man in MI Five engineered it all. He said MI Five had a mole in the IRA they had to protect, who had actually informed on the arms shipment. He said that this MI Five fellow—I don't have his name—arranged for a meeting in Washington with the American ambassador, the head of customs, the FBI director, to shift the blame on somebody else. On my son, as it turned out."

The tears had started streaming down Ingrid's face, and he reached over and gripped her hand.

Whitson slouched back in his leather chair, tapping a pencil.

"How can you support this?" Healy said. "Why should we believe you?"

"I shot Ahearn."

"You?"

"Yes." And then Michael McGuire precisely recounted what had taken place in Ahearn's New Hampshire retreat. "If it hadn't been for Ingrid, I wouldn't be here," he said. "But I'm the one who killed Ahearn and the other guy. The paper said his name was Quinn."

There wasn't a sound in the office. Even Whitson's pencil was motionless. Tucker broke the hush. "Mind me asking you a question, Mr. McGuire? When you got that gun, were you going up there with the intent of using it on Ahearn?"

"To be honest, I don't really know. All I think I know is that I was going into his world, and if I could find out what happened to Jamie, I wanted to be able to walk out of it."

"What you're admitting to, true or not," Healy said, "could land you in a lot of trouble. You're fully aware of that?"

"I intend to hold a press conference about what I've just said."

It was as though Whitson had purposely let the other two do the cross-examining while he listened. "I'd advise against that," he said now.

"Why?"

"Going public right away will make everything more difficult. Alert some of the people you've mentioned. Give them a chance to circle the wagons. You always have the option of going to the press if you're unhappy with what we're doing."

"Then you're going to do something? You believe me?"

"These are very serious allegations you've made. As for believing you, I know for a fact Tommy Ahearn is dead, and you've told me how, in some detail. That makes you very credible."

"I'm gratified. I guess I've gotten a little cynical."

"I can understand that. We try to run this office differently. Are there any specific leads you can give us?"

"A Boston customs officer, Angelo Bertelli. He interrogated my son out of the blue on a Saturday, at Ingrid's apartment, and a couple of days later Jamie disappeared. Just like that. There's got to be a connection. I saw Bertelli myself and he seemed ready to jump out of his skin. He was the first to tell me MI Five was involved in this."

Whitson said, "I'd like to turn you over to some investigators for a formal session. I have my own investigators, and there are agents in the FBI loyal to me. I know who they are. How do you feel about that?"

"If you're giving me a choice, I'm not so sure I'd feel comfortable with the FBI. I got a runaround when Jamie was reported missing. And I can't forget the director was at that meeting."

"All right. We'll use my people, at least for now." Whitson got up and walked around the desk to shake hands. "I appreciate you coming in, and, of course, Miss Gerhard."

"That's all? You're letting us go?"

"I assume neither of you are running off to someplace where we can't reach you. Just leave us phone numbers and addresses."

"But what about Ahearn? I know murder isn't a federal crime, but don't you have to inform the local D.A. in Nashua, or wherever?"

"Yes, eventually. I'll hold off, for the time being. Might be helpful to you, and Miss Gerhard, depending on how things work out."

Afterward, in Whitson's office, Healy said, "What's the statute?"

"Ten-oh-one, for starters," Whitson said.

"Old reliable," Tucker said.

Section 1001 of Title 18, U.S. Code, made it a crime to cover up a material fact by "any trick, scheme, or device," or to willfully concoct "any false writing or document knowing the same to contain any false, fictitious or fraudulent statement or entry."

"Lee," Whitson said, "first thing, have a chat with our friend Bertelli about what he reported after his interview with Jamie McGuire. If that pans out, we can start thinking about obstruction of justice. And by the way, contact the State Department. See when the ambassador was over here last, who he might have met with."

Healy waited until Tucker left before he said, "Do we really need this?"

"No, but we've got it."

"I can just see the shit hitting the fan in D.C."

"I appreciate your concern, Denny. But how does a headline like 'Boston U.S. Attorney Participates in Cover-up' grab you? Besides, I like to think we're better than that. I didn't take this job to play games."

Two days later, Tucker said, "I never saw anyone cave in so fast. Bertelli says he was only following orders. Barry Goldfarb, the regional commissioner, told him to write up a report fingering the McGuire kid. He says he had no idea the kid would end up dead, which he didn't know. He thought the kid was only missing. Bertelli says he doesn't want a lawyer. In return for his cooperation, he wants us to help save his pension."

"And Goldfarb?"

"Oh, he wants to come in with counsel to make a deal. He's worried about his pension, too. But he did give up the MI Five guy. Brian Forbes."

"Tell you what," Whitson said. "Get a cable off to the London embassy. Say we want the British government to provide us access to a security officer named

Brian Forbes regarding a conspiracy investigation. That should rattle the cages."

In London, when Whitson's request arrived on Roger Gravesend's desk, Gravesend could barely contain his glee. Forbes had become insufferably arrogant over these past weeks with his grandiose plans to infiltrate the IRA, and there hadn't been anything Gravesend could do about it. Not even the discovery of Billy Dugan's body had humbled Forbes. "Fortunes of war," he had said.

But now the director general was in full agreement. Forbes had gone too far. Gravesend summoned Forbes and showed him the cable forwarded by the embassy's legal attaché. "I'm afraid, Brian, that this is your last day in the office. As a matter of fact, at this very moment, your files and safe are being sealed. Your personal belongings are being gathered up. You can find them in reception. Your accounts will be drawn up to date and you will, of course, receive whatever is due you. I'm afraid, however, that the normal channels for private security employment will not be available to you."

Gravesend glanced at the scarlet-faced Forbes. "Fortunes of war, you know."

The return cable from the embassy for Whitson's attention said: "Home Office advises that if, in fact, one Brian Forbes was ever employed by Her Majesty's Government, he no longer is. His present whereabouts are unknown."

. . .

In Washington, in the J. Edgar Hoover Building, Whitson sat opposite Judge William Tallman. "Judge, that's quite a desk you have. I don't remember seeing it before."

"Shelby, how far are you going on this?"

"As far as it takes me."

"I don't know any of the specifics at that meeting. I left before any of it was discussed. Terry McDonell can attest to that."

"It's a shame you didn't raise a cautionary voice. Might have prevented a number of problems."

"You think you're some hotshot, don't you?"

"I'll let posterity decide that."

"You know, Shelby, it's going to be mighty tough to pursue cases up there in Beantown without the active cooperation of the FBI."

"On that basis, how would you like it if I formally requested that you remove yourself from every investigation I undertake? I'm sure some alert reporter would want to know why."

"You going to subpoena me?"

"I'd prefer a voluntary appearance."

"I'll think about it."

The day after the indictments against Winston Taylor Groome III and Alan Nyquist were announced, a grand jury sitting in Manchester, New Hampshire, declined to indict Michael McGuire, on the grounds of self-defense, in the homicides of Thomas Ahearn and Bernard Quinn. It was later learned that Shelby Whitson, unseen by reporters at the time, had slipped into a side door to testify. Michael McGuire was then given a one-year suspended sentence for the illegal possession of a firearm.

Reporters swarmed around him as he left the courthouse. On the advice of Whitson, he said, "I prefer not to comment."

That night in Boston he had dinner with Ingrid at the Ritz-Carlton. "I ate here with Jamie the night I met you," he said.

"Yes, I know."

"My God, what don't you know?"

"I don't know what I'm going to do." She reached over and put her hand on his arm. "You know, that night after we did what we did," she said, "I wanted to make love with you."

"Yes, I know."

"I thought it was the only way I could reach Jamie, through you. You find that shocking?"

"No, we've been through a lot. But aside from everything else, I could be your father."

"Isn't that funny?" she said. "I was too old for Jamie and too young for you."

"You'll get over this. You've got to get on with your life."

"So do you."

"Yes, I guess it's easier to give advice than take it." He looked at her. "There's one more thing I have to do for Jamie," he said. "I want very much for you to be part of it."

"Of course. Anything."

Chapter

20

The next day in New York Michael Mc-Guire telephoned the marina manager out at the beach. "I'm calling about the boat," he said.

"I've been trying to reach you about her. I left a couple of messages."

"Yes, I know. I've been away."

"I don't think there's anything to worry about. It's been pretty mild this fall. But I don't think you should wait putting her up much longer. By the way, how's Jamie doing?"

"Jamie's dead, I'm sorry to tell you. That's why I didn't get back to you."

"My God, what happened?"

"It was kind of an accident. It's a long story."

"Is there anything I can do?"

"Yes, that's why I'm calling."

"I'll get one of the men to put up the *Mary Alice* right away."

"No, I'm going to be needing her tomorrow. I just want you to have somebody go over to make sure the engine's okay and so forth. After tomorrow, you can take her in."

"No problem, Mr. McGuire. You can count on it. Gee, that's terrible about Jamie. I want you to know you've got my sympathy, all of us here. He was some kid, not really a kid anymore the last time I saw him."

"Yes, thank you."

Then he and Ingrid drove to the beach together. The thermometer on the outside of the house registered forty degrees. The sky was overcast, ash gray, as if smudged by a worn eraser. The bay, rippled by a breeze, was the color of old pewter.

The inside of the house seemed colder than the outside, damp and still. He turned up the heat and made a fire. She sat hunched over by it.

"Do you want some coffee?" he said. "I forgot about milk."

"No, I'm fine."

He looked at the clothes she was wearing. "You'll need something warmer," he said, and rummaged around and found a heavy sweater that had been Mary Alice's and also her hooded foul-weather jacket.

He went to the station wagon and lifted out the cardboard box and carried it to the boat, and he helped her into the boat and turned the ignition key and pressed the starter button. After a couple of tries, the engine whined into a cough and then caught, expelling water through the exhaust.

He untied the lines and circled away from the

dock, heading west down the bay. "You all right?" he said. "Not too cold?"

"It's okay. Don't worry."

He pointed to his left, toward the beach. "That's where I took Jamie fishing for the first time," he said. "Right over there. That was some day."

"Yes, he told me."

"He did?"

"Yes."

He turned at a channel marker and moved into the inlet. They went between the rocky groins where the inlet met the ocean. The tide was ebbing. There weren't any other boats. Gulls perched somberly on the rocks, like professional mourners.

Michael McGuire eased the boat close to the first line of breaking waves and told her to take the wheel. He opened the box. There was a wreath inside. A ribbon was attached. It said, "Jamie."

He tossed the wreath out over the wave line as far as he could. For a second, it seemed as though the wreath would come right back in, but it didn't. It floated indecisively, and then began to drift seaward.

"Goodbye, son," he whispered. His eyes blurred. He could not bear to look at Ingrid.

Together, side by side, they watched the wreath bobbing in the swells until they could no longer see it, and then he eased the throttle forward and brought the boat around, and they slowly went back up the inlet.